THE SEDUCTION OF MIRIAM CROSS

W. A. Tyson

e·LITBOOKS

This book is a work of fiction. Names, characters places and incidents either are products of the author's imagination or are used fictitiously. Any resemblance to actual events or locales or persons, living or dead, is entirely coincidental and not intended by the author.

THE SEDUCTION OF MIRIAM CROSS

Copyright ©2013 Wendy Tyson

All rights reserved.

Published in the United States by E-Lit Books.

www.e-litbooks.com

Except as permitted under the U.S. Copyright Act of 1976, no part of this publication may be reproduced, distributed, or transmitted in any form or by any means, or stored in a database or retrieval system, without the prior consent and permission of the publisher.

Art and Cover Design by Frank Montagna
For information on subsidiary rights, please contact the publisher at info@e-litbooks.com

ISBN 9781492758785

*For Ben, Ian, Jonathan and Matthew,
without whom I would be lost.*

PROLOGUE

The sound, a subtle scrape of metal against metal, drilled through her subconscious, jarring her awake. She picked her head up off her desk, rubbed her eyes, and looked around the dim room, telling herself to focus. Outside, the wind howled. The branches of the big pine hit her window in a rhythmic *tap*, *tap*, *tap*. She tried to listen beyond the wind, beyond the falling rain, beyond the pounding of her own heart. She heard only silence.

Quickly, fervently, she organized the materials she'd been working on into a pile and fastened them with a binder clip. She shoved everything into a desk drawer and locked the drawer with a small silver key. Her computer screen was black, so she tapped the mouse and waited impatiently for the screen to come alive. Just to be safe, she hit the save button, exited the document and shut down her computer. All of this took her a minute, tops. It felt like forever.

She stole a glance at the clock on her desk. 2:48. Had she bolted the doors and windows before she'd gone into her study? It'd been around nine, so no, probably not. She cursed herself for falling asleep.

She made her way through the study and out into the hallway that divided her one-story house. The darkness felt thick and viscous, enveloping her in dread. Try as she might, she still heard nothing beyond the storm.

Perhaps it had been a dream. But her gut said that wasn't the case – and once upon a time she'd been a woman who trusted her gut.

She didn't dare turn on a light. Feeling her way along the walls, she passed the open doors to her bedroom and bath, each room a dark abyss in the early morning hour. She held her breath. A few more feet and she would be in the living room. Beyond that, the kitchen and the back door. She needed to check the locks. Then she could return to her study and finish what she'd needed to finish in the first place.

A table lamp in the living room cast shadows across the small, carpeted space. Her gaze flew from one end of the room to the other, pausing in the darkened corners. Nothing looked disturbed. Relieved, she crept to the front door and fastened the bolts, stopping only to take a deep breath in a failed attempt to calm her jittery nerves. A year of running had made her paranoid. A year of relative anonymity had, perhaps, made her careless.

Paranoia was fine. But she could ill afford to be careless.

She turned, pulling her cardigan closer against a sudden chill. For the briefest of moments, her mind flitted to another time, to feelings of warmth and contentment. But some things were bigger than one person's feelings and she forced herself back to the present. To her own safety. To the safety of others.

The kitchen was dark.

Her pulse raced. She could have sworn she'd put the light on over the stove. Yes, she was certain. She'd retired to her study after a dinner of bread and soup and had left the dishes out to be cleaned later. The light had been her reminder.

But the light was off.
That meant . . .

"Hello, *Emily*."

She jumped. While her eyes scanned the darkened kitchen for the person associated with the disembodied voice, her mind spun with more practical matters. What had she left out? What would they find?

He said, "This place is very . . . quaint."

She spotted him in the shadows. He sat sprawled on a chair by the back door, his legs out in front of him, something long and metal on the table by his side. In the dark, his face was hidden. But she recognized the voice.

"How did you find me?"

"Does it matter?"

She ironed the shakiness from her voice. "It does to me."

"We have our sources."

"We," she repeated.

"Does that bother you, *Emily*?"

She remained silent, her eyes on the back door, which, she noticed now, stood slightly ajar. How long would it take her to reach it – could she get there before he did? Even if she did, what then? A run to the neighbor's house? To what end? So that she could knock loudly on the locked door and wait until the frightened woman finally agreed to open up? By then he'd have caught her. Perhaps her bolted front door? But her car keys were in her purse . . . and what if he wasn't alone?

"What do you want?" she said.

"You know what we want."

"No."

He smiled. It was a shark's grin, full of cold-blooded malice, a reminder of who he was and all that he stood for. She knew then that she could tell herself whatever lies gave her momentary comfort, but the truth was, she was going to die in this house, far from everything she held so dear.

Oddly, this sudden understanding gave her strength. She forced herself to meet his gaze. She smiled. "Killing me will do you absolutely no good."

He raised his arm. In his hand was a needle. Another icy smile. "I beg to differ."

She shook her head, thankful for her forethought. He – they, she reminded herself – could take what they could from her. But it wouldn't be everything.

He rose and took two steps in her direction. She saw now that the glistening metal object on the table was a knife. An impossibly long knife. She swallowed, again measuring the distance between her and a door.

In a burst of desperation, she stepped toward the back door, then quickly turned and ran toward the living room. She fumbled with the bolts, forcing jittery hands to steady as she jammed the locks away from their resting places.

The last bolt in her hand, she felt him behind her. Strong fingers clasped over her mouth, hot breath on her neck. She struggled against him, but it was no use. He was too big, too powerful. Her only weapon was retreat.

"Oh, *Emily*," he said. A hand slipped down her side, cupped her breast, continued down to her waist. There it stopped. "What were you thinking?"

She remained quiet and closed her eyes. He tugged at her sweater, pulling it off. Her bare arms prickled in the chilly air. He grabbed her forearm. She felt the sting of the needle and waited for the haze that would no doubt descend. He picked her up, carried her to the back of the house. Toward her study.

She knew what he wanted. What *they* wanted.

She wouldn't give it to him. That much she could do.

ONE

"Delilah Percy Powers, never in a million years did I think I'd find you doing something like this. Your momma was right! You *have* lost your mind."

"My mother has a narrow view of sanity, Katrina."

Delilah sank back in her office chair, amusement and irritation battling it out. She'd agreed to see her old school mate only because the woman had driven hours for a consultation. For what purpose, Delilah still wasn't sure. Getting information out of Katrina Straub – now Katrina Rice – was like prying a bone from a rabid dog.

"Well, never mind that, you haven't changed a bit." Katrina laughed, a gesture that did nothing to soften the horsy look of her face. "Your momma is worried about you, you know. After everything . . . " Katrina shook her head. "Back home, we understand your need to get away. But here? Never expected to find you running to a place like Philadelphia."

"This is Jenkintown, not Philadelphia. And I'm not running away from anything."

Katrina looked pointedly around the office. "Well, sweetie, it doesn't look like you're running *to* something, either."

Delilah refused to bite. As she recalled, Katrina had been mean-spirited in high school. *Seems some things never change.* Delilah took her time straightening the papers on her desk, careful to keep her face neutral. No good would come of saying more, even if the words were burning a hole in Delilah's mouth. As satisfying as it would be, Katrina would scurry back to their hometown, full of half-truths and syrupy anger. And then Delilah's mother really would have her Spanx in a twist.

Delilah said finally, "What do you want Katrina?"

Katrina sniffed. "That's all I get after almost twenty years? Down to business already?"

"Most potential clients are in a hurry to discover some truth or another." Delilah folded her hands on the desk, strained patience losing out to frustration. "But maybe you're the exception."

Katrina pursed her lips, clearly deciding whether or not to be offended. She held out a magenta-manicured hand in supplication. "It's Hank. I think he's desirous of other women and I mean to prove it. Your momma told me about what you do, and I thought, well . . . I thought maybe you could do something to help me out. I'll pay, of course."

Delilah thought about this. She remembered Hank Rice as a tall, balding, dour-faced young man. While he didn't seem to be much of a catch, he also didn't seem like the cheating type. But Delilah knew that a pickle could be a cucumber and vice versa; you had to be close enough to smell the difference.

"Do you need him followed?"

"Not exactly."

"Pictures?"

"Kind of." Katrina looked away. Delilah and Katrina were the same age, but Delilah could see the thinker's crease etched between Katrina's thirty-five-year-old eyes. She didn't look like a woman who feared her love was betraying her. Delilah smelled a scheme.

"I can't help you, Kat, unless you tell me what you need."

"Your momma said you're a private investigator."

"That's right."

"You have women who . . . who can nab men?"

"I hire professional detectives."

Katrina stood up. She walked to a bookshelf in Delilah's office and scanned the photos that lined the top. She picked up a picture of a young man standing in front of a rocky cliff. His smile was generous, his eyes focused on something just beyond the camera. An involuntary shudder coursed through Delilah. She held Katrina's stare.

"Have you ever fallen in love again, Lila?"

"No."

"You were lucky with him, you know. Had things turned out differently" Katrina flashed an apologetic smile - "he'd probably be a bastard like the rest of them."

"That's enough, Kat. Whatever your problems, don't involve Michael."

Delilah's voice was quiet, but Katrina must have heard the underlying steely threat because she put the picture down and turned back to face the desk, suddenly all business. She sat down.

"I want one of your sexiest women to come on to Hank in a bar. I can give you the name of the place where he hangs out, I can tell you the type of women who excite him, I can give you any information that will make it more likely that he'll bite. And then I want pictures."

"You want one of my investigators to sleep with him?"

"Whatever it takes to get incriminating photos." Katrina took a deep breath and continued. "I can't be married to him anymore, Lila. I'm miserable. I dread every day waking up next to that man. But we have a pre-nup and the only way out is if he's cheating. You understand - it's for the kids."

"Does he hurt you?"

"No, of course not."

"The kids?"

"Never."

"You suspect him of having an affair?"

"Not exactly."

"Homosexual trysts?"

Katrina laughed. "Why would you even ask that?"

"So you want me to set up what amounts to a sting operation?"

Katrina nodded.

"For money?"

Katrina smiled. "What other reason is there?"

Delilah said, "No."

Katrina let out a strained laugh. "You're refusing?"

"Yep."

"If you don't want your girls getting sexual, hire a prostitute. I'll pay. There are women out there who can be bought, I assure you."

"But I'm not one of them." Delilah stood and pushed her chair back from her desk. It was after six o'clock and her stomach was rumbling. She had another two hours of muggy daylight to get the horses settled down and she still had her other chores to do. She wanted Katrina and all she represented out of her office - and out of her life.

"I offended you. I'm sorry," Katrina said. She stayed seated on the chair and looked up at Delilah with beseeching eyes, fluttering unnaturally long lashes. "I couldn't go to someone near home for fear that Hank would find out. I knew I could trust you to be discrete, being school friends and all-"

"Look Katrina, I'm sure you have reasons for wanting out of your marriage, but at Percy Powers, we don't set men up to fail. Lord knows, they do that often enough on their own. Hank may be an honest man. I won't have a hand at turning him."

"I drove almost four hours to get here."

Delilah opened the office door. "Then you should have called first."

#

"What was that about?" Margot asked in her typical matter-of-fact way, but Delilah heard the undertone of concern.

"Just an old acquaintance."

"Didn't sound too friendly."

"Business."

"Or turning away business?"

"Let's just say it wasn't a case for us."

Margot nodded, clearly not satisfied. The older woman reached under the receptionist's desk and pulled out her purse. She slipped on a pair of driving glasses. With her shapeless brown skirt, dowdy cream sweater - even now, in early June - and wedge-sole shoes, Margot looked every bit her seventy-two years. But Delilah knew what a spitfire Margot McDentry could be. She only worked for Percy Powers part-time, mostly doing administrative work and research, but she was smart and could operate under the radar. Two attributes that came in handy at a detective agency.

"A few more applications came in," Margot said, peering at Delilah over the top of her glasses. "I put their resumes on your desk."

"Thanks."

"Some have solid backgrounds."

"Great."

"Try to hide your excitement, Delilah."

Delilah gave her a weary smile, Katrina's caustic reference to Michael still on her mind. Fourteen years had done nothing to dull the ache. Or the anger.

"You're turning away cases because we're understaffed, yet you've been looking for someone for nearly three months." Margot shook her head. "You're stalling."

Delilah sighed. "We're a well-oiled machine. If anyone should understand that, it's you. Barb, you, Natasha . . . If we introduce a new person, it'll upset the mix."

"I left the convent for a reason, summed up in one word: control. But clergy aren't the only ones cornering *that* market. Perhaps it's time you stop holding so tight to everything and let the world in."

Exasperated, Delilah turned away. While Margot, an ex-nun and former headmistress, was not shy with her opinions, it was rare that she voiced them in business matters. Yes, Delilah had been turning away business, real business, not like Katrina's offer, for months now. But introduce someone new and the chemistry she valued would disappear.

Delilah glanced in the mirror behind the desk. The woman staring back at her looked tired and worn, her red hair more tarnished penny than fresh copper, her skin pale, circles like bruises under her eyes. She *was* tired. It had been a long day and tomorrow would bring with it new crises.

"Margot," she said finally. "I appreciate your concern. When the right person comes along, we'll hire her."

"Or him?"

Delilah sighed. "Or him."

Margot gave Delilah an appraising stare. She straightened her skirt, tossed Delilah a curt nod and marched toward the door, stopping short of the threshold. "In life, Delilah, there is no bigger thief than fear." With that, she left.

Delilah walked back to her office, mulling over Margot's words. It had taken eight years to build this business into what it was today: one of many private investigative firms near Philadelphia but one of the few places women could go to find justice. Was Margot right – was she afraid to relinquish control? No. If she was turning away paying cases, it was because she had to, plain and simple. If she expanded too much, she'd lose what she'd set out to do in the first place. The personal touches, the tough but caring atmosphere, would be gone.

Why am I spending time thinking about this nonsense? But Delilah knew why. Margot had uncanny intuition. And between Margot's comments and Katrina's visit - specifically, the mention of Michael and her mother and, like entwined vines, all the suffocating pain they represented - Delilah felt rattled.

Delilah locked away the few files still on her desk. She glanced around at her cramped office. One large mahogany desk, a yard sale find, and two upholstered arm chairs filled most of the space. A bank of filing cabinets lined one wall, rows of neatly sorted book shelves the other. Matted and framed photographs of her father's ranch in Wyoming were scattered about, roots in a crazy world.

The entire room measured 90 square feet. Katrina had been right about one thing – the office was nothing to look at. Her employees shared one large office and, other than the two rooms and reception, there was just a tiny kitchenette and an even tinier bathroom. But this place felt like home.

Damn it, Lila, you're getting sentimental. Cut it the hell out.

Delilah turned off the lights to her office and walked through reception. On impulse, she went back to her desk and grabbed the stack of resumes. She'd give them a quick glance. At least then she could tell Margot she'd considered everyone.

And that the answer was still no.

#

It was well after nine when Delilah closed her front door, finally in for the evening. Night had fallen fast and hard on her little farm, and Delilah, exhausted, wanted nothing more than dinner and a hot bath. She'd driven up the gravel driveway that led to the two-hundred-year-old house in Ivyland nearly two hours ago. After running inside to throw on jeans, sneakers and a tank top, she'd headed back outside to feed the animals.

Delilah rode the horses, brushed each horse down and picked the mud out from their shoes. Chores finished, she leaned back against the small barn and inhaled the clean scent of fresh hay. If only everything in life were so simple. Millie, her rescue horse, an old brood mare, nuzzled Delilah's hand with her soft muzzle, searching for the carrot that Delilah offered at the end of each day. Delilah fished the vegetable out of her back pocket and watched the mare devour it. Millie had lived on the ranch for over a year, but it was just recently that the haunting had left her eyes.

Millie's treat got Spur worked up and he whinnied, poking at Delilah's stomach with his nose. She stroked the white star on his head. "I have one for you, too, old boy." Spur had been her childhood horse and the first thing she came back for when she moved north. He was an old man now, nearly thirty, but he had the spirit - and manners - of a young stud.

"What would I do without you two?" she asked aloud. The horses, chewing contentedly in their stalls, simply stared at her with a mixture of innocence and old-soul wisdom. Delilah locked the barn gate behind her and walked briskly back to her house. She heard a meow and turned to see Mittens, the stray that had adopted the horses, following her. "You, too, huh?"

Two dogs greeted Delilah at the front door. She smiled at their noisy hellos and went inside. She scooped a bowl of cat food from inside a pantry and placed it outside, next to a bowl of water. She gave the skittish cat a quick stroke, then closed and locked the front door. The dogs - Sampson, a small Terrier mix and Goliath, a Great Dane - sat next to each other in the kitchen, waiting expectantly for their own food. Delilah fed the dogs and then poured herself a tall glass of Pinot Grigio. In her bedroom, she traded her jeans and tank for pale green cotton pajamas. Back in the kitchen, she put together a ham and cheese sandwich. She sank into the sofa, sandwich in one hand, remote in the other. The time on her BluRay read 9:33.

Her cell phone rang. Work. Reluctantly, Delilah stood back up, the muscles in her legs and back complaining loudly, and picked up her phone, half expecting it to be Katrina. Not a number she recognized.

"Delilah Percy Powers."

There was a moment of silence. Delilah was about to hang up when finally a soft voice said, "Delilah? Lucinda Mills. Do you remember me?"

Indeed, Delilah did remember Lucinda, a quiet, unassuming woman with extensive burn scars on her arms and neck. Lucinda had been one of Delilah's first *pro bono* cases. Lucinda's ex-husband Butch had been the worst kind of abuser: an abuser with power. A cop. Terrified that if she asked for a divorce, Butch would get the kids, Lucinda had put up with the beatings for years. Desperate, she showed up on the firm's doorstep convinced that she needed proof of the abuse to get her divorce and keep custody of her boys.

At first, Delilah had said no. How could she sit idly by while a client was beaten? But Lucinda had insisted that they could intervene *after* they got photos. She just needed proof. They got proof alright – proof that Butch beat his wife and harassed the homeless, runaways and prostitutes he encountered on the streets. When all was said and done, Delilah and Barb had the pleasure of giving Butch a tiny taste of the hell he'd spread like cholera in a developing nation.

It'd been a troubling case, but in the end, Lucinda got her divorce and full custody of the kids. Butch Mills was fired from the Philadelphia police force.

That was three years ago. Delilah hoped that Butch was not back in Lucinda's life. While she liked to believe that her clients were able to move on and create new lives, she was pragmatic enough to know that abusive relationships, like all relationships, were complicated. Some women could not resist the call.

As though reading her mind, Lucinda said, "It's not Butch, Delilah. Haven't seen him since the divorce." Lucinda paused. "But I can't talk about this over the phone."

"Why?"

"I just . . . can't."

"Are you in danger?"

"I . . . I don't think so. I don't know. Listen, Delilah, I can make this job worth your while, but I need to talk to you, explain everything. Can you meet me? Please?"

Delilah looked at Sampson and Goliath lying on the cool stones of the hearth by a dormant fireplace. Content. Happy. A knot of anxiety twisted in her stomach. Lucinda sounded nervous, and the fact that she couldn't explain the job over the phone made *Delilah* nervous. Either Delilah was stepping into a hot pile of manure or she was dealing with a paranoid and unstable woman. Neither option seemed attractive.

Still, Delilah was not one to turn away someone in need. She could at least get the facts before making a decision.

"Where do you want to meet?" Delilah said finally.

"Center City. I'll email you the location."

"Fine. Nine a.m. sharp." Even as she clicked off her phone, Delilah wondered what she was getting herself into.

TWO

Delilah arrived to find Lucinda already seated. The woman was even tinier than Delilah remembered, with a slight overbite and brown hair cut into a short wedge that exposed the raised red scars on her neck. Lucinda motioned toward the seat across from her, a tight smile of recognition on her face.

They were at a ubiquitous Starbucks on Sixteenth Street in Philadelphia. Center City was bustling at this hour, the day promising to be soupy and hot. Aromas of street vendor food - frying bacon, soft pretzels, eggs – mingled with the lingering odors of damp, exhaust and urine. Delilah had driven for ninety minutes to go the forty miles it took to reach the city from her house, then another fifteen minutes to find parking. Inside Starbucks, she looked around, scanning, out of habit, for exits and suspicious-looking people. Two women wearing business black and carrying serious leather briefcases waited for their orders, tense expressions on tired faces. A group of college students took up a table in the back, their conversation punctuated by fits of laughter. Nothing ominous. Satisfied, Delilah sank into the chair opposite Lucinda.

"Thanks for coming." Lucinda pushed a steaming cup toward Delilah. "Coffee. Black."

"You remembered?"

Lucinda smiled. Warmth lit up world-weary features. "You saved my life. I think it's the least I can do."

"I didn't save your life."

"Yes, you did." Lucinda touched the scars on her neck absentmindedly. "You and my Aunt Miriam."

"Aunt Miriam?"

Lucinda nodded. "It was her idea for me to contact you in the first place. She wanted to stay out of it, so I never mentioned her. After everything with Butch, Miriam took me and the kids in. She was a smart woman. Brilliant, even."

"*Was?*"

"Was." Lucinda tore at the edges of a brown paper napkin, rolling tiny twisted strips between her fingers. "She died."

"I'm sorry."

Lucinda nodded. "She's the reason I called you."

A tall black man sat down at the seat next to them. He pulled a Netbook out of a saddlebag and spread papers on the table, beside the computer. Lucinda watched him before continuing. "Do you recognize the name Miriam Cross?"

"The author?" Delilah said, understanding sinking in. "*Miriam Cross* was your aunt?"

"My mother's youngest sister - more like a big sister than an aunt. All the family we had. Only forty-nine when she died."

Delilah recalled seeing something online about Cross's death. "I'm sorry to hear about your loss, Lucinda. But how can Percy Powers help?"

Lucinda sat forward. She spoke in an urgent whisper, looking around as she did so. "Aunt Miriam was murdered almost a week ago. Beheaded."

Delilah thought about the headlines of the last seven days. "Then why haven't I seen anything in the news?"

"Exactly! Something's going on. Press has been minimal, the police aren't getting anywhere. That's why I need help. Before Aunt Miriam disappeared-"

"Disappeared?"

Lucinda nodded. "At first I didn't see anything sinister in it. Aunt Miriam was . . . quirky. She often disappeared for periods of time when she was working on a book."

"She'd just leave?"

Lucinda nodded again. "Miriam tackled some serious issues. Genocide, religious extremism, crooked politicians. She'd dig up a scandal and then include a thinly veiled version in her novels. Along the way she made enemies. And she witnessed the worst of human nature. It had its effects."

Delilah leaned forward. "Meaning?"

"Meaning she was given to . . . moods." Lucinda stared straight ahead, avoiding Delilah's eyes. "Bouts of black depression followed by feverish activity. I'm sure a psychiatrist would have called her bipolar, but we just called her different." Lucinda shrugged. "Like most artists, I guess."

So true, Delilah thought. Many gifted people struggled with internal demons. But being different was, perhaps, what made them special. The key was turning those demons into something productive, which Miriam Cross had certainly done. Delilah had been a huge fan of Miriam's work once upon a time. Neither liberal nor conservative, Miriam pointed out bullshit, whoever the purveyor. A staunch feminist, she'd written literary novels that entertained and educated. But in recent years, her novels seemed rambling, paranoid.

"Why did she disappear this time?"

"That's just it, I don't know. At first I thought it was because of us. She wasn't used to having kids around, and I was preoccupied . . . afraid Butch would try to get revenge. A lot fell on Aunt Miriam, things she wasn't emotionally equipped to deal with. I thought maybe she needed a break."

Lucinda's hands strayed back to the torn napkins, as though of their own volition. She frowned. "About eighteen months ago, Miriam said it was time for me to go out on my own. She found me an apartment, paid a year's rent and gave me a $5,000 emergency fund. After that, we talked on the phone once in a while, saw each other sporadically. Then about a year ago, she took off."

"Did you hear from her at all?"

"For a while. Her cell was disconnected, which was typical. She liked to remove distractions when she was writing. I'd call her house, she'd call me back eventually . . . or I'd get an email with a quick update. Like I said, I wasn't too worried. She'd done that before. But then about three months ago, things changed."

Delilah waited for Lucinda to continue. The other woman seemed lost in thought, her eyes projecting loss, confusion and hurt. Delilah wanted to comfort her, but she knew silence would be more productive.

Eventually, Lucinda said, "Aunt Miriam stopped returning my calls. A week went by, then two. When I swung by her house to see if maybe she was there, she wasn't. In fact, much of her stuff was gone and her house looked deserted. Things not put away, dishes in the sink, office packed up."

"Did she normally take her belongings with her?"

Lucinda looked thoughtful. "Not like that. She normally left the house neat. Like you would if you were just going on vacation."

"Did you ever hear from her?"

Lucinda shook her head. "I kept waiting. Eventually my worry turned to panic. I called mutual acquaintances. No one knew anything. I was going to call you . . . I should have. But I didn't have the cash and I couldn't ask you for another favor." Fat tears trekked down her face. "I might have prevented her death."

Delilah reached a hand out to touch the other woman's arm. "Finding her may not have prevented her death. It sounds like she went to great lengths to disappear."

Lucinda looked unconvinced. She sniffed, wiped at her eyes with a crumpled napkin and shrugged her shoulders. "I need answers, Delilah. Who killed my aunt? And why?"

#

Delilah watched the barista - a skinny girl with three silver rings through her lip - while she mulled over what she'd just heard. A well-known, eccentric author is murdered and there's barely a ripple in the news? There were holes, lots of them, and no solid leads. Where would she even begin? And how would Percy Powers be compensated? Delilah might be willing to forgo her fee, but this wasn't a job she could do on her own. She couldn't expect her employees to work for free.

"Why Percy Powers, Lucinda?" Delilah said finally. "Murder's not exactly our sweet spot."

"I know I can trust you."

Delilah shook her head. "I don't think-"

Lucinda's hand shot out and grabbed Delilah's wrist. "Please, Delilah. I want justice for my aunt. But I'm also worried about my kids. Until I know who was behind this, I won't know if we're in danger, too."

Delilah thought about Lucinda's cryptic call the night before, her insistence that they not discuss the matter over the phone. There was more to the story than what she'd divulged so far.

"What happened to make you so nervous?"

Lucinda's mouth clamped shut. She shook her head.

"If you think I will even consider taking this case - and there are no promises, mind you - you had best come forward with everything. And I mean everything." Delilah fixed her best Southern mama stare on the startled woman. "Now 'fess up. What happened?"

Lucinda sighed. "Someone's been calling my house. They don't say anything and after a few seconds, they hang up. The caller I.D. says 'unknown caller.'" Lucinda shrugged. "It may be a coincidence, but I have a bad feeling."

"When did the calls start?"

"The day I learned about Miriam's death. The police wanted me to identify the body. What was left of it."

Delilah knew how traumatic that must have been. But she also knew that Lucinda still wasn't telling her everything. "You're sure that's it, Lucinda? Just those phone calls?"

Lucinda hesitated. "And then there's my son."

"*Out with it.*"

"He swears he was followed on his way to school. May have been his imagination, he's only ten, but it happened the day Aunt Miriam's lawyer called me. Coincidence? Again, I just have a nasty feeling."

"Did your son recognize the man?"

Lucinda shook her head.

"Did the guy approach him?"

"No."

"What did Miriam's lawyer say?"

"He told me that Miriam left me a sizable estate. But it's frozen while the murder is investigated. In case . . ."

"In case you're the killer."

Lucinda nodded. Delilah took in the slump of her shoulders, the tilt of her head. While Delilah was sure a desire for justice and fear for her family were significant

21

factors for requesting this meeting, she was just as sure that self-preservation was at work here. Lucinda was scared. And she her only support person was now dead.

"You said one of her heirs. There were others?"

"A nonprofit . . . Miriam left it a few million."

"What nonprofit?"

"I don't know. Miriam was involved with a number of charities. She had a thing for helping people. Liked to make grand gestures."

Delilah considered this. If Lucinda was owed a sizable estate and the nonprofit was still getting a few million, Miriam had tucked away a lot of cash. And money was a great incentive for murder.

"Lucinda, have you told the police about the calls? About your son?"

Lucinda snorted. "Please. Why would I trust the police? They've never helped me before."

Butch. Of course Lucinda would avoid police. Eight 9-1-1 calls over the course of three years and yet her husband was never charged. Never even taken into custody.

"But this isn't about Butch, Lucinda. Surely the police are investigating Miriam's murder. You need to call them. They may know something that can help you."

"They say they're investigating. They asked me to keep things quiet, so I don't jeopardize their work. Still," Lucinda shrugged, "I'm not contacting them. For all I know, the police are involved somehow."

"The lack of press coverage?"

Lucinda nodded. "How could they manage to keep things so quiet? Even if I didn't say anything, someone would. Things have a way of leaking out."

True enough. While Miriam may not have been in the spotlight the way she once was, the media loved a murder, and the murder of a celebrity should garner some attention. In the local papers, if nothing else.

"Unless people are afraid to say anything," Delilah said. "Was Miriam working on something controversial?"

"Who knows? Miriam was always involved in some project or another. I have no idea what she was up to."

"Is there anything else, Lucinda? Anything you can tell me about Miriam that might help?"

Lucinda shook her head, a pained expression on her face. "For as close as we were, I'm embarrassed to say that my relationship with Miriam revolved around my life, my boys, my problems. Miriam was self-sufficient. The picture of self-control and discipline. And very private. I guess you could say I respected that privacy." She gave a half-hearted smile. "And now . . . and now I am pretty much useless to you."

Delilah thought about Miriam's disappearance. "Is there any chance Butch could have been involved?"

"I thought of that. I don't think so. He's living in Arizona. The boys have contact with his parents. I'd know if he headed back east. Plus, he never knew Miriam was involved. It's me he would have gone after."

Delilah thought Lucinda was probably right. Logic said Miriam disappeared for a reason and Delilah doubted it was out of fear of Butch Mills. She said, "Where was your aunt living before she was killed?"

"That's the other weird thing. A small neighborhood outside of Allentown. Willston, Pennsylvania. Miriam was a sophisticated woman, independent and cultured. She'd traveled all over the world. Why Willston?"

"And why disappear to somewhere so close by?" Delilah said. "Unless . . . "

"Unless she was investigating something local." Lucinda finished Delilah's thought.

"Exactly. Something . . . or someone." Delilah glanced at her watch. She had an eleven o'clock meeting with another client and it was already after ten. She needed to go. "I have to think about this."

"If money's an issue, I can pay. For the work you did before, too. Every penny. Once the estate goes through."

"It's not just the money, Lucinda."

Desperation colored Lucinda's face. "Please? There's no one else I turn to."

Delilah gave her a long look. "No promises. I need time to think. But I'll call you later today." Delilah rose. "For now, watch your surroundings. Drive your kids to school. Keep your doors locked. If you don't have an alarm system, now's the time to get one."

Lucinda gave Delilah a noncommittal nod before handing her a piece of paper she pulled from her pocket. "My new address and my employer's number. You can reach me at work."

Delilah tucked the paper into her purse. Gently, Lucinda grabbed her arm again. "One more thing," Lucinda said. "Before her death, my aunt had altered her appearance – cut her hair short and bleached it blond, changed her clothing style. And she also changed her identity."

Interesting. "Her new name?"

"Emily Cray."

THREE

Barb Moore had three daughters, none of whom took after their mother. The youngest, Dee, was on the computer. Again. Barb threw down the towel she was folding. She poked her daughter on the shoulder.

"Off the computer. Now. Outside."

"It's hot."

"Sun and fresh air are good for you."

"We live near Philadelphia. There is no fresh air." The thirteen-year-old smirked. "And sun gives you skin cancer."

Barb shook her head, unimpressed. "Then use your inhaler and wear sunscreen. Outside. Now."

"My friends aren't home."

"Doesn't matter. I want you to weed the flower garden. You don't require company for that."

Dee stared at her mother, venom in her eyes. She slammed her hand on the desk, huffed out an exasperated sigh and, finally, walked toward the door all the enthusiasm she'd give an extra hour of Sunday school.

Barb called, "I'll be checking. Any weeds left in the garden, and you'll do this tomorrow, too."

Slam.

"I love you!" Barb called after her, chuckling to herself. She did love her girls, but the truth was, things came much too easily for them. To all teenagers these days. Too many distractions, not enough discipline. Barb didn't believe in coddling. It made for soft, lazy kids, and later, soft, lazy adults. There was nothing Barb hated more than laziness.

Barb picked up another cream towel and carefully matched the ends. Next she would organize the linen closet and bag clothes for donation. Yep, people would be surprised at how much they could accomplish if they just turned off the darn television.

Barb's cell phone rang. She answered.

"Can you come in?" Delilah said.

Delilah's voice held the soft lilt of a Southern accent. Although Barb knew Richmond, Virginia was not the hometown of Delilah's heart, it was rare for Delilah to begin a conversation without at least some niceties. Enough of the Southern belle persona had rubbed off to see to that. Something hot was brewing.

Barb glanced at the clock. 4:53. "I'm about to start dinner. Can it wait until tomorrow morning?"

"I promised to get back to someone today. I can come to you, if that's easier."

Barb dismissed that option – no privacy. She did a quick inventory of her evening: dinner of pork chops, rice and salad, overseeing homework and an hour of needlework so she could finish the christening blanket for her sister's baby. She hated to disrupt a schedule, and work was not on the schedule for today, but Delilah sounded pressed. Fred could put together dinner. The girls were old enough to do their own homework. And the christening wasn't for two weeks yet. And besides, wasn't being more flexible on her to-do list?

"Give me an hour. I'll meet you at the office."

Barb went outside to tell Dee she'd be leaving. Her daughter would be ecstatic.

#

If Barb was expecting Delilah to be pacing the floor in front of her desk, waiting for her, she was wrong. Instead her boss was on her hands and knees in front of the little flower patch that marked the entrance to Percy Powers LLC pulling up weeds from around the impatiens and pansies with all the ferocity of a mother lion protecting her wee-ones.

"What's gotten to you, Delilah?"

Delilah stood up and dusted her hands against one another. Barb had known Delilah for six years now, since Barb had been a stay-at-home mom in need of extra cash and flexible hours. Meeting the feisty Delilah Percy Powers at a charity function had seemed like a godsend. But rarely in those six years had Barb seen her boss more agitated. Her red hair, long and straight and normally wrestled into a neat ponytail, hung loose around her face. Her typical outfit of tailored pants and a plain blouse had been replaced by dirty jeans and a gray USC t-shirt, stretched tight over small breasts. Her feet were bare.

Delilah noticed Barb staring at her feet. She looked down and said, "My muckers were full of crap."

Barb laughed. That meant Delilah had gone home mid-day to ride her horses. That also meant Delilah was in thinking mode, mulling over something to the point of distraction.

"So what did you decide?"

"Don't you want to know the question first?"

"Why waste time? I'm a bottom line kind of girl."

Delilah grinned, her smile brightening jade-green eyes. "That you are, my friend." She nodded toward the front door. "Shall we? I may have to bore you with the question anyway. For context."

Barb followed Delilah through the small receptionist area and into Delilah's office.

"Coffee?" Delilah said.

"None for me."

Delilah walked around her desk and sat down, tiny against the mammoth piece of furniture. Unlike Delilah, Barb was a large woman, over five-foot-ten and more than two hundred pounds - mostly muscle. Mostly. Barb never wore make-up, had given up on contacts years ago. She was about as fashionable as Wilma Flintstone. Sitting so close to Delilah, she felt like Gulliver next to a Lilliputian.

But she was too practical and too busy to worry about things like that.

"The answer," Delilah said, "is that we have a new engagement. And I need you. But it's not our usual case and if you're not interested, I understand."

"Whoa, back up. What's the assignment and why is it different?"

"Potentially dangerous. And I don't mean crazy-husband-with-a-gun dangerous."

Barb thought for a moment. She had three kids to consider. But Fred was a local cop, so he'd understand, and for the most part, Barb trusted her own instincts and her physical abilities. She'd worked for a security firm until Dee was born and had been a gym teacher and volleyball player before that. She had a good head on her shoulders and a no-nonsense attitude. But she also wasn't one to step into a cow pasture without looking down first.

"Tell me more," Barb said.

"Remember Lucinda Mills?"

"Is this about Butch Mills again?" Barb remembered the slippery, cowardly bastard and the hell he'd put his family through.

"No. Nothing that simple."

Delilah relayed her conversation with Lucinda. "So you can understand my reticence. A murder. Not our typical gig." She looked pensive for a moment. Her head turned and Barb followed her gaze to the picture of Michael on the bookshelf. "Plus there's the small matter of my employees. I don't want anyone getting hurt."

"We're all grown-ups, Lila. We can decide for ourselves." Barb shrugged. "Besides, all of the nonsense about phone calls and someone following the kid may be just that - nonsense. Sounds like Lucinda may be excited over what probably amounts to nothing."

"Seems awfully coincidental that the calls would start the day Lucinda learned about her aunt's death."

"Memories are fragile. She *thinks* the calls started the same day. Maybe it was two days before or a day after. Maybe she's in debt and someone on the other end is trying to harass money out of her. Who knows?"

Delilah tilted her head to the side and Barb could see the internal debate raging within. Between the wild hair, the t-shirt and the large desk, Delilah looked like a well-developed little girl play-acting at life. But Barb knew she took this seriously and decisions weighed heavily on her. Delilah was nobody's fool.

"You're right," Delilah said finally. "We'll divide this up and see how far we get. If things get out of hand, I'll give you my cases and I'll take it myself." She looked satisfied. Tired, but satisfied. "Now you can go home to that brood of yours. But come in at eight sharp tomorrow. We'll get started then."

#

Only Delilah didn't wait until the next morning to get started. She needed a plan of attack, and that meant facts. She'd talk with Lucinda again, but for the time being, she wanted a better handle on Miriam Cross. Who she was, what she wrote, what her habits were. She'd start with the Internet. After she took care of Millie and Spur.

The horses kept her rooted. They were like large alarm clocks: if she was late, they'd be pacing in their stalls, anxious and agitated. So she tried not to be late. Which was why Delilah decided to do the Internet research from her house rather than the office.

Still in jeans and a t-shirt, she grabbed a glass of cranberry juice, a Slim Jim and a bag of pretzels and sat at her computer to enjoy a well-balanced dinner. Then she logged on.

As she surfed the Net, she considered what she knew. Not much. Miriam Cross had her first critic's hit with a literary historical novel called *Temptations*. It dealt with the changing role of women after World War II and was written from a biting feminist perspective. Before that she'd published two novels, both more journalistic than fictional. One looked at female circumcision in Muslim nations and the other was a documentary-like fictional account of the treatment of women during the Great Depression. Neither sold well.

Miriam hit her peak as a commercial author about ten years ago with a book called *Mourning*, the story of one woman's struggle in a post-apolocolyptic world run by an extremist sect of the Catholic Church. Delilah had read it. Like *Temptations*, it was thought-provoking, unabashedly critical of religion and politicians and could have been called a feminist novel. But unlike *Temptations*, it had an entertaining plot-line. It had been a financial success.

Everything since then had flopped.

Delilah was no literary critic, but since *Mourning*, Miriam's books seemed too dark, too pessimistic, and too unapologetically esoteric. They were books devoid of hope. But considering the number of online fan pages, Miriam still had a cult following. Some seemed drawn to the *noir* aspects of her novels, others to her championing of women's rights.

Yet the only thing mentioned on the Web was the fact of her death, not *how* she died. No big hoopla over her passing, either. Small pieces on CNN and other news sites, a few tributes here and there to a great author, and every one of them simply said she died of unknown causes. Very odd.

Delilah stretched her arms over her head and yawned. It was almost midnight and she'd arranged for Barb, Natasha and Margot to meet her at the office at eight the next morning. She needed to be up and riding by six. She should head to bed. After she tried one more search.

She typed in a string for Willston area news. If Miriam Cross died in Willston, there should be an obituary or death announcement, or, at the very least, a news piece on her death. Again, not one relevant hit.

That could mean the news was simply not in the online version – and she'd need to look at the hard copy papers. Or it could mean nothing had been published.

She tried a broader search using the terms "Emily Cray" and "murder." Still nothing. She was beginning to wonder of Lucinda was crazy and had simply made up the whole story. But when she used only the words "death" and "Willston" and the month of Miriam's murder, she came across a short piece on a local news website: *The Lehigh Valley Reporter*. In the section called

Police Log, the site noted that a woman was murdered in Willston. The date matched Lucinda's account. How many women could have been murdered in Willston on that day? Odds were, not more than one. No details about the death were provided. But the article did include a street address. The fourth block of Lacy Lane.

Delilah had a starting point.

FOUR

"So we have an eccentric old author who changed her name, moved to some bum-fuck town and was killed, execution-style? And our only connection is a crazy woman who let her husband beat her?"

Delilah smiled. Leave it to Natasha to get to the heart of things. "Yes, Natasha. Although I wouldn't call Miriam old. Old to you, maybe. She was forty-nine when she died. And despite being beaten by a psychopath, Lucinda is quite lucid."

"Whatever." Natasha sat back in her chair before glancing over at Margot. "What do you think, Sister?"

"I'm not a nun anymore, Natasha."

"Once a nun . . . ."

Margot glowered, otherwise too smart and too accustomed to Natasha's provocations to react.

Delilah shook her head. Anyone looking in on the scene would wonder how they ever got any work done. They were a disparate group of women: Margot, the ex-Catholic nun, Barb, the militant mother and Natasha, the special case.

"So what do you want us to do?" Natasha said. She raked her hand through her thick dark hair. It was a hot, humid June morning and Natasha was wearing military cargo pants and a black sports bra. Her abdominal muscles stood out like tines on a fork.

"I'll take the lead on this one," Delilah said. "Barb, you'll work with me. We'll see what we can find out about the crime scene and Miriam's disappearance. Margot, I want you to research Miriam Cross. I did some preliminary work last night and found info on her as an author, but see if you can't find out more - particularly about Miriam as a person. What she liked, whom she associated with, any skeletons."

Margot nodded.

"And me?" Natasha said. She jutted her chin out. The morning light spilled through the blinds and fell in liquid lines across her face. Although Natasha was not conventionally pretty, she had a raw sexuality that made her striking, beautiful even, and she knew it. Which was, in part, what made her such a valuable member of the team.

Delilah said, "I don't need you yet."

"Seriously?"

Delilah stood. "Seriously. But I will. Sit tight."

Natasha rose and grabbed her gym bag. She looked ready to storm out. After a few tense seconds, she said, "Are you leaving me out because of Sam?"

Delilah shook her head. "I'm not leaving you out. I just don't know what I need from you yet."

"Because I can take care of myself. You let me worry about my son."

Delilah took a step closer, ignoring Margot's tight smile and Barb's disapproving frown. She moved directly in front of the taller, fitter woman and looked her in the eye. "I am not leaving you out, Natasha. Once we have a better handle on what's going on, I'll have a role for you. If you want it."

"I'm not just a dumb kid. I know what you all think" – she looked pointedly at Margot, then Barb – "But I know how to handle myself."

It was true. Mostly. Delilah took a long look at Natasha, the desire to nurture competing with the need to set limits. Natasha only moonlighted as a private investigator. These days, she made her living as a bartender and masseuse, but before Delilah met her, before Sam was born, she'd been a stripper. Natasha was the toughest woman Delilah had ever met, but she'd had to be. On the streets since she was fourteen, pregnant by a drug dealer boyfriend at seventeen. And Delilah could only guess at the abuse she'd suffered at the hands of her parents before she ran away from home. Natasha never discussed that period of her life.

Because of her looks and street-smarts, Natasha often took the bar roles, following men into sleazy joints to photograph equally sleazy hook-ups. But Natasha had a good head on her shoulders, especially when it counted. Like a high-strung filly, she just needed some careful handling and a bit more TLC.

Delilah said finally, "We all know you're capable, Natasha. That's why you're part of the team. That's why I called you here today."

Natasha stared at Delilah for a moment, her face a portrait of indecision. "Alright then. I'll wait to hear from you."

Delilah watched Natasha walk out the door. She turned back to the other two women. "Not a word."

Barb held up her hand. "I know you have a soft spot-"

"I have no such thing. This is just business."

Margot cleared her throat. "If we're done with the group therapy session, I'd like to make a suggestion." Margot got up from her armchair and walked to the window. She pulled open the blinds and looked out onto the small patch of grass and the street and sidewalk beyond. "I can do basic Internet research on Miriam, but it's not enough. We need to trace Miriam's movements online."

Delilah saw immediately where Margot was headed. "Not again. I looked at the resumes and no one had credentials-"

Margot held up a hand. "A new one came in today. The man's a trained hacker, Delilah. Google searches won't be enough. We need a computer forensics expert."

"Margot-"

Margot smiled. "Just business, Delilah. You said so yourself."

#

Reluctantly, Delilah looked at the paper on the desk. Margot was right. Usually they were following a live person in real time. But in Miriam's case, it was forensic surveillance. The ability to re-trace Miriam's electronic footsteps before death would be invaluable. While Delilah's team could do the footwork, no one was a master on the computer. They needed a master.

Delilah skimmed the document. Margot was right again. The new applicant's credentials were all there, in bold black against crisp ivory parchment.

Matthew Anderson. Based on his college graduation date, he would be in his late thirties. Based on his work history, he was either laid off or had voluntarily chosen to stay home. He now worked very part-time as a reporter, covering sporting events for local papers. But what interested Delilah, and what surely interested Margot, was his background.

Fifteen years as a freelance journalist for a variety of well-known magazines. Investigating war crimes in Bosnia, environmental dumping in Nebraska and New York, misappropriated union dues in California. A brief stint as a contractor for the government around Y2K.

And beneath it all, included in a smaller font, was his CEH certification. Certified Ethical Hacker.

Delilah picked up the phone. Missing X chromosome or not, Matthew Anderson could be an asset.

#

Natasha drove down the turnpike at nearly ninety miles per hour, as fast as her little Toyota would go. She had a mild headache and her thighs still ached from her night with Amelia. But mostly, she felt pissed. She knew Barb and Margot respected her. They hadn't worked together for this long without coming to understand each other's strengths and weaknesses, and she was pretty sure they'd both want her beside them if things turned nasty. Still, when it came to the brainy work, she was never the first choice.

She understood. She was the youngest. And she didn't even have a high school diploma. But neither did Quentin Tarantino. Or Dave Thomas, the Wendy's guy. Or plenty of other rich, famous people, for that matter. So fuck them. She could figure shit out just as well as anybody. Better. How else had she survived this long? There was no daddy's money for her. In fact, she didn't even have daddy's name. Not anymore. She ditched that when she stopped being his victim. A lifetime ago.

Natasha exited the Turnpike, downshifted into fourth, then third, and barely slowed through the EZPass lane. That was it! There were lots of ways to change your identity. Some worked, some didn't. Sometimes the change needed to be official. And sometimes it just needed to *look* official.

At fourteen, when she'd left home and needed work, she'd needed to be eighteen. No one wanted to take a chance on an underage stripper. Lots of perverts had a thing for teens, but real teenage girls were a liability. Jake had helped her back then. And he could very well help her again. Jake was a thug, but he may have some ideas about how Miriam Cross became Emily Cray.

She dialed Jake's number. No answer. She left a message. Ten to one she'd never hear from him. He was a slimy son-of-a-bitch. But you never knew with Jake. Fathering someone's child was kind of a big deal. The way Natasha figured, Jake Morowski owed her.

#

Matthew Anderson agreed to come in at four o'clock for an interview. He had a deep voice and sounded pleasant enough on the phone. Still, Delilah remained skeptical. It wasn't clear why he wanted a PI job or why he'd applied at Percy Powers. But Delilah's father had taught her never to judge a horse before you got the opportunity to ride him. And while she could see the humor in the analogy, she also saw the wisdom. She'd find out what Matthew Anderson was made of – and then she'd make a decision.

It was after eleven. That gave her almost four hours to scope out Emily Cray's neighborhood, and then another hour to complete her notes and prepare for the interview. The day was quickly turning from warm and humid to warm, humid and overcast. Gray clouds bruised the sky and a light breeze rocked the dogwood outside her office window. Delilah grabbed an umbrella from the coat closet and set out to her car. She'd left the Wrangler at home today, opting instead for the six-year-old black Honda Civic she kept for these occasions. Better to be forgettable - and nothing blended better than a common car.

The route to Willston took over an hour. Row upon row of residential streets made up the town, with a Main Street that snaked through the middle like a jagged spine. Garages, gas stations and convenience stores, plus two beauty salons and a thrift shop aptly named Second

Chances, perched along Main Street. And a Walmart. Always a Walmart.

Delilah followed her GPS directions. Lacy Lane ran parallel to Main Street and acted as a second thruway. Like suburban sentinels, two types of houses lined Lacy Lane: tiny one-story homes with carports and stone facades and slightly larger split-levels. The houses sat close to the street, with only small front yards and narrow driveways to separate them from the traffic.

Delilah drove her Honda the length of Lacy Lane to get a full picture of the road. The street curved right before ending at a traffic light. In the fourth block, first house after the bend, no one seemed to be home. Delilah pulled into the driveway and killed the engine. She rolled down her windows. Overgrown grass encircled a weedy flowerbed. Unlike the neighboring homes, no air conditioning hum emanated from within.

Delilah backed out of the driveway and drove a tenth of a mile to the nearest cross street. She wanted a chance to look around, but leaving her car in the driveway would be too conspicuous. All it would take was one overly vigilant neighbor to take down her license plate number. Better to walk.

She pulled the car alongside the curb, put the manual transmission in neutral, pulled up the handle for the parking brake and got out. She left her purse in the car, under a notepad. She locked the doors. Although the sky still threatened rain, she left her umbrella in the car, too. Sometimes it came in handy to be stuck in a downpour. Played on people's sympathies.

There was no sidewalk, so Delilah walked along the street. When she neared the curve that led to the vacant house, she hopped up onto the grass. An old Buick sat parked in the split-level closest to Emily's house, but the front door was closed and the buzz of a window air conditioner could be heard from the street. Delilah kept walking.

The vacant house - 406 Lacy Lane - was a one-story home with white wood siding and a stone façade in a patchwork of brown, beige and peach. A black wrought iron handrail ran from the driveway up a short flight of concrete steps to the front landing. A single clay flowerpot, empty, sat on the landing. Delilah tried the doorbell. Broken. She knocked hard on the door. No answer. She tried again.

Silence.

Delilah turned the knob. Locked. She backed up and surveyed the property. The house to the left looked temporarily empty: no cars in the driveway but the lawn was freshly mowed and a hose lay unfurled by the back door. On the other side of that house stood another ranch with two cars in the driveway. Next to that home, just the corner traffic light. To the right of 406 Lacy was the home with the Buick. The curve of the street and a pie-shaped wedge of lawn protected Delilah from its inhabitants' view, but Delilah suspected that around back, the homes were in each others' line of sight. She'd take her chances.

Delilah looked quickly at the windows on the front façade of Emily's house. Drawn blinds blocked her view. She walked around the left side of the house. Unruly Azalea shrubs stretched out towards her, their branches unevenly populated by tiny white and pink flowers. In the back, a massive pine tree shaded parts of a lawn clearly in need of a mow. The pine and a small concrete patio took up most of the rear yard. Indeed, Delilah could clearly see the Buick owner's backyard from this angle. Only a broken chain-link fence and a dying row of rose bushes separated the two properties.

Delilah saw no signs of police chalk or tape, but, as she made her way to the carport, she noticed the dirty outline of trash cans on the smooth cement. The cans themselves were missing.

She had the right house. Emily/Miriam had lived here, Delilah could feel it. But why? What was the famous author doing in Willston, a town Delilah had not even heard of before yesterday? Delilah decided to try the neighbors. She'd start with the Buick people.

It began to rain fat, cool drops that scrolled down her face. Delilah sprinted across the front yard and to the front door of the Buick people's house and tried to shield her body under the small awning that covered the entry. She rang the bell. A young boy answered.

"Are your parents in?" Delilah said.

He shook his head. The child was probably ten or eleven, on the chunky side, and still in his pajamas. Delilah figured Mom or Dad was in bed, sleeping off a night shift or a hangover. She decided to press.

"You're home alone?"

Another head shake.

Delilah didn't want to upset the kid. He'd probably been told a thousand times not to talk to strangers and, certainly, not to tell a stranger he was home alone. And the car in the driveway said he was not.

"It's about my cat," Delilah said. "She's lost. I was hoping your mom or dad could help."

That sparked his interest. He seemed to be weighing whether a lost cat was enough of a reason to disturb his parents. Finally, he said, "I'll get my mom. She's taking a rest."

A few minutes later, the boy's mother arrived at the door looking disheveled and mildly annoyed. She wore black cotton sweatpants and a white Mickey Mouse t-shirt that hugged a thick mid-section.

"Billy said you lost your cat?"

Delilah nodded, doing her damnedest to look simultaneously distraught and apologetic. "Binky. A tabby. Someone said your neighbor had her, but no one seems to be home next door."

The woman wiped her eyes, which looked red and bleary from sleep. "Over there?" She motioned toward the house Delilah had just left. Delilah nodded. "You wasted a trip. Emily's dead. If she had your cat, the ASPCA's got it now."

"Dead?"

"Yep. Murdered." The woman lowered her voice. "I'm the one who found her, too."

"That must have been awful."

"You're telling me."

Rain started to come down in sheets, driven by a biting wind. A June thunderstorm. There wasn't enough space under the awning to stay dry, and Delilah could feel water soaking her blouse and the backs of her legs. She huddled closer to the door.

"Where are my manners?" The woman said. "You're gonna catch cold out there! Come in out of the rain for a minute. Maybe you can give me a description of your cat in case she turns up."

Delilah smiled gratefully. She followed the woman through a small entry hall and into a kitchen decorated in a country theme that would make any farmer proud. Green gingham curtains hung on the windows. Matching placemats lay on the table around a wicker basket full of unnaturally shiny red apples. A dried flower wreath hung on the wall over the table. From glass Yankee candles – cinnamon and pine – the scents of winter wafted into the room. The apples made Delilah think of Snow White and for a brief second she wondered whether this woman could be the killer. She dismissed the notion as unlikely.

The woman introduced herself as Janie and offered Delilah a seat. Delilah accepted.

"Coffee?"

"If it's not too much trouble."

"Not at all. Billy and I don't get much company these days. Not since . . . not since my husband left." She turned away from Delilah and spoke while she put water on to boil. She took a jar of instant coffee out of the pantry and placed two mugs of coffee, a carton of mocha-flavored non-dairy creamer and a small bowl of sugar on the table. She poured the water in the mugs and sat down across from Delilah.

"Billy's your son?"

Janie nodded. "I didn't know Emily very well. She was friendly enough. Always had a treat for Billy. Not that I let him go over there too often. But Emily said he reminded her of her nephews, so I figured once in a while was okay." Janie paused. "In fact, that's how I found Emily to begin with."

Janie looked like she wanted to talk about it, so Delilah urged her on with a quiet, "What happened?"

"I couldn't find Billy, so I went knocking on Emily's door. Only her back door was open, so when no one answered, I went in." Janie paused, took a sip of her coffee, looked around the room at nothing in particular. "Emily was in her bedroom. She was fully clothed, thank God for that, but her head . . . her head was cradled in the crook of her own arm. And her face" – Janie gulped – "so swollen and misshapen. I almost didn't recognize her."

"I'm so sorry you had to see that."

Janie's head was bent over her still-fill cup, but she nodded. "Me, too. Someone had beaten her bad. And then . . . and then cut off her head. Blood was everywhere. On the ceiling, in her hair, soaking her bed. I'm afraid I didn't handle it too well. I didn't know where Billy was and I kept thinking . . . I kept thinking, what if Billy had been there when it happened. If he was dead, too."

"But Billy was safe."

"Out riding his bike. Thank God for that."

Delilah could see that the conversation had upset the woman and she tried to shift it to less emotional ground. "Did Emily have family, other than her nephew?"

"Don't know. That nephew was the only mention Emily ever made of family."

"How long did Emily live next door to you?"

"A few months. Three, maybe four."

That seemed to align with when Miriam stopped all contact with Lucinda. "Was Emily a good neighbor?"

Janie took a sip of coffee. "Standoffish. Kept to herself, mostly."

"You must have had reporters swarming the neighborhood."

Janie frowned. "Now that you mention it, no. Only the police. That's odd, isn't it? You'd think something like that in a town like Willston would be big news."

Delilah agreed. "Did Emily own the house, Janie, or was she renting?"

"Oh, she was renting. The owner lives in some fancy town near Philly. I'd rather have Emily as a neighbor, if you know what I mean. Don't need the high maintenance type right in my backyard."

"Do the police have any clue who the killer might be?"

Janie shook her head. "Not that I'm aware." Janie was quiet for a minute. She looked around before speaking, as though checking to be sure her son was not within earshot. "I don't think it was random, though. Emily was an odd one. I may be wrong, but I think she was into something. Something bad."

FIVE

Delilah took a long sip of coffee, forcing herself not to look too interested in Janie's thoughts on the matter of Emily Cray. She was, after all, there for her cat.

"Emily was into something bad? Nothing to do with animals, I hope?" Delilah said casually, after swallowing the rancid concoction in her cup.

"Oh, your cat. No, of course not. Nothing to do with animals." Janie took a swig of coffee, wiped her mouth daintily with a paper napkin and said, "Mind you, I'm not one to spread gossip, especially about the dead." She crossed herself quickly. "It's just that I watched that house. When you have kids, you pay attention to your surroundings. For their safety."

"What did you see?"

"Foreigners."

Delilah's eyes widened. "Men or women?"

"Both, I think." Janie thought for a second. "Actually, now that we're talking about it, mostly women. Maybe all women. I can't really remember."

"How did you know they were foreigners?"

"They dressed funny. Different. Strange color combinations. Head scarves. Even one of those head-to-toe things."

"A burka?"

"Yeah, that. And they were mostly dark-skinned. Indian or Arab, maybe."

"So why did you think something bad was going on?"

"Two reasons." Janie leaned in conspiratorially. "One, they always went to the back door. That's how come I could see them. Our yards are close back there."

"And two?"

"I never saw them leave."

Delilah let that sink in. Foreigners, arriving quietly, leaving, most likely, in the dead of night. Drugs? A terrorism connection? Or simply Miriam's friends?

"Did you tell the police this, Janie?"

Janie nodded. She finished the last bit of her instant coffee and sat back in her chair.

"And what was their reaction?"

Janie cocked her head. "They didn't seem surprised."

#

Frustrated, Barb stared at her computer monitor. It was a Saturday, so the county courthouse was closed. But the same records should have been available online on Pennsylvania's website. Birth, death, social security records. Home purchases. But she couldn't find anything for Emily Cray. Which told her one thing: Emily Cray never existed. At least not legally.

Barb opened a new window on her computer. From downstairs came the murmur of a baseball game. The Phillies. Fred would be sitting on his favorite recliner, Phillies cap on backwards, Cherry Coke in his hand, eyes glued to the set. The Phillies must be winning, she thought, otherwise I'd hear screaming: *You idiots, what are you thinking? My daughter could hit better than that!* But Fred was quiet. She considered running this by him, but decided against it. For now, the less he knew, the better.

She performed another Google search for "Emily Cray" and, after sorting through about one hundred irrelevant results, decided it was pointless.

Emily Cray had been an alias, that was it. Miriam Cross had not officially changed her identity - merely her name. But why? If she was truly running from something or someone, why not go the distance. Anyone could have done what she'd just done and figured out that Emily Cray in Willston, Pennsylvania had no history, no documentation.

And they would have gone right back to Miriam Cross.

Unless that was the point.

Barb stood and stretched. Her back ached from too many hours in one position. Outside, the rain had stopped. She thought about going for a walk and decided against it. While Emily Cray didn't exist, Miriam has been living under that alias for a reason. What had been the point?

After a few minutes of toe-touching and back-arching, Barb sat back down at the computer. She re-opened the Commonwealth's website and repeated her search, but this time for Miriam Cross. *Bingo.* She came up with a host of results. Date of birth. Date of death. Marriages (none). Lawsuits (one – libel – nine years ago). And two addresses in Philadelphia.

Barb opened a new window and did a search of the first address. The Chestnut Hill section of Philadelphia. *This must be where she'd lived with Lucinda.* From what she could tell from the satellite views, it was a beautiful old stone row home in a nice neighborhood. Worth a small fortune, given the location. Next, Barb searched the second address. Old City, in downtown Philadelphia.

Barb compared the dates of purchase. The house in Chestnut Hill had been in Miriam's name for over fifteen years. The house in Old City, eleven months. Which meant that Miriam had bought that house after she disappeared.

So where had she been living? According to Lucinda, it wasn't in Chestnut Hill. So had she been living as Miriam Cross in Philadelphia or as Emily Cray in Willston?

Barb pulled up White Pages in a new window on her computer. She typed in "Miriam Cross." The address that came up was the one for Chestnut Hill. With a phone number. Out of curiosity, Barb picked up the extension next to her computer and dialed the number listed. As she expected, no one answered, but voicemail did pick up. The message said that Miriam Cross was not at home and to please leave a message.

Barb sat and stared at the computer screen for a long moment. She thought she understood what was going on. But there was one thing she needed to check out. Barb stuck her head in the living room. Fred was there, splayed out on the couch, a contented look on his scruffy face. On the television, a Bud Light commercial blared. *Yup, the Phillies must be winning.*

Barb decided to take advantage of his good mood. "I have to head out for a bit."

His gaze didn't leave the screen. "Okay. Where are you going?"

"To the city," Barb said. "To run an errand for Delilah."

Fred sat up, suddenly alert. "What are you up to? It's a Saturday, Barb."

Barb smiled. "Window shopping. See you around five."

#

Raymond Street was one of those quaint Philadelphia cobblestone roads lined on both sides with brick row homes, each three stories, tall and narrow. Most had freshly painted trim and doors – crisp white or dark green – and bars on the windows. A few sported potted plants in matching window boxes on the second or third story. Only two homes looked worn and tired. One, an end unit with a broken screen door and a front stoop of crumbling cement, would have appeared vacant except for the child's tricycle chained to the porch railing. The other, 2129 Raymond Street, looked occupied, although the pile of banded store circulars on the doorstep, too big to fit through the mail slot, and the dying plant in the living room window hinted at a different story.

Miriam's house.

Barb climbed the three steps to the front porch. She knocked loudly and, as she suspected, no one answered. She hopped from the stoop to the empty flower bed in front of the living room picture window. Curtains were drawn, but there was enough space on either side of the dying plant to get a glimpse inside. She could only see a brown couch and the edge of a chair.

Barb skipped down the sloped garden area and stepped back on the sidewalk. She looked up. A third floor light appeared to be on, though it was hard to tell from this vantage point and in broad daylight. Blinds covered the second floor windows. Barb glanced around the neighborhood. She'd parked her minivan a few blocks down because there was no parking on this block of Raymond. But that meant there would be an alley.

An alley with a parking area and back door access.

Barb walked down the block, toward the house with the tricycle. At the corner, she turned right. Sure enough, about halfway down the next block was a narrow unnamed street. She made another right. Along the back, each of the row homes had a paved area that ran the length of the home and was about twelve feet deep. Enough space to parallel park one car. Miriam's house had been the fourth house on the block. The fourth home had a navy blue Toyota Camry parked in the narrow lot. The tires were slightly flat, as though the car had been sitting, abandoned, for quite some time.

Barb glanced in the car, which had, no doubt, been thoroughly searched by police and any evidence removed. Likewise for the house. But Barb wasn't interested in evidence. She had a theory she wanted to prove.

A small brick landing sat a few feet from the Camry. This led to a wooden door, painted deep red. Curls of peeling paint hung in strips along the frame. Barb climbed the two steps and peered through the door window into a tiny kitchen. A row of cabinets, very old from the look of them, stood against one wall. A worn Linoleum countertop with metal trim topped the cabinets. An apartment-size refrigerator abutted one end of the workspace. Two coffee mugs stood next to the metal sink, clearly visible from the back door.

Barb tried the door knob. Locked. She glanced around to make sure no one was watching. Satisfied, she stooped over and pulled a pair of kitchen gloves and a small lock-picking set out of her handbag. The gloves were the same ones she wore to wash dishes. The lock-picking set had been a gift from Natasha and it came in handy on the rare occasions she needed to get in somewhere uninvited. She had practiced on her own front door until she could pick a lock in less than one minute. This time it took her forty seconds.

She hadn't seen an alarm system sign. And if Barb's theory was correct, Miriam had purposefully left the house unprotected. Miriam wouldn't have wanted to blow her cover if someone came sneaking around the property, and an alarm system meant contact information and police involvement. Still, Barb held her breath for the first few minutes, hoping no alarm would sound. She'd know if her theory was right soon enough.

Barb entered, closed the door behind her and made her way into the middle of the kitchen. It was dark, but enough sunlight showed through the back door to guide her way. Barb opened cabinets. Boxes of macaroni and cheese, pasta, cans of soup and jars of sauce had been neatly placed inside the upper cabinets to the left of the sink. In the cabinets on the right, dishes – FiestaWare in different earthy colors – were stacked next to matching coffee mugs and cereal bowls. In the sink sat a small plate; the two coffee cups were on the counter. She opened the dishwasher, knowing what she would find. Sure enough, inside a small load of dishes sat clean and dry.

A tile-topped bistro table perched against one wall. On it, magazines and envelopes sat next to an open paperback novel. Barb glanced at the magazines. Most of them were from the last year. Same with the post marks on the mail. The paperback was a Margaret Atwood novel.

The house was laid out like a train car. The kitchen led to a small dining room, which led into the living room. A set of steps that led to the upper floors and down to the basement were positioned between the kitchen and the dining room. Barb glanced at her watch. It was almost four. She needed to get a move-on.

She did a cursory inspection of the dining room and living room. Same story. The dining room housed an antique table and a small buffet. A majolica vase stood on the buffet, a fine coating of dust covering its surface. The living room was sparsely furnished, containing nothing but a brown couch, a matching chair and a set of end tables. A blanket had been thrown across the chair, made to look as though someone had gotten up to go to bed and couldn't be bothered to fold it. Pieces of mass-produced pottery sat upon the tables along with books on architecture and travel. Framed pictures hung on the walls. Everything wore a fine coating of dust.

No television. But then, maybe a woman like Miriam Cross didn't watch television.

Barb could hear the roar of police sirens. Logic told her the sirens had nothing to do with her. Still, her heart raced. She still needed to check out the bedrooms. She ran up the steps, two at a time. On the second floor she found two bedrooms and a small bath. The first bedroom stood empty except for a twin bed, which was unmade. The second room had been turned into an office. A desk sat against one wall, its top covered with file folders, books and a printer. No computer. Everything had been freshly sorted and moved, probably the work of police detectives. A file cabinet stood against the far wall, its drawers open, folders sticking at odd angles from its depths. Barb knew that anything of interest would already have been taken.

The sirens were getting louder.

Barb ran up the last set of stairs. A master bedroom and bath. The bed was unmade, the sheets and blankets turned down several times and slightly rumpled. One pair of shoes had been carelessly thrown near a cherry wood dresser. Photographs lined the bureau, mostly of Miriam with various famous people. No family shots – which would make sense. Barb ran her finger across the dresser's surface. Dust. The room had been made to look lived-in, but it had the institutional feel of a furnished apartment.

Quickly, Barb opened closet doors. Women's clothes – skirts and suits and blouses – lined the narrow enclosure. Stacks of neatly folded sweaters had been placed on shelves. In the bathroom, one towel was draped across the shower stall, as though left to dry after use. The medicine cabinet door was already open and empty – police handiwork.

The sirens stopped. Barb took a deep breath and headed back toward the stairs. She had been careful, but it only took one witness. Her heart was in her throat and sweat trickled between her breasts. She had confirmed her suspicions. *Time to go.*

On her way out, something caught her eye. Light had fallen across one of the pictures on the dresser. The glass was cracked into a dozen fine lines and the pattern caught the light in flickering bursts. Barb picked it up and stared at the photo. A picture of Miriam with a man. He stood in the shadows, all that was visible a long, thin, dark hand and the suggestion of height. Miriam looked happy. On impulse, Barb stuck the picture in her bag before running down the stairs and out the back door. For some reason, she felt the need to get out of that house like she was in a race for her life.

SIX

Delilah was looking at a hurting man.

Matthew Anderson had chestnut-brown eyes that shone bright with intelligence behind a small pair of wire-rimmed glasses. Tall and slim, with broad shoulders, short, dark hair and a strong jaw that hinted at a day's worth of shadow, he was handsome without being fussy. But Delilah's assessment had nothing to do with his outward appearance. A sadness lingered around Anderson that affected the atmosphere in the room and made Delilah wonder what had broken him so.

"Why Percy-Powers, Mr. Anderson?"

"Please, call me Anders."

"Okay, Anders. What sparked your interest in Percy Powers?" Delilah skimmed his resume. "You have an impressive background. Why do you want to shift gears now and become a private investigator?"

He cocked his head to the side. "Because I'll be good at it."

"I imagine you were good at those other things, too."

Anders nodded. "But right now, I wouldn't be."

"I don't understand."

Anders didn't respond at first. Delilah watched his jaw clench and unclench, matching the action of his fist. The tension was contagious. But she brushed it away as anxiety over the Cross murder – what reason did she have to doubt Anders, after all? She'd just met him. Besides, she had promised herself – and Margot – that she would give him a chance.

"I need to be in the Philly area right now," Anders said. "And I need the money."

"And you figured investigative journalism would translate well to investigating?"

Anders nodded.

"It's a tedious business. Sometimes you sit in your car for hours tailing someone and nothing happens. And it's not dirty bombs or toxic dumping. It's cheating spouses and abusive boyfriends and deadbeat fathers. It's not pretty and it's not uplifting, and honestly, there's no glory at the end of it all. No byline with your name on it."

"Just a paycheck."

"Just a paycheck." Delilah smiled. "I assume that's enough?"

Anders re-positioned himself in the chair, turning to face her, and locked his eyes onto hers. She felt a jolt from the intensity of his stare.

"You won't find a better forensic investigator. I know my way around a computer. I can handle tedious. I can handle physical threats. I can handle whatever you throw at me. I need this job, Ms. Powers. But beyond that, I think you could use me."

Delilah returned his gaze with as much icy calm as she could muster. Part of her resented his forthrightness. She didn't *need* anyone, much less this man. The other part felt sympathy for him. It wasn't in her nature to look upon someone so wounded, whatever the reason - and it was clear he wasn't in a sharing mood - and simply turn away.

She stood. "I think I have everything I need."

He rose slowly, unfurling his long body like a rope. "Thanks for meeting with me."

She walked toward her office door, uncomfortably aware of his presence behind her. In reception she stopped and turned. "If I decide to run a background check on you, Mr. Anderson, what will I find?"

"Anders, please." He seemed unfazed by the question. "Three trespassing violations, one fine for disorderly conduct and a citation for disturbing the peace. If you really dig, you might find a few speeding tickets and a probationary status one semester during college."

"Nothing else?"

He met her gaze. She felt that jolt again. "Nothing else."

#

"He's full of shit, I just know it," Delilah said later. She and Barb were at Delilah's. Delilah had dinner in front of her - a frozen diet meal that was supposed to be chicken but tasted like salted cardboard. She'd tried to convince Barb to eat with her, but it was late - almost nine o'clock - and the other woman had supper waiting for her. Looking down at her plastic dish now, Delilah couldn't blame Barb for declining. This wasn't food.

"What makes you say that?" Barb said.

"Just something about him. Great credentials, seems smart, didn't have three heads or pick his nose during the interview. So why us? Why a PI when he could go back to the glory and excitement of journalism?"

"Because it's not that glorious and it's not that exciting? That's one possibility. Or maybe he pissed off the wrong people and he's been blacklisted."

"I called his references – impeccable."

Barb considered this. "Well, he told you he needs to stay around here for some reason. I bet working for a PI firm pays a hell of a lot better than being a desk jockey for the local paper."

"Maybe." Delilah shrugged. "I guess it's his business. I'm running a background check, and then I'll decide."

"He sounds like a catch."

"He sounds like trouble."

Barb laughed. Delilah liked the sound of someone else's laughter in her kitchen. She liked the way the dogs snuggled at Barb's feet, hungry for someone's attention other than her own.

Delilah said, "On to Miriam?"

Barb nodded.

Delilah recounted her trip to Willston. "Don't know how reliable the neighbor was. She seemed lonely and maybe a little bored, looking for drama. But I don't think she was making up the bit about the people coming to Miriam's door."

"So *someone* knew Miriam lived there. Even if they knew her as Emily Cray."

"Exactly. She wasn't a complete recluse." Delilah thought for a moment. "The neighbor, Janie, said they were foreigners. And efforts had been made to hide their comings and goings. If Janie's right, that could add a whole different wrinkle."

"Terrorism?"

"That's what comes to mind, though I find it hard to believe. Janie said they were mostly women."

"That she saw."

"True. Maybe Miriam was interviewing people for a book."

"Then why not be upfront about it?" Barb said. "Why all the secrecy?"

Delilah stood, stretched and stifled a yawn. "Could have been controversial or dangerous. That would fit her M.O. And she *was* murdered. We have to assume for the time being that everything is connected to that simple fact. *Someone* wanted Miriam Cross dead."

"Or," Barb said. "Someone wanted *Emily Cray* dead."

Delilah walked to the sink. She ran the tap for a moment and rinsed her hands before pulling a wine glass from the cabinet. "Pinot?"

"Trying to quit."

Delilah smiled. She grabbed the chilled bottle of Pinot Grigio out of the fridge and poured herself a glass. The moon was full, and she caught a glimpse of its soft glow from her open kitchen window. A soothing breeze rustled through the dense woods that surrounded her farm. Delilah enjoyed the momentary relief from the heat.

She said, "Were you able to find anything about Miriam's identity change?"

"Emily Cray doesn't exist. Plain and simple. The name was an alias. There was no history of an Emily Cray in Willston. Not even an address listed. Miriam still had her house in Chestnut Hill on file as her address. She must have been renting the house in Willston."

"She was. The neighbor confirmed that. I plan to talk with the landlord tomorrow." Delilah considered the news about the Chestnut Hill property. "So Miriam Cross kept up appearances despite her disappearance?"

"I think she went a step farther than that. She wanted it to look like she'd set up house in another location, on the run. As a ruse. She kept the original address – Chestnut Hill. But someone who came looking for her and had half a brain would realize she wasn't there. So she bought a second property. In cash. No listed phone or address and it was on a busy, secure block in Philadelphia."

"Did you check it out?"

"Inside and out."

Delilah smiled. "Cameras or security?"

"None that I saw. But it looked like the cops had searched the place."

"What was it like? No, let me guess," Delilah sat down across from Barb and stretched her legs in front of her. "Sparsely decorated, but Miriam had tried to make it look like someone was living there."

"Right. Unmade bed, dishes in the sink, just enough clutter." Barb shook her head. "But there was a solid coating of dust on everything. Whoever Miriam had been paying for upkeep had become lax. Either that, or Miriam was doing it herself. And she stopped going weeks ago."

"Did you get the sense that she had lived in that house at all?"

"Maybe for a little while between the time she left Chestnut Hill and her stay at Willston, if I had to guess. Not recently, though. Honestly, I think the Philly house was meant to be a decoy."

"To throw someone off the trail and protect Emily Cray."

"Exactly."

Delilah thought about what Lucinda had said when they'd met a few days ago, about Miriam's periodic disappearances. Had she gone to these lengths before?

Three whole months without any contact seemed extreme, even for an eccentric like Miriam.

Delilah said, "Any other real estate history that you could find?"

"Not in Pennsylvania. Could be assets in other states – or overseas – that we don't know about. Wouldn't show up on the Commonwealth's website."

"We need to find out. Her niece mentioned that disappearing for stints at a time was Miriam's style. I want to know whether this time - the name change, the fake address - was special or whether Miriam had been living this way for years."

Barb was silent for a moment. She drained the last of her coffee and put the mug down with a light thud. "I thought of that, Delilah. And I did what I could to search records, but I came up with *nada*. I hate to sound like Margot, but she's right. We could use a computer expert."

"I know."

"Matthew Anderson. He's here, interested and has the right credentials." Barb smiled. Delilah considered Barb an old and true friend. She could be salty and bitingly no-nonsense, but she was also smart and kind and always had Delilah's back. Delilah trusted her unconditionally, which said a lot. When it came down to it, Delilah didn't trust many people.

"Margot's a smart lady," Barb said, rising. "You should listen to her."

Delilah waved her hand in dismissal. "Next steps. I'll track down the landlord. See what else you can find online about Miriam's assets, bank accounts, etc. I'll ask Natasha to ask around Miriam's Philadelphia neighborhood, to see whether the neighbors remember seeing her there. I need to find a role for her, anyway."

Delilah accompanied Barb to the front door, the dogs nudging her legs from behind. Barb stood in the doorway, her plain, square leather purse under one arm, a spiral-bound notebook in her hand.

Barb said, "It's almost harder following a public figure."

Delilah nodded. "The real Miriam Cross was a mystery. Before we can find out who killed her, we need to cull the public image from the private person. Seems like that will be more difficult than I'd hoped."

SEVEN

Enid Bartholomew was not the type of landlord Delilah expected. She lived on the Main Line of Philadelphia, a wealthy suburb of old money estates, the nouveau rich and ladies who lunch. Enid was clearly not the latter. Thin as a stick figure, with a razor-sharp chin and enough silicone for a manufacturing plant, Enid eyed Delilah with a look of disdainful curiosity.

"Who did you say you are?" she asked.

"A friend of Emily Cray's niece."

"Like I told the police, I don't pry into the background of my tenants. I'm afraid, therefore, that I will not be of help to your friend."

"Just a few questions. I promise I won't take up more than fifteen minutes of your time."

Enid sat across from Delilah at the local Barnes and Noble, the picture of practiced nonchalance. It was Monday morning, a little after ten. Tracking Enid down had been easy enough.

Miriam's neighbor, Janie, had given her a name. And Enid's number was listed. Not a whole lot of Enid Bartholomews in Pennsylvania. Delilah had called on Sunday night and received a half-hearted agreement to meet Delilah for coffee. But Delilah was beginning to think that getting the woman to talk would be another matter.

Enid took a weak sip of her skim latte. "What do you want to know?"

"How long ago did Emily contact you?"

Enid thought for a moment. "Four months tomorrow."

"That exact?"

"I'm a business woman. Rentals *are* my business. The house on Lacy had been vacant for almost three months. I'd just cleaned it up, was looking for the right kind of person. Older, no parties, no kids, no pets." She took another sip of her coffee, puckered her skinny lips and put the cup down. She wagged one finger at Delilah.

"Of course, I can't really ask about kids. Can't discriminate and all that horseshit. Damn lawyers. So when Emily showed up, I was relieved. Happy to have an older woman. Responsible. No kids."

"So you didn't run a credit history on Emily?"

"Why in the world would I do that?"

"Isn't that normal procedure when you're renting to someone?"

"Only when you're not careful about whom you're renting to. But I'm careful. No single parents. No kids. No one under twenty-five."

Delilah looked at her questioningly. "Still, weren't you worried she wouldn't be able to pay?"

63

"Not at all. She paid me a year in advance. In cash."

"How much was that worth?"

"Fourteen hundred a month. Twelve months. You do the math."

Sixteen thousand, eight hundred. A lot of money. "Cash again?"

Enid nodded.

"And you didn't find that odd?"

"Like I told the police, I don't get involved in my tenants' affairs. They keep the place clean, pay their rent, I mind my business."

"But you had to wonder."

Enid looked down at her coffee. When she looked back up, Delilah saw shrewdness in her eyes. For all her plastic surgery and make-up, Enid was still rough around the edges. Probably not from the Main Line, but making a go at staying there.

"Sure, I wondered. But some women don't choose men too well. She looked a little shaken, a little lost. So I thought maybe she was running from a beater, you know what I mean?" Enid shrugged. "She paid up front. She had good manners and clean clothes. She seemed smart and sane. What did I have to lose?"

"And now?"

Enid shrugged again. "Something happened. Had nothing to do with my house or me. Do I feel bad for her? Yeah, of course. Do I feel pissed that my house is tied up with the police for a while? That I've got a mess to clean up and the chance that no one will want to rent a house where someone was murdered? Hell, yeah. But what can I do?"

Delilah considered this. If Enid was telling the truth, she'd had little contact with her tenant during the months Miriam lived there. Still, so far, Enid was their lone connection to Miriam's alter ego.

"Can you describe Emily when you met her?" Delilah said.

Enid looked surprised at the question. "Short platinum hair. Thin. No make-up. Kind of attractive – or she could have been, with a little effort. Soft spoken." Another shrug. "Like I said, she seemed a little sad, a little shaken. We met at the house. She took a minute to walk around, and then she said she wanted it. Just like that."

"Didn't that spark your curiosity?"

"Curiosity doesn't pay the bills. Like I said, she offered a year up front. Good manners. Not a lot of stuff."

Delilah sat up a little straighter. "Stuff?"

"Yeah, I like that. Hate to be left with a tenant's belongings after they leave. This lady was traveling light."

"What does that mean?"

"It means she didn't have a lot of stuff."

Delilah was getting impatient. "I understand that. But how would you have known that at the time?"

"Because she wanted to move in immediately. That day. And she had her stuff with her in her car. A suitcase. And a few boxes – books or papers or something. And a laptop case. That was it."

"Didn't you think that was odd?"

Delilah knew what Enid would say before the words were out of her mouth. "Her business, not mine."

Delilah didn't believe her. A savvy business woman would ask some questions, want some personal information. But Enid wasn't budging. Delilah said, "So you simply handed her the keys that day? What about furniture?"

"Already furnished."

"She must have given you some form of identification, a cell phone, something."

Enid stared at her, clearly exasperated. "Why do you want to know this stuff?"

"Because a woman was murdered, Enid. Like I said, I'm a friend of her niece. Did the police tell you that Emily Cray was an alias?"

"Yeah, so? A runner, like I figured. Where there's a runner, there's a beater."

"Not just any runner. Emily was really Miriam Cross. The author."

Enid stared blankly.

"The *famous* author."

Enid sat back, her expression unreadable. "So?" She said finally.

"So it seems odd that a famous author showed up at your house with a car load of stuff and a lot of cash, don't you think?"

"There was a beater involved," Enid said. "I'm telling you, there's always a beater."

#

Natasha stood on the corner of Raymond and Arch, hands in the pockets of her black sleeveless hoodie, and turned her face toward the sun. She closed her eyes and pictured the layout of the neighborhood. From this spot, she could hear the traffic rushing by on Route 95. Over a few blocks, on the other side of Columbus Boulevard, would be the Delaware River and Penn's Landing. To the south, South Street and Society Hill.

Natasha had dressed to blend, which wasn't hard. She wore low-slung jeans, a white tank and the hoodie, her naked arms embroidered in tattoos. Her hair was pinned back from her forehead. She'd left the silver studs in her lip, nose and ears. A switchblade sat tucked into her pocket, within easy reach. She patted it now.

You never know.

Miriam's house was fourth on the block. Seemed like a nice neighborhood. Natasha mentally calculated how much Miriam must have paid for this house and the Chestnut Hill house, plus rent for the Willston place. *Chick was loaded.* Natasha had read one of Miriam's novels, she couldn't remember which, and found it preachy. She hated preachy, even if she agreed with the preacher.

Natasha checked her watch. She'd been standing on the corner for almost ten minutes while she waited for a neighbor to come outside. People were funny about opening the door for a stranger, especially in the city. Now she'd have to start knocking on doors. Just as she was taking a step toward the house next to Miriam's, she caught movement out of the corner of her eye. She stopped, watched. Then she saw him. Or, rather, she saw his shadow in the hot noonday sun. She followed the shadow, splayed black against the bleached cobblestones, until she located the source.

A man was tucked next to the bushes between two houses, facing Miriam's property. He wore a black t-shirt and a black baseball cap. He could've been a cop, but he looked more like a goon. Natasha whispered thanks that she'd seen him before she started knocking on doors and asking about Miriam. She debated what to do next.

She couldn't very well approach the neighbors unless she went around back, into the alley. But if someone was watching the front of the house, chances were good that someone was watching the back of the house, too. And she didn't want to bump into *that* someone. Natasha patted the knife again. She wouldn't hurt anyone unless she had to. But if she had to, well, it wouldn't be her fault.

What the hell was he doing there, anyway?

Still debating her next move, she saw her mark glance around and step out of the bushes. She made a show of checking her cell phone, throwing a sideways glance at the stalker. He started walking toward her. She ignored him. When she sensed him pass, she turned her body slightly so that she could follow his movement. Sure enough, he was joined by another man - this one shorter and stockier - at the entrance to the alley. Together they walked down Arch, not talking.

Natasha thought about her bike, locked onto one of the bike racks. She opted to walk. She'd lose them if she went to get it. She let the men have a half-block head start, and then she followed them, matching her pace to theirs.

On the corner of Arch and Fifth, by Independence Mall, the two men stopped. The taller one pulled a cell phone out of his pocket. He glanced around. Natasha stepped back into the shadows. She watched him make a call. He spoke briefly into the phone and, after a few seconds, snapped the phone shut and nodded to the other man. The taller man raised his hand and waved for a taxi. He got in and was gone.

The shorter man stood there for a few minutes. Crowds bustled around him. A teenaged boy carrying a skateboard bumped into the guy, but the goon shrugged it off. Suddenly he turned and looked right at Natasha.

She stood pressed against a wall in the doorway of a church, but she felt completely exposed. She toyed with the idea of running but decided against it. He wouldn't dare shoot her here in full view of the public. She pulled the knife from her pocket but kept it hidden.

It took him fifteen seconds to get to her. By that time, the blade was positioned against her palm. One flick of her wrists and she could jam it wherever it needed to go. If he tried to lead her somewhere, she'd use it. She knew better than to leave a public place with a would-be attacker. She'd made that mistake once before. *Never again.*

He grabbed her right arm.

"Let go or I'll scream," she hissed.

"Tell me why you're following me."

"I'm not following you, you fucking idiot. Let go of me."

"I saw you. On Raymond Street." He tightened his grip on her arm. His breath smelled of cigarettes and salami. Natasha moved her hand to the side, gripping the knife tightly. She was glad she was left-handed. He thought he was disabling her ability to fight back. He was wrong.

"You're coming with me. Play it nice and easy. bitch, or you're gonna get a quiet bullet through your side."

Natasha couldn't see his left hand, but the right one was gripping her arm. She hadn't seen a bulge on his t-shirt or jeans, and he hadn't reached down to pull anything from his pant leg, much less a pistol with a silencer attached. *He's bluffing.*

"Where are you taking me?"

"This isn't twenty questions."

He had a faint New York accent. "Follow" came out as "folla." *What are New York goons doing outside Miriam's house?* But Natasha didn't have time to ponder that thought. The guy twisted her arm around her back. Pain tore through her shoulder blade.

"Let's go, bitch. You're coming with me."

Magic words. "The fuck I am."

Natasha flicked her left hand and heard the satisfying click of the knife. With as much momentum as she could muster in this small space, she jammed the knife into his thigh. He gasped and let go of her arm. Natasha didn't waste time. She pulled the knife out, snapped it shut and ran. She headed for Independence Mall.

Natasha zig-zagged through the park, trying to blend into the crowd. Goon number one wasn't going anywhere far or fast – she'd gotten him good. But she figured that goon number two taking a taxi was a ploy. He was waiting for goon number one somewhere nearby.

He may have even seen her escape. She wasn't about to fall into his trap.

But her bike was by Miriam's house. No way she could go there now.

And she had no money for a train, taxi or bus.

Damn.

She headed for the Quaker Meeting House and ran to the back of the building. She pulled her hair out of the clips, quickly unzipped her hoodie and threw it into the dumpster. It wasn't much, but any alteration of her appearance would help. She kept the knife closed, but held it against her palm. Just in case.

She needed to get out of the area. Fast.

She looked around the side of the building and scanned the park. No sign of either of them. Goon number one would need medical attention. He could tell the cops she attacked him, but if he was a bad guy, and she was sure he was, he wouldn't risk police involvement. And if he went to the hospital, they'd call the police. They always did for a knife wound. So he would dress it himself or, if he was Mafia, he would head for a Mob doctor.

But goon number two would be more worried about her than about goon number one. That was the nature of those guys. And they would make her look a lot worse than goon number one looked.

If they caught her.

Natasha ran through her options in her head. Hiding was out of the question. They would out-wait her. She needed to go now, while they were still off-balance. She jogged down the Mall until she got to Market Street. There, running would be too conspicuous. She walked, quickly, side-stepping pedestrians and looking over her shoulder for her assailant. Her heart was pounding but her attention was razor-sharp, a benefit from years of living on the streets. She angled her way toward Penn's Landing, her eyes on the riverfront.

Once she got past the crowds, Natasha broke back into a jog. It wasn't until she sprinted her way across Delaware Avenue that she let herself slow down. She looked behind her. No sign of either asshole. She tucked the knife into her front pocked and scanned the marina. There, on the side of the river, she saw what she was looking for. A stray kayak, its paddles thrown carelessly alongside the fiberglass craft. Before she could talk herself out of it, she picked up the small boat, pushed it into the water, and wedged inside. She'd never kayaked before, but she'd figure it out. How hard could it be?

She pushed away from the edge and headed downcurrent. She didn't need to go any great distance – just far enough to put some miles between her and the goons. She paddled hard, trying to blend with the other boats in the marina. She felt bad about stealing the boat – but she'd had no choice. She blamed herself for coming into the job with no back-up money.

Never again. Natasha always made a point to learn from her mistakes.

She looked up. Route 95 followed the Delaware River. She'd get out along the way, dump the boat, and hitch a ride. Things would work out.

No sweat.

EIGHT

Natasha stood outside of Delilah's barn, clearly terrified of the horses. Considering what she'd just been through, Delilah found this current fear amusing. She was proud of the girl for her resourcefulness. But she was annoyed that Natasha had followed the men at all. It'd been a huge risk.

Delilah finished brushing Millie. She stroked the underside of the mare's muzzle and listened to Natasha's recounting of events. It was late Monday afternoon. Clouds were crowding the sky and Delilah braced herself for a rash of evening thunderstorms. The humidity felt like a wet, heavy cloak. At least with rain there'd be some relief from the oppressive heat.

"Any sense of who they were?"

Natasha shook her head. "Goons. Hired ones, if I had to guess. At first I thought they might be cops, staking out the place. But neither of them looked too gifted in the brains department. And the short one had a New York accent."

"Funny that Barb didn't see anyone Saturday. So why would they be watching Miriam's house now?" Delilah said. "And why risk coming after you?"

Natasha shrugged. "I thought I was being inconspicuous. I stayed back a full block" – she pointed at her clothes – "and I dressed like a student. Maybe they *were* there Saturday and Barb didn't see them."

"Doubtful." Delilah thought for a moment. "Either you saw something they didn't want you to see – or you happened along at the wrong time."

"Drugs?"

"It does sound like they were waiting for a delivery. But why would Miriam be mixed up in drugs?" Delilah gave the horse a gentle pat. "Did you see anything else suspicious?"

"No. Just the men."

Delilah threw a saddle blanket on Millie's back and a saddle on top of that. She buckled the belt that went underneath the horse and slid a finger between Millie and the girth to check for tightness. Gentle Millie leaned in toward Delilah, making the process easier. When Millie was saddled up, Delilah turned to Natasha.

"Want to give it a go?"

"No way." Natasha backed up so that she was tucked into the trees that lined the other side of the fence. "Me and horses don't mix."

Delilah smiled. Natasha didn't look any worse for wear after today's ordeal. But she *had* stabbed a man. That was serious. And had the men caught her . . . Delilah didn't even want to think about what could have happened. She purposefully hired competent women, women who could blend and be unobtrusive, but who had guts and wits and a dose of common sense. Barb was heavy on the common sense. Margot was big on wits. Natasha had enough of all three, but guts were her thing. And sometimes guts needed to be tempered with a strong dose of reality.

"No more going after people like that, Natasha. Until we know more about what we're dealing with, we keep it clean and simple. You should have let them go. We gained nothing by your little adventure, other than risking your life."

Natasha looked angry. "Is that an order?"

"I admire your courage. And your quick thinking. But yes, it's an order."

Delilah put one foot in a stirrup, heaved her weight onto that leg and swung the other leg over the horse's back. She wiggled in the saddle, shifting forward to get comfortable, and grabbed the reins. She was in the mood for a ride through the woods. She'd get Millie some exercise, clear the cobwebs from her own head, and then go back to work. Natasha's misadventure had made her curious. She wanted to speak with Lucinda again. There were a few things she needed to know.

When Delilah looked up from the reins, she saw Natasha staring at her. She looked like she'd swallowed nails.

"What?" Delilah said.

"You gave me an order."

"I give you a paycheck, too," Delilah said.

"You never give me orders. It makes me think you're nervous."

Delilah nudged the horse forward. Millie responded with a slow walk toward the fence where Natasha stood.

"I'm not nervous, Natasha," Delilah said. "This is a game of chess. But until we know who our opponent is, we don't what we're up against. And we can't be sure of our strategy."

"Nothing's going to happen if we just sit around, waiting for them to make a move."

Delilah smiled. "Who said anything about sitting around? Besides, as our opponents proved today, whatever Miriam was mixed up in, it didn't end with her murder. It's just a matter of time until our opponents make their next play."

#

After Natasha left, Delilah called Lucinda. She didn't answer her cell phone, so Delilah tried her work number. Someone picked up on the third ring.

"River Crossings Assisted Living, where the golden years are golden," a flat voice said. "How may I direct your call?"

"Lucinda Mills, please."

"One moment."

One moment turned into three minutes, but eventually Lucinda came on the line. She spoke so softly that Delilah had trouble hearing her. In the background, Delilah heard the constant murmur of voices and the clang of metal against ceramic. She assumed Lucinda was in the nursing home's dining room.

"I can't really talk," Lucinda said. "Did you find out anything?"

"I'll update you, but not on the phone. We need to meet."

"I get off work tonight at seven. I can meet you then. At Starbucks again?"

"No. At Miriam's house in Chestnut Hill."

Lucinda hesitated for a moment. "Why there?"

"You have a key?"

"Yes."

"I want to look around. Meet me there at seven."

"I don't think that's a good idea. The police-"

Delilah cut her off. "I need to look through her things, Lucinda."

"There's really nothing there. Nothing of importance, at least."

Delilah persisted. "Trust me. Seven in Chestnut Hill?"

"If you say so," the other woman said finally. "I'll see you then."

#

Delilah arrived at the Chestnut Hill home at six o'clock. She wanted time to stake out the place while it was still light outside, to make certain it wasn't being watched. If Natasha encountered henchmen at Miriam's Center City house, they could be here, too. She drove the nondescript Honda around the block until she'd located the property. Then she parked a block and a half away and watched for any signs of visitors.

The house was a three-story stone row home on a quiet city street. Anend unit, and obviously old but, like the other houses in the neighborhood, well cared for. Flagstone steps led to a small landing. Wooden double doors marked the entrance, which had a peep hole and a bell, but no windows in the door. Instead, sidelights flanked the doorway, the trim around them painted a deep burgundy. No newspapers on the front porch, no piles of store circulars or UPS packages stacked by the door, no lights on inside. The house looked buttoned up and empty.

At six-thirty, Delilah decided to take a walk around the property. She rarely carried a gun, but she'd brought her .38 snub nose today. She tucked it into the holster around her ankle and pulled the leg of her boot-cut jeans down to conceal the bulge. Then she got out of the car, locked the doors, and pushed her key down into her front pants pocket.

Outside, the afternoon sun sat low in the sky. Bands of pink and orange rose from the horizon. Delilah squinted in the glare. She walked down the block, attentive to her surroundings. There were few hiding places on this street – no rows of overgrown shrubs or ivy-covered iron gates. Just the rose bushes that lined the neighbor's stoop. Still, she scanned the street for parked cars or unmarked vans. All clear. If someone was watching this property, they were well hidden.

Delilah checked the front door to Miriam's house. Locked. Windows in the front were intact. Delilah walked quickly around the concrete path that led to the back of the property. A detached stone garage sat at the back edge of a small yard, a paved parking spot in front of it. Like the house, the trim on the garage had been recently painted. The doors were in good shape and locked. There were no windows.

Delilah walked around the perimeter of tiny back yard, alert for sounds or movement. The grass was overgrown and weeds had sprouted between unkempt perennials. A koi pond sat empty next to a small stone patio. The only adornments were a weathered iron bistro table and two matching chairs.

Three concrete steps led to a back door, its window barred. Delilah tried the knob. Locked. She scanned the back of the house for signs of a break-in. Nothing looked disturbed. The house seemed desolate and lonely, but solid. Delilah took a deep breath. It was six forty-eight. Lucinda should be here soon. Delilah walked around the front of the property and waited.

Lucinda arrived ten minutes late.

The other woman ran up the steps. She still wore her work uniform and her rubber clogs made a hollow sound against the stone. She nodded at Delilah and pulled a key from her purse. Once inside, she flicked up the light switch and a soft glow flooded the front foyer.

"I figured the power would be off," Lucinda said.

"It'll take a few months before the power company gets around to cutting off service."

"But that means she kept the power on when she wasn't living here. Why?"

"Appearances," Delilah said. "She wanted people to think she still lived here. Your aunt went to a lot of effort to throw somebody off her trail. I just wish we knew who." Delilah pointed toward the kitchen. "Mind if I look around?"

Lucinda shook her head. "No. I'm going to sit for a few minutes. Been standing all day."

Delilah took off down the hall. The front door opened into a small foyer, outlined with white and gray marble tiles. Through an open closet door, Delilah saw coats and shoes on the floor. One scarf, fuzzy purple wool, lay half in and half out of the cramped space.

The entryway led into a large living room. On one end stood a baby grand piano. The other end was designed to be an intimate parlor: a loveseat and two upholstered chairs faced each other across an antique coffee table. Stacks of books, their jackets now dusty, had been scattered across the table. A notebook sat on the floor next to a Bic pen, its cap off. Delilah flipped through the notebook. Mostly blank.

Delilah walked through a small dining room and into the kitchen. Clean but cluttered. Stacks of books were scattered on a small tiled table. Mostly fiction, but Delilah also saw a photography book on Russia and a treatise on investing. Two kitchen towels hung crookedly from the stove handle. A sauce pan sat in the sink, its bottom covered with a cloudy liquid. The small countertop was covered with dishes and cups. They were all clean, but someone – either Miriam or the police – had laid them haphazardly on the granite surface. Two cabinet doors stood ajar, their dark interiors mostly empty.

Unlike the Philadelphia property Barb had described, this house looked as though its owner left in the midst of everyday activity. Delilah thought about what Enid, Emily Cray's landlord, had told her: Miriam arrived with only a few boxes of belongings. And that matched the look of this house, which said she'd left most of her belongings behind. Why?

There was a beater involved, Enid had said. *There's always a beater.*

Delilah was beginning to wonder.

#

At 8:10, Delilah finished her walk through the property. The rest of the house looked like the downstairs. Closet doors open, cabinets half empty, towels scattered on the bathroom floor, medicine cabinet empty. Books and magazines were strewn everywhere, but none of them gave Delilah any clue to what Miriam had been working on. There were no themes, no red flags. Just the eclectic collection of an educated, intellectual woman.

Miriam's bedroom was the only oddity. The bed was stripped – the police again, probably looking for semen or some other DNA sample that might offer a clue. But other than that, the room was largely intact. Someone had folded the comforter over a taupe armchair. The room itself was decorated in browns, taupe and ice blue. The furniture was a rich cherry wood, simple, with antique brass pulls. It looked custom made.

Most of Miriam's clothes were still in the closet and the drawers. Suits, jeans, sweaters, many of them designer pieces, size 6 petite, hung on black matching hangers in a closet that seemed small by today's standards.

The closet was stuffed to capacity. Why hadn't Miriam taken more clothes when she left? And why hadn't she come back again to pack them up? The full closet supported the notion of a fast escape and backed up Enid's story that Miriam had showed up with only a few suitcases. Maybe Miriam wanted to change her name *and* her image. She wanted to blend in with the norm in Willston. And $500 silk blouses would not have helped her to do that.

Or maybe she was afraid to return.

Finished with the closet, Delilah glanced around the room. Only Miriam's tall dresser remained. Delilah opened the top drawer and did a quick inventory of cotton underwear and flannel nightshirts. Nothing interesting. In the second drawer though, Delilah found lingerie. Not simply Victoria's Secret, the kind Delilah might buy for herself, but expensive French lingerie, some of it risqué. Peek-a-boo teddies and silk chemises and corsets with matching garter belts from Agent Provocateur. And tucked way in the back, behind the lingerie, were the toys.

Padded handcuffs, a black satin blindfold and beautiful silk scarves with colorful, intricate designs. It wasn't a lurid collection, which was probably why the police had left it all here. Rather, the items in the back of Miriam's drawer were fairly tame, well-made and had been carefully wrapped and stowed.

Delilah had the feeling that these items represented something to Miriam.

Something she was willing – or needed – to leave behind.

Delilah heard footsteps on the wooden floor in the hallway. Hastily, and for reasons even she was unsure of, Delilah tucked the items back in the dresser, covered them with lingerie, and closed the drawer.

"Find anything?" Lucinda said. She looked and sounded exhausted. In the watery bedroom light, Delilah could make out dark bags under her eyes, gray hair at her roots. Delilah felt a tender concern.

"I need to ask you a few personal questions about Miriam."

Lucinda nodded warily.

"Did your aunt have a lover?"

Lucinda looked startled. "Aunt Miriam? No."

"Never?"

"None that we ever met. I often wondered if . . . if Aunt Miriam was gay."

"Did she have girlfriends?"

"No, it wasn't that. She just seemed asexual, I guess. Like relationships weren't important to her."

"So why would you think she was gay?"

Lucinda walked to her aunt's closet. She fingered one of her blouses, ran her hand down the length of the sleeve. Delilah saw an escaped tear glistening on her cheek. "I thought maybe she was a closeted gay woman. That would explain her disinterest in men."

"Disinterested how?"

Lucinda looked at Delilah sharply. "Are these questions really necessary?"

"Your aunt was murdered," Delilah said softly. "There may be parts of her life she'd kept hidden. I'm trying to figure out if there could have been a man involved."

With clear reluctance, Lucinda nodded her understanding. "If Miriam was seeing someone, I would have known. Had Aunt Miriam had been a religious woman, she could have been a nun. She was *that* celibate."

Delilah thought of the sexy lingerie, the padded cuffs. Not the belongings of a celibate woman. Unless she wore them to fantasize . . . but that seemed unlikely.

The simple answer is usually the right one, her father, James Percy, used to say. It was a mantra Delilah lived by. And the simple answer was that Miriam Cross had had a lover. Or several lovers.

"I looked through her belongings," Delilah said. "But there's not much personal stuff here. Papers, notebooks. The police must have confiscated most of it."

Lucinda nodded. "She probably took anything important with her to Willston."

"Did she leave anything with you? Papers, a computer . . . anything?"

"No. She left without a word to me. I stopped by this house and it looked deserted. Much like you're seeing now." She rubbed her temple. "I'm tired, Delilah. I want to get home to the boys."

"I know. And I'm sorry for the twenty questions. Just a few more and we can leave, okay?"

"Okay."

"The other times Miriam disappeared, can you get me dates?"

"Why?"

"I'd like to see if the pattern is the same. There seems to be no public trail during this disappearance. It would help to know whether that was always the case when she left or whether this time was different."

Lucinda nodded. "I'll try to remember some rough dates. I don't have them written down anywhere."

"Whatever you can come up with." Delilah leaned against the wall, her mind going over and over the details, trying to make sense of what she'd found out so far. "Lucinda, the police. How did they know Emily was Miriam Cross?"

"They said Miriam's personal effects, including identification, were in the Willston home."

"Did they turn those personal effects over to you?"

Lucinda shook her head.

Delilah sighed. No files, no papers. Just a bedroom full of abandoned clothes and an attic full of books. "Okay. If you think of anything else, please call me. Even if it doesn't seem important at the time, it might be."

Lucinda nodded.

"Are you and the boys okay? Anymore calls?"

Lucinda looked down at the floor. "No," she said a little too quickly.

"We talked about honesty, Lucinda. If someone is bothering you, we can call the police" – at the mere mention of the cops, terror clouded Lucinda's eyes – "or I can have someone watch your house."

"Not necessary. The boys are staying with Butch's mom for a few weeks when school lets out. Part of our divorce agreement. And I'll be fine."

Delilah reluctantly agreed to let it go. For now. "But call me if there is even the hint of trouble."

Lucinda smiled her agreement, but the smile did not reach her eyes.

NINE

Tuesday morning, Delilah stretched her way to awareness. It was nearly five. She'd overslept by thirty minutes and the horses would be anxious. But her head hurt and she'd been plagued by dreams all nights. Weird sexual dreams in which a young Miriam Cross bedded one monster after another.

The lingerie. And the toys.

Delilah knew her reaction had as much to do with her own situation as it did with her perception of Miriam. She believed Lucinda was telling the truth, or at least her version of the truth. To Lucinda, Miriam *was* celibate. Clearly Miriam had not shared her personal life with her family. Maybe she was into kink. Maybe Miriam preferred women. Or, perhaps, she simply did not want to expose her private life to others, even those closest to her.

Delilah could certainly understand.

Michael had been dead almost fourteen years and still Delilah ached for him every day. Sex for her now was a release, something she did with a casual acquaintance or someone she'd just met when the loneliness or the stress became unbearable. Sex meant nothing to her anymore.

She'd dated since Michael, of course. Not much – maybe half a dozen guys over the past decade. But always they were too distant or too boring or too emotional or too controlling or too laid back.

In other words, they weren't Michael.

Delilah wasn't surprised that Lucinda thought Miriam celibate. People made assumptions when they didn't have all the facts. Delilah's own mother, her step dad and her sisters – all of them saw her as some kind of androgynous recluse. In her family's circle, a person simply did not *choose* to stay single.

No, in the Powers family, marriage was pragmatic. One gave up niceties like independence and personal goals for the greater benefits of security and procreation. So when Delilah left Virginia a few years after Michael died so that she could go to law school in Philadelphia, her family waited for her to come to her senses. They waited for her to get over Michael, find a nice, respectable man and give up the silly notion of independence.

They were still waiting.

Delilah stayed in Philadelphia. She had wanted to return to her roots in Wyoming, to take up where her own daddy had left off, on a ranch with horses. But that had been her and Michael's dream and back then she couldn't bear the thought of living that dream alone.

Still couldn't.

Had Miriam had a Michael in her past? Was Miriam running from her own feelings of loneliness and anger and betrayal?

Delilah just didn't know. She closed her eyes and thought about the puzzle pieces. A house in Chestnut Hill suddenly abandoned. Another in Philadelphia made to look occupied. A rental home in Willston, Pennsylvania. The foreign visitors. The thugs who chased Natasha. And the damn lingerie. *There's always a beater.* How the hell did it all fit together?

Delilah's cell phone rang. She picked it up off the bedside table and squinted at the caller I.D. Lucinda.

"I do have some of Miriam's stuff," Lucinda said, sounding breathless. "I checked this morning. I must have taken a box of her belongings by accident when I moved my things from her house last year."

Delilah sat up. "What's in it?"

"I haven't even opened it. It's secured with duct tape. I'm running out the door now. I won't have time to go through it until tonight."

"How about if I go through it?"

"Sure, but don't get your hopes up, Delilah. It's too small to be anything important." Lucinda paused. "I'm heading to work now - the early shift. Can you meet me at the nursing home at ten? I have a break then. I'll bring the box with me. If there's anything inside worth keeping, you can give it to me later."

#

Barb was the first to arrive to the eight o'clock staff meeting. She walked into Percy Powers wearing nylon sweat pants and a golf shirt, carrying something loaf-shaped and wrapped in foil. This she put down next to a stack of papers on her tiny desk.

Barb unwrapped the banana bread and sliced it with a knife from the kitchenette. She arranged the slices on a small platter and set them out on the conference table.

"What's the occasion?" Delilah said, nabbing a slice.

"Peace amongst the tribes."

Delilah laughed. "Good luck with that." Yes, it was true that Margot and Natasha frequently argued, but Delilah wasn't so sure breaking bread together would help.

As though on cue, the two women came into the room. Margot was dressed in a long-sleeved black cardigan and gray pants. She carried an oversized LL Bean tote bag stuffed with papers. Delilah noticed her stiff gate and wondered whether she'd hurt herself again. Last time, Margot had tried kickboxing at her gym and pulled a hamstring.

Natasha didn't bother with hellos. She grabbed a piece of banana bread and stuffed it in her mouth. Then she pulled up a chair, swung it backwards and straddled it. She was wearing her signature cargo pants and a sports bra. Margot gave her an exasperated stare but didn't say anything.

Delilah sat down. "We'll keep this brief. The Cross murder. Let's go through what we have so far."

Delilah filled the group in on her visit to Miriam's house in Chestnut Hill. Barb and Natasha related the details of their trips to Center City. When they were done, Delilah turned toward Margot. "Any luck with the online research?"

Margot pulled a stack of papers out of her tote. "Lots of interesting stuff. Whether it's helpful or not is another story."

Margot passed a set of stapled pages to each of the women. "Here's what I was able to find on the Web. Facebook, LinkedIn, author sites, Publishers Weekly. I didn't print out everything, just the stuff that would give us a sense of who Miriam was, what she did in her free time, her work, that sort of thing."

The women took a few minutes to skim the papers. Delilah saw lots of stuff about Miriam Cross, the public persona. But she wanted to know about the *private* Miriam Cross. The woman who emerged behind closed doors. The woman who'd worn the lingerie and dabbled in bondage.

Barb shook her head. Echoing Delilah's thoughts, she said, "Facebook pages are unremarkable. No candid photos, no ranting diatribes, no political affiliations. We already know what she writes."

"Actually," Margot said, "that's where it does get a little more . . . interesting."

Margot sifted back through her tote. She pulled out several slim books, different colors and sizes. Delilah recognized them from her English literature classes. Literary magazines, those purveyors of a struggling art form: the short story.

"Miriam wrote short fiction?"

Margot nodded. "Under the pen name Erica Moss."

"Emily Cray. Erica Moss." Natasha grabbed one of the books off the pile. "She had more fake names than my bookie."

Natasha skimmed until she found the page with Erica's byline on it and then began to read silently. After a minute, her eyes widened.

"Did you read this?" she said to Margot.

"I did."

"This is some heavy stuff." She tossed the book to Delilah. "Check it out."

Delilah read about half the story. It was about a futuristic state where women were slaves and a handful of powerful men ruled. Delilah found it reminiscent of Margaret Atwood - very dark, very ominous, very realistically drawn. Still, it wasn't that far removed from Miriam's main body of work. "Why publish this under a pen name?"

Margot shrugged. "I wondered the same thing. It's very Miriam Cross, if not a bit darker. If that's possible."

"The graphic sex," Natasha said. "Rape. Humiliation. If her novels were usually tame, maybe she didn't want to offend her readers."

"Good point." Delilah checked the date on the magazine. Two Decembers ago. Around the time she asked Lucinda to leave the Chestnut Hill home. "Did she publish any others?"

Margot nodded. "Six that I could find, all under the pen name Erica Moss. All had similar themes: hopeless future states where women are subservient to men. Almost militaristic in their feminist ideology. As Natasha pointed out, all had almost startling sexual undertones."

Barb said, "How did you put it together that Miriam Cross was Erica Moss?"

"I found a blog by her agent, Liam McMaster, linking the two names to the same author."

Delilah sat forward in her chair. "Did you call Liam?"

"I did. He hasn't returned any of my calls yet."

Delilah considered the date. "When were the stories published?"

Margot picked through the literary magazines. "That one you have is the oldest." She held up two more booklets. "The rest came out a month or two later. And I found a poem online, published under the pen name E. M. Moss. Last June, I think."

Barb said, "Around the same time she left Chestnut Hill."

"Right-o, although she probably wrote it well before. I called the magazine and they said there is a three-month lag time before an accepted piece is published."

"Interesting," Delilah said. "Do you have the poem?"

"Right here. I printed it out." Margot shuffled through her bag again. She pulled out a red folder. Inside was a single sheet of paper. She handed it to Natasha. "You read it."

Natasha sneered. "Give it to the whore, Sister?"

"That's not what I meant. I don't have my glasses."

"Sure, that's why-"

Delilah held up her hands. "*Please.*"

Natasha looked back at the paper. When she spoke, her voice was tight with anger. "He comes. I break under his tutelage, a slut, a whore" – Natasha glanced at Margot – "an angel, pure and innocent and so full of need I swell and grow in fury and anger until I am no more. He fucks me frontward, backwards, and I succumb to the madness. Like Chinnamasta, split in two, cognition separate from sensation, pleasure entwined with shame. I know only him."

When she finished reading, Natasha looked up. "What the hell does that mean?"

Barb said, "Darn if I know. Sounds like she was writing with a particular person in mind."

Delilah said, "Who is Chinnamasta?"

"I looked her up," Margot said. "This gets even weirder. She's a Tantric goddess. I read varying accounts, but the bottom line? She symbolizes both sexual control and sexual energy."

"Like a sexual awakening?" Natasha said.

Margot nodded.

Delilah stood. Now some of this was beginning to make sense. "Exactly like a sexual awakening. The lingerie, now the writing." She turned toward the group. "Miriam Cross took a lover."

"Sounds like sexual infatuation to me," Barb said.

Delilah's mind flashed to the scarves and the blindfold, the way everything was neatly and lovingly folded despite the violence suggested by the items themselves, items of bondage.

"But to Miriam," Delilah said, "a woman who never married, who, according to her niece, was asexual, it must have felt like a loss of control. A wild, sensual loss of identity."

Natasha repeated the lines, "*Like Chinnamasta, split in two, cognition separate from sensation, pleasure entwined with shame.*"

No one spoke. Delilah thought about Miriam, so full of intellectual curiosity, political ideals. Who could this man have been? Very special, indeed, to have captured Miriam's heart and body so fervently.

Delilah turned to Margot. "You called this 'coincidental.' Why?"

Margot looked from one woman to another, her gaze finally resting on Delilah. "Chinnamasta is also known as 'she whose head is severed.'"

Delilah's looked at her in surprise. "Come again?"

"The goddess is usually pictured standing on a copulating couple. But always, she has her own head in her hands."

#

Barb pulled Delilah aside after the meeting, Margot's words still reverberating in her head. Barb wasn't easily shaken, but the thought of Miriam, beheaded like Chinnamasta, gave her the chills. There had to be a connection. It was too much of a coincidence. Which was why she felt compelled to push the issue with Delilah now.

"We're in over our heads," Barb said.

Delilah motioned toward her office. They left Margot and Natasha at the table, reviewing the materials Margot had collected and searching for any additional information. Delilah closed the door.

"Lucinda won't trust the police," Delilah said. "And I can't say I blame her, after everything she went through with Butch."

"But we can't solve this, Delilah. We don't have the resources."

"Look what we've managed to discover in just a few days. Anyway, weren't you the one saying we can handle it just a week ago?"

"Still." Barb chose her words carefully. "You asked me to look at Miriam's assets outside of Pennsylvania. I've been trying to find more online – bank records, property. Her electronic footprint, if you will. Dead ends at every point. I'm not a computer expert. None of us is."

Delilah took a deep breath, her eyes searching Barb's. Barb knew that Delilah took her employees' safety seriously, but that she also felt compelled to help the underdog. And, in this case, Lucinda was clearly the underdog. But there was a solution. Delilah either needed to drop the case – or hire help.

"Matthew Anderson?" Delilah said finally.

"Yep."

"I've already hired him on a contract basis. He starts immediately."

Barb nodded, relieved.

TEN

River Crossings Assisted Living was situated next to an industrial park on the northeast edge of Philadelphia. Flat and drab, the building was one story of plain concrete. Delilah turned the Jeep into the parking lot and drove over enough ruts and bumps to feel like a rodeo rider. She pulled into a space in the nearly empty parking lot, jammed the transmission into first gear and turned off the vehicle.

Chinnamasta. Delilah had looked the goddess up online and now she couldn't get the thought of Miriam, beheaded like the symbol she'd written about, out of her mind. Delilah had to consider the possibility that someone had read that poem and become obsessed with the author. Obsessed enough to kill.

Were they dealing with a stalker?

That might explain the name change and the sudden move, but what about the evening visitors whom Emily Cray's neighbor claimed to see? Unrelated? And if Miriam was being stalked, why had she not simply involved the police? Unless she didn't know someone was following her.

But then how to explain the alias?

Delilah grabbed her purse and climbed out of the Wrangler. She sent Barb a quick text asking her to have her husband check whether Miriam Cross had made any recent complaints to the police.

A stalker would be the simple answer, but Delilah's gut said it wasn't going to be that straightforward. Maybe the box Lucinda found would contain some answers.

#

The reception area of River Crossings was no more welcoming than the exterior. Six mustard-yellow vinyl chairs had been placed around two cheap coffee tables. Stacks of frayed, out-dated magazines – *Outdoor, Newsweek, Family Circle* – lay in neat piles on the tables. The floor was scuffed brown Linoleum, the walls had been painted institutional white. Shoddily framed posters with clichéd sayings like "You can do it!" and "Love is the answer" hung around the room. An elderly woman in a floral nightdress dozed in the corner, her wheelchair blocking the emergency exit.

The place depressed Delilah. She hated to think of all the people who worked so hard their whole lives only to end up somewhere like this, waiting out their end of days in a home with all the warmth of a dentist's office.

Finally, at ten thirty-three, Lucinda showed up. She looked anxious and more than a little nervous. Her eyes darted to the receptionist, a heavy-set woman with short gray hair and a noticeable black mustache.

"I'm taking my break," Lucinda said to the receptionist.

"Keep it short," the woman replied. "Mike's watching."

Lucinda nodded obediently. Delilah followed her outside.

"What was that about?"

Lucinda shrugged. "That's the manager's sister."

"Seems like a real peach."

"Yeah, likes to use her power to dock our pay."

They were standing in the parking lot by Lucinda's Chevy. Delilah looked at the building, and then glanced around at the barren industrial park next door.

"Do you like working here?"

Lucinda opened the trunk of her car, her face a practiced neutral. Years of being Butch's punching bag, of never knowing what emotion or comment would cause a flare-up of his horrific temper, must have taught Lucinda to have a damn good poker face.

"It pays the bills, Delilah. And with Aunt Miriam gone and her estate tied up, I have no alternative. This job is the only thing that stands between us and a shelter."

Lucinda reached into the trunk and pulled out a box. It was small, roughly the size of a shoebox, and taped with layers of duct tape. No name was written on the box. No identifying markers at all. Delilah was disappointed. She'd been hoping for files or something. This box was far too small to hold anything significant.

"How do you know this is Miriam's?"

"It's not mine," Lucinda said. "Who else would it belong to? One of my boys must have grabbed it by accident when we moved our things from her attic."

Delilah nodded. "I checked the attic when I was at her house. A few boxes of books and some household junk. Nothing important."

"The police must have taken the rest. She had a stack of boxes up there, all secured like this one."

Delilah thought for a moment. "Any idea of what was in them?"

"I asked her once. She said 'past lives.'"

"Didn't that seem like a curious comment?"

"It didn't at the time. Aunt Miriam could be dramatic. But now, yes." She looked at Delilah with tired eyes. "I got another call last night."

"Home or cell?"

"Home."

Delilah wasn't surprised. The men Natasha had clashed with had been hired by someone. That someone was clearly still associated with whatever Miriam had been up to.

Before Delilah could respond, Lucinda said, "Have you made any headway?"

Delilah gave her a bare-bones account of Natasha's run-in with the goons in Philly. She didn't want to alarm her, but Lucinda needed to know whom she was dealing with.

"I think you should call the police," Delilah said. "You and your boys could be in danger. These guys aren't fooling around."

"I'm not calling the police."

"Then how about going somewhere for a while? Until we get this straightened out?"

"I have no where to go. Besides" – she pointed at the nursing home – "I can't leave my job."

"Then let someone stay with you. We could hire a security guard for a few weeks."

Lucinda slammed down the trunk. "No. Look, Delilah, I appreciate your concern. But until Miriam's estate is freed, I have nothing. And I don't want anymore loans. It's bad enough that I can't pay you until the will is settled."

"Your safety comes first."

"I live in a secured building. The boys will be with their grandmother beginning next week. I'll be careful. I promise."

Delilah nodded, but she couldn't shirk the feeling of dread that clung to her like a wet shirt.

Lucinda reached into her pocket and pulled out a piece of paper. "Before I forget, here are the dates you requested. Each set represents a period when Miriam was away. At least, as close as I could remember." She glanced at her watch. "I have exactly four minutes before the receptionist tattles on me. Anything else?"

Delilah debated whether to tell her about the sexual writing, about Chinnamasta. Not yet, she decided. Not until she had a better idea of what it meant.

"Nothing concrete. Just watch your back, Lucinda. And call me if you need help. No matter what the time."

Lucinda gave her a weak smile. Delilah watched the woman square her shoulders and enter the bleak building, as though preparing to do battle within.

#

Delilah had one stop to make before going back to the office. She pulled into the parking lot of Tenner Security, a small firm whose store-front property was just a few miles into the city limit. Delilah had known Joe Tenner for twelve years, since they'd both done a stint at the Pennsylvania State Police Academy. Joe had completed his course and gone on to be a state trooper for four years before opening Tenner Security. Delilah had been fine with the grueling physical routine, a welcome change from law school, but she'd quit weeks shy of completion. Too many rules for an ex-cowgirl, too much pressure to conform. She'd had that at home with family. She didn't want it in her career, too.

But the cadet training had stayed with her.

And it served her well. She could disarm an assailant. She could handle a gun. And she could stay calm under extreme pressure. Such skills sure came in handy on occasion.

Delilah pushed open the front office door and was met by a surly boy with an anemic beard wearing too much cheap cologne.

"You need an appointment," he said, not bothering to look up from his desk.

"Tell Joe that Lila's here to see him."

"You need an appointment." Still no eye contact.

Delilah walked to the desk and slammed her hand down on the scuffed metal. The boy-man looked up.

"Tell Joe it's Lila," she said again, slowly. "Or I will pull you into his office by your sorry whiskers and tell him myself."

The boy swallowed, his Adam's apple bobbing up and down like an ocean buoy. "I'll tell Joe you're here."

A few seconds later, a burly man with a full beard and a sweet smile bounded into the room. "Damn it, Delilah, why do you always pop up at the worst times?"

"You married again, Joe?"

"I am, I'm sorry to say. But at least it's a pleasant one this time." He held up a wedding ring.

Delilah laughed. She and Joe had been lovers at the Academy. Even after he graduated and she dropped out - one the lowest points in Delilah's life – she'd often found solace in his arms. They'd had to call off their on-again, off-again relationship, a friendship with benefits, really, when Joe married his first wife. Delilah and Joe hadn't slept together since. Delilah figured Joe was on wife number three or four by now. He was a giving and gentle lover, but apparently not so great in the husband department.

It looked like the new wife was a good cook, though. Delilah's slim Joe was a little huskier in his proportions.

The extra bulk suited him. As though reading her mind, he looked down at his belly and smiled.

"Contentment. See what it does to a man?"

"You look great, Joe. Still a killer with the ladies, no doubt."

Joe tilted his head and looked Delilah up and down. It was a friendly, how-is-life-treating-you gesture, but it left Delilah feeling exposed and unsettled.

"No man for you, cowgirl?"

Delilah shook her head. "I have the horses and my job. That's all I need."

"You're as lovely as ever."

Delilah smiled. *Same old Joe.* "You mean as hard-headed as ever?"

"That too."

They stood looking at each other, and Delilah felt the warmth of friendship and the subtle nagging of regret. There'd been a time when Joe wanted to marry her and she'd said no. Michael was still too fresh, too real. Marriage would have felt an awful lot like infidelity. But if she had given a different answer, by now she'd have kids and someone to curl up with at the end of the day. Maybe it would have been worth the price of guilt.

The boy-man cleared his throat, startling Delilah into remembering he was there, too.

"Can I have a few minutes of your time, Joe?" She gave the boy a hard look. "In private."

Joe led Delilah to a cramped back office. He sat on the edge of another metal desk and motioned for her to take the only chair. She moved two files off the seat and sat down. The office was cluttered. Stacks of files and stray papers competed for space with old aluminum cans and yellowed newspapers. The room's only window caught the late morning sun, bathing the place in light and highlighting a thick coating of dust. Joe had never been a neat man.

"I know that face, Lila. You're chewing on something."

Delilah nodded. "I have a job for you, if you can staff it. Client of mine. I'd like someone to tail her. Someone who can handle a gun. I'm pretty sure some bad people are watching her."

"Bad as in-"

"Not sure yet. Mob, maybe."

"She doesn't want the protection?"

"She can't pay for it and doesn't want any favors. This is on me. I have a real bad horse-is-down-and-not-gonna-get-up kind of feeling. I want her protected."

The way Joe was looking at her, Delilah knew he was wondering why she didn't tail Lucinda herself.

"I haven't gone soft, if that's what you're worried about. I'm short-staffed."

Joe nodded slowly. "Okay, then. I can give you someone."

Delilah opened her purse and pulled out her checkbook. "Like I said, this is on me. Not my firm."

Joe started to wave his hand in protest and Delilah stopped him.

"Don't even say it, Joseph Tenner. You have mouths to feed, too." She wrote him a check, and then she wrote Lucinda's work and home addresses on a separate slip of paper. "This should cover a week's worth of surveillance. If we need more, I'll pay. Do me a favor, though? Have your guy stay in the background. I don't want Lucinda to know you're there."

"Like a guardian angel?"

"Like a guardian angel."

On impulse, Delilah stood up to give Joe a kiss on the cheek. With her lips pressed against him and her body so close, something in her stirred, something primal and urgent. For a second, she toyed with kissing him on the lips, waiting for him to wrap his arms around her and hold her close, like old times. But he was married now. And that was one complication neither of them needed.

Delilah pulled away and backed toward the door, her pulse racing.

"Later, cowgirl," Joe said. He looked as flustered as Delilah felt.

"Later, Tenner," Delilah said and, reluctantly, headed back to her car.

ELEVEN

It was nearly one o'clock when Delilah returned to Percy Powers LLC, ready to lock herself in her office and get some work done. She planned to go through Miriam's box, make a few phone calls and check on how Margot was making out with her attempts to contact Miriam's agent, Liam McMaster. But instead she arrived to find Anders sitting at the small desk in the reception room. She stopped in front of him.

"I thought you were going to work from home."

Anders looked up, his hair tousled and the sleeves of his button-down shirt rolled nearly to the elbows.

"I don't have the workspace right now. Margot said it was fine if I camped out at the office."

"It's too crowded here already."

Anders looked surprised. Delilah instantly hated herself for speaking so curtly, but the damage was done. And the truth was, she didn't want him here. Anders' presence would mean change and she was quite happy with the way things were.

Anders just sat there, so Delilah moved past him toward her office. Once inside, she laid Miriam's box on her desk. She could hear Anders rustling around in the reception area. Her gaze fell on the photo of Michael, her fiancé, presumed dead after a freak kayaking accident in a West Virginia river. They were to be married exactly two weeks from the date he disappeared, his kayak found miles downstream from where he started. The authorities believed he'd been tossed from the kayak and sucked under, caught in one of the hollowed-out rocks that lurked beneath the rapids. But he'd been a strong kayaker. It took Delilah years to accept his death.

A death that may not have occurred if Delilah had been with him, like she would have been had it not been for her mother's insistence that she stay home. *A bride-to-be needs to be focusing on the wedding, Delilah, not traipsing around the wilderness.* So he'd gone alone. Wasn't that what she'd loved about Michael? His independence. His strength. His refusal to care what others thought. Friends since eighth grade, when she'd arrived in Richmond as the freaky horse girl from Wyoming, an outsider in a foreign land, newly fatherless, newly friendless. But Michael had become her friend. Bound by a love of animals and a mutual desire to escape, their friendship eventually turned to love. They'd been inseparable.

Until the accident.

But that wasn't Anders' fault.

Damn it, Delilah. You're acting like a scared child.

Her mind wandered to the first time she fell off a horse. Delilah had been twelve. The horse's name had been Whisper and he'd been traded to her father by a local Indian chief in return for cattle. Whisper had been a stunning stallion: ebony, with a white star on his face and, to her twelve-year-old sensibilities, endlessly long legs. The horse bolted whenever her father drew near, but he'd let Delilah pet and brush him, nuzzling her with his aristocratic head. So finally, after weeks of begging and pleading, James Percy agreed to let her saddle up.

She lasted nine minutes before the horse bucked and she fell. She refused to get on again.

"Why not, Delilah?" her father said. "What's got you so scared?"

Delilah shrugged.

"There's a lesson here, Lila."

Delilah, feeling betrayed by Whisper, said, "Don't ride a mean horse?"

James Percy had looked at her with those emerald green eyes made brighter by the tan, crinkled skin around them. "Nope."

"Get back on again?"

"Nope."

"Then what?"

"Delilah Percy, someday you'll know what kept you off Whisper. And then you'll have one of the keys to a peaceful life."

James Percy died six months later. She never did find out what the lesson was.

But today she thought she knew.

Figure out what you're afraid of, silly, she thought. Back then, she hadn't really been afraid of falling off Whisper again. She'd been terrified of embarrassing herself in front of her daddy, of being less of a cowboy than he was. If she could have identified that fear, she could have articulated it. She could have beat it. Instead, Whisper was sold along with most of the other horses, the ranch and all the cattle when her mother married

Virginia businessman Paul Powers and the family moved east. She never saw the horse again.

Oh, Daddy, if you're up there now looking down, you'll see your daughter's still nursing the hurts instead of facing her fears.

Only problem was, Delilah couldn't quite name this current fear.

But that wasn't Anders' fault, either. Delilah would apologize to Anders. She turned around, ready to march back out there and eat crow, when there was a strong knock on her office door. Anders stormed in before she had a chance to respond.

He handed her a letter.

"What's this?"

"My resignation."

Delilah ripped the paper. "I don't accept your resignation."

"You can't do that."

"I can and I did."

"It doesn't work that way."

"You can't quit," Delilah said. "We need you."

Anders stared at her as though her head had spun a full circle on her neck. Then he started to laugh. After a moment, Delilah laughed, too.

"I'm sorry," Delilah said. "I didn't mean to be so abrupt. Fresh start?"

Anders nodded. "Fresh start."

"You're not resigning?"

"I'm not resigning."

"Good." Delilah pointed to the chair next to her desk. "Sit, Anders. Please."

She watched as he folded his lanky body into her chair. *Know what you're afraid of, Delilah.* Maybe she did. Anders reminded her of Michael. He had the same slow smile, the same easy presence and the same sad aura. *Like a man who knows his time is short.*

Delilah picked up Miriam's box. It was better that she put her energy into something constructive.

"What's that?"

Delilah sighed. "I guess it's time to fill you in on the case we're all working on, rather than giving you bits and pieces." She took a seat at her desk and went through the facts, from Lucinda's initial call until Delilah's visit with Joe.

"The poem led you to the stalker hypothesis?"

"Yes. Barb's husband is checking to see whether there are any police reports on file. He's a cop for another precinct but can usually get basic information now and again, when he's willing."

"Was Miriam married?"

"No."

Anders looked troubled.

"What is it?" Delilah said.

"The foreigners showing up at Emily Cray's house. And now the men hiding outside the Philly property."

"Drugs?"

"It's a possibility you can't ignore."

"We've had the same thought. Although I find it hard to believe a woman as bright and educated as Miriam Cross would involve herself in something like that. She's rich already. To what end?"

"Hmmm. How about terrorism?"

"We thought of that, too. But why?"

Anders shrugged. "You said it yourself. Her books are pretty paranoid. She was an offbeat lady with a warped view of the world. People get involved in extremism for lots of reasons."

Delilah nodded. "I agree that it would seem to fit, but I still don't believe it." She thought of the lingerie, of the erotic stories and poem. There was a personal element here and Delilah was pretty certain it was relevant. "We're hoping that's where you come in,

Anders. We need to reconstruct Miriam's actions over the past year."

"Hard to do without her computer."

"But not impossible?"

Anders gave her a bashful smile. "No, not impossible."

"Well, then, do it." She caught herself. "I mean do it, please." She pulled Lucinda's paper out of her purse. "You can start here. These are the dates of previous disappearances. See whether there is any pattern, especially between those dates and her most recent vanishing act."

Anders tucked the paper in his notebook. Delilah reached for a pair of scissors and began cutting through the duct tape on the box Lucinda had given her. When she had the lid off, she placed it carefully on the floor. Then she cleared a large space on her desk, took out a pad and pen and handed them to Anders.

"Would you mind cataloging what I take out of the box? Make a list. We'll put a copy in the file and give a copy to Lucinda."

"You want me to play secretary?"

Delilah looked at him sharply. "We all pull our share of the load here."

Anders gave her a maddened look. "Are you always this touchy?"

"Are you always this difficult?"

"My wife would say yes."

Delilah tensed at the mention of his wife. She glanced at his left hand. No ring. He'd caught her off guard, that was all. She forced her attention on the box. *Business first.*

"One copy of *The Economist*, dated last August." Delilah put the magazine to the side. She'd take inventory and then she'd consider what the items meant, if anything. "Three pairs of women's silk stockings, size small."

"Silk stockings?"

Delilah shrugged. "They're not in the package. For padding, I guess?" She put the stockings with the magazine. "A hairbrush. A pair of women's leather gloves, size small."

"This is just a random box of stuff," Anders said. He picked up the gloves. "Like the crap from the junk drawer that you move from house to house and never actually sort through."

"Could be. Although the magazine is relatively recent."

"True."

"We'll check through the contents, see if any of the articles seem relevant." Delilah continued sorting. "One stapler, two boxes of staples, a small, blank notebook and a mug that says 'Miriam' on the outside." She put the items to the side. "Three plastic binders, all empty."

"That it?"

"Almost." Delilah pulled out the last two things: an over-stuffed envelope marked "bills" and a recordable DVD in a clear plastic case.

Anders leaned over. "There's something else in there," Anders said. "I can see it tucked up against the side."

Delilah felt along the cardboard until she found the paper. It was a ticket stub for a political dinner in New York City. From about a year ago.

"Could this be relevant?" Anders said.

Delilah turned it over. She didn't recognize the candidate's name. Still, it could provide some clue as to Miriam's recent activities.

Delilah shrugged. "Anything could be important at this point. Research the candidate. See if we can't get our hands on the guest list. Confirm that Miriam attended."

Anders nodded. "Tickets were $1,000 a seat. I may be able to find evidence of payment." He took the stub and made a note of the pertinent information on a separate sheet of paper. Meanwhile, Delilah handled the envelope marked "bills." It was too heavy to have bills in it. She used her opener to tear the edges and then she placed the contents carefully onto her desk. Two Indonesian passports.

"What the hell?" Anders said.

Delilah opened them. One belonged to a woman named Cinta Wahid and the other, Kemala Gunawan. Both women were young, maybe early twenties, at the time their pictures were taken.

"Check the dates."

Delilah paged through the passports, trying to decipher the stamps. "It looks like Cinta entered the Unites States in December of 2006. No exit date."

"How about the other woman?"

"It says she arrived in October of 1998." She looked up at Anders. "So why would Miriam have these?"

"That *is* odd." He picked up the documents, looked through the pages, and then put them down on the desk. "I should be able to find out something about the women, though. Whether they're alive. Whether these are stolen passports and their embassies had to get involved in order for them to go home."

"The names-"

"Muslim? Like you said, right now anything could be relevant. We can't ignore a possible terrorism connection."

Reluctantly, Delilah nodded. There'd certainly been other American women who'd joined extremist groups in a misguided effort to right the wrongs of the world.

Miriam wouldn't be the first. Still, that possibility didn't *feel* right to Delilah.

Delilah said, "Why would she have these secured in a box in her attic? What if the sole reason for the box was to keep these passports? What if she'd taken them from these women for who-knows-why and she put them in the box and taped it shut to keep them hidden?"

"You said Lucinda has no recollection of taking the box?"

Delilah nodded.

"So, taking your theory one more step, what if Miriam put the box in Lucinda's house? For safekeeping?"

"There would only be one reason to do that," Delilah said.

"If you thought someone was after its contents."

"So whoever murdered Miriam wanted these women's passports? The most likely candidates would be the women themselves." Delilah stared at Cinta's picture. Pretty, with long black hair and a hopeful smile. Was this girl out there somewhere, in trouble? Or was she a willing participant in something evil?

Anders took the passports. "We'll see what we can find out about the women. It's a start." He nodded toward the envelope. "How about the DVD?"

Delilah had almost forgotten about the disc. "I'll pop it into the computer now."

"Maybe it's related to these women."

"I guess we'll know soon enough."

TWELVE

Delilah clicked on the small triangle that indicated "play." She and Anders sat in silence, waiting. The screen remained black. After about thirty seconds of nothing, they heard a series of grunts followed by a woman's scream. Then a snap. More grunts. Another scream. The screen stayed dark.

Delilah could feel the skin on the back of her neck prickle. This was a murder or a skin flick. She felt ill.

Suddenly a picture emerged on the screen. The camera panned back and the image slowly came into sharper focus. It took Delilah a moment to adjust to the change. She could make out a woman lying on a bed, naked, her arms bound to an ornate iron frame, her eyes covered by a black blindfold. She was grimacing with pleasure. Her legs were spread, a man's head buried between her thighs. The camera caught only his naked torso and the back of his head. He had thick blond hair.

"My turn?" A deep baritone voice asked. Pronunciation was crisp, the accent British. Presumably the cameraman.

In answer, the woman struggled against her binds and raised her hips. The man kneeling between her legs lifted himself up so that he was over her. Delilah could see his penis, hungry and erect. He entered her violently.

"Jack," the cameraman said, warning in his tone.

Anders reached for the mouse. "We don't need to watch this."

She paused the DVD. Jack – for the man having sex must have been Jack – was gripping the woman's hair so that her head was forced backwards at a painful angle. A blurred shot of her face, frozen in a look of agony or ecstasy - Delilah couldn't tell which - filled the screen.

Delilah stared at that image. "This is the biggest lead we've had so far. If you want to leave, Anders, I understand."

"That man is raping her."

"I don't think so."

"I do."

Delilah looked at Anders. She saw only concern and disgust reflected in his eyes. Not lust. She was glad . . . if he had been turned on by this, she *would* have asked him to leave.

Anders said, "Do you recognize her?"

"Not with the blindfold. Hopefully we'll get a clearer look at her face."

Anders turned his attention back to the video and Delilah clicked the play button. They watched the sex continue, Jack's motions increasingly rough. At one point, he put one hand over her mouth and twisted her nipple with the other hand, hard. The woman gave a muffled scream. Anders sat forward, his hand reaching out as though to stop the action on the screen.

"*Jack,*" the cameraman said again, his tone stern.

Jack slowly backed off. He moved out of the camera range, back to the camera, his penis still engorged. The woman continued to lay there, her breath ragged and uneven, her legs open. She had red welts where Jack had slammed his hand over her mouth. One small breast looked pink and bruised.

"Now?" the clipped British voice said. That one word conveyed so much emotion: desire, tenderness, even a certain amount of insecurity. The woman on the bed smiled. It was an inviting, joyous, *happy* smile.

But more than that. It was Miriam Cross's smile.

"That's her," Delilah whispered. "Miriam."

"Are you sure?"

"I know that smile. It's on her book jackets. Even with the blindfold. That's Miriam, I'm sure of it."

They watched as Miriam moved her slim hips in time to the caresses of the new man. From the back, he appeared tall and thin, with coffee-colored skin and jet black hair. He leaned in to kiss Miriam, lingering on her mouth and then drawing his tongue down to her breasts. Unlike Jack, his touches were soft and fleeting. Miriam moaned in response.

They heard harsh breathing from Jack, now the cameraman, a sharp intake of air and an abrupt, "Oh no." And then the screen went blank.

Delilah and Anders sat there, staring at the darkened computer monitor.

Anders spoke first. "Jack was masturbating. When he climaxed, he shut off the video."

Delilah nodded. "I think that's right." She still felt sick. She stared at the blank screen. Her image of Miriam Cross - feminist, intellectual, author - in total turmoil. A ménage a trois? Lucinda thought her aunt was celibate, but clearly Miriam had a life she'd kept hidden from her niece, from the world. The lingerie in her Chesnut Hill home, the erotic poetry, that all made more sense now. But how was the DVD connected to the passports? And the visitors to the Willston house? Miriam's murder? Things seemed murkier than ever.

"Want to get a beer?" Anders said, interrupting her thoughts. "I could use a drink after that train wreck."

"Or a cigarette."

Anders flashed a weak smile.

"A beer sounds good," Delilah said, her mind still on the DVD. She looked at Anders. "Though it *is* the middle of the afternoon."

"A shot of espresso, maybe?"

"Espresso works."

Anders stood. "Give me a minute to get my things."

While Anders was in the other room, Delilah gathered the DVD, the dinner stub and the passports and locked them in the safe. Images from the film flashed in her mind, leaving her feeling uneasy. She was most troubled by two things: the sadistic violence of the first lover – why would Miriam engage in that willingly? – and the obvious bond Miriam shared with the second man.

And perhaps most importantly, who were these men? And why had Miriam Cross kept this recording when she was the only identifiable person in it?

#

"Blackmail?" Anders said. They were sitting on the patio at a local burger joint, having opted for the beer after all. Despite the large table umbrella, the sun poured down upon them. Beads of sweat formed along Delilah's brow and the back of her neck. She was finding it a little hard to sit casually across from a man she'd just watched a sex tape with, but Anders's relaxed manner made it easier.

"Could have been blackmail, I guess," she said. "The men – anyone, really – may have been holding other tapes, threatening exposure." Delilah picked at her French fries. Something was troubling her. "But then why move? Why go to all the trouble of changing your name, running away? If the tape went public, her real identity – Miriam Cross, the author – would be affected. Living under an alias wouldn't help."

Anders took a swig of beer and pushed a half-eaten burger across his plate. "Agreed. But why else keep that tape?"

"And what does the tape have to do with the two passports?"

The waitress, a young, perky girl with a limited vocabulary, came back to refill drinks. When she was gone, Delilah said, "What if has nothing to do with the passports? What if she kept the movie for sentimental reasons?"

Anders laughed. "Sentimental? You saw the same tape I did. That was sex, pure animalistic sex."

"But what about the end? Miriam's response to the British guy? She looked . . . happy."

Anders was quiet for a moment. His hands danced over his napkin, active while the rest of him stayed still. Echoes of Michael. Delilah tried not to think of her fiancé, of the way Michael used to close himself off when he was immersed in an idea or a project. He, too, would have a nervous energy about him, as though his body and mind ran on separate circuits.

Anders said, "He *did* seem protective of her. Maybe they were lovers . . . either before or after the recording was made."

"The first man" – Delilah struggled to put her confusion into words – "was . . . degrading."

Anders nodded.

"And that doesn't fit. Miriam Cross, at least the persona that she projected, seemed sure of herself and her ideals. A strong woman. Not someone who would let herself be subjugated sexually."

"Unless it was a turn on, Delilah. The things that turn people on sexually . . . well, they don't always make sense. Politicians who hire a dominatrix, teachers into kiddie porn, firemen who wear women's panties. There's a whole world of different out there."

"I don't know. I think there's more to the story." Delilah shook her head. "We need to find out who those two men are. They could be connected somehow." She met Anders' gaze. "I know we have almost nothing to go on. Not even faces. But see what you can dig up."

He looked skeptical. Still, he nodded.

Delilah took a long, slow swallow of her Amstel Light. The restaurant was quickly emptying. She glanced at her watch. After three o'clock. But she felt no great urgency to leave. Anders was easy company.

"So how'd you end up in this field?" Anders said finally, breaking the silence.

Delilah looked down at her beer. "I wanted to be a cowgirl, but life, it seems, had its own agenda."

"A cowgirl?" An amused smile spread across his face. "Really? With a name like Delilah?"

"My parents had a sense of humor." Delilah looked up at him. "Anyway, that's the long answer. The short answer is that I was studying to be a lawyer, but wanted something more visceral. So I trained to be a cop. But I hated all the structure."

"Like the Goldilocks of the legal world."

Delilah laughed. "You could say that. I had done some sleuthing for my sister a few years before – her husband was cheating. He ended up back in the family's good graces, God knows how, but it occurred to me that a legal background plus cop training plus investigative skills could equal a career. I learned the business through trial and error and here I am."

"What's the long answer?"

Delilah sighed. "Do you really want to hear the gory details of my very boring life?"

"I really do."

"Then I'll expect reciprocation."

Another smile, but this one, Delilah thought, seemed overcast. "Fair enough."

"I grew up in Wyoming," Delilah began, her gaze on the now-empty courtyard. "In a little town east of Jackson. My father was a rancher, but in my eyes he was the world's greatest cowboy. I have three sisters and none of them particularly like the outdoors, so mostly it was me and my father and the animals. To a little girl, that ranch was a magical place. The Tetons off in the distance, a broad expanse of plains around us, the sunsets . . . and the freedom."

Delilah stirred her iced tea, her mind lingering on the bittersweet memories of youth. "But when I was thirteen, my father died. Kicked in the head by a horse while trying to get a puppy out from under it. He saved the puppy, but a week later, my father died of brain trauma."

"I'm sorry."

Delilah nodded. "The worst part? It was my fault the puppy had been out in the first place. I was supposed to be watching her. I got distracted." Delilah forced a pained smile.

Anders eyes reflected nothing but sympathy. "You were a *kid*. Kids get distracted."

"Maybe." The waitress brought the check and Delilah waited for her to leave before continuing. "Had enough?"

"Keep going."

"My mother never liked Wyoming. She was a city girl who'd met my dad in college. Six months after my father died she became engaged to businessman Paul Powers. Do the math, Anders, and you'll understand my anger at my mother. Anyway, Paul moved us all to Virginia. I went to a private school. The teachers there – along with my mother – did their damnedest to breed to cowgirl right out of me."

"Didn't work?"

"Not very well, I'm afraid. I never did marry a rich man and settle down to a wholesome life. My hypocritical mother's still waiting. She calls me often to remind me of what a colossal failure I am in her eyes." Delilah smiled. "What can you do?"

Anders sat back in his chair. Delilah felt uncomfortable under the burden of his stare.

"So you never returned to Wyoming?"

Delilah thought of Michael, of their plans together, of the things that happened after his death. Some things were best untold. "Nope."

Anders pulled out his wallet. Delilah shook her head. "Business expense." She picked up the check, took her American Express out of her wallet and placed the two back on the table. Seconds later, the waitress whisked the bill and credit card away.

"She must be waiting for us to leave."

"Too bad. My turn now. How about you? What's your story?"

Anders hesitated, staring down at his hand. He flexed his fingers and Delilah's gaze rested on his naked ring finger.

"It's pretty simple, really. Boy has promising career in investigative journalism. Boy meets beautiful girl. Boy marries girl. Boy and girl have a baby with a severe birth defect. Child dies. Boy and girl can't deal with the stress of a sick child or the anguish of losing her. Boy and girl separate."

"Oh, Anders."

"It sounds pretty awful, doesn't it? The reality is, most of it was okay. When Missy was born, the doctors gave her two years, max. She lived to be eight. Kathryn – my wife – had the stable job with medical benefits. So I took a hiatus to take care of Missy. She passed away in January."

Delilah didn't know what to say. Losing a parent had been a nightmare, as had losing her fiancé. But she doubted either compared to the pain of losing a child. That explained the hurting she'd recognized in Anders when they first met. Walking wounded meets walking wounded.

The waitress came back with the bill. Delilah took her time signing the receipt. When she was done, she said, "So you decided to change careers?"

"Not exactly. I told you I needed to stay in the area. That was the truth. Kathryn and I separated after Missy died, but we're trying to figure out if there is anything left of our marriage. I can't really do that if I'm traveling and my kind of journalism requires a lot of travel. This position made sense." He shrugged. "I couldn't exactly tell you all of that in an interview. You never would have hired me."

Delilah smiled. "You never know."

Just then, her cell phone rang. "Hold on." She answered. It was Barb.

"Nothing on the stalker," Barb said.

"I'm not surprised."

"But Fred did come up with something we may want to check out."

Delilah waited.

"A few days before Miriam left Chestnut Hill, a neighbor called in a complaint. Domestic disturbance."

Delilah's heart jumped. "Details?"

"Nah. Bare bones report. Screaming, crashes. But when the police showed up, Miriam said everything was fine."

Delilah's mind flitted to the video images. "Interesting."

"Follow-up?"

Delilah looked at Anders, at the soft way he was looking at her.

"Yes. Talk to the neighbor. But be careful, though. Natasha's goons are still out there."

Delilah hung up and stared at her cell phone for a long moment. Enid's voice rang through her head. *There's always a beater.*

Could it really be so simple?

THIRTEEN

It was Wednesday afternoon before Barb had a chance to check in with Miriam's neighbor, Inez Freeman. She expected to find an empty house. It was, after all, two o'clock and, to Barb, there was no reason to be home during a weekday afternoon unless you were cleaning or planting your garden or attending to a child. But apparently Inez thought differently.

The woman came to the door in a light blue house coat, the cheap fuzzy kind, with matching slippers that looked like something a cat had vomited. Her hair was knotted on the top of her head and dark shadows - or old mascara - encircled her eyes. From the groggy way she looked at Barb through the crack in the door, Barb figured she'd been sleeping one off. Barb held up a business card.

"Ms. Freeman, my name is Barb Moore. I was hoping to ask you a few questions."

"About what?"

"About Miriam Cross."

The woman frowned.

"I'm a friend of Miriam's niece."

"I don't really know Miriam." Inez tried to slam the door, but Barb beat her to it. She stuck her size eleven foot in the small space and pushed against the door with her palm.

"It will only take a minute, Ms. Freeman. I promise."

"Whatever you want to know, just ask Miriam."

"She's dead."

The shock on Inez's face seemed genuine. She took a moment to compose her features back to neutral and then said, "Come back later."

Barb knew there wouldn't be a later. "Did you call the police the night of June seventh? That would be *last* June seventh?"

"How would I remember?"

"Do you call the police often?"

"No."

Barb smiled. "Ten-fourteen at night. You told the officer, and I'm quoting your words, 'There's screaming and crashing and I hear someone crying through the walls.' Does that ring a bell?"

"Maybe." Inez backed away from the door.

"Inez" – Barb used her best calm-the-irrational-daughter-voice – "I just want to know if you'd heard any other disturbances from Miriam's house before."

The woman eyed her warily. "No. Never."

"Why didn't you call Miriam instead of the police?"

"I thought she was being hurt."

"By whom?"

Inez shrugged.

"A man?"

Inez laughed, and it came out like a snort. "Miriam didn't have lovers, if that's what you mean. She didn't have friends, either. At least none that we ever saw. Just that niece and her two boys. No men, though."

"You're sure?"

Inez looked out at the street beyond Barb. In the harsh afternoon light, Barb saw yellowed skin and branching wrinkles and realized Inez was much older than she'd originally thought.

"In this neighborhood, we called her Sister Miriam. She was so damn self-righteous."

"What was she self-righteous about?"

Inez shrugged. The collar of her robe slid down. Barb got a glimpse of tan, leathery bare skin underneath. "Stuff. Everything. It doesn't matter now – look, I gotta work in five hours. I need some rest, okay?"

"Just one more question."

"I said-"

"The night you called the police, do you remember seeing another car at Miriam's? Besides her own?"

Inez rolled her eyes. "Look, Miriam was a strange bird. She didn't talk to people much, especially not to me. Ever since my husband and I split, well, I've been working two, three jobs. Miriam, she had money. She didn't understand what a working girl goes through to stay in a neighborhood like this."

Barb waited for her to continue.

Inez let out an exasperated sigh. "Fine, if I tell you will you leave me the hell alone?" She crossed her arms over her chest. Barb nodded.

Inez said, "Miriam drove a Saab. The night I called the police, her Saab was in the parking spot behind her house, like usual. Behind it was a brand new silver

Mercedes. I remember thinking she'd gotten herself another car, lucky bitch. But then I heard the screaming. And when I went outside to talk to the police, I saw the plates. They weren't Miriam's."

"What state?"

Inez stared at Barb's foot. Barb removed it from the doorway in a gesture of good will.

"New Jersey. Or Pennsylvania." Inez said shrugged again. "It was late and I was tired, so I can't really remember."

"Can you tell me anything else? Anything distinguishing about the car?"

Inez wrapped her fuchsia talons around the edge of the door. "Not a Phillies fan, whoever it was. Had a Yankees magnet on the rear bumper."

#

Delilah hated Philadelphia traffic. Unlike the endless straight roads and quiet mountainous highways of her home state of Wyoming, here the city streets formed a grid, designed in pre-Revolutionary America to accommodate horses, not cars. The highways were narrow. They twisted and turned, a remnant of yesteryear, giving way to an urban, high-speed nightmare. Or total gridlock.

Delilah jammed the Jeep into fourth gear and careened around yet another person driving under the speed limit in the left lane. That was the other problem with Philadelphia – the whole damn East Coast, really. No one cared that the passing lane was a *passing* lane.

Delilah yelled a few choice phrases at the driver after he tossed her a one finger salute. She threw some muscle against the gas pedal. Margot had finally reached Liam McMaster. Delilah had promised Margot she could meet with Miriam's agent at exactly five o'clock at a small bar outside of the University of Pennsylvania. He was in the city for a writers' conference and could spare no more than fifteen minutes.

Delilah pulled off the University Drive exit. She followed traffic around the hospital and, after fifteen minutes of searching for parking, finally found a spot four blocks from the bar. She was going to be late.

Delilah sprinted across the street, ignoring the crosswalk, and into Rooney's Pub. The bar was of the type you'd find in a college town. Wooden benches, scarred picnic-type tables and the permanent stench of stale beer. She looked around the room until she saw a man who – slightly – matched the photograph on the literary agency's website. She waved. He gave her a stony wave back.

"Liam McMaster?"

"You're three minutes late."

"Sorry."

He glanced at his watch. "That means you now have twelve minutes."

Delilah slid into the bench across from him. Liam was a jowly man, with a reddened complexion and a thick head of graying hair. He was nursing some type of mixed drink, its cloudy brownish liquid punctuated by three small ice cubes and a lonely slice of lime. He looked at her through narrowed eyes, a man of the world waiting for the riffraff to get on with things.

Delilah said, "What can you tell me about Miriam Cross?"

"Ah, yes. My favorite client."

Delilah ignored the undisguised sarcasm. "You knew her well?"

Liam laughed. The sound was bitter and, to Delilah, rather nasty. She took an instant dislike to this man and wondered how Miriam could tolerate working with him.

"Miriam was a crazy, bull-headed bitch, pardon my French. We worked together for nine years. *Nine years*, Ms.-"

"Percy Powers. Delilah."

"Delilah. Nine years. And in the end, the only thing Miriam could do was throw up her middle finger at success."

"How so?"

Liam took a long, slow sip of his drink. He looked around the room for a moment, his gazing lingering a few seconds too long on a very young brunette across the bar.

"Do you know how many agent queries I get each week?"

Delilah shook her head.

"Upwards of five hundred. *Five hundred*. That's five hundred desperate writers eager to have me – *me* – represent their work. Ninety-nine percent of them can't write their way out of a garbage can. But the other one percent? Potential. The world likes new talent, with fresh ideas and enthusiasm."

He took another long swallow of his drink, wiped his mouth with the back of a beefy hand and said, "Do you know how agents get paid?"

"On commission?"

"Smart lady. That means we only get paid when our clients get paid. And the more our clients get paid, the more we get paid. But we can only have so many clients. They're like children, you know. Each needing attention, guidance, reassurance . . . and Miriam was no exception. Only Miriam didn't want to do her part. She didn't want to *sell out*, she was a woman of *ideals*."

Again, Liam made no attempt to hide the contempt in his voice, letting Delilah know exactly what he thought of *women of ideals*.

"Did she have enemies?"

126

He thought for a moment. "She had people who disliked her work. People who thought she was a leftist femi-Nazi."

"Anyone who might want to see her dead?"

"All of them, probably. But do I know of any specific threats against Miriam? No."

A waiter came over with a fresh drink for Liam. "Anything for you?" the waiter said to Delilah.

Delilah ordered an iced tea, hoping to prolong the meeting. She opened her purse and pulled out the erotic poem Miriam had written. She slid it across the table to Liam.

"Ever see that?"

Liam scanned the paper. He frowned. "Never. Miriam wrote that?"

"She did."

"I didn't see any commission." He paused, clearly thinking of all the other things Miriam may have submitted on her own. "Where did you find it?"

"My colleague found it on the Web. Had Miriam written erotica before?"

Liam shrugged. "Miriam wrote what she wanted to write, whether or not anyone gave a damn about reading it."

"Did you know her to have . . . lovers?"

Liam looked surprised at the question. "As a matter of course, I don't get involved in my writers' affairs. My own version of 'don't ask, don't tell.'" He let out a bemused chuckle. "But if I had to pick my client least likely to have an active sex life, it would be Miriam, hands down. A real man-hater."

A man-hater, or a Liam-hater? "In what way?"

"How many ways are there to be a man-hater, Delilah? If you've read her books, you'd understand."

"I have read her books."

"Then you know that Miriam thought the world order was stacked against women. That male domination causes global strife, war, famine . . . beached whales on the coast of Massachusetts. You name it."

"That might be a slight exaggeration."

"Hardly." Liam picked up his new – now empty – glass and swirled it around as though it was still full. "Miriam was an active member of the Women's Creative Initiative for Change in Politics. Ever heard of it?"

"No."

"Right. Know why? Because it's a fringe group. WCICP is made up of dykes and crazies convinced that female subjugation is the root cause of all the world's ills." Liam smirked. "Miriam had been a member for the past fourteen years."

"What are you saying, Mr. McMaster?"

Liam leafed through the bills in his wallet. He threw a twenty down on the table.

"I'm saying that Miriam was a nut job. She turned her nose up at anything mainstream. Marriage, heterosexual relationships, success. She was a recluse, a *chienne misérable*, a misanthrope."

"But you know of no one who had a specific grudge against Miriam?"

Liam stood. He bent over, his hands on the table in front of Delilah, his face close enough to Delilah's that she could smell the bourbon on his breath.

"You're at minute sixteen."

Asshole. "If you don't know the answer to the question, Mr. McMaster-"

"If you're trying to figure out who offed Miriam Cross, you're in for a long, boring ride. The woman had no friends, no life. My guess?" - Liam straightened - "A random murder. Miriam was in the wrong place at the wrong time."

"Then how do you explain the name change? She'd been living under an alias."

Liam shrugged. "Who knows? That doesn't mean it wasn't random."

Liam turned abruptly to leave. Delilah stood and grabbed his arm. Liam shrugged her hand away.

"If Miriam was such a terrible client, Liam, why did you continue to represent her for *nine* years?"

He smiled, but it was a smile that turned Delilah's lunch into something sour and heavy in her stomach. "Because she had me by the balls, *Delilah*. But not anymore. The twisted genius of Miriam Cross is dancing with the devil now. And we're all the better for it."

FOURTEEN

Delilah was standing mid-thigh in stinky hay when she saw Barb's maroon Honda minivan pulling up her driveway. It was almost dusk and nearing the longest day of the year. Bats swooped overhead, their black bodies silhouetted by a sinking orange sun. Delilah wiped her hands on her soiled jeans and balanced the pitchfork against the barn walls. For Barb to show up unannounced, whatever it was had to be important.

But Barb wasn't alone. A person sat next to her in the passenger seat. Anders.

Delilah placed Spur back into his nearly-clean stall. Millie was already safe in hers, and the old mare looked up at Delilah as though sensing her anxiety, a few long strands of hay hanging from her mouth.

"You're past caring about men, aren't you, girl?" Delilah bent to give Millie a gentle kiss on the head, her gaze on the figures coming toward the barn. Barb entered first, her tall form moving self-assuredly through the piles of clean hay on the floor. Anders followed behind. He eyed the horses with wary interest.

"Sorry for showing up so late," Barb said. She patted Spur. "Some things can't wait."

Barb volunteered at the school marching band, and she still wore the navy t-shirt with the red crest and the words "Falcons" emblazoned across her chest. As always, Barb's hair was neatly combed, her jeans pressed.

"What's got you so worked up you'd leave a band event to come here?"

"We have a lead."

"What would that be?"

Barb motioned toward the house. "It will take some explaining. Can we talk in there? You might want to freshen up . . . you smell like horse and look like something the horses have been stepping on."

"That bad, huh?" Delilah glanced at Anders. "Welcome to my sorry excuse for a ranch."

He looked toward the house and Delilah suddenly saw it through a stranger's eyes. Three stories of field stone in need of re-pointing. Small, deep window sills, a peeling front porch. A house of shadows, one that ghosts could call home. A place children might avoid on Halloween, had there been any children within a mile. It was a house with history and scars, and Delilah felt a certain kinship for those very reasons. Had ever since she'd first come upon it four years ago.

The house had been cheap, purchased from the prior owner's quarreling heirs. It had a decent barn, a pasture for the horses and, perhaps best of all, no neighbors too close by. Delilah liked her privacy. And right now,

Anders' presence was infringing on that particular preference.

"Come on up," she said to Barb and Anders. Outside the barn, she swung herself over the fence and headed up toward the house, lingering to wait for her colleagues. No one spoke until they were inside.

Delilah didn't have central air, but the thick stone walls and low downstairs ceilings kept the home cool. Still, to keep her guests comfortable, she turned on the one window air conditioner in the living room. She asked Anders and Barb if they wanted a drink. After handing Anders a Yuengling and Barb a glass of cranberry juice, she excused herself so that she could peel off at least some of the grime.

She returned fifteen minutes later, showered, her wet hair combed straight, wearing sweat pants and a tank top. Her nipples hardened from the cool air in the living room and she crossed her arms over her chest, suddenly self-consciousness.

"Are you going to sit?" Barb said.

Delilah grabbed a beer for herself and then sank into the couch. "Happy now?"

"Happy as I get." Barb turned to Anders. "You want to start?"

"Sure." He looked at Delilah. "I'll begin with the dates you gave me. During each of the two periods that Miriam's niece said she'd disappeared, she still had a limited public presence. A lecture series, a published story, was quoted in an article . . . something."

Delilah was not surprised. "Not this time?"
'No. Mostly."

"Mostly?"

"Seems our girl had quite a history of philanthropy. I was able to trace her activity. She used the name Miriam Cross - her real name - for official business.

132

Miriam had been an active member of four organizations over the last decade."

"Not surprising. Fits her character - and Lucinda told me that she'd left money to a charity."

"But there are two things I found curious. One, three of the nonprofits are very well-known. Habitat for humanity. Amnesty International. And Women for Women International."

Delilah said, "Nothing ominous there."

Barb, who had been quiet up until that point, sat forward in her chair. "Anders says she'd been a generous benefactor of all three."

Anders nodded. "In fact, I'd say very generous. She donated most of the royalties from her last book to Amnesty International."

Delilah frowned. "Her *last* book? It wasn't very popular."

Anders smiled. "You're right. Her last *two* books were not as popular as her second novel, *Temptations*. That book, along with a generous movie option, has earned her millions over her life time. Even so, she only kept a fraction of it."

"And the rest?"

"That's curious fact number two. Have you ever heard of Women's Creative Initiative for Change in Politics?"

"Miriam's agent, Liam McMaster, mentioned it today. Said it was a fringe group."

Anders nodded. "It is a fringe group. Made up of mostly women - from dozens of countries. The group itself is fairly vocal on the issue of women's rights, but not recognized as mainstream."

"Okay, and Miriam was a member. How does that relate to her murder?"

Barb said, "Miriam was a founding member."

"Was she active during her disappearance?"

"Not exactly."

"Then I'm still not following you." Clearly Barb and Anders had already walked through the significance of these facts together, and Delilah was starting to lose patience with both of them.

"Have you ever heard of Women NOW?"

"You mean NOW, the National Organization for Women?"

Anders shook his head. "No, I mean Women NOW."

Delilah shook her head.

Anders explained, "It's a sub-group of Women's Creative Initiative for Change in Politics. A *small* subgroup."

Delilah frowned. "Look, you two may understand why this is important, but it's not clicking for me. Miriam was a member of a fringe nonprofit. She helped create it. And there was a small subgroup of women who made up Women NOW. So why is this so critical that you showed up late to tell me about it? Spell it out."

Barb said, "We don't know."

"You don't know," Delilah repeated. "But clearly you know something, or you wouldn't be here."

"Anders followed the money. Miriam was a founding member of a fringe nonprofit, and one of seventeen members of a subgroup called Women NOW. But Women NOW is different, Delilah. We're not sure it means anything yet. But it sure is an eyebrow raiser."

"Why's that?"

Anders cleared his throat. "Because Women NOW is, effectively, like a secret society. It exists, but there are few public records of its existence. It seems to influence politics, though. Largely because of its members."

"Who are?"

"Former world leaders. Prominent women in exile. Women with money – or who have the backing of people with money. This isn't a group of do-gooders. This is a group of women who understand how to get shit done. They have power, Delilah."

"And you think Miriam's murder is somehow a result of membership in this group?"

Barb shrugged. "We think it's too important to ignore."

Delilah nodded. She agreed. "And Miriam surfaced during her disappearance as part of Women NOW?"

"From what I could tell," Anders said, "she never stopped contributing. She may have receded from the public eye, but she stayed active in Women NOW."

Delilah considered this. "But what about the sex tape? Chinnamasta and the beheading? Is there a connection?"

"We don't know," Barb said.

"And that's the truth. We don't know." Anders stood and pulled something from his pocket. "Look at this."

Delilah took the paper. A print out for a political dinner held to raise money for Juan DeMarco. Last April - *before* her disappearance - in New York City. Five courses, a wine tasting and a speech by DeMarco. Introductions by the esteemed literary author, Miriam Cross.

"This matches the dinner ticket we found in Miriam's box," Delilah said. She stood, excited. They were right . . . this was something, at least. A hint of Miriam's life before her murder. A name, a connection. "What do we know about DeMarco?"

"Ardent supporter of Habitat for Humanity," Anders said. "Worked in the field constructing houses, has given thousands to the cause. Makes great press. In fact, DeMarco himself has a nice rags-to-success story. I'm still looking into it, but I'm guessing that Habitat for Humanity was his connection to Miriam."

"Is DeMarco a Democrat?"

Anders shook his head. Barb gave a half-smirk. "Republican?"

"Neither. Juan DeMarco is a nobody in politics. Not yet, anyway. He's running again next year. On the Libertarian ticket."

#

An hour later, after hashing and re-hashing the seemingly random facts they'd pulled together, Barb rose to leave.

Delilah said, "Can Fred contact the Lehigh County coroner's office to confirm Miriam's cause of death?"

"He can," Barb said. "But I'm pretty sure being separated from one's head would do the trick."

"She could have been shot or poisoned beforehand."

Barb shrugged. "I can ask, but whether he'll cooperate is another story." Barb glanced at her watch. "Anders, you need a ride home?"

"I do."

Delilah knew that Barb's house was forty minutes in the opposite direction. And she had a family at home, waiting for her.

"I'll take him," Delilah said.

"You sure?"

Delilah nodded. "Doylestown, right?"

Anders nodded. "My car died earlier today. If it's too much trouble, I can call a cab-"

"Don't be silly."

Delilah put her beer bottle in the recycling bin – thankfully she'd only had one – and slid her flip flops on. When she walked back into the living room, Barb and Anders were huddled together. They looked like a pair of kids caught showing each other their goods in a closet.

"What's going on?" Delilah said.

It was Barb who spoke. "We need to go to New York City for a few days."

"Out of the question. This client can't afford to reimburse us for overnight stays."

Barb shot Anders a *told you so* look. "We need an audience with Juan DeMarco, see if we can get a hold of the attendance sheet for his fund raiser."

"You think a trip to New York is necessary?"

Barb told Delilah about Miriam's Chestnut Hill neighbor and the car with the Yankees magnet.

"That could be anyone."

"But it makes sense that one of the men on the sex tape could be the same person who was at Miriam's house the night the cops were called." Barb shifted to lean against the wall. "We know one of the men was named Jack. If Anders can wheedle information out of DeMarco, I can help him cross-check the attendance records. See if any of the guests is named Jack, if there is a connection to Miriam, to her women's organizations, or even to the same Habitat for Humanity chapter that Miriam belonged to."

"It's a long shot."

"It's all we have."

Delilah thought for a moment. It wasn't *all* they had, but what they did have wasn't much. They had to begin connecting the dots. New York would at least represent movement.

She said, "It'll have to be a day trip."

Anders looked thoughtful. "I have a friend in New York who will put us up." He turned toward Barb. "Is that okay with you?"

"You know the saying. If it's free, it's for me."

Delilah smiled, suddenly remembering something. "What about the passports? The ones in Miriam's box along side the DVD?"

Anders shook his head. "Nothing. I looked for missing person reports, any kind of electronic trail, and found zilch. It's as though neither of them ever existed, here or abroad."

"Odd."

"Maybe not," Anders said. "These are foreign women from a developing country where electronic records are not as readily available. It's possible the women entered the United States and have been staying here illegally, with friends or relatives. They might be using cash, which isn't traceable."

"But you would think there would be *something* once they arrived in the States."

Anders said, "Whatever they've been doing, it's been on the down low. For now, those passports are a dead end."

Barb picked up her black backpack that doubled as a purse. "With everything settled, I've got to go. Let's make it Friday. Anders, I'll pick you up in the early afternoon?"

Anders agreed. They settled on a time and, with that, Barb left. Delilah took a few minutes to refill the dogs' water dish and find her car keys. Anders was waiting for her by the front door. Delilah broke through a pregnant silence by jingling her keys and saying, "Jeep. Top down okay?"

"Sure."

Delilah led the way outside, and down the dark driveway to the alcove where she parked the Jeep. Delilah waited while Anders fumbled with his seatbelt. Then she started the car.

"Your house is beautiful," Anders said.

"If by that you mean old, you're right."

"By that I mean it's beautiful. All the millwork, the stone walls, the deep sills. It may be cliché, but they really don't make houses like that anymore."

"Character is an old-fashioned, out-dated concept, it seems." *Wow, Delilah, you really come up with the killer lines.*

They drove under another quiet spell, only the hum of the engine and the whoosh of the wind penetrating the uncomfortable hush. Finally, it was Delilah who broke the spell.

"I think the men in the tape are connected somehow to Miriam's murder. I'm not opposed to the New York plan, but I wish to hell there was another – quicker – way to find out who they are."

"Short of releasing the tape?"

Delilah looked at him sharply. "That's out of the question."

"Unless we go public with the tape, we have two voices and a couple of naked asses. Not a whole lot to go on."

"I know. But if we do go public, we have no idea what kind of hornet's nest we'll be stirring up. Besides, there's Miriam's reputation to consider."

"What about Miriam's niece? What's her name . . . Lucy, Laura-"

"Lucinda. I doubt she'll know. She swears her aunt was celibate. I hate the idea of showing her that tape."

"We could edit it, so that she only hears their voices."

"That would still be traumatic and unproductive. Plus, she'd want to see the tape and I can't do that to her. Not now. We need to come up with another way."

"Don't get your hopes up, Delilah-"

"I don't work based on hope, Matthew." She glanced in his direction. "Gave that up long ago."

"Spoken like a bitter woman."

Softly, Delilah said, "You don't know anything about me."

"I know that you have a hell of a tough shell."

Delilah downshifted to third to take a corner and then accelerated on the straightaway. *Damn him.* Keeping her gaze on the road, she said, "Anders, if this is

139

going to work, stop analyzing me, okay?" She hated the iron in her voice. It made her sound defensive.

"Got it."

They drove the rest of the way in silence

FIFTEEN

Thursday morning, Barb, Margot and Natasha watched Miriam's sex tape for the fourth time, convinced that they were missing something that would help them identify the men. Barb, forcing herself to watch Jack's sadistic coupling with Miriam, kept her eyes on the larger picture. She hoped some reflection or extraneous bit of background would provide a hint. She tried not to judge, but she couldn't understand why a woman like Miriam would put herself in that situation. But experience had taught Barb that the choices people should make and the ones they do rarely match.

She said, "Stop and back it up, Margot. I'll tell you when."

Margot replayed the same sequence. It was then that Barb realized she'd been focusing on the wrong thing. She knew what had been bugging her. "There." Barb pointed to the screen. "Jack's ring."

On screen, Jack was slapping his hand over Miriam's mouth while the other hand twisted her nipple violently. Miriam cried out.

"Pause."

Margot hit the pause button.

"Can you blow this picture up?"

"Which part?"

"Jack's hand. Zoom in." Barb squinted at the screen. Where were her reading glasses when she needed them? "There. Look."

Barb pointed to the hand clasped over Miriam's mouth. On the third finger of the left hand was a ring. At first glance it looked like a plain gold band, easily mistaken for a wedding ring. It was on the wrong finger for a nuptial band, though. And upon closer inspection, Barb could see the blue stone in the center. She had a hunch.

Margot said, "Even when I enlarge it, the quality of the picture is terrible."

Natasha stood and went over to her desk. She picked up her purse, rummaged through its contents, and pulled out a magnifying glass. She handed the glass to Barb, who held it over the screen.

"I think it's a class ring," Barb said. She could make out thick striations of gold interlaced with black. And that blue stone. But even with the magnifying glass, she couldn't make what looked like squiggles on the sides. Too blurry. "But it could be any class, from any school. I wish we at least had a graduation date."

"We can ballpark his age," Natasha said, uncurling her long, toned legs and stretching them out in front of her. "From the sound of his voice and the look of his back and penis, Jack's in his forties or early fifties."

"You can tell that by looking at his genitals?" Barb said.

"I've seen a lot of dicks."

Margot stayed quiet, for which Barb was grateful.

Natasha took the magnifying glass. "The guy's hair is dark blonde, but there's gray in his pubes. You can see it even though he trims."

Margot back-tracked until she reached the shot of Jack getting ready to enter Miriam. Indeed, now that Natasha mentioned it, Barb could see streaks of gray in the neat mound of pubic hair. She had to hand it to the girl, she knew her genitals.

"Okay, so that would mean he probably graduated from college in the eighties," Barb said.

Natasha said, "Unless it's a high school ring."

Margot shook her head. "He speaks with an air of command. If I had to guess, I'd say he's well-educated. And the only way he would be wearing a high school class ring is if he didn't have a college one to replace it."

Barb nodded. "Good point."

Margot skipped ahead, back to Jack and his ring, and then continued to forward the DVD in the hopes that another frame would provide a sharper view of his hand. No luck.

"One thing is odd," Natasha said. "He's wearing the ring on his left hand. I thought class rings were worn on the right hand."

"I think she's right," Margot said, looking at Natasha with surprise.

"Hey," Natasha said, "Just because I didn't graduate doesn't mean I haven't dated a few high school jocks in my time."

Barb said quickly, "We need a way to blow up the picture of that ring to get a better look at the etchings."

Natasha frowned. "Delilah won't let that DVD out of her sight."

"Anders. He can do it when he gets back from New York. We can email the frozen frame to him." Margot stood. "Now, if you'll excuse me ladies, I've had enough pornography for one day."

Barb held up a hand. "Just one more thing, Margot." Barb had brought the picture she'd stolen from Miriam's Raymond Street property, the one of Miriam and a dark stranger. She pulled it out of her briefcase. Because of the broken glass, she had wrapped it in cloth, which she carefully pulled back. She showed the picture to the other women.

"Think it could be one of these men?"

They all stared at the photograph for a long, silent moment. From beneath the cracked glass, Miriam looked back at them, her smile radiant, totally unaware of the awful fate awaiting her.

"It's not Jack," Natasha said. "His skin is too dark. I bet it's the second guy in the tape. The one Miriam seemed to like."

Margot nodded her agreement. "Too bad we can't see his face. Without that, neither the picture nor the video is of much help."

Barb's cell phone rang. It was her daughter's school – never a good thing. Quickly, she re-covered the picture, careful not to disturb the shards of glass, before answering. A class ring, an aging penis and a set of voices. That's all they had. Right then, it didn't seem like much.

#

Thursday evening, Delilah called Joe. It was late – after nine – but she had been meaning to check on Lucinda all day. And if she were being honest with herself, she was lonely, plain and simple. She wanted to hear a friendly voice.

"Hey cowgirl, I was going to call you first thing in the morning."

"Well, then, it's good I got to you first. What's up?"

Delilah was curled up on her couch. She'd turned the air conditioner off and opened all of her windows – those not painted shut, at least. She was enjoying a rare cool June breeze. On the television, she'd muted the *Biggest Loser*. She watched tortured overweight people teeter their way across a balance beam. *Only in America*.

"We haven't seen anyone following the target."

"Well, that's good."

"Not exactly."

"Explain."

"My man saw one of the target's sons talking to a guy."

"What'd he look like?"

"Mid-thirties, rough, walked with a limp."

Delilah sat up. *The guy Natasha had a run in with?* "Dark-haired?"

"Didn't say. But he definitely got a bad vibe. He was told to watch the mother, so he didn't follow the boy. I wish he had."

Delilah pondered this. "This happen outside their apartment building?"

"About a block away. What do you want me to do?"

Delilah had a dilemma. Lucinda didn't know she had a tail, one hired by Delilah, so calling her about her son would throw her into a panic. And it *could* be nothing. At the same time, Delilah had to do something.

"If it happens again, follow the son, even if that means leaving Lucinda. I suspect it's the same guy one of my employees had an, um, moment with."

"Done."

"It could be dangerous, Joe."

"So can driving, but we do it every day."

She laughed. "True enough."

145

There was a moment of silence. Delilah's business was over. She knew she should simply hang up.

"You okay, cowgirl?" Joe asked.

No. "Yes. Just worried about my client."

"No worries, Lila. We got it covered."

#

It was almost eleven when Natasha got home from the bar. She found Amelia at her apartment already, naked except for a white t-shirt and a pair of pink panties, her small, slim form sprawled on the living room couch. She'd agreed to come over and watch Sam while Natasha tended bar. But there would be a price. Natasha smiled. There was always a price.

Natasha slipped her bag off her shoulder and onto the small dining table. She walked the nine paces to where the other woman dosed. She knelt down and, softly, kissed Amelia on the lips. A slow smile spread across Amelia's face, one that made even Natasha's ice-cold heart melt. Just a little.

"Hey, sleepy head. Want to stay the night?"

Amelia moaned *of course*, her voice husky from sleep. Despite the exhaustion brought about by working three jobs in one day, Natasha felt a thrill shoot through her body. She ran a finger down the length of Amelia's cheek, continuing down her neck, across her breast and down to the mound covered by the pink panties. Amelia raised her hips in reply.

"Let me check on Sam," Natasha whispered. "I'll meet you in bed."

Natasha watched as Amelia stood, stretched and walked gracefully into the bedroom, her tight little bottom swaying deliciously from side to side. Amelia was Natasha's first woman. Natasha was pretty sure she wasn't going back.

Natasha crept her way into Sam's room. She'd given him the bigger of the two bedrooms in the cramped

Northeast Philly apartment. Someday she hoped that he would have a house, a real home with a yard and a dog – he was always begging for a dog – and a separate room for his toys, so his friends could come over and play. She knelt down over Sam's sleeping form and pulled up the covers, tucking the sheet around his shoulders. Nope, he won't be playing with toys much longer, she thought. Her blonde angel was growing. Too quickly.

Natasha kissed Sam's head, letting her lips linger on the warmth of his skin. She thought of the woman in the bed in the next room and the boy she loved so much and, for the briefest of seconds, let herself pretend this was a family. A real family. Not like the one she ran away from when she was a different Natasha, one with a past she'd rather forget.

Except that her past gave her Sam. The best thing in her life.

Her phone rang. Natasha popped up and sprinted out of Sam's room. "Damn, who the fuck is calling me at midnight?" she said to herself.

"I ain't paying you no more fucking child support, bitch," said the voice on the phone.

Ah, the message she'd left for Jake earlier in the week. "I wasn't calling for child support, Jake. Not this time." Natasha sat down on the edge of the table, her warm family feelings suddenly replaced by icy disgust. Jake had that effect on her.

"Then why the fuck were you calling me?"

"Nice to talk to you, too."

"Yeah, well." But his voice had softened. Jake had wanted to marry her, once upon a time. After he knocked her up, put a bun in her oven, committed statutory rape, whatever you wanted to call it. But she'd been a willing and eager fifteen-year-old. Anything to create a new life for herself - even sleeping with Jake, a bookie, con-man and twenty-five-year old thug. Jake hadn't beaten her. And he'd always fed her afterwards. Back then, she was only getting one meal a day, if she was lucky. So a screw for a cheesesteak seemed like a pretty good deal.

"So what do you want, Natasha? You in trouble?"

Natasha relaxed. A little bit. The thing about Jake Morowski was that he was unpredictable. Sweet and gentle one minute, a raving lunatic the next. Plus, he was stupid. That had been the deal breaker for Natasha. And she thanked God that Sam had gotten her brains, not Jake's. Otherwise, life would have been tough for her son.

"I called you days ago, Jake. I need to find out about a woman."

"You a dyke now?"

Natasha smiled. "Not that kind of woman. A dead woman. Miriam Cross. That name pop up in your circle?"

"No."

"How about Emily Cray?"

She could almost hear the wheels creaking away on the other side of the mobile. "Nope, don't know that name, either."

"Can you do some digging for me, Jake?" She lowered her voice, soft and sexy, the way she used to in her dancing days.

"I don't know."

"*Please?*"

"Jeez, Natasha. You're giving me a boner. Stop that."

She smiled. "Then you'll help me?"

"What'll you give me?" And from the tone of his voice, he had something very specific in mind.

"I won't pursue child support with the lawyer for at least another six months."

"Damn it, Natasha. Enough about the fucking child support for a kid you won't even let me see."

"You want him to have a good life, don't you?"

"Yeah, sure."

"Then stay the fuck out of it, Jake. I'm raising him good."

"How so?"

"School, routine, three squares. A hell of a lot more than either of us had."

"Does he know you were a whore?"

Natasha closed her eyes. Only words, she said to herself. "Will you look into this woman or not?"

"What do you want me to dig for?" He sounded annoyed, but resigned. That was good enough for Natasha. Moron or not, Jake had connections in the criminal underworld. It'd take Delilah years to find the kind of word-of-mouth information Jake could get in a week.

"Anything. A hit, a heist, drugs. Just put the name out there and see if you make a connection."

"I'll be looking for a pay back, Natasha. A fucking big one."

Natasha smiled, but there was no joy in it. "You always are, Jake. Just like everybody else."

SIXTEEN

The next morning, Delilah awoke to the sound of her conscience having a meltdown. The night before she'd decided not to tell Lucinda that some creep was talking to her kid. *Wrong, wrong, wrong.*

Problem was, she was convinced that, logically, it was the *right* decision. There was the small fact that Lucinda hadn't wanted protection. She would view that as meddling – fair enough. But that's not what was stopping Delilah. Rather, it was the fear that Lucinda would shrug off the danger and order her to cease and desist all surveillance.

Then Lucinda's son would really be in trouble.

So Delilah had to play it differently. But how? That's what had kept her awake half the night. That's what was weighing on her now, even in the promising sunlight of a new day, in the comfort of cotton and down.

She sat up. *That was it!* She reached for her phone, blowing away the mental cobwebs that usually came with early morning.

Lucinda picked up right away. "Have you found something?"

"We're making progress, Lucinda. But I called for another reason. When are your sons leaving for their grandparents?"

"Today's their last day of school. I was going to take them upstate this weekend."

"A favor?"

"Anything."

"Make it today. Right after school."

"Why?"

"Because we've found out enough to know that this is bigger than Miriam, Lucinda. And right now you and your family are exposed. Get the boys – and yourself, if you can – out of here for a while. Let us finish with all of you in a safe place."

Silence on the other end. Delilah waited it out. She watched a breeze blow open her bedroom curtains and ticked off, in her head, the morning's chores. The horses, a run, and then an early start at the office. She could handle everything better if she knew Lucinda's kids were safe.

"Okay," Lucinda said, finally. "Them, not me. I'll have to call my in-laws to make sure it's okay, but I don't see a problem with bringing them up today."

"Great!" Delilah tried not to sound too relieved.

Another pause. "Can you tell me what's going on?"

"I can tell you this. Your Aunt Miriam was a complicated person. I think what you saw – the eccentricities, the disappearances – were only icing on a very large cake."

#

Delilah's relief was short-lived. An hour later, while feeding the horses, her stepfather, Paul Powers, called. "Your mother is headed your way, Delilah."

Holy hell. "Great."

"You don't mean that, and I knew you wouldn't. That's why I'm calling you."

"And here I thought you just wanted to say hello to your favorite stepdaughter."

"Always with the sarcasm, Lila darling."

Delilah settled against the barn wall. She wanted to tell Paul not to call her Lila, but she kept her mouth closed. It would only lead to an argument, one she was not prepared to have. Instead she said, "When will she be here?"

"You know her. When she gets around to it. And if she knew I was calling you, she'd likely divorce me. So keep it under wraps, okay?"

"Sure." Delilah thought for a moment. "Why now?"

He sighed. "Because some nitwit named Katrina Rice came back here saying what a stuck up witch you are and your momma almost had a stroke. She wants to check on you personally."

"And she decided to surprise me? Is she mad?"

"Your momma's always been a little bit mad. We both know that."

"An understatement."

"You need to get over your anger toward your momma, Lila. It's been an awful long time."

"It's not just that. She'll come. She'll meddle. She'll tell me my job is too dangerous, the house is a money pit, and that I need a husband."

"True. All of it. But you're whining, baby. It doesn't become you."

"*Ugh.*" He was right. She hated when he was right.

Delilah could picture him in his man-cave, their spotless garage where he housed a Porsche and an old Ford Mustang, neither of which he drove on a regular basis. He had a Ford F-150 for that. His ample belly would be spilling over a pair of too-dark blue jeans, a checkered shirt neatly pressed and tucked in, the whole thing cinched with his brown leather belt. To be fair, Paul had always treated her fine, but she could never – probably would never – forgive him for his part in her mother's betrayal of her father.

"Darn it, Paul. I don't want her here."

"I know. Your momma means well, but she can't hold her tongue. And when it comes to you . . . well, I think she sees your daddy in you." He paused. "And it both pains her and scares her at the same time."

"Paul-"

"Paul, nothing. I have no illusions about your father, kitten. He was like a John Wayne character to your momma. Bigger than life, but also distant and unattainable."

"Like me?" Delilah said, suddenly tired despite the early hour. "The distant and unattainable part, I mean."

"No. Your momma just doesn't understand your chosen path. She wants each of her girls to have a safe, wholesome life."

Delilah snorted. "If she's looking for wholesome, maybe she should start with herself."

"Delilah!" There was real anger in his tone. It took a lot to get Paul Powers angry, but Delilah usually succeeded. He lowered his voice. "Look, Delilah, you're bitter. After losing your daddy and Michael, I understand. But your momma doesn't. She thinks you need to move on. Seeing you so angry still . . . well, if she makes it up there, it'll damn near break her heart. So do me a favor and put on a happy face."

#

"I *cannot* have her here," Delilah said into the phone.

Delilah turned the handle on the shower spigot in her bathroom. With the ancient plumbing that she kept meaning to replace, she needed at least five minutes for the water to warm up to a tolerable temperature. In the meantime, she sat naked on the closed toilet, a Little Mermaid beach towel draped across her legs.

After her conversation with Paul, she'd hopped on Millie and ridden bare-back through the woods and fields that surrounded her house. An hour later, both she and Millie were panting and the edge was finally gone from her anger.

Then Barb called at 8:38.

"Well, you're in luck, Delilah. You won't be there to greet your mom."

"What are you talking about?"

"I'm talking about Miriam Cross. New York City awaits."

"I thought you were going?"

"The best laid plans and all." Barb sighed. "School called yesterday. Dee has strep throat. And Fred is on call. I need to be here."

"Can't." Delilah stood up. She watched her image in the mirror as it made its way across the bathroom. A little more jiggle in her step than she'd like. Time to increase the mileage and reduce the wine. "Who's going to take care of the animals?"

Barb said, "I'll do it. I've taken care of the horses before. And the dogs can stay with me."

"Really?"

"Really."

"Okay, then."

"Great!" Barb sounded genuinely relieved.

"Gotta go." And don't you dare kill my animals, Delilah thought. She stuck a hand under the shower spray. Plenty hot.

"I appreciate this, Delilah. Don't forget to pick up Anders."

Delilah felt a shock run down her spine. "Anders?"

Barb laughed. "It's his friend you're staying with. I'm the only loser who had to back out."

Great. Delilah clicked off the phone and climbed into the shower. She let the warm water snake down her back, and run, unfettered, through her hair, streaming into her eyes and mouth. The sting felt cleansing.

What was she trying to wash away? The unease caused by her mother's impending visit? Even if the New York trip delayed it, inevitably she would come raging into Delilah's life like a storm surge. Maybe it was the trip itself and days without the horses. Delilah, the homebody.

Or maybe it was Anders. They hadn't spoken since she'd driven him home two days ago. She wished she knew why his presence turned her into an awkward teenager, snappish and inarticulate.

Delilah reached for the shower knobs, turning the handle as far left as it would go. She wanted the burn. She wanted the water so hot that she could hardly stand it.

#

Anders was late.

Delilah pulled up outside of his Doylestown apartment at one o'clock in the afternoon. She drove the Honda and had the air conditioner on full-blast to try and combat the scorching mid-day sun.

Anders lived above a bookstore in a historic building two streets off the main drag. The quaint Doylestown shopping district - street after street of brick, stone and stucco buildings, some dating back two hundred years or more - bustled at this hour. Delilah waited in a no-parking zone, her briefcase and lap top bag on the back seat, one small suitcase in the trunk. Where was Anders?

Delilah felt the weight of someone's gaze on her. She looked up, expecting to see Anders, and instead caught a glimpse of a bald-headed man, scalp as bare as a baby's bottom, in a nondescript car across the street. He was parked in a red zone. The guy was now looking down at a newspaper he held in his hands, but Delilah could have sworn he'd been staring at her. She looked down at her lap, watching him out of the corner of her eye. Sure enough, a few seconds later he was watching her again.

Just another guy waiting for someone, a guy with a wandering eye? Or could he be-

Tap, tap, tap.

Startled, Delilah glanced at the passenger side of the car. Anders stood outside the Honda, dressed in khakis and a faded red Life is Good t-shirt that said: *Not all who wander are lost.* He flashed a tired smile.

"Sorry I'm late. I had some stuff to deal with."

Based on the way he said it, having stuff to deal with was not good. His wife? None of my business, Delilah thought, and turned her attention back to the bald man. His car was gone.

"Something up?"

Delilah shrugged. "Probably nothing." She looked around one more time, searching for a flash of bald scalp. The coast was clear. Still feeling uneasy, she started the car.

SEVENTEEN

An exotic-looking woman with long, silken black hair met Delilah and Anders at the door of a posh Upper East Side townhome. The woman hugged Anders with a warmth that seemed both sensual and maternal. Anders grinned like a boy on his first date. He turned to introduce Delilah.

"Tula Rajav, this is my boss, Delilah Percy Powers."

Tula took one of Delilah's hands in both of hers. Her fingers felt smooth, warm and dainty, the nails buffed to a shine. Delilah felt conscious of her own hands - nails clipped short, fingers callused from working with the horses – but she squeezed back, Tula's warmth contagious.

"Matthew, you must tell me all about your life now. Your job, your lovely wife." Her eyes saddened beneath impossibly long black lashes. "And I am so very sorry for your loss."

Anders nodded slowly. Tula seemed to take the cue that he didn't want to talk about his daughter. She touched his arm, gave a half smile, and turned to lead them inside.

The townhouse was a three-story mix of contemporary and Asian. Artistic treasures from what Delilah assumed were Tula's home country of India had been woven tastefully with modern furnishings. A cream-colored sofa and matching chair had been paired with a handmade rug, its Oriental pattern accented with vibrant shades of ruby and jade. On the wall, framed Indian folk art prints took center stage against ecru walls. The overall effect pleased the eye and emanated tranquility. Like Tula herself.

As Tula led Anders and Delilah to the guest quarters, Delilah studied their host. Her age was impossible to tell: somewhere between thirty-five and fifty. She had sharp cheekbones and a prominent nose that would have been large on another face but that seemed regal on hers. Lips full, thin frame, breasts round and high against a pink caftan. Delilah found herself wondering whether Tula and Anders had been lovers.

Really Delilah?

Tula opened the door to a small bedroom decorated with a teal silk comforter and matching curtains. In the corner sat a writing desk of carved walnut. "For you, Ms. Powers."

"Delilah. Please, call me Delilah." She smiled at the woman. "This is very generous. Thank you for allowing us to stay here."

Tula smiled back, but it was Anders she was looking at. "It is my pleasure. Matthew here is an old friend. One I have not seen in far too long."

Was Anders blushing? Delilah decided then and there that the relationship between the two adults was none of her business.

"The bathroom is there"- Tula pointed to a door in the hallway -"and towels and toiletries are in the linen closet. Please let me know if there is anything you need."

Delilah thanked her again and excused herself. She wanted to get started on her research. She'd allotted two days to get an audience with Juan DeMarco and figure out what the hell Miriam Cross was up to before she died. Delilah hoped DeMarco could provide some answers.

#

Delilah's estimate of forty-eight hours proved way too optimistic. Tracking down DeMarco proved harder than she'd imagined. The man was as slippery as a newborn colt.

Anders said, "We know his office is in New York City."

Delilah nodded. "But his secretary doesn't know how to reach him."

"That's bullshit."

"Agreed, but what can I do?"

It was nearly ten o'clock Monday morning. They'd spent the last hour at DeMarco's headquarters with a surly secretary who seemed put out that anyone actually wanted to reach DeMarco, especially on a Monday. When they'd asked her for the guest list for the dinner at which Miriam spoke, the woman clammed up and shook her head. "Not without Mr. DeMarco's permission."

Now Delilah stirred her scrambled eggs around on her plate. The smell overpowered her senses and after only two or three bites, she placed her paper napkin over the whole pile.

"Not hungry?"

She shook her head. The diner – like so many in this corner of the city – was stuffy, crowded and noisy. She and Anders sat side-by-side at the counter, sharing a carafe of coffee and a small silver pot of cream. Anders was having no trouble powering through his omelet and bacon.

"You okay?" Anders looked genuinely concerned.

She *was* okay. But it was less than three days into their trip and already the sheer bustle – the madness, really – of the city was getting to her. The first night, Tula had suggested they eat in. Tula had prepared a wonderful, fragrant meal of homemade naan, lentil stew and tandoori chicken. Sensing that Anders and Tula wanted some time alone to catch up, Delilah had excused herself after dinner. She had no idea what time Anders finally went to bed, but from the shadows on his face the next morning, it'd been late.

Then over the weekend, they tracked down DeMarco's headquarters and spent an unsuccessful day trying to get an audience with DeMarco, whose office, not surprisingly, was closed. Monday began a new week. They were trying DeMarco again. But even with his headquarters open, it was looking more and more likely that New York had been a wasted trip. They were racking up time and money, neither of which Lucinda could afford.

"I'm fine," Delilah said finally and forced a cheerful smile. "You? Seems like you and Tula have a lot of catching up to do."

Anders gave her a funny look, as though he was trying to decide whether there was hidden meaning beneath her words. "Tula was my best friend Ahmed's wife. She lost Ahmed last spring."

"Was Ahmed a journalist, too?"

Anders nodded. "A casualty of the trade, you could say."

"I'm sorry."

"I'm sorry, too. At the time, I was so wrapped up in my daughter - in my family's problems - that I didn't do the things I should have. For Ahmed. Or for Tula."

"What could you have done?"

Anders looked at her for a long time. When he finally spoke, his tone conveyed much more than his words. "I should have acted, Delilah."

She waited for him to say more, but he didn't. Instead, he waved the waitress over and asked for the check.

"Back to DeMarco's headquarters?"

Anders shook his head. "Not quite. On to Plan B."

Delilah smiled. She thought she knew what Plan B was.

She was right.

#

Juan DeMarco agreed to see the journalist Matthew Anderson at noon in a small Caribbean restaurant in Greenwich Village. Juan's secretary had been more than happy to give Tula DeMarco's phone number when she told the woman in her soft, accented voice that she was trying to arrange an interview for the up-and-coming politician. DeMarco was happy, too . . . happy enough to meet with Anders and his assistant that same day.

"So how will you break the news that there is no article?"

"Who said there won't be an article?"

Delilah smiled. "Moonlighting?"

Anders laughed. Delilah liked seeing him smile. "We'll see what DeMarco gives us. I still have my journalistic integrity to think about."

They were waiting inside Caribbean Village. Anders had ordered a Sprite, Delilah a mango iced tea. They sat in a brightly-colored corner booth. Reggae music played overhead – Bob Marley crooning *No Woman, No Cry* – and Delilah could feel Anders's leg tapping to the beat. She stared at the menu, mentally preparing the questions she wanted to ask DeMarco, who finally arrived at 12:27.

Anders saw him first. He stood and waved. DeMarco was not what Delilah expected. She had an image in her mind of a stodgy man of Latin descent, someone with a thick mustache and an even thicker accent. Instead, DeMarco was tall – well over six feet – and scarecrow thin. His skin was ebony black, his head completely bald and he had an almost frenetic energy about him. When he saw Delilah, he broke into a grin.

"You didn't tell me your assistant was so lovely," he said to Anders.

Anders, clearly enjoying the change in roles, grinned. "That's why I keep her around." He winked at Delilah. She glared back, not amused.

DeMarco slid into the booth across from Anders and Delilah. "So what can I do for you folks?"

Anders threw Delilah a look that said *trust me*. She threw him one back that said *fuck you*.

"With respect to your candidacy, I'm interested in a particular angle, Mr. DeMarco."

"Call me Juan."

"Juan, this city gets its share of congressional candidates. But what interests me – and what will interest my readers – is your particular philanthropic history. You don't simply write checks to various foundations and then fall back on your haunches and announce how much you care. You're actually out there, in the trenches, volunteering."

"I am, indeed." DeMarco sat back in the booth. He looked from Delilah, to Anders and then back at Delilah again. "But that hardly seems like news."

"People love a rags-to-riches story, Juan. Yours is an Everyman's dream."

"And how do you know that?"

"I did my research."

DeMarco turned his head to follow the progress of a young, attractive waitress dressed in a yellow and white-striped rugby shirt. The waitress stopped at their table, order pad at the ready. "What can I get you?" she said.

DeMarco ordered mango iced tea and codfish fritters, Delilah, hungry after her uneaten breakfast, jerk chicken, rice and beans. Anders stared at the menu again before saying "curried shrimp" without enthusiasm.

DeMarco looked at Delilah. "I like a woman who's not afraid to eat."

"And I like a man who keeps his opinions to himself."

DeMarco smiled. "Spirited, aren't you?"

Delilah met his grin with an icy stare of her own. DeMarco turned his attention back to Anders.

"What if I told you that I've decided not to run for office. Not next year, maybe never."

Anders paused before responding. "I'd say you're full of shit."

Tense silence followed. Then DeMarco laughed, a deep, mirthless laugh that almost drowned out the hip-hop music now playing over the loudspeakers.

"Look, Matthew Anderson and his *assistant*, I did my research, too. I know Matthew Anderson, the journalist, hasn't written a damn thing worth a second of my time in over six years. I also know that even in your heyday, you never gave a damn about the lives of unknown politicians like me. So stop bullshitting me, *please*, and tell me what this is about."

Delilah and Anders exchanged a look. On to Plan C: honesty.

"Miriam Cross," Delilah said.

"Miriam Cross?" For the briefest moment, a look of fear passed over DeMarco's features. But like that, the smooth persona was back. "Miriam Cross, yes. The author. She spoke at a fundraising dinner I hosted."

Delilah nodded, grateful that he was up front about at least that fact. "Why Miriam? She seems an unlikely choice."

"I needed a name. If you haven't noticed, I'm not some hot shot politician pulling in millions in contribs. I don't get the major celebrities."

Anders said, "Was she paid to speak?"

DeMarco shook his head. "She did it on behalf of Habitat for Humanity. We're both active members." He smiled. "But you already know that."

Delilah nodded. "Did she speak at more than one dinner?"

"No."

Anders said, "Do you remember when this one took place?"

"Man, I don't remember the date. Does it really matter? Why do you two give a damn that Cross spoke at a fund-raiser for some dude from New York who we all know doesn't have a chance in hell of making it to Washington?"

"Precisely for that reason," Anders said. "It makes no sense."

Delilah said, "Mr. DeMarco, Miriam Cross is dead. She was murdered a few weeks ago."

DeMarco didn't respond. Instead, he stared down at his dinner plate-sized hands, turning those hands over like he was inspecting a manicure. When he finally looked up, the shadow of something that Delilah saw

164

earlier was more pronounced. And it *was* fear. Plain old, self-serving fear.

"I ain't getting mixed up in this shit," DeMarco said. "I got nothing to tell you."

"We want the guest list for that dinner. That's all."

"I can't give you that. I don't even have it anymore."

"That's a lie, Juan, and you know it. You have to keep those lists for tax purposes," Anders said. "You give us the list, we walk away. This meeting never happened."

Just then, the waitress walked over, a large tray in her hand. She placed the iced tea and fritters in front of DeMarco and the other two dishes in front of Delilah and Anders, oblivious to the tension wafting in waves from the table.

When the waitress left, DeMarco said, "See what you've done? Made me lose my appetite."

Delilah leaned over the table. "Look, Juan, Miriam was *murdered*. And the person who killed her is still out there. If she met this person at your dinner, you could help us by sharing that guest list. I think we would all feel a little safer if whoever killed Miriam was behind bars."

"What makes you so sure it was one person, Delilah? Because I have a hunch of my own. My hunch is that there are some bad-ass people out there. People who manipulate the system for their own ends. People who attend political dinners because they want favors, they want access to the decision makers. They want a fucking puppet whose strings they can pull."

"And they wanted you to be that puppet?" Anders said.

DeMarco's eyes widened. All the blood was gone from his lower lip, and his skin seemed a shade paler.

"You told them no," Delilah said, suddenly understanding DeMarco's role. "They said they could get you elected if you cooperated. But you refused, didn't you, Juan?"

"I did. And they didn't much like it."

"Who were they?"

"I can't tell you that. I really can't. Or I will end up like your Miriam Cross."

"Was she one of them?" Anders said.

"No. At least I don't think so."

"Was she even involved?"

"I don't think so. I don't even think she knew them."

"Can you give us the list? Just the list," Delilah said, aware of the pleading in her voice. "You don't need to tell us who had been pressuring you. We just want the guest list. We'll figure it out from there. Your name never has to come up."

"Why do you care? What's your stake in all of this?"

"I'm a private investigator. My firm was hired by one of Miriam's relatives to find her killer."

"That's it?"

Delilah met his gaze. "That's it."

DeMarco stabbed half-heartedly at a fitter. He swirled the bite around on his plate. "I'll think about it," he said finally. "That's the best I can do. But don't expect anything. I'm a survivor, and sharing information with you . . . well, man, that could be my ticket to the morgue."

Anders looked at Delilah. She nodded. "I hope you change your mind," Delilah said. "A woman's life could be in danger."

"More than one life is in danger," DeMarco said. "Believe me on that one."

EIGHTEEN

Barb's heart sank. Almost three days on an antibiotic and her daughter still had a fever. Barb suspected something more than strep was going on – perhaps a virus on top of the pesky bacteria. She pulled off the plastic tip to the ear thermometer and placed the device back in its box.

"Back in bed," she said to Dee. "Let's go."

"I feel fine."

"You may *think* you feel fine, but on a cellular level, you're not so good. Rest and fluids."

Her daughter rolled her eyes, but with less zeal than normal. Her long, blonde hair hung straight and lank against her skull and her pale skin looked ghost-like.

Barb felt another stab of concern. *The heck with the doctors.* She picked up the phone.

Fred answered on the third ring. "Let me guess. On my way home, you want me to grab an old Jewish grandmother and bring her home to make soup."

"Close. I need two whole chickens and a bag of carrots. I already have the celery and onions. Oh, and some fresh ginger root and two lemons."

"Ginger-lemon tea again?"

"You know it."

"Barb, the doctor said-"

"Don't Barb me, Fred. We both know doctors don't know everything. Besides, you like chicken soup, too."

"True. But that tea tastes like vomit."

"Be glad you don't have to drink it. Are you leaving soon?"

"Not soon enough."

Barb heard her husband yawn. He'd been working long shifts for the last few weeks and it was beginning to catch up with him. If he wasn't careful, he *would* be sipping ginger lemon tea before long.

Before Barb hung up, Fred said, "One more thing, Barb. I contacted the Willston Police Department. They confirmed the cause of death for Miriam Cross. Shock and hemorrhage from the severed neck."

"No surprises there."

"Well, there was one surprise."

Barb tensed. "What?"

"A drug screening detected amobarbital. The coroner used gas chromatography-mass spectrometry to determine the concentration of the drug in her body fluids and tissues."

"And?"

"Levels that exceeded a therapeutic range."

"Translation, Fred."

"Your girl had barbiturates in her system."

"Enough to kill her?"

"Probably not. Based on the amount of blood at the scene, she was alive when the perp beheaded her."

"*Shit.*"

"Look, my buddy at Willston wanted to know what was up with all the questions. I think they have a pretty tight operation going on over there, Barbie. There's even a gag order in place. I can't be turning in chips anymore or someone's gonna start to wonder."

"Why the gag order?"

"Don't know and I ain't asking."

"Got it."

His voice softened. "I love you, you know. Pain in the ass that you are."

Barb smiled. "Fred, do you think Miriam was taking drugs?"

He took so long to answer that she thought maybe he'd hung up. But then he said, "I've seen a lot of crazy shit. Some lonely rich lady swallowing Amytal to dull her jittery nerves wouldn't surprise me in the least. But-" he hesitated.

"I want to hear the *but,* Fred."

"But you have to think about this in context. The woman was murdered."

"If she was taking drugs, especially if they were illegal drugs, that could explain why she was murdered-"

"No one said anything about illegal drugs, Barbie. Amytal can be used to treat anxiety and insomnia. Perfectly legal, with a prescription. But it has another use. It's far-fetched."

Barb waited.

"Some people believe it acts as a truth serum."

"I thought truth serum was a thing of fiction writers."

He sighed and she loved him then for his infinite patience. "Fact or fiction, Barbie, you have to consider all your options. When you're dealing with reality . . . well, anything can happen."

#

Delilah and Anders drove back to Tula's home, but no one was there except the housekeeper, a quiet Hispanic woman named Maria who spoke limited English. Anders let them in with the extra key Tula had given him and Maria greeted them at the front door.

"Something to drink?" Maria said.

They both declined and Maria retreated to the kitchen. The house felt cool after the stale urban air, and Delilah sank into the couch gratefully. Anders disappeared down the hall. He reappeared a minute later with his laptop and a notebook.

"I'll need an hour or so," Anders said. "Something DeMarco said-"

"The guy sure seemed nervous."

Anders nodded. "Shitting bricks, as the saying goes."

"Gotta give him credit for turning down whoever was trying to buy him off," Delilah said. She was thinking of DeMarco's face: the wide eyes and drained pallor. "An honest politician? Too bad he's not running."

"Oh, he'll be running alright, just not in the way we might like."

Anders placed the laptop on the square coffee table and sat cross-legged on the floor in front of it. Criss-cross applesauce, Delilah thought, for no reason at all other than the faint recollection of her niece saying that every time she sat that way. Delilah watched Anders unfurl a mouse and plugged it into the computer. Then he sat back and waited for the computer to boot up.

Anders said, "But why did he say no?"

"Ethics?"

"Maybe, but something more than morals was at work."

Delilah considered this. "Fear."

"Exactly." Anders typed something into his computer. When he was finished, he looked up at Delilah and smiled. The unexpected warmth threw her off guard. "You were good in there. With DeMarco."

"It's my job."

"Of course it is. It was just a compliment, Delilah. Why do you have such a hard time with the personal stuff?"

"I don't."

"You do."

Delilah waved him away. "Do you think the Mob is involved?"

"I think you're changing the subject."

"Stop."

"Stop what? All I did was say something nice and you turned it around. What is it with you?"

Delilah looked away. She didn't want to be like this. And if this was going to work, she needed to stop letting him get under her skin. After a few seconds, she said, "Sorry."

Anders sighed. "Yes, I think the Mob could be involved. But how Miriam Cross got involved with the Mafia is anyone's guess."

"And which Mafia? The Italian Mobob, the Russian Mob . . ."

"Exactly."

Delilah put her head back against the couch cushion. It was only two-thirty in the afternoon but she felt tired and cranky.

Anders was back to typing on his computer. He looked preoccupied.

"What are you working on?"

Without looking up, Anders said, "If we can't get that list from DeMarco, we'll need to figure out who the men in the sex tape are some other way."

"You know how?"

"Not exactly, but I may be able to pull a few leads out of the cybersphere . . . with a secure connection and an hour or two of time."

Delilah stood up. She stretched, and then slipped her shoes back on her feet. "I'll leave you and your laptop alone, then."

"What will you do?"

"I have an idea. Call my cell when you're finished. I'll meet you back here later."

#

Delilah didn't really have an idea. She was feeling uneasy in Tula's house and wanted time away from Anders. But where to go?

On her way out the door, she swung by the kitchen to talk to Maria. She asked her where the nearest bookstore was located. A large coffee and some space to think might provide inspiration. She'd leave the car – finding parking in this city was a feat – and walk. She could use the exercise.

Maria shook her head. "I do not know book store."

It occurred to Delilah that, although Maria worked here, she probably lived in another area of the city. "Thanks anyway," Delilah said.

Maria nodded solemnly.

"Where are you from originally?" Delilah said on impulse.

Maria's eyes widened in fear. She backed up against the long, granite counter and knocked a wine glass onto the tile floor. It shattered.

"*Idios mío*," Maria mumbled.

Delilah bent down to help Maria pick up the scattered pieces of glass. They worked together in silence, placing shards in a paper bag to be discarded in the garbage. Delilah chided herself for mentioning the woman's home country. If she was an illegal alien, of course the mere thought of deportation would be enough to terrify her.

"*Lo siento*," Delilah said. "I didn't mean to scare you."

"It is fine," Maria said. "*Gracias*."

"I only asked where you were from because . . . because I was interested."

"Colombia."

Delilah watched as Maria removed a broom from a narrow cabinet and leaned on it, her shoulders rounded in the slump of someone used to hard days on her feet. Delilah noticed that, despite the circles under her eyes and the creases around her mouth, Maria had youthfulness to her skin and brightness to her eyes. Delilah had initially guessed Maria to be about her age – mid-thirties – but she realized the woman was much younger. Mid-twenties, perhaps.

Maria pulled something from a drawer and held it up.

"The telephone book? Ah, to find the bookstore." Delilah smiled gratefully. "That's okay, Maria. I'll just walk around. I have some thinking to do."

"Do you have children?" Maria asked shyly.

"No children. Just horses and dogs. You?"

Maria gave a tentative nod. "Two boys." She smiled – the first real smile Delilah had seen from her – and it brightened her face. "In Colombia. With *mi madre* – my mother."

Delilah, struggling to follow the rest of Maria's story, learned that Maria came to America because the money she earned working for Tula was enough to support her mother and her children in a way that they otherwise could not afford in Colombia. Delilah hoped Tula was paying a fair wage. She had to believe a friend of Anders would do so. Still, Tula had to be getting something for the risk of hiring an illegal. And that something was surely financial savings. Delilah gazed at Maria with renewed respect. She could only imagine the heartbreak of leaving your children behind. Feeding your children versus raising them yourself . . . what a Sophie's choice.

"*Tenga cuidado en las calles*," Maria said. She lifted the broom and started sweeping, her demeanor business-like again, the conversation over.

Delilah knew very little Spanish, but she thought Maria just told her to be careful on the streets. *An odd thing for her to say.* But still feeling the woman's loss, Delilah simply said good bye and headed back outside.

#

The day had turned from hot and humid to hot and windy. Scraps of garbage whipped through the streets. Pedestrians, dressed in the rainbow of garb one would only find in New York, swarmed the sidewalks. Delilah, her weather senses tuned like that of an animal, could sense a storm coming despite the clear sky. She wished she'd brought an umbrella.

Delilah walked briskly, unsure where she was headed. Her mind felt cluttered with images: DeMarco's insouciant smile, Emily Cray's plain little house in Willston, Miriam's naked body tied to that bed. Somehow they were all interrelated. Delilah pulled out her cell phone, dialed Lucinda's number and then cupped the phone near her ear, waiting for Lucinda to pick up. When there was no answer, she left a message asking Lucinda to confirm that the boys were with their grandparents. Then she called Lucinda's work only to learn from the grouchy receptionist that Lucinda had called in sick. Next, Delilah tried Joe. No answer there, either. She left another message.

She felt useless in New York – too far away to help the people who needed her and unable to assist Anders in tracking down DeMarco's list. She toyed with heading back to Philly now. Anders could stay and work on DeMarco.

She needed some way to get that list.

She stopped mid-step. *Keep it simple, stupid.* There was a way. At least it was worth another shot. Delilah dug through her purse until she found the scrap of paper with the address for DeMarco's headquarters written hastily on it. She raised her hand to hail a cab. A yellow car stopped a foot away from where she stood and she climbed in quickly, providing the address as she did so. It was getting late in the afternoon and Delilah didn't know how long anyone would be at the DeMarco headquarters. She wanted to catch DeMarco or his receptionist before they left for the day.

Delilah looked up from the scrap of paper just as the cabbie was pulling away from the curb. A man was staring at the cab. Bald scalp, chiseled face. Delilah squinted through the rear window, trying to decide if it was the same man she'd seen back in Doylestown. Was she being followed?

Delilah felt pretty certain it was the same man.

Damn. While the cab driver wove his way too slowly through the streets, Delilah wondered who'd hired her tail. Who would already know that her firm was investigating the case?

"Just pull over here," Delilah said about twenty minutes into the ride. They were still two blocks from headquarters, but traffic had slowed to a stop and she was far too impatient to wait. She'd walk.

She was in Hell's Kitchen. Delilah jogged down 10th Avenue, constantly checking for a tail. All clear. Still, she was careful, keeping her head up and attention focused.

At DeMarco's office, she stopped before entering and took one last look around before going. The bells on the door announced her arrival.

She didn't see DeMarco.

The office consisted of a cramped reception area with a broad desk, a row of filing cabinets behind the desk and two beat-up orange vinyl chairs against the front wall. Juan DeMarco fliers were tacked to the walls. Stacks of literature on everything from Habitat for Humanity to Hispanic Gay Pride to the Libertarian party were scattered around the office on tray tables. Behind the front office, a doorway hid the rooms beyond with a set of colorful beaded strings – the kind Delilah's roommate had in college. If DeMarco was trying to appear the working man's candidate, his digs –from the odd location amidst actors, industrialists and restaurants to the humble interior – supported that image. He seemed like a straightforward, hardworking, colorful man. She wished him luck.

Delilah rang a small bell on the desk. After a moment she heard a "be right there" ring out from the back room. It wasn't the annoyed tone of the older woman who had greeted Delilah and Anders earlier. Someone much younger was manning the booth now.

While she waited, Delilah glanced around the room. The message light flashed on the phone. A stack of pink slips sat neatly next to the receiver. A shredder perched near the desk area, a pile of papers next to it on another folding tray table. A streaked and battered coffee maker had been placed on a table in the corner. The machine was off, but two stained mugs and a pint of milk sat on a paper plate beside it.

Seconds later, a pretty young face interrupted Delilah's assessment of the office. No more than twenty or so, she had short, curly black hair and caramel-brown eyes. Chubby, with the rounded belly that said she was either pregnant or had recently given birth. A shrill cry in the back room confirmed Delilah's suspicion.

"Sorry to keep you waiting," the woman said. "Can I help you?"

"I'm looking for Juan."

"You and the rest of the world."

"Is he here?"

"Nope. Haven't seen him since I arrived."

"What time was that?"

"After one."

Delilah glanced back at the coffee machine. The woman, following Delilah's gaze, shook her head. "That was me and Agnes, the morning volunteer. She always makes me coffee." She shrugged. "I guess she figures I'd fall asleep on the job without some caffeine, the baby and all."

"Congratulations on the baby. Are you a volunteer here, too?"

"Hell, no. I'm the paid labor." The woman held out her hand and Delilah shook it. "Elena, Juan's sister. The cherub in the back is Juan's nephew, Miguel."

Delilah smiled. "So maybe you can help me find Juan. He and I met this morning-"

"Then you're the only one who's seen him all day." The baby gave another wail and Elena cringed. "I need to feed him. He's a pig, that one. Do you need literature or something? We have all kinds of stuff on the Libertarian party" – another wail – "or on Juan. He's a good guy, you know. He could win if only he would make up his mind to run. The people like him. He's real."

The baby started to scream. Delilah said, "Elena, go take care of him. I'll grab some literature and let myself out."

Elena gave her a grateful smile and disappeared through the beads.

Delilah needed to act fast. She scanned the room for a security camera. Deciding that it didn't matter, she pulled her phone out of her bag and tapped the camera setting. She walked around the desk and, as quietly as she could, started to sift through the shredder pile. That was her first guess for where the list would be, especially if Juan had somehow rushed back here after their meeting or directed his staff to dispose of the information. She found memos and bills but otherwise nothing. She moved on to the filing cabinets, trying to figure out how such a document would be filed. She looked under "D" for dinner, then "C" for charities. Nothing. Likewise, "F" for fundraiser was a dead-end, as was "H" for Habitat for Humanity.

"You have what you need?" Elena's yelled through the curtain.

"Just about. Mind if I take a few of the gay pride brochures?"

"Help yourself!"

Delilah opened the last cabinet. She sifted through the T's, looking for tax information. This cabinet contained a jumble of tax returns, receipts and handwritten notes about donations. Delilah could hear the baby's now contented murmurs and Elena's shuffling. At any moment Elena would walk through the beads.

"Damn, come on," she muttered to herself. To Elena she said, "Do you want me to lock the front door when I leave?"

"No need!"

Bingo! Delilah pulled out a file that said "Tx - Fundraising Dinners." Inside were three sets of documents. Each contained a set of receipts – guest payment information, credit card numbers, etc. – and a master list of attendees. She pulled out her phone, ready to snap pictures of the master lists. Elena's shuffling became more pronounced. Delilah stuck her phone in her pocket, pulled the master lists away from the receipts and shoved the rest of the documents back in the file cabinet. She closed the door softly.

Elena came in just as Delilah was grabbing a handful of Libertarian brochures – the biggest ones they had – to cover the stolen papers.

"You're still here," Elena said.

"I think I have all I need now."

"Can I give Juan your number when he calls?"

Delilah glanced at the file cabinet. Closed. Relieved, she nodded. Giving her number was a risk, but she'd still like to talk with Juan.

Delilah scribbled her name and cell phone number on a scrap of paper. "Tell him anytime he's ready, to call me."

Elena gave her a curious look. She nodded and stuck the paper with the other pink slips by the phone.

"You should lock the door," Delilah said.

"Nah, it's fine," Elena said. "No one is interested in robbing Juan's headquarters. We don't have anything here. Nothing anybody wants, anyway."

NINETEEN

The bald man was back.

Delilah felt his presence before she saw him. Slowly, nonchalantly, she looked left, then right. The street was nearly deserted. A lone homeless man lay on the sidewalk, his body propped against a brick building, a brown army-issued blanket tucked under his head. In the other direction, three young dancers in bodysuits, their lithe bodies nearly naked in the stifling afternoon air, talked in a circle, their laughs clashing against the distant sounds of traffic. Behind the women, Delilah caught a glimpse of a tall man with a bare scalp. The same man from that she'd see in Manhattan and before that, Doylestown. He had a strong resemblance to Mr. Clean.

How did he find her here? She'd made sure she wasn't followed. There was no way for him to locate her unless he knew where she'd be headed. That meant that Mr. Clean was aware of the DeMarco – Miriam connection.

Which meant that there *was* a DeMarco-Miriam connection.

A bolt of lightening flashed in the distance. Delilah heard the distant rumble of thunder. A wave of tension passed through Delilah's body, leaving her breathless. She felt rigid with attention, poised at the brink of flight or flight.

She didn't know the area and she didn't have a weapon.

She stole a glance at Mr. Clean. Gone. *Shit.* Delilah started walking.

Unlikely she could outrun him. Her only option was to outwit him. Delilah tucked the dinner guest list into the pocket of her jeans. *Think quickly.* The subway! Her one advantage at this point was that he didn't know she'd seen him. She had to keep it that way.

Despite her racing heart, Delilah forced herself to walk slowly. She paused to glance at a brochure outside a small dance studio. She crossed the street and walked the next block as briskly as she dared. She could see the subway entrance on 8th Avenue. She had her pass from yesterday, but it was in her purse. How to get it out now without tipping him off?

Delilah kept walking until she was just beyond the subway entrance. She stopped, glancing back as subtly as she could. He was about a block behind her, pretending to stare intently at a map. Delilah opened her purse. She fished inside for her cell phone and Metrocard. She slid them together in the confines of her bag, and pulled out her phone. She made a show of sending a text. Mr. Clean didn't move. Clouds converged overhead, darkening the sky. Delilah waited, hoping like hell that the storm would hold off.

Then she felt it. The rumble of a subway car moving underground. She continued to stare at her phone, forcing herself to act casually, all the while calculating how much time she would need to make it through the crowd and onto the subway. It had to be last minute. She had to be fast.

The rumble slowed. She had, at best, twenty seconds. With one last glance in Mr. Clean's direction – he was looking at her candidly now, pretenses gone – she took off. She sprinted down the steps. Out of the corner of her eye, she saw Mr. Clean run toward her, the map flung to the ground.

Delilah was short, but she was in shape. She took the steps two at a time and jumped the last four. She pushed through the crowd, eyeing the line of people waiting at the turnstiles. "Police!" she called out. Jaded New Yorkers didn't move. "Police!" she yelled again. "Move!" She ran through the line and swiped her card. The subway car was still there, though it wouldn't be for long. Delilah sprinted inside just as the doors were closing.

Looking out the window, she saw Mr. Clean vault over the turnstile. Curious onlookers parted for him as he ran for the train. He spotted her through the window. Their eyes met. Then, thankfully, the car pulled away and he was gone from her sight.

#

Delilah called Anders from an ancient payphone. Despite the adrenaline rush, she felt oddly calm and focused.

Anders said, "Where are you?"

"Not sure yet. I got off some random stop. But listen, Anders, you need to get out of there. Clearly this guy followed me from Tula's house. That's probably where he's headed now."

"I can't put Tula in danger."

"Exactly. Leave the car. We can get it later. Too conspicuous."

Delilah walked along the street. She was somewhere in Brooklyn. She'd taken the first train only two stops before switching to another line. Then she'd done the same three stops after boarding that train. She hadn't wanted Mr. Clean to have any inkling of her direction. That meant she didn't have any clue where she was, either.

"Make your way back into the city," Anders said. "And meet me at the Mason Hotel on Broadway. I'll be there in an hour."

"Watch for a tail. My guy is tall, completely bald, wearing a gray t-shirt, but there could be others."

"I'll be careful," Anders said. "Just get there safely, Delilah. And soon."

#

The Mason Hotel was a dump. Delilah stood in the lobby, still feeling the rush from her earlier escape. She watched the hotel clerk, a wisp of a man with a thin black mustache and heart tattooed on his skinny bicep, as he read a magazine. She couldn't see the title, but she caught glimpses of skin. Lots of skin. Finally, the guy tore himself away from the girlie magazine long enough to acknowledge Delilah.

"Can I help you?" he said.

"I'm waiting for someone."

He tossed her a lascivious smile, one that said he knew exactly what she was waiting for.

Jerk.

Anders finally showed up looking infuriatingly unruffled, a Phillies cap on his head and a navy blue backpack thrown over one shoulder. He carried his laptop case in one hand and her overnight bag and lap top bag in the other.

"I took the liberty of packing for you," he said. Anders walked over to the clerk. "I need a room."

"Two rooms," Delilah said.

"One room," Anders corrected.

He and the clerk whispered back and forth, out of Delilah's earshot. Every once in a while the clerk gave Delilah a slimy, appraising glance. After a few minutes, he and Anders reached some agreement. Anders pushed a short stack of cash across the desk. The clerk grabbed it and handed him a key.

Anders pointed toward the elevator at the back of the lobby. "Let's go."

Delilah followed. When they were behind closed doors and the elevator was hemming and hawing its way to the ninth floor, Delilah said, "What was that little charade?"

"What charade?"

"You know what I'm talking about. You and the clerk and all that whispering."

Anders smiled. "I told him we were lovers and needed a room for a few hours. That you were embarrassed and worried that your husband would find us."

The elevator doors opened. They climbed out.

"And the cash?"

"The clerk's cut - the room fee and money to keep our little secret." He winked. She frowned.

"You gave him cash so there is no record of a room rental?"

"Exactly. At a place like this, there are always unrented rooms that management will let out for a few hours, off the books."

Delilah shook her head, both because of the unscrupulousness of some people and Anders' resourcefulness. They were walking down a poorly-lit hallway that stank of damp and urine. Rusty-orange carpet, walls covered with Internetfaded metallic wallpaper that had probably once been grand but looked sickly now. Anders stuck the key into the door of room 928. So much for electronic access, Delilah thought, and braced herself for the room's interior.

It didn't disappoint. A stained orange floral bedspread on the full-sized bed. A beat-up desk and an old television, both chained to the wall. Matted green carpet dotted with bald spots and cigarette burns. The smell of mildew competed with stale smoke and ammonia.

Delilah eyed the bed warily.

"It's not pretty, Delilah, but no one will find us here. At least not right away."

"How long do we have?"

"I paid him for two hours."

Delilah nodded. "Then let's get started." She sank down on the bed. The springs creaked beneath her. She tried not to think of all the things that went on in that bed. Or that lived beneath the mattress. She tried not to think about how seldom the comforter had been washed.

Delilah pulled out the list of attendees. "Here."

"You got it?"

Delilah nodded. She gave him a bare bones account of her trip to DeMarco's headquarters and her escape from Mr. Clean's tail. Anders looked at her for a few seconds too long, the look in his eyes unreadable. Then he skimmed the paper.

Delilah said, "Jack is probably short for John. There are nine Johns on the guest list ."

"And it's possible that none of them are the Jack we're looking for."

"Possible – but there might be a way to find out."

Anders, who had been pacing the floor in front of the bed, stopped. "How?"

"I spoke to Barb an hour ago." Delilah filled him in on Barb's discovery of the class ring. "If you can figure out which school it belongs to-"

Anders snapped his fingers. "We can cross-reference graduate names against the guest list."

"Bingo."

"Brilliant, Delilah. Call Barb. Have her email us a snapshot from the video."

"Already done."

"Great. I'll see what I can do to enlarge the picture." Anders smiled. "I found some interesting facts of my own. But they can wait until later."

TWENTY

The hotel room had a certain charm. Delilah especially liked the cockroaches that poured from the bathtub drain like tiny, marching soldiers. She'd been debating whether to use the facilities for a quick shower – who knew when the next opportunity would present itself – but the presence of these little pets helped her make up her mind. She closed the bathroom door, stifling a groan.

The digital clock read 8:14 p.m. They'd paid for an extra two hours in their little love shack, to the amusement of the clerk, but now they were nearly out of cash and Anders still didn't have a match on their man Jack. Delilah stood next to the bed and watched Anders's form, bent over his laptop, a look of intense concentration on his face. He'd been like that for three hours.

Anders motioned for her to sit next to him. "Look at this."

She sat on the bed, close to the desk, her knee just inches from his. A close-up of a ring glowed on the screen, the stone a deep azure, the band gold, its etchings now clear. West Point. 1981.

"You got it?"

Anders nodded. "Barb has a good eye. This would have been easy to miss." He moved closer to the screen. His knee pressed against hers. She thought about moving away but didn't.

Anders said, "Of course, it's possible to inherit a class ring, but 1981 seems about right."

"Our Jack would be in his fifties now."

"Right. A fit fifty-ish, which corresponds to the man we saw in the sex tape."

Delilah thought for a moment. "So can we cross reference all the Johns and Jacks who graduated from West Point in 1981 against the guest list for DeMarco's dinner?"

Anders smiled. "Done."

"And?"

"And take a look at this."

He pulled up another window. On it was a webpage for Domino Venture Partners LLP. The President and CEO was one John S. Cashman.

"And John Cashman was on the guest list?"

Anders nodded. He twisted to pick up the master list for the fund raiser. His leg pressed harder against Delilah's. She moved away slightly. Suddenly the room felt very warm.

Anders put the list on Delilah's lap and traced the names with his finger. "When I compared the guest list to the names of West Point alumni, I came up with two who matched." His finger skimmed down the paper, stopping at John D. Brown.

"John Brown graduated from West Point in the fifties. He'd be in his eighties now."

"Not our guy."

"No, too old." His finger continued to trace the master list, this time stopping on John Sylvester Cashman. The pressure on Delilah's thigh was maddening. She shifted in her seat, but he kept his hand in place.

"The year on the ring matches the West Point alumni information I tracked down for John Sylvester Cashman. John – or Jack as he was known in school – was originally from Boston. His father served as a Captain in the Marines. Jack went on to get an M.B.A. from Wharton. He started Domino Venture Capital about twelve years ago."

"What does Domino do?"

"I'm still looking into that. At first glance, it's your average venture capital firm, providing seed money to high-potential start-ups."

"National or international?"

"Good question." Anders placed DeMarco's list in his laptop bag and unplugged his computer. "But we don't have time to figure that out now."

Delilah glanced at the clock. Anders was right – they had less than fifteen minutes before the clerk would come banging on the door. She said, "Let's head back to Tula's and get the car. Head home."

"Domino is in New York. I say we stay and confront Jack Cashman tomorrow. Besides, I don't want to make our way to Tula's. Not now."

"We're out of cash, Anders. We can't use credit, not after my run-in with Mr. Clean. We don't know who he belongs to."

Anders thought about it for a minute. "I think we can borrow from Tula without getting her involved – *and* get your car. Give me a minute to reach her. Then be ready to roll."

#

Delilah and Anders used their last seventeen dollars for a cab ride to the Bronx. There, Tula's maid met them outside of a small pawn shop called simply, Pawn Shop. Delilah appreciated the directness.

A young man stood next to Maria. Hair trimmed close, he had the peach fuzz kind of beard common to dark-skinned teens who mature early. The kid tried to look threatening but managed only to look awkward.

"Miss Tula asked Maria to give you this," the boy said. He handed Anders a bag of groceries and Delilah's car keys. "She said be very careful. She said she knows what you are doing and she doesn't want you to do it."

A strange look crossed Anders's face – embarrassment or shame, Delilah couldn't tell which. When he spoke, he looked at Maria, not the boy. "Tell her thank you. We'll be careful."

The youth shifted from foot to foot. His jeans hung so low on skinny hips that Delilah wondered whether they were glued to his thighs. How else did they stay up?

She also wondered what Tula had meant when she said she knew what Anders was doing. But that was a question for later. For now, they had to find another hotel for the night. Then tomorrow they would visit Domino – and hopefully get some answers.

They found a haven on the Upper West Side, just a few blocks from Central Park. Run down, anemic air conditioning . . . but clean. This time Delilah insisted on two rooms. The only rooms available were adjoining.

"It'll have to do," Delilah said to the clerk. They paid in cash.

Anders stayed quiet on the way to the fourth floor. At Delilah's door, he smiled. "You were great today. Finding the guest list, getting away from your tail, the connection between the ring and the list."

"It's my job," Delilah said, but this time she softened it with a smile.

Anders nodded. He held up one hand and brushed it gently against her cheek. "Soot."

"I'm sure I look fabulous."

Anders leaned in, closing the distance between them. Delilah felt an involuntary shudder course through her. "You're beautiful," Anders said. He smiled. "Soot and all."

Words stuck in Delilah's throat. She stepped back, toward the door, and waved the room key in front of the digital lock. "Good night, Matthew." She closed the door softly, before either of them could do something they couldn't take back in the morning.

TWENTY-ONE

Delilah awoke at six the next morning to the discordant *beep*, *beep* of her phone alarm. She reached for the device and shut off the noise.

She and Anders were out of the hotel by 7:12, setting off for Madison Avenue, the location of Domino's corporate headquarters. Traffic was heavy, so they walked side-by-side, quiet purpose in their strides, conversation limited to directions, the tension of the night before replaced by an easy companionship.

They arrived at Domino by eight. A burly guard on the ground floor of the Baker Building asked for their names.

"Matthew Anderson. Jack's expecting me."

The guard called Domino's office. After explaining that guests were here to see Mr. Cashman, he put his hand over the receiver.

"Receptionist says Mr. Cashman isn't in yet."

"I'll wait upstairs for him."

"Lady says you're not on Mr. Cashman's calendar."

"Then he didn't inform her of our appointment. That doesn't change the fact that he's expecting me."

"What's your business with Mr. Cashman?"

"I'm a journalist. I'm writing a feature article on Domino."

The guard flicked his thumb at Delilah. "What about her?"

Anders flashed Delilah a mischievous smile. "My assistant."

Delilah gave him a smile of her own. She said, "That's right. I'm the brains behind the operation. He asks the questions and I write the stunningly good prose."

The guard chuckled. "I bet." He mumbled something into the phone. A few seconds later, he hung up and asked for their drivers' licenses. Delilah hesitated, but only for a minute. She had come too far to turn back now.

The guard printed out two passes and handed them back their licenses. "Third bank of elevators. Thirtieth floor. Left side."

Delilah and Anders rode up to the thirtieth floor in silence, feeling distinctly out of place in jeans amongst all the suits.

When the doors opened, Delilah emerged first. To the right was a law firm. To the left, glass doors led into a small reception area. The plaque on the wall said Domino Venture Partners LLP. Delilah pushed open the door.

A perfume-doused young woman greeted them. Model-tall, with long, gangly limbs and tiny, neat breasts, her blond hair twisted into a chignon. She wore a black business suit and fashionable red-rimmed glasses aimed, Delilah figured, at making her look smart. Instead, she looked like an actress playing the part of a banker in a B-movie.

"Ms. Powers and Mr. Anderson?" the woman said.

Delilah nodded.

"Please have a seat."

Delilah and Anders exchanged a glance. The room was small. Four chairs lined one wall, across from the receptionist's desk. No magazine-strewn table, no piped in music. Clearly they didn't get many visitors. They sat next to each other on matching leather and chrome chairs and waited.

After about twenty minutes, the receptionist's phone rang. She answered it and then disappeared through another glass door into an office beyond. Delilah took advantage of the moment. She rose and grabbed one of each of the four business cards propped on the receptionist's desk. She stuck these in the pocket of her pants. Then she scanned the minimal papers on the woman's desk, aware that there was probably a security camera aimed at her at that moment. Nothing other than their names, scribbled in neat, rounded cursive on a pad of Domino letterhead.

The woman sauntered back seconds later, but Delilah was already in her seat.

"Mr. Cashman says he has no appointment with you, Mr. Anderson."

Anders stood. "Maybe I have my days mixed up. Since we're here anyway, we'd like to see him."

"I'm afraid that's impossible. Mr. Cashman's not here at the moment. He's on holiday."

Delilah said, "When do you expect him to return from *holiday*?"

If the woman caught the sarcasm in Delilah's voice, she didn't let on. Instead, she shrugged. "If you leave your number, I'll ask him to call you when he has a free moment."

Which would be never, Delilah thought.

Anders gave the woman a phone number. The receptionist opened the glass door for them and waited in the hallway until they entered the elevator. Disappointed, Delilah knew they would have to find another – less direct – way of tracking Cashman down.

Clearly Anders had had the same thought. When they were back out on the humid streets of New York, Anders said, "Another tact?"

Delilah nodded. She looked around, her eyes locking on something in the distance. "Well, this wasn't a total waste," Delilah said.

"Why's that?"

"Because we know something we didn't know before." Delilah put her sunglasses on. "Don't look now. Mr. Clean at three o'clock. Behind the falafel cart."

Anders kept his gaze straight ahead. "Wonderful."

"At least now we know that Domino is behind our tail."

Anders started walking toward the Starbucks across the street. "How do you figure?"

"I kept watch for him while we walked here and when we arrived. No sign. And then that receptionist kept us waiting in Domino's office. I bet the receptionist was told to keep us there just long enough to get Mr. Clean back on our tail."

"You may be right. We can lose him again, though. But first I need to look something up."

"Cashman's home address?"

Anders nodded. "If he's on vacation, his family probably is, too. That means we can check out his property. And if he's not on vacation-"

"We question his wife, if she's there."

"Assuming he's married."

Anders opened the door to Starbucks. The aromas of coffee and cinnamon were enticing, but Delilah had no appetite. She headed for a free table in the back. Anders joined her and slapped the laptop on the wooden top.

"Anders, Mr. Clean will expect us to head to Jack's home address, especially if he works for Domino."

"We're not going straight to Cashman's house. We have a detour to make first."

Delilah sank into a wooden chair. She eyed the front door of Starbucks, half hoping Mr. Clean would be brazen and stupid enough to come inside. Sometimes a frontal assault was the most efficient way to handle a tail.

She said, "You followed the money trail for Women's Creative Initiative for Change in Politics?"

"I did. That was basically a dead end. WCICP has its hand in a lot of different pots, most of them overseas, most of them pretty innocuous. Women's health clinics, fair trade initiatives and the like. But I also dug deeper into the finances of Women NOW."

"The subgroup?"

"More like a spinoff. It has its own corporate entity, its own governance board and its own very intricate funding and investments."

"A terrorist organization?"

Anders shook his head. "I don't think so, though I imagine a terrorist organization would be set up similarly."

"So where are we headed?"

Anders looked around at the faces nearest them. He scribbled something on a napkin. Delilah squinted at his blocky writing in the soft overhead lighting. The Poconos. *Interesting.* She wondered what, exactly, Miriam's nonprofit was financing in the mountains of eastern Pennsylvania.

#

Natasha got off work at eleven. It was now 11:30. She was moonlighting at Brighton Day Spa and Hair Salon, a step up from the happy ending parlor where she'd spent the last two years as a fill-in for the regulars. Not that *she* ever gave a happy ending. Those days were long over. But Brighton wasn't so bad. Lots of blue haired old ladies, South Philly brides-to-be wanting a day of pampering and working girls looking to get their mustaches waxed or their bikini areas bare as a baby's ass. The women didn't tip well, but Natasha got 30% of every treatment she did. That added up.

She was up to almost $7,000 in her bank account. Another year and she'd be buying a house. A hell of a lot better than living in the basement of an abandoned brownstone. *You've come a long way, baby.* People said you couldn't escape your past. Not so. She was living proof.

Natasha opened her locker and pulled out jeans and a black t-shirt. Today she would be following some asshole who was cheating on his wife with men. His wife had found his membership to ManHunt.com and called Delilah. Natasha got the assignment. Her mark left his corporate desk jockey job at noon every day and headed to a local bath house for a lunch time sauna. *A sauna - yeah right.* She'd been following him for three days and every day the same thing. Today she would catch him red handed. Well, red something, anyway. Natasha laughed at her own little joke.

Outside, the air was hot and city-stagnant. Natasha threw her backpack over both shoulders and buckled it around her waist. She unlocked the double thick chain that secured her bike to the fence and climbed aboard.

She had nineteen minutes to get across town. Plenty of time.

Natasha had one foot on a peddle and the other still on the ground when she felt a shove from behind. Her bike toppled, her head hitting the cement.

"What the fuck!"

Dazed, she felt hands grab her beneath the arm pits and pull her to a semi-standing position.

"You little cunt." Another shove, this time in the direction of the shed behind the spa. "What the hell did you think you were doing? Trying to fucking get me murdered?" Another shove. "What the hell!"

Jake.

He shoved her toward the shed. She didn't resist. She needed to get her wits together. Jake was a lot of bad, bad things, but he wasn't a murderer or a rapist. But Natasha smelled desperation. And that made her curious. Curious *and* angry.

He pushed her into the side of the shed. Her nose hit the wooden siding. She turned quickly and shoved him back. "What the fuck, Jake? Get your slimy paws off me."

He grabbed the collar of her t-shirt, twisted and slammed her back against the shed. "Look, bitch, I don't know what kind of games you're playing. Is this about the fucking child support? 'Cause if it is, it ain't working. You ain't gonna blackmail me, hear that?"

"I don't know what you're talking about."

"You know exactly what I'm talking about."

Natasha had had enough. She leaned into the shed wall and rammed her knee into Jake's balls.

"Fuck, Natasha!" he screamed. "What was that for?"

Natasha grabbed Jake's finger and pulled it back. His whole arm followed. When she had Jake pinned against the shed, she stood on tiptoe and got in his face, "Read my lips, asshole. I don't know what you're talking about."

Trapped against the wall by a woman half his size had a paralyzing effect on Jake. Still, Natasha kept his arm twisted. He stared at her, breathing more evenly now. He looked the same: same spiky blonde hair, same dull brown eyes, same semi-handsome, scruffy appearance. Natasha let go.

"Are you ready to tell me what's going on?"

Jake rubbed his arm. "Jeez, you been learning martial arts or something?"

"Get on with it, Jake. I need to be somewhere in ten minutes."

"That name you asked me to look up? Emily Cray? Nearly got me killed."

He had Natasha's attention. "What happened?"

"Just putting her name out there like that . . . raised some interest. And not the good kind. Know what I mean?"

"No, Jake. I don't."

"Mob, Natasha. The fucking Mafioso. Now you get it?"

"Why would the Mob be after Miriam Cross?" She said it more to herself than to Jake. She wasn't really surprised. Hadn't she suspected the same when that guy came after her in the city?

Jake raised his eyebrows. "What do you got our son involved in?"

"Nothing."

"Sounds to me like maybe I should have custody of Sam. You should be the one paying child support."

Natasha slammed her knee into Jake's groin again. Harder this time. He screamed.

"Don't you ever threaten to take my son." She punched him in the stomach. "Got it?"

Jake reached toward his pocket. Natasha grabbed his hand and flipped his wrist backwards, pinning him against the shed again. He moaned.

"Leave Sam out of this. Understand?"

Jake looked pissed. Natasha didn't care. She was stronger than ever and he'd gotten soft. Natasha could take him. She let go of his arm. "Had enough?"

"You're a crazy bitch, know that?"

"Want more?"

Jake shrugged. "Stop already! I don't want the little brat anyway."

"Tell me the rest. And keep your hands where I can see them."

"Ain't nothing to tell. I put the name out there like you asked. Next thing I know, I got some Neanderthal after me, threatening to kill me if I don't come clean."

"What did you tell him?"

"Nothing. Said I was paid to ask a few questions."

"You give my name?"

Jake rubbed his wrist. "Think I'm a total deadbeat, Natasha? You got my son. Of course not."

"Did he believe you?"

"Roughed me up, but yeah." – Jake pulled up his shirt, showing a flabby stomach and star-shaped bruises on his ribs – "Eventually he let me go."

"Learn anything else?"

"Jeez, Natasha. An ounce of sympathy?"

But Natasha was late and not in the mood for sympathy. Jake had threatened to take her son. Natasha didn't forgive so easily. "What'd you learn, Jake?"

He shook his head. "The goon works for Guy Franko. Mobster out of Camden. Heard of him?"

Natasha nodded. Franko was the nephew of Dominic Moroni, rumored to be the Mafia boss in New York City.

Natasha moved toward Jake. He took a step back. She said, "What else? What about Emily Cray?"

Jake threw up his hands. "I found out there had been a hit out on her."

"*Had been?*"

He nodded. "Pulled."

"So the Mob didn't kill Emily Cray?"

Jake shrugged. "Don't know who killed her. I just know that Franko had a hit out on her and it was pulled. Make of it what you want. But I sure as hell ain't asking any more questions. Not for you. Not for the fucking pope."

TWENTY-TWO

Hawley, Pennsylvania, one of a string of tiny towns in the Pocono lake region, had all the normal charms of a small rural tourist town - antique shops, restaurants, parks - as well as the standard eyesores, like rundown trailer parks and oversized billboards advertising candle outlets, massage parlors and the second coming of Jesus Christ. But the thing that most appealed to Delilah about Hawley was the silence. After three days in New York City, the lack of traffic noise seemed a welcome change.

Delilah drove down the main street, keeping a wary eye for a flash of bald head, a tailing car or anything else that seemed suspicious. They'd managed to lose Mr. Clean back in New York using a meandering detour through the Bronx, where Tula had provided a gun and two cans of pepper spray, but they weren't sure whether their current destination was in any way linked to Miriam's murder. And they weren't taking any chances.

From the main street, Delilah made a left down a narrow residential road. Small one-story houses lined each side, their beat-up exteriors advertising a depressed economy and harsh weather. They continued driving. Soon, houses gave way to fields and, eventually, woods. Anders had her turn down an even narrower road, paved in pebbles. A power sub-station sat close to the street on one side.

"Keep going," Anders said. "I think it's a mile or two down this road."

"And what, exactly, will we find when we get there?"

"I don't know exactly."

Delilah simply looked at him.

"Really. Like I told you before, I followed the money trail from Women NOW. Someone – Miriam, presumably – took great pains to make it hard to follow. I finally traced it to a Sister Anna Berger with a P.O. box in Hawley.

"A nun?"

"Seems like it. I was able to find the address for the owner of the P.O. box."

"And that's where we're headed?"

Anders nodded. "The P.O. box is registered to a company called Lynchpin at an address in Hawley. There's no street address. Just a rural route." He gestured toward the road ahead of them. "The road we're on now."

Delilah considered these new facts. What would Miriam be doing funneling money to a Catholic nun? Miriam's novels scorned organized religion.

"Were you able to find anything on Anna Berger?"

"Nothing particularly helpful. Spent years working abroad in various orphanages. Has a background in psychology and a law degree."

"Pretty accomplished."

"Many nuns are. Especially those in leadership roles."

"Is she a leader within the Church?"

"Not that I could tell, but she moved around a lot. Whether of her own volition or that of her superiors" - he shrugged - "can't say."

The street dragged out ahead of them. Delilah glanced at her cell phone. No reception. Afternoon was quickly giving way to dusk. They hadn't brought a flashlight.

The road changed from gravel to dirt. It curved to the right. In the distance, Delilah could make out the peak of a rooftop beyond the trees.

Anders said, "This must be it."

Delilah pulled into the driveway, nearly hidden in tall grass and weeds. She edged the car as close to the surrounding woods as she could without hitting a tree. Delilah liked the wilderness, but when she killed the engine, she realized just how secluded this place was. Secluded and creepy.

No other cars sat in the lot and the house had no garage. The building, a vacation-style Cedar home, stood tall, with over-sized windows and sharp roof peaks. Shingles covered the outside and a long porch flanked one side. A pile of firewood sat stacked next to the porch. The house looked empty. Delilah patted the gun, tucked in the holster on her ankle. She gestured to Anders. They approached the front door.

"Shall we knock?" Anders whispered.

Delilah nodded. She rapped on the door. No answer. She knocked again, harder. Still no answer. Anders tried the handle. Locked.

Delilah pulled the gun from her holster and walked around to the porch. The windows were large but veiled with blinds. Another door stood at the rear of the house. It, too, was locked.

Anders pointed at the door. "Ready?"

Delilah held her gun close to her side, tip up. She nodded.

Anders kicked in the door. Delilah went in first, gun now raised, safety off. The back door led directly into a mud room. Darkness enveloped her. A mask of silence hung over the home's bleak interior. They walked single-file through the mud room, into a laundry room and then stopped at the cusp of the kitchen. Delilah held up one finger and gestured toward the upstairs.

"Listen for movement," she mouthed.

Anders nodded. His body pressed against hers. Despite the current situation, for a second she flashed to last night, to the feeling that snaked across her skin when he'd moved close. She forced the thought out of her mind. *Concentrate, Delilah.*

"Let's make sure the place is empty first," Anders whispered. "Then we can search it."

Delilah agreed. They walked through the downstairs, alert for signs of movement. Shadows danced around the kitchen. Small and tidy, a bank of cabinets, stove and a sink sat on one side, a large refrigerator on the other. The floor was cheap vinyl, the countertops scuffed Formica. A large farmhouse table perched at the other end of the kitchen, its wooden surface scarred with knife gouges and stains. Someone had placed twelve mismatched chairs around its perimeter.

The kitchen led into a large great room where four couches were arranged into two separate seating areas. None of the furniture matched. Between two of the couches sat a square coffee table. On it were three candles, a book of matches and what looked like a sewing kit. The room was otherwise empty - no pictures on the walls, no tchotchkes, no effort at personalization. The place felt decidedly institutional.

Anders led the way up a set of narrow wooden steps. They walked quietly through the upstairs. Delilah's body felt tense and ready. She half expected Mr. Clean to pop out from behind a closed door.

The first bedroom held four single beds, the mattresses stripped bare. A single dresser had been stuffed into a corner. A long closet with two folding doors stood open, its interior bare.

"Women," Delilah said. She walked to one of the mattresses and pointed to a reddish stain. "Menstrual blood? Not recent."

A coating of dust blanketed the furniture, as though someone had skipped several weekly cleanings. The place smelled stale and buttoned up. An aura of despair lingered like a low-lying fog. Delilah realized she had been holding her breath. She forced herself to exhale.

The second bedroom looked much like the first. Three single beds, a dresser and a footstool. No linens, no personal effects. Two other bedrooms were nearly identical.

Only the fifth bedroom was different. No bigger than a closet, it held a Futon, a small Ikea-type dresser with a Bible on it and a bookcase. Books still lined the shelves.

"Interesting," Delilah said. She squatted next to the books and read their titles aloud. *"English for Dummies, The United States Constitution Made Simple, Home Economics, How to Create the Perfect Resume, Your Body, Your Choice."* She pulled a book out of the case and turned it over. The cover was battered, the pages yellowed and torn. *"Basic Home Remedies."*

"Some sort of half-way house?"

Delilah shrugged. She had her suspicions, but she wasn't ready to voice them yet. "It'll be dark soon. Let's do a more thorough inspection of the house and get back on the road."

They split up. Delilah took the upstairs, Anders the downstairs. Delilah started with the first bedroom. She looked under the beds, inspected the closets and opened the dresser drawers. The room was completely empty. If it weren't for those rusty blood stains on the mattress, Delilah would question whether anyone had been staying here at all. The other bedrooms and the bathroom held the same number of clues: zip. Delilah headed for the steps, too aware of the echo of her footsteps against the bare wooden floors.

At the banister, she changed her mind and went back to the first bedroom. She lifted the mattress. Clear. She did this to the rest of the beds. Nearly convinced that this was a fruitless exercise, she hit pay dirt on bed number eight. She saw something tucked into the far corner. Carefully, Delilah lifted the thin mattress up and pulled out the item.

It was a photograph of a young girl, maybe three or four years old. She had Asian features and heartbreakingly gleeful smile. The picture had yellowed with age, but no stains or creases marred its surface. Delilah ran her finger gently across the little girl's face. Someone had treasured this picture.

Delilah felt a pit forming in her stomach. She thought of Tula's maid, Maria, and of women leaving their children behind. She thought of Miriam, with her erotic poetry and her sex tape and her decapitated torso. She thought about the goons going after Natasha and her own escape from Mr. Clean in New York.

She thought about this mysterious Sister Anna Berger.

If her suspicions were correct, the pattern that was emerging had implications far bigger than a single murder. It was an ugly pattern, full of greed and cruelty. She hoped to hell she was wrong.

They needed to find the nun. Anna Berger held the key to many unanswered questions. Delilah was sure of it.

"Delilah!" Anders called from downstairs. Delilah jumped at the urgency in his voice. She tucked the photograph carefully in her pocket, next to the pepper spray, and pulled the gun from its holster. She ran downstairs, alert for any noises that would say they weren't alone.

"Delilah! In the bathroom!"

Delilah reset the safety on the gun but kept the weapon in her hand. She jogged through the kitchen and into the downstairs half bath. She found Anders bent over the toilet.

Anders looked up. "Take a look at this."

Delilah knelt next to him in the cramped space. The room had one small window. The remnants of afternoon sunlight flowed weakly through dirty glass. She looked at the spot he was pointing to, next to the toilet.

Even in the dim light, she could make it out. Blood. A dried pool, at least six inches in diameter and a half inch deep, lay at the base of the toilet. Smears of dried blood streaked the side of the porcelain.

Delilah stared at the floor, thinking of the women who must have stayed here. "It's as though someone tried to clean it up in a hurry." She looked at Anders. "Any signs of violence downstairs?"

Anders shook his head. "But I don't think this was violence, at least not directly."

"A miscarriage?"

"Yep." He stood. "My wife had an early miscarriage during her first pregnancy. She lost the baby at home." Anders looked around, then hugged himself. "Do you feel it, Delilah? It's as though the walls have soaked in whatever misery lived here."

Delilah couldn't agree more. "Let's go," she said. "I think I know what we need to do next."

"Find Sister Anna?"

"After we visit Cashman. If he is the guy in the sex tape, the bastard owes us some answers."

"It's late Delilah. Even if we leave now, we won't get there until midnight."

"Then we get to his house first thing in the morning. Before he has a chance to avoid us."

"Another hotel?"

Delilah pulled the wad of cash from her pocket. She still had over $400. This was supposed to be a cheap trip, but the expenses were quickly adding up. But what choice did they have? Cashman lived in New Jersey, southeast of Hawley. They could get there in two hours from here, but driving all the way to Philly and back would be a waste of time. Suddenly exhausted, she nodded. "Let's find something inexpensive and on the way. We can be at Cashman's by six and still have the rest of tomorrow to track down the good Sister."

#

Inexpensive seemed hard to find in Cashman's upscale neighborhood, so Delilah settled for a one-bedroom at Homewood Suites off the highway nearby. She and Anders trudged up the short stack of steps to reception and barely spoke on the elevator ride to the fifth floor. Delilah's mind latched on to those blood stains in the bathroom. Together with the photo and the barren feel of the house, the nasty picture that was forming had solidified. But she felt too tired to make sense of anything right now. Sleep. She needed sleep.

Anders opened the door to the suite. Cold air blasted from within. The suite held a small bedroom and an open living room with a couch. A small bathroom was off the living room. Simple, but the rooms were clean and cockroach-free.

"You take the bedroom, I'll take the living room couch," Anders said. He sounded tired and looked as beat as Delilah felt. Delilah didn't argue.

While he used the only bathroom, Delilah unpacked. She pulled shorts and a tank top from her overnight bag. She wanted to be ready in case they needed to leave suddenly. There had been no sign of Mr. Clean since Domino. Still, she thought of Natasha's thugs and Miriam's lifeless body. Whoever they were up against, trailing was the least of their intentions.

The digital clock read 12:09 a.m.

Delilah took a quick shower, brushed her teeth and dressed for bed. When she opened the bathroom door to head back to her bedroom, she saw Anders, already asleep on the couch. She smiled. They'd been together for four days now and hadn't killed each other. Pretty impressive.

Delilah crawled into bed, her head swimming with details from the case. She tossed and turned, shivering in refrigerated air. Her head hurt and she rolled over, hoping a new position would ease the pain. It didn't work. She needed another blanket and less air conditioning. An Advil would be nice, too.

As quietly as she could, she slid off the bed and opened the closet. No blankets. She opened the door to the living area, hoping to find the air conditioner control in the dark. She could make out the panel, beyond the couch.

She was halfway there when Anders said, "I can't shake the feeling of desolation in that house."

"I thought you were asleep."

"Trying."

"Sorry if I woke you."

"You didn't."

Anders sat up. In the watery neon light seeping through the blinds, Delilah saw broad shoulders, his bare chest. She closed her eyes.

She said, "What happened to Tula's husband?"

Anders took so long to respond that Delilah thought maybe he'd drifted off to sleep. But when she looked his way again, she saw him staring at her. He was still sitting upright, his arms behind him, supporting his weight. His head was cocked to the side.

She said, "You don't want to talk about it."

"I don't want to think about it." He sighed. "Have a seat."

Delilah perched on the edge of the sofa bed, the only seat in the room. She waited.

"Ahmed was a good man. A decent journalist, ethical, but not street smart. And it got him killed."

"Had he been in the Middle East?"

"At one time. He covered the Gulf War, stints in Afghanistan. He spoke seven languages, including Pashto and Arabic. This made him an incredible asset. It also made him vulnerable."

"To terrorists?"

"To anyone looking to cash in on the Middle East unrest."

"He was Indian?"

Anders nodded. "Ahmed and I met in school. Cornell."

"Tula, too?"

"No. He and Tula met in New York. They're both Indian, but Ahmed was a Muslim, Tula is Hindu. Their marriage made for interesting . . . family issues."

"Tula's beautiful."

"And very successful in her own right. A hematologist. Ahmed loved her fiercely."

Delilah turned to face Anders. His voice had grown hushed. She waited for him to say more and thought about Michael, about what it meant to lose the one person who tethered you to the world. It was a crazy pain, a searing, bottomless, invisible wound. A wound that never really healed.

"Ahmed called me a few weeks before he died. He said he thought he was in danger. He said people were following him."

"What did he want you to do?"

Anders climbed out of bed. He began pacing the room, his hands behind his back.

"That's just it. I don't know." He looked down at Delilah. "I don't know because I never asked."

She waited.

"Missy wasn't doing well. The doctors said she had three, maybe four months to live. Her pain seemed unbearable. So much pain. Until you see someone you love go through that . . . the sheer impotency is torture." His tone was crisp, but the underlying anguish was unmistakable. "I listened to Ahmed, but I didn't really hear him. I could only think of Missy, of my own pain. I missed the fear in his voice. But looking back, it was there. Terror, really."

"Ahmed was murdered?"

Anders sat on the edge of the sofa, next to Delilah. His leg pressed against hers. The sensation was maddening.

"Ahmed drowned in a river a few miles from his home."

"An accident?"

Anders shrugged. "Things didn't add up. During the autopsy, there were signs of abrasions, broken fingernails, as though he had fought an attacker. A broken arm. Things that maybe could have been explained if he had fallen from a bridge or been dragged over rocks, but that wasn't the case."

"What did happen?"

"His body was caught under a log in an inlet. It was spring, though, and the water was high and cold. Why would Ahmed go into a river when the weather was so cool?"

"Maybe he fell?"

Anders stared at her, the intensity in his eyes searing. "That's just it, Delilah. It makes no sense. Ahmed was an expert swimmer. A triathlete. If he had simply fallen into the river, he would have been fine."

"Not if he hit his head."

"No signs of a head injury."

Delilah saw the inconsistencies. She understood why Anders would question. But she also understood guilt and the way it could twist and distort reality. She reached out and touched his hand. His skin felt warm.

"Do you know what Ahmed was working on before he died?"

Anders shook his head slowly. But Delilah sensed he wasn't being completely honest. She decided not to push it.

"Then there was nothing you could have done, Matthew. You have to let it go. Even if it wasn't an accident, no friend would expect you to leave your dying daughter-"

"I could have done *something*. I could have listened."

Delilah pressed a finger against his chest. "Don't do that to yourself. It's over. You did the best that you could under the circumstances. Now you have to let it go."

Anders was quiet for a moment. "Could you let it go?"

Anders' eyes bore into her own with a conviction she understood. She thought of Michael, of the body they never found, of the years she spent searching, hoping. And she gave the only answer she could. An honest one.

"No."

He kissed her.

Delilah kissed back.

Anders leaned in, pressing his chest against hers. Delilah's body reacted to the sensations. The roughness of his face against her smooth skin. The radiating warmth of his body. The hardness of his arms, now circling her back. His growing excitement.

She found the strength to push him away. "You're married."

Anders gave a wry smile. "She left me a long time ago, Delilah."

They stared at each other.

Anders whispered, "It's the truth."

Delilah nodded. She believed him. She felt Anders's hand, now curved against her breast. She saw raw hurt in his eyes. She felt her own hurting, still open and sore. Delilah's brain said *stop*. Her body wanted him to continue.

Her body won.

TWENTY-THREE

Cashman's house stood empty. A contemporary home in an elite New Jersey suburb, it had the requisite complicated roofline, two-acre acre yard and enough room to house six families - all with the charm of a McDonalds. Delilah was duly unimpressed. She and Anders spent twenty minutes knocking, but finally gave up. The empty driveway and garage broadcast Cashman's absence. The security signs in the windows broadcast the reason they couldn't break in. Frustrated, they headed back to Pennsylvania.

"Maybe he is on vacation. Let's try again later today, after work hours," Delilah said as they pulled next to the curb outside her office. She'd arranged to meet Barb there for an impromptu meeting. Then she'd drive Anders home.

"Sounds good." Anders was about to say something else when his expression changed. Delilah followed his gaze.

She saw Barb standing outside the building, her tall form clothed in sweatpants and a Minnie Mouse t-shirt. Next to her stood another woman. Short, pretty, with long, caramel-color hair pulled into a loose ponytail. She was watching Delilah's Honda with an anxious half-frown on her face. Delilah knew who she was even before the woman's stare locked on Anders. Kathryn Anderson, Anders' wife.

Delilah thought of the night before, of Anders's tenderness and their feverish lovemaking. Of her own stupidity.

The woman didn't move until Delilah and Anders joined their little circle. Then she smiled tentatively at her husband.

"I thought I'd surprise you," she said. "After the way we left things, I called your office and Barb was kind enough to tell me you would be here. I thought I'd drive you home."

Anders nodded. He looked at Barb, at the ground, at his large calloused hands. At anything and anyone but Delilah.

"How did it go?" Barb said. By the forced joviality in her voice, Delilah could tell that even Barb had picked up on the tension.

"No luck on Cashman," Delilah said. *Be your father's daughter, Lila.* She pulled her shoulders back, head up and held her hand out to Anders's wife. "Delilah Percy Powers."

Kathryn shook it, her grip flaccid. "Kathryn Anderson."

To Anders, Delilah said, "Find the whereabouts of the nun, Anders. When you have something, let me know."

"I thought we were giving Cashman another go?"

"Barb and I can handle that."

Anders looked surprised, but Delilah didn't care. She was being rational, not vindictive. Something she should have been all along. Anders, the newcomer, didn't have the experience. She'd hired him because of his hacking skills and that's what she would have him do.

Once inside her office, though, her resolve wavered. Was she being unfair? He'd earned her respect these past few days. More than earned it. Still, she reasoned, better for each of them to stick to their roles. Sex was sex, business was business. What was best for the business was best for everyone. Plain and simple.

"You slept with him," Barb said, startling her. It was a statement, not a question. Delilah, who tried always to be honest, said nothing in reply.

#

Delilah and Barb waited until later that day to head back to Cashman's house in New Jersey. It was early evening when Barb finally pulled her minivan in front of the home's stuccoed façade. The sun's orange glow was starting to set beneath the western horizon. Cashman's house still looked empty. Delilah feared they'd be zero for two.

"Ready?" Barb said.

Delilah nodded.

Barb looked at her, her face a mask of disapproval - quiet and silently judgmental. Barb had been this way since their brief conversation that morning. Delilah knew her friend had her best interests at heart - and sleeping with an employee *was* just dumb - but Delilah was a big girl. She could clean up her own messes.

"Stop," she said to Barb. "Please."

"Stop what?"

"The silent treatment. You're acting as though I bedded a priest."

"You may as well have."

"That's ridiculous."

"He's married, Delilah. And you're vulnerable." Barb shook her head. "I saw the look on your face when you noticed Kathryn. You weren't just angry. You were hurt. *Hurt*. That Anders' *wife* came to get him. Think about that."

He said she'd left him. Delilah wanted to defend herself. But the words struck a hollow chord, even to her.

Barb flashed a weak smile. "I'm sorry, Lila. Maybe this murder has gotten to you, I know it's gotten to me." She wagged a finger in the air. "But whatever you two did, it wasn't just a silly fling. Don't kid yourself into thinking that. That look on your face said everything."

"Are you finished?"

Barb took a deep breath. "For now."

#

Delilah scoped the place before knocking. If Domino was involved somehow in Miriam's murder, and if the company had hired Mr. Clean, then Cashman would have every reason to expect a visit. She'd wanted to catch him off guard. She knew the chances of anyone answering the door would be slim.

"If he's not here, we park up the street and wait. We'll pounce when he arrives."

"You don't think a Honda minivan will look conspicuous in this neighborhood?"

Barb had a point. Even the minivans in this neighborhood screamed money. "It's the best option we have right now."

But when Delilah finally knocked, a woman in a maid's uniform answered Cashman's door. The woman had dark hair, ashy brown skin and a face that had probably once been beautiful. Thin as an exclamation point, her were shoulders hunched like she carried the weight of the world - literally - on her back.

Delilah introduced herself and asked to see Cashman. The woman said he wasn't at home in a thickly accented voice. She made no attempt at eye contact.

"Is his wife here?"

"Mr. Cashman have no wife."

That was a surprise. "He's not married?"

The woman shook her head.

"What is your name?" she said.

The woman shook her head again. "Mr. Cashman not home."

"This is very important, ma'am. I need to talk to him as soon as possible."

Another head shake. Still no eye contact. Delilah noticed the way the woman cradled her left arm protectively.

Barb pulled a picture out of her purse. "Does this woman look familiar?"

The maid glanced at the photo and there was an instant change in her demeanor. The woman tensed, eyes widening like those of a nervous colt.

"Her name is Miriam Cross," Barb said. "She died a few weeks ago. We'd like to speak with Mr. Cashman about her."

The woman stood statue still for a moment. Her eyes went from wide to narrow to blank, all in the space of an instant. Then, with surprising strength, she slammed the door in their faces. Barb and Delilah stood there, stunned at the sudden ferocity.

"Talk about rude. What do you make of that?" Barb said.

"She definitely recognized Miriam."

They were walking back to the car. A peek through the garage window confirmed Cashman's absence. And clearly the housekeeper would be of no help. Delilah had an idea.

Back in the minivan, Delilah rummaged through her purse until she found the business cards she'd taken from Domino. There were two U.S.-based partners at the venture firm. She called Anders from her cell phone. He answered immediately.

"I need you to look something up for me."

"Delilah, I have been meaning to call you. About last night -"

"Forget it, Anders. I have."

"No you haven't. And neither have I."

Delilah glanced at Barb. "Things are not what I thought."

"I wasn't lying about Kathryn."

"It doesn't matter."

"But it does."

"Drop it. *Please.*"

Silence.

Delilah forged ahead, before he could change her mind. "Remember the business card we picked up at Domino? I need you to find an address for me. For Jay Patel."

"The other U.S. partner?"

"Yes. Barb and I struck out with Cashman again – he's not home. But it's worth paying Patel a visit, too. If he lives close enough."

During the conversation, Delilah watched Cashman's house. She hadn't seen so much as a curtain part since they'd left. Why had the maid slammed the door that way? What caused her agitation?

To Anders, Delilah said, "Anything on Anna Berger?"

"She doesn't have much of a Web presence."

"You couldn't find anything?"

"Still working on it. So far, not so much as a photo."

The photo!

Delilah pictured the maid's face, the sudden burst of anger. Or was it anger? Maybe it was shock. Not shock, more like disappointment. Bone-crushing disappointment. She thought of the house in the Poconos, of the hidden picture of the child, of the book titles on that shelf in the bedroom. Cashman's house remained quiet. Suddenly the stillness seemed ominous. *Very* ominous.

"Anders, I have to go."

She hung up, comprehension exploding.

To Barb she said, "Come with me." Delilah flung open the car door and raced toward the house, Barb behind her. When they reached the front entrance, Delilah pounded on the wooden entry and slammed her palm against the door bell.

"Come on, damn it. Come on."

No answer. Delilah stood back and surveyed the house again. Still no sign of life - no parting drapes, no flickering lights. Dead quiet.

She pounded again. When she got no response, she tried the knob. Unlocked. She ran inside.

"Delilah, what are you doing? Are you mad? We're breaking into someone's house in broad daylight."

"Call an ambulance!"

Barb was right behind her. "An ambulance? What are you talking about, Delilah?"

But Delilah was already making her way through the maze downstairs. Living room - empty. Dining room - empty. Library - empty.

She found her in the kitchen. Delilah raced to her side, afraid it was too late. Blood coated the maid's arms and pooled around her body like a hellish snow angel. She still had a pulse.

"Did you call 9-1-1?"

"Done."

Barb stood over them. Quickly, she reached down and grabbed the woman's wrists. She placed her hand over the vertical gashes, stemming the blood flow, while Delilah made two tourniquets out of kitchen towels. Once the towels were tied, Delilah cradled the woman's head in her arms and whispered in her ear. The words were nonsense, but she kept her tone soft, comforting.

"Look." Barb lifted the woman's arm. Delilah saw bruises the size of plums along her upper extremity. They disappeared under the sleeve of her shirt.

"She was favoring her side, too."

"Cashman?"

Delilah remembered Enid's words: *There's always a beater.* "I suspect so."

Barb made a sound of disgust. "How did you know?"

"Her reaction to the picture of Miriam. I should have seen it before. Terror. Pure, animal terror. And grief. I recognized the look from the pictures of me after . . . after Michael died." Delilah's voice trailed off. She looked down at the woman, who lay with her eyes closed. "I don't want to say anymore now. Not here."

Barb nodded.

The ambulance arrived minutes later along with the local police. Delilah knew the rest of her evening would be shot. She and Barb would be grilled about their reasons for being here. Delilah would be honest – kind of. She just hoped the maid survived. She didn't want Miriam's efforts to be for nothing.

TWENTY-FOUR

In the safety of her office, Delilah watched Miriam's sex video again. She needed something, anything, she could use the next day when she and Barb went to see Jay Patel. Anders had tracked down Patel's address and some bare-bones information about the man. Originally from India, he came to America to get his MBA from Wharton. He stayed here, married, and worked for several large corporations, all in the Boston area. Now he lived in Pennsylvania, in an affluent Bucks County suburb not too far from Delilah, with his wife and three daughters. Delilah and Barb planned to surprise him in the evening, when, hopefully, he would be home with his family.

Delilah stood. It was after midnight and she needed rest. The horses had been the only bright spot in her day. When the police were finally through with her, she'd come home and fed them. Then she rode Millie in the dark until her legs ached and her fingers bled from rubbing against the leather reins. Now she would return home, have a glass of wine, and try to get a few hours of sleep.

The problem was, she couldn't get Cashman's maid out of her mind. The woman had lost a lot of blood, but she'd lived. Delilah feared that physical exhaustion would be the least of the woman's problems.

Delilah wasn't sure the police believed her half-truths about following up on an investigative lead. She'd admitted to looking into the connection between a client's aunt and Jack Cashman. But she'd said nothing about Miriam's murder.

And apparently Cashman told the police the bruises on his maid were due to her own clumsiness. She'd fallen down the stairs, he'd said. The woman refused to speak against her employer, so the police had no evidence to the contrary. And the way the cops presented it, they assumed Jack was telling the truth.

Bullshit. *There's always a beater.*

As Delilah had explained to Barb - but not the police – she'd gone back into that house because of Miriam's picture. More specifically, because of the maid's reaction to Miriam's picture.

The fact that the woman had recognized Miriam meant that she'd met her before. This most likely happened at Cashman's house. Delilah felt pretty certain that if she had explored the upstairs of that home, in one of the bedrooms she would've found a wrought iron bed that looked exactly like the one in the sex tape. Cashman, unmarried, could have hosted the tryst between Miriam and the mysterious stranger. And the maid was a live-in, which the police confirmed, so she would've been there to witness Miriam's comings and goings.

She probably talked with Miriam. A woman with Miriam's worldly sophistication and curiosity would have asked the maid questions.

And if Delilah's suspicions were right, then the maid was also counting on Miriam. She believed Miriam would help her. And when she found out Miriam was dead . . . hope vanished, too.

Delilah knew too well that when hope is gone, truly vanquished, it can seem like there is nothing left to live for. Despair – that bottomless pit from which it feels like there is no escape – can set in. And now the maid could be in greater danger than ever before. This thought fueled Delilah's resolve to find the solution to the puzzle. Quickly.

Delilah locked the front door of Percy Powers LLC and walked outside. The new moon bathed the evening in thick gloom, punctuated only by the hazy artificial glow of street lights on the deserted block. Delilah headed toward her car. She considered what they knew so far. Miriam had promised Cashman's maid escape, Delilah felt certain of that. Then there was the house in Hawley. Anders was almost right when he thought it was a halfway house. It was a shelter, not unlike the secret safe houses used for abused women. Only these women, if Delilah's hunch panned out, were foreigners, probably in this country illegally. That would explain the people Miriam's Willston neighbor saw showing up at all hours. It would explain the passports Delilah found in Miriam's box. It might even explain Miriam's connection to Women NOW.

But it didn't explain why these women needed help in the first place. What did Domino have to do with Miriam's death? What about the Mafia? And if

Natasha's source was to be trusted, why had the Mob placed a hit on Emily Cray, A/K/A Miriam Cross, only to pull it? Whatever Miriam was up to, nothing yet explained her murder.

Which is why they needed to talk to Cashman and Patel.

And Anna Berger.

Delilah had one hand on the Jeep handle and the other on the key when she felt a presence behind her. She tensed, her mind flitting to the goons Natasha had run into in Philadelphia. Stupidly, Delilah had left her gun at home. But the pepper spray sat in the Jeep.

The Jeep's roof was down. Delilah used her leg muscles, strong from hours spent running and horseback riding, to hoist herself over the side, using surprise to her advantage. As she went head first into the open Wrangler, she struck backwards with her left leg. She kicked her stalker full-force in the chest. She heard a sharp intake of air and then a thud. Delilah grabbed the pepper spray and turned.

Mr. Clean lay sprawled on the ground. He didn't stay down for long, though. Before she could take aim, he kicked his leg out, whacking her behind the knee. She fell. He stood, pulled her up roughly and pinned her to the car. Delilah's grip held tight to the canister of pepper spray. She rammed a knee to his groin. Mr. Clean blocked it. She tried to get her arms in front of her, but his weight bore down on her. She couldn't move. He had a ten inches and a hundred pounds to his advantage.

Delilah stopped struggling. Mr. Clean relaxed. Delilah slammed her head forward, hitting Mr. Clean square in the nose. He brought his hands to his face. Delilah pulled the pepper spray from behind her and sprayed his eyes and nose. He yelled. Delilah reached for her cell phone but, before she could get to it, Mr. Clean was backing away, his hands covering his face.

"You're a fool," he growled. "You have no idea what you're dealing with. Let it go."

Delilah shook her head, too winded to respond.

The man spat. Blood dripped from his nose. "Then expect a visit from people far more dangerous than me."

Delilah watched as Mr. Clean disappeared into the shadows.

#

Barb gripped the end of the conference table, furious. "They know where the office is. That's to be expected, Delilah. But it's not exactly brain surgery to figure out where you live."

It was the next morning. After a cursory review of their cases, Delilah finally got around to telling Barb, Margot, Natasha and Anders about her visitor the night before. In daylight, her street seemed much less menacing. In fact, it was hard to believe that he'd approached her just feet from her office front door.

"Look," Delilah said. "This guy did us a favor."

Natasha frowned. "How do you figure?"

"We know he wasn't out to kill. He seemed unarmed. He could have easily taken me – I was an open target. For all I know he just came to talk with me and I provoked him with the kick."

Anders shook his head. "He's been following you for days."

"Ah, but why has he been following me for days? We assume he works for Domino, right?" Anders nodded. "So obviously Domino is interested in what we're finding out. But that doesn't explain why they're interested. Maybe they want to know what we know, and it's as simple as that."

"Or," Natasha said. "We've stumbled onto a hornet's nest."

Delilah looked around the room at each of her employees from her perch on the edge of the table. She had the tiniest inkling of what Domino's role was, but nothing that would explain Miriam's death. Miriam had become a threat to someone or something. Her financing of women's shelters – if that's what the place in Hawley was *and* if Miriam was the financier? But why would that make her someone's target?

Quietly, Anders said, "What if Miriam knew something. Something big, something she was willing to make public?"

Margot looked skeptical. "Like what?"

Natasha said, "If that were the case, journalists would be sniffing all around Miriam's murder, which they're not."

Anders said, "Not necessarily."

"There's a gag order," Barb said. "Fred told me. Explains the lack of media attention. The police have withheld nearly all of the details."

Delilah stood. She paced the length of the room, thinking. Something set the murder into play. But until they knew what the *it* was, it would be hard to understand a journalistic angle.

Delilah looked at Anders, meeting his eyes with a cold stare. "Any luck with Anna Berger?"

He shook his head. "I've been able to dig up some basic biographical information on her, but she has led a very limited virtual life."

Margot cocked her head. "Meaning?"

"Meaning she has almost no online trail. And her religious order isn't talking. It's been dead end after dead end."

"Her bio? Anything there?"

"Not really. I'll send the file to you later, Delilah, but it's mainly family history and the like."

"She's in hiding?"

Anders shrugged. "Maybe. Maybe she's met with foul play. And maybe I just can't locate her. Do you want me to keep searching?"

Delilah thought for a moment. She only had so many human resources. "I do. Based on the condition of the house in the Poconos, it was recently abandoned. Assuming she was there, it seems awfully coincidental that Anna would leave around the same time Miriam was killed. And I'm sure that Anna has some critical pieces of information. Including Miriam's connection to Women NOW."

Anders nodded.

Delilah was about to adjourn the meeting when her cell phone rang. She checked the caller I.D. Joe. She held a hand up to the group and hit the receive button.

"What's going on?"

"Lucinda's missing."

Delilah's pulse quickened. "How did that happen?"

"My guy was positioned outside of her apartment, like we agreed. Lucinda normally leaves by six-thirty in the morning. When she didn't come out by eight, he got nervous. Called me."

"Maybe she doesn't have work today."

"That was our first thought. We confirmed that she was expected at seven this morning. I drove over to the site. Door was unlocked. She's gone."

"Evidence of a break in?"

"No."

"Anything missing that you could tell? Suitcase, clothes?"

"Nothing obvious."

"No recent visitors?"

"No, Lila."

"*Damn.*"

Delilah looked around the room. Everyone was watching her, intent on her conversation. "Look, Joe, maybe Lucinda left without your guy noticing."

"Doubtful. He's my most senior PI." Joe paused. "Whoever nabbed Lucinda was a pro."

"Did you call the police?"

He hesitated, but only for a second. "No."

"Good." Delilah took a deep breath. "Things are starting to add up, Joe. And I smell something rotten. I need the name of the guy we went to the Academy with. The one who went Fed. Remember him?"

"FBI? Mansaro."

Delilah snapped her fingers. "Carl Mansaro." She pictured a bone-thin man with bushy eyebrows and a perpetual sneer. "Get me Mansaro's number?"

"Will do. Anything else?"

"Keep your man outside Lucinda's place. Just in case she comes back or someone tries to get in. They may show up to toss the place."

"Already done. And Delilah?"

"Yes, Joe?"

"Be careful. I don't know who *they* are, but I think you have your hands full with this job."

"I'll be careful." Delilah hung up. Joe was right, of course. But there was no going back now. At least not for her.

"What's happening, boss?" Margot said.

"Change in plans."- Delilah pointed to Margot and Barb – "You two will go speak with Jay Patel. See what you can get out of him. Anders, find Sister Anna Berger. Call her parents, the Pope, I don't care, but we need to talk with her."

"And me?" Natasha said.

"You're coming with me." Delilah opened the conference room door and motioned for everyone to get going. "After I make some calls about Lucinda, we're going to pay another visit to Cashman."

Natasha smiled. "You want me to convince him that it's not nice to beat up women?"

Delilah sighed. "It just may come to that."

TWENTY-FIVE

Barb had exactly two hours and forty minutes to deal with Jay Patel in Bucks County and then fight traffic back to Phoenixville to get her daughter to band rehearsal. Marching band was an unforgiving mistress and her daughter's career in the color guard had just begun. She couldn't afford to stray now.

The problem was, Jay Patel was stalling. And Barb felt her Irish temper, usually well-suppressed, bubbling to the surface.

"Look, Mr. Patel, we know you have a business relationship with Jack Cashman. And we know that Cashman and Miriam Cross were lovers."

"While you are most correct that Mr. Cashman and I are partners in a joint venture, I no more keep track of his comings and goings than I do my next door neighbor's."

They were seated in Patel's home office, a spacious room that housed floor-to-ceiling book cases, an oversized mahogany desk with matching credenza and a fireplace. Patel sat at his desk. He was a charismatic man in his early fifties. Tall and lanky, he had even features and coal-black hair that was brushed thick and straight off his forehead. Patel projected an air of confidence when he spoke – with a distinctly *foreign* accent. Barb couldn't be sure – frankly, many accents sounded the same to her – but it could very well be the voice she heard on Miriam's ménage tape.

Before arriving about fifteen minutes prior, Margot and Barb had decided to be up front about the reason for their visit. They expected resistance, but, to their surprise, were let in immediately. An elderly woman in a ruby and yellow sari answered the door. She was joined seconds later by a younger woman wearing plum-colored velour sweatpants and a silver t-shirt. The younger woman, also Indian, had bland features and even blander countenance. After checking with her husband, she asked no questions of her guests, simply led Margot and Barb to Patel's office. She reappeared now with three glasses of iced tea.

"Thank you, Guna," Patel said.

After his wife placed the drinks on the small table that sat between Margot and Barb, she waited for her husband to dismiss her. He did so with an absentminded flick of the hand.

When the woman had gone, Barb said, "Your wife seems very . . . loyal."

"I value loyalty in a relationship, Ms. Moore. Marital or otherwise."

"I wonder . . . would she be so loyal if she knew about you and Miriam?"

Patel gave Barb a look of practiced and condescending patience. "What exactly is the purpose of your visit, ladies? I've already told you all I know."

Margot said, "All you've told us is that you work with Cashman. We want answers about Miriam. As we said at the beginning, we've been hired by Miriam's niece to investigate Miriam's untimely death." Margot looked at Patel over the top of her glasses. "We're speaking with anyone who may have had a relationship with the author."

"I assure you, there was no relationship between Ms. Cross and me."

Frustrated, Barb said, "Mr. Patel, are you aware that Miriam kept a video? A rather incriminating video of a sex act between you, her and Mr. Cashman?"

Patel looked Barb square in the eyes. "That is quite impossible. I never had relations with your Miriam Cross. Now if you'll excuse me-."

"Was Mr. Cashman involved with Miriam? Perhaps you met through him?" Margot said.

"Jack and I are business partners, not social friends. I appreciate that you want to find who killed Ms. Cross, but I am afraid I cannot help you with that effort."

"Does the name Anna Berger ring a bell?" Barb said.

"I'm afraid not."

"Emily Cray?"

The slightest flicker in the eyes, but otherwise, nothing. Barb sighed inwardly. Patel was as cool as a Canadian Christmas.

Patel stood. "I have another appointment, ladies. If you will excuse me."

"We understand. Thank you for your time, Mr. Patel." Margot rose slowly to her feet. "One last thing, if I may. The woman who answered your door. Very sweet lady – who is she?"

"My mother." He gave Margot an appraising stare. "Don't look so surprised. It is an Indian tradition for women to care for their husband's parents. My father is dead. My mother has lived with us for almost fifteen years."

He was herding them toward the double doors that led out of the library. Barb followed him, her eyes scanning the books on the floor-to-ceiling shelves. If the guy had read all of these books – classic novels, treatises on business, art and history, Greek and Shakespearean tragedies – he was Barb's new hero.

But then her gaze locked onto one shelf in particular. *Bingo*.

"Does the name Chinnamasta ring a bell, Mr. Patel?" Margot was saying.

Catching the tail-end of the exchange, Barb glanced from the shelf to Patel. She could have sworn she saw another crack in his plaster at the mention of the Hindu goddess.

"Any educated Hindu knows of Chinnamasta." He opened the door. "Guna," he called. His wife arrived seconds later, looking no more curious about the reason for their visit than she might be about the way glue dries.

"Do you know how Miriam Cross died?" Margot said. "She was beheaded. Beheaded like Chinnamasta-"

"Good evening, ladies." Patel shut the office door, quietly but firmly.

"Well, I guess that's all we're going to get out of him," Margot muttered.

The women followed Guna to the front door. Once outside, Barb took a quick detour down the driveway and made a mental note of the two cars parked there: a baby blue Jaguar and a silver Mercedes. Then she joined Margot, anxious to get on the road.

Margot slipped behind the driver's seat of her two-door Miata. Fire engine red. Manual transmission. Barb could never reconcile the car and the woman, but both of them could move, and right now Barb needed speed.

"What did you think of Patel?" Barb said when they were back on the highway. Margot's speedometer read ninety-two. Barb hoped Margot could keep it up. Band practice would start in less than an hour.

"That was too easy."

"You think he was expecting us?"

"I don't know. But I am surprised he let us in." Margot adjusted the radio. She stopped when she found the local public station. Her gnarled fingers tapped the steering wheel to the folksy beat of Dar Williams. "The man is a liar if I'm a day over seventy. I think he told us two truthful things. One, his wife's name."

"And two?"

"That the woman who answered the door was his mother."

"Why did you ask about her?" Barb said, although she thought she knew the answer.

"Just looking for patterns."

"Like Cashman's housekeeper?"

Margot nodded. "Nothing there, though." She paused. "How about you? Telling the truth about Miriam?"

"Oh, he's lying all right."

Margot gave her a sideways look. "You sound pretty confident."

"Not because of anything he said, really." Barb paused. "Whoever was at Miriam's Chestnut Hill house the night the neighbor called the police was driving a Mercedes with a Yankees magnet on the back."

"And Patel had Yankees magnet on that show car of his?"

"No. But they're easy to remove and a smart man like Patel would go to lengths to cover his trail."

"So what's the relevance?"

"Patel had a whole shelf dedicated to baseball books and paraphernalia in his office. *Yankees* books. Philadelphia is a Phillies world."

"I don't know. There are lots of Yankees fans in this area, Barb. Bucks County is full of New York commuters."

"Maybe. But I can't help but wonder." Barb held up a hand and counted on her fingers as she spoke. "Look, the guy works with Cashman. He has a British accent, like the man in Miriam's sex tape. And he reacted ever so subtly to two things – the mention of Emily Cray and the Hindu goddess Chinnamasta" - Barb shrugged - "in my book, all of this adds up to suspicious."

"Did he strike you as capable of murder?"

"To me, everyone seems capable of murder . . . under the right circumstances. At the very least, he knows more than he's letting on." Barb glanced at her watch. "Step on it, lead foot. I've got an appointment with someone far more important that Jay Patel. And if I don't get there soon, the next murder in the tri-state area will be mine."

#

Delilah's head hurt, both from worry about Lucinda and a growing concern for her staff. She'd gotten her people involved, and now they may be in danger, too. For what? A sizable fee – if they ever got paid. And to assuage her own blasted sense of duty.

Delilah pressed down on the gas pedal. She knew this trip was likely to be pointless. They could drive two hours to find the house empty. Or Cashman would refuse to see them, if he was even home. But Delilah had to give it another try. And driving to Domino's headquarters in New York City seemed senseless. There, it was unlikely they'd get past the ground floor security. And besides, she'd had Natasha call Domino beforehand. Cashman was still out of the office. Code for *he doesn't want to see you.*

Delilah followed a silver BMW onto Cashman's street. She slowed. Natasha yawned. She'd been silent for most of the trip to New Jersey.

"Rough night?"

Natasha smirked. "Not in the fun way."

"Sam?"

"My ex."

"Jake still bothering you?"

Natasha shrugged. "He's on the Mob's radar now. I don't care so much about Jake – he's a jerk. But the bastard is Sam's father."

Delilah slowed to a stop. She turned to the younger woman. "Do you want out, Natasha?"

"What are you talking about?"

"This job. Do you want to stop working on it?"

"It's a little late now, Delilah."

"No, it's not. Think about it. Your son. Jake. Your own life. One of us could end up like Miriam."

"Are *you* pulling out?"

Delilah shook her head. She knew she couldn't stop until they had answers. But she would do it alone. If it came to that.

Natasha gave her a funny look. Then she turned her head toward Cashman's house. Her eyes widened. "Delilah, the silver BMW. It just pulled into Jack's driveway."

Delilah looked ahead. Sure enough, there it was. With two people inside.

Delilah pulled her binoculars out from under her seat. Cashman's housekeeper sat beside him. Delilah waited until Jack and the maid were out of the car. Cashman grabbed the older woman by the elbow and began leading her up the steps toward the front entry.

Delilah put down the binoculars. She looked at Natasha. "Answer me. Do you want out? If so, no hard feelings. We have plenty of other work."

"Damn it. No, I don't want out. None of us do. This isn't the Wild West, Delilah, and you're the only cowboy who can handle the ranch. We're a fucking team."

Delilah nodded. Natasha was right. "Okay, then. I won't ask again." She turned back toward the house. Cashman and his housekeeper were halfway up the steps. "Here we go."

Delilah pulled the car up Cashman's driveway and killed the ignition. She and Natasha got out and jogged toward Jack's house. He and his maid were still walking, slowly, up the stairs. When Jack saw her, he tried to hurry the woman up the walkway. She fumbled, her movements hunched and stiff. He pushed her.

"Always beat up helpless women, Jack?" Natasha yelled.

Delilah shot her a warning glance. Delilah shared Natasha's sentiment, but they had to tread carefully. One, they needed Cashman's cooperation. And two, she didn't want him to take anything out on the maid later.

Cashman looked at Delilah. He said, "You're the woman from the precinct. The one who found my housekeeper yesterday."

The voice from the sex tape! Delilah tried to keep her voice even, despite her growing excitement. This was their guy. The authoritative tone was unmistakable. "We're private investigators, Mr. Cashman. And we'd like a few minutes of your time."

"You can see I'm busy."

"We'll wait."

The housekeeper looked over at Delilah. She made eye contact for the briefest of moments, but in that split second, Delilah saw an awful, pleading despair. Delilah's heart twisted. She closed the distance between her and Cashman.

"Natasha, give me a hand." Carefully, she took the housekeeper's free arm. "We'll help her. Sometimes a woman needs another woman."

Jack, too stunned to speak, moved back. Delilah smiled at the woman reassuringly. The woman didn't smile back but she didn't shy away, either. Natasha took the woman's other arm. Gently, they helped her to the front door.

Cashman unlocked the door and punched in a security code to disable the alarm system. He stepped inside and motioned for the housekeeper to follow.

"A few minutes of your time?" Delilah said.

Jack looked back and forth between Delilah and Natasha, his mouth smiling and his eyes stone cold. A handsome man, tall and muscular with a full head of dirty blonde hair and intelligent marine-blue eyes, but Delilah sensed that underneath that dashing exterior lurked something sinister. She couldn't shake the feeling that she was looking at a monster.

Finally, Cashman said, "I won't be able to get rid of you otherwise." He frowned. "Five minutes." To the housekeeper, he said, "You can get upstairs yourself, Rosa. Take your time. I don't want you falling again."

Head bent, the woman nodded.

Jack said, "What do you want?"

Delilah pointed toward the stairs. "Let me help her."

"She's fine."

"She needs help."

"I said she's fine." Jack took a step, putting himself between Delilah and the stairs. "You have ten seconds to get to the point. Then I am calling the police."

"Does the name Miriam Cross ring a bell?" Delilah said.

"The author?"

"Bingo, smart man." Natasha smiled. "Now, three points if you can tell us who starred in a sex tape with the famous Miriam Cross."

"Is this some kind of joke?"

"We know you and Miriam were lovers, Jack," Natasha said. "We have proof. Miriam died a few weeks ago. Murdered."

Jack looked at Natasha, then back at Delilah. "Does the smart ass here work for you?"

"She has a name. Natasha. And yes, she does."

"You should find some better help."

Delilah ignored him. "We're looking for insight into Miriam's last months. Who she knew, what she was doing."

"I have no idea."

Delilah said, "We think you do."

"Then you think wrong, Ms. Powers."

Delilah could see Natasha's hands balling into fists. She had no doubt Natasha had a knife strapped somewhere. For all Delilah knew, she had nunchucks up her lady parts. Natasha didn't go anywhere unprepared. That's why Delilah valued her so.

But now she gave Natasha a second warning glance. If things went south, they wouldn't get any information out of Cashman. And right now, they needed information more than they needed a fight.

"Look Jack, a few straight answers and we'll be out of your hair."

"What, exactly, do you want to know?"

"How did you meet Miriam?"

"I don't know what you're talking about."

"We know you were acquainted with Miriam."

Natasha said, "In fact, we have proof that you were lovers."

"Nonsense."

Delilah smiled. "Did you ever see her speak publicly?"

"Not that I recall."

"So you never attended a function – say a political fundraiser – at which she was the featured speaker?"

Jack stared at her a moment, wheels turning. "I may have. I don't remember every function I've attended."

"Let me jog your memory," Delilah said. "Juan DeMarco. Last spring. Miriam Cross was the main presenter. Ring a bell?"

Silence.

"Look jackass," Natasha said. "We know you knew Miriam. We know you tied her to a bed and fucked the hell out of her. We know you're a cruel son of a bitch who likes to beat up women. So you might as well cut the crap and admit to it."

Jack's face colored. He took a menacing step forward. Delilah tensed. She considered how long it would take her to grab her gun if necessary. But it wasn't necessary. Like that, Jack transformed before their eyes. The banker version of Jekyll and Hyde.

"You're right," he said. "I knew Miriam. We dated for some time. A brilliant woman. Intelligent, articulate, passionate. I was sorry to read of her murder in the papers. Sadly, we hadn't spoken for months."

Delilah decided to take advantage of his unexpected change of heart. "Why the denial a second ago?"

"I don't owe you information about my private life. Miriam is part of my past. She has no relevance now."

"How about Jay Patel? Your business partner."

"What about him?"

"Did he have a . . . relationship . . . with Miriam?"

"Jay is married with children."

Natasha snorted. "We know *that* doesn't mean a damn thing."

Cashman looked down at her over the bridge of his aristocratic nose. "Maybe in your circles."

Delilah interjected before Natasha could react. "There's a second man in the sex tape. Could that be Jay Patel?"

Cashman's anger returned. "Let's be real clear, ladies. Whatever tape you're talking about, it wasn't me she was with. I wasn't her only lover."

"So Patel *could* have been her lover?"

Cashman shrugged. He walked toward the door and opened it, looking pointedly at his watch. "I promised you five minutes. That's come and gone. Now leave."

Delilah didn't budge. "How's your housekeeper feeling?" she said.

"I guess I never did thank you for helping her."

"No, you didn't." When Cashman didn't respond, Delilah continued. "What Rosa did to herself is serious. She needs counseling. Someone to help her cope. There are services out there -"

"What my maid needs is none of your business. Now go. Please. Before I call the police."

Natasha took a step toward him. Delilah placed a calming hand on her shoulder.

"You were friends with Miriam," Delilah said. She edged toward the door, stalling. "Don't you want her killer brought to justice?"

"The police will see to that."

"Nevertheless" – Delilah held out a business card – "please call me if you want to talk. If something triggers a memory, something that might help."

Cashman took the card. He looked it over and then stuck it carefully in his wallet. He regarded Delilah with amusement. "So someone hired you two to find a killer? Seems a little farfetched to me. You don't look like pros."

Delilah smiled. "Looks can deceive."

Jack smiled back. "Indeed they can, Ms. Powers. Indeed they can."

Back in the car, Delilah placed a quick call to Anders. "Check the papers and online news. Confirm for me that nothing new has been published about Miriam's death."

"Will do," he said, his tone icy. So be it, Delilah thought. No time to worry about Anders now.

"Any word from Lucinda?"

"I'm afraid not."

Damn. Earlier, Delilah had confirmed that Lucinda never showed up for work. Delilah had also contacted Lucinda's in-laws. The kids were safe, but they hadn't heard from Lucinda in days. Delilah had been contemplating whether or not to call the police. Her gut said not to involve local officials. Not yet, anyway.

After she hung up, Natasha said, "What was that all about?"

"Jack said he found out about Miriam's *murder* in the papers. That was a slip. There's a gag order. Mainstream media hasn't mentioned the cause of death."

"Why the gag order?"

"Either the police are hoping that details of the murder – details unknown to the public – will help solve the murder."

"Or?"

"Or someone high up, someone with a stake in what happened to Miriam, ordered the suppression of information."

"Police?"

Delilah shrugged. "Maybe. Or politicians. Either way, someone with clout has reason to keep this out of the news."

Natasha looked thoughtful. "So Jack was lying. Surprise, surprise. If he didn't find out about Miriam in the news, then how did he know?"

Delilah nodded. "The billion dollar question." She pulled out onto the main drag, happy to be out of Cashman's suffocating neighborhood.

TWENTY-SIX

Delilah dropped Natasha off at her apartment in Northeast Philly before heading home. Something was niggling at her brain like a hungry goldfish. She pulled over into a Wendy's parking lot and dialed Joe's number. "Anything more on Lucinda?"

"Sorry, Lila. We watched her place all day. Nada."

Delilah tapped clipped fingernails against her dashboard. "Do me a favor, Joe?"

Joe chuckled. "With all these favors, you should have married me back when I asked you. At least then you could have repaid me with sex."

Delilah smiled despite herself. "I was a silly girl back then."

"And now?"

Delilah thought of Anders. "Not much has changed."

Joe paused before saying, "What can I do for you, Cowgirl?"

"I need you to pull some phone records for me. I want numbers for all calls made to or by Lucinda from her cell and her home number in the past three weeks."

He was silent for a minute. Delilah knew that was a lot to ask. He'd have to use connections, call in some favors.

"Okay. I'll do it."

"And can you check for a trace on her home number?"

"That may be harder."

"If you can, Joe, do it. If you can't . . . no worries. I appreciate the help. And I'll pay you, of course."

She hit the off button on her cell phone before he could object and sat back in her seat. It was dark outside and the blackness around her felt heavy and unfamiliar. She was in new territory, literally and figuratively. Somehow her life had spun out of control. A missing client, tension with Anders, her staff in harm's way . . . and Cashman's maid. The haunted look in that woman's eyes. As though she'd been through living hell.

Living hell. Something clicked. Delilah picked up her phone again and scrolled through her numbers. She called Margot and got the number for Miriam's agent, Liam McMaster. He answered on the third ring.

"What do you want this time?" he said, his syllables slurring into one another.

"When we met to talk about Miriam, you mentioned that you couldn't dump her as a client because she had you by the balls. What did you mean?"

"Exactly that."

"How? What was she doing?"

He let out an obnoxious laugh. "Isn't it obvious?"

"Miriam was blackmailing you?"

Another bellow. "Heavens, no. I may have a lot of vices, but I assure you, all of them are legal."

Another call beeped in. Delilah ignored it. What else could make Liam feel trapped? Sex? *Doubtful.* Money? "She was working on a new book," Delilah said.

"Aren't you a little genius? Yes. Miriam was working on something big. Only this time, it wasn't another of her rancid novels."

"Memoirs."

"*Pah-lease.*" Another snort. "No. An exposé. Something juicy, something scandalous. Something fucking fresh for once."

A knife twisted in her gut at the implications. *All* of the implications.

"What was the topic?"

"You think she told me? I am, after all, only her agent. I'd barely heard from her in months."

"Do you think it was something that could have gotten her killed?"

Liam made a gulping noise into the phone. Delilah heard a sigh, then a series of clicks. She repeated her question, afraid she'd lost him to a bottle of whatever he was downing. "Mr. McMaster, do you think whatever Miriam was working on could have gotten her murdered?"

But McMaster was still there. "I guess we'll never know, now will we?" He laughed. "Our only source is dead."

#

Delilah pulled into her driveway, exhausted, angry and feeling used, her conversation with McMaster still echoing in her head. She parked next to the barn, got out and slammed the driver's side door. Inside the barn, she flipped on the lights and hoisted herself over the side of Spur's stall. Like a lucky talisman, the old horse calmed her down. The connection to her father. Somehow, irrational as it would sound to others, being with Spur allowed her to feel her father's spirit. And right now, Delilah wanted her daddy.

She looked around the barn. She still had chores to do, but first thing's first.

She dialed Anders' phone number. He picked up immediately.

"Anything more on Lucinda?" he said.

"No." She paused, unsure how to continue. "Can you come to my house?"

She heard his light breathing on the phone and the sound sent a mix of feelings through her. Was Kathryn there, too? She didn't care. She *shouldn't* care. Her reasons for calling Anders went well beyond their night together.

"Is everything alright?" he said finally.

"We need to talk."

"Is it about what happened in New Jersey? Because-"

She cut him off. "Can you come over?"

Another pause. "I'll be there in half an hour."

Delilah kicked off her shoes and replaced them with the muckers she kept in the barn. Then she got to work cleaning Spur's stall. The horse whinnied beside her. He wanted dinner and his nightly carrot. She'd wait for Anders here and then head up to the house to let the dogs out and get the horses their treats. Right now, she wanted – no, needed - the release of physical labor.

Delilah remembered the phone call that she never answered. She put down her pitchfork and picked the phone up from its perch on a bale of hay. The call was from New York. She had to listen to the message three times to understand Juan DeMarco's sister, her voice was so garbled by grief.

One thing was clear: DeMarco was dead.

Delilah sat down hard on the hay bale. They found Juan's body on shore a half a mile from the Tappan Zee Bridge. Suicide. Or so his family thought.

Another piece of the puzzle connected.

Poor Juan. Delilah pictured the gregarious man with the broad smile. He'd tried to resist whatever forces of evil were at play in his district. To no avail. They got him in the end.

And those same forces were connected to Miriam Cross. An unlikely pairing.

Spur pushed his head under her arm. She reached up to stroke the silky soft spot under his chin and heard tires crunching gravel. Anders. Delilah made no move to meet him. He would follow the light and find her. He was, after all, a resourceful man.

Millie greeted Anders' arrival in the barn with a warning shake of her head. Anders looked nervously from the horse to Delilah and back again.

Delilah pointed to a bale of hay. "Sit."

Anders stared at it for a second, and then perched on the edge. He tilted his head, waiting, clearly picking up on Delilah's anger.

"When we were in New York, you said Kathryn had left you long ago. Those were your exact words. Do you recall?"

Anders nodded. "That was the truth."

"Why did she leave you, Anders?"

"What do you mean?"

"Was it really a result of the tension over your daughter, or was there something else?"

"I still don't understand the question."

Delilah walked the length of Millie's stall and climbed over the rail so that she was in the same enclosure as Anders. Then she leaned against the barn wall, watching his face as watched her. Once upon a time, he'd reminded her of Michael. She felt foolish now to have made that connection.

"Could it be that you were preoccupied, Matthew? Not just because of your daughter, but with other things? Guilt? Things that haunted you to the point of distraction?"

"Delilah, you're not making sense."

Delilah raised her hand to silence him. "How many private investigator jobs did you apply for?"

Anders looked away, sudden understanding reflected in his eyes. "One."

"*One*. Interesting. Any reason in particular that you chose my shop?"

Anders didn't respond.

"Then let me help you remember. I made a call to Miriam's agent today and you know what he told me? Miriam had been working on a project. A secret project – an exposé. I started to think about that. Miriam had uncovered something scandalous, according to McMasters. Something big."

"So-"

"So it dawned on me that your arrival at Percy Powers was no coincidence."

"Delilah-"

She shook her head. "Don't Delilah me. I've asked a friend of mine to pull Lucinda's telephone records. If I had to guess, I think I'll find a trace on her line. I might not be able to track it to you, but how else would you have known about Lucinda's connection to me?" Delilah threw her hands up. "Maybe you'd been following her and saw us have coffee together. Maybe you asked her directly. Maybe you did your homework and figured out our past connection, when we followed her husband. I don't know. But somehow you found out and figured joining my firm would get you closer to the truth."

"It wasn't like that. I tried to reason with Lucinda. I called her and asked what her aunt had been working on. She didn't know. So I followed her, thinking perhaps she was lying . . . and there you were. It was a win-win for both of us, Delilah. Surely you see that."

"I trusted you."

"So did Ahmed."

Delilah shook her head. "Regardless, you used me. You have been using my firm to find Ahmed's killer."

Anders twisted his hands into a ball between his knees. He spoke softly. "Before he was killed, Ahmed called me. I was a mess, I didn't listen. Just like I told you. That was all true, Delilah. The only name I remembered from our call was Miriam Cross. But when I went to find her"- he shook his head - "She'd disappeared. By the time I located her niece, Miriam was murdered."

"You could have been honest with me. Told me the real reason you applied for the job."

"Would you have hired me?"

Delilah slid down the wall until she was on the floor. She wrapped her arms around her knees. "Probably not."

They sat there, quietly, for what felt like ages. Anders' story added up. She never quite believed that he wanted to be a private investigator to save his marriage. Had she been so taken with his quiet demeanor and resemblance to Michael that she'd let herself be snowed? Maybe. The thought disturbed her.

He said, "What are you going to do now?"

"We're in it this deep. I suppose we keep going."

Anders nodded.

"But you can no longer work for Percy Powers. My loyalty is to my client, Lucinda. Clearly your loyalty is to Ahmed and his family. There may be a time when we realize our goals are not the same."

"I haven't hidden anything from you, if that's what you're worried about. Anything related to Miriam's murder."

"That's just it. You have. The piece about Miriam's collaboration with Ahmed is important. And that's something you knew all along."

Anders stood. "I had no idea what their relationship was. I just knew that there was some connection."

"A fact *we* didn't have."

Anders nodded slowly. "I see your point."

"So from now on, total honesty. We cooperate by sharing resources and information. But only because we've come this far. Otherwise, Anders, *our* collaboration will be over."

Anders looked shaken. Whether his shame was sincere or contrived, Delilah didn't know. But ever since she'd realized that Anders had been lying to her – only not about Kathryn, as she previously thought – she'd been trying to come to some solution that would salvage the case. Because the truth was, they needed him.

Anders dug in his satchel and pulled out a manila file. "Anna Berger's biographical information. Nothing earth shattering, but who knows."

Delilah took the file. "I have to head up to the house to feed the dogs and get the horses their evening dessert. Before you leave, though, you should know one more thing. DeMarco is dead."

Anders took in a sharp breath. "What happened?"

"His family is saying suicide. But he drowned, Anders. His sister says he was a strong swimmer, which is why they believe he took his own life. Ring any bells?"

"Ahmed."

Delilah nodded. "I'm beginning to think we have two forces at work here. Domino and the Mob. I'm just not sure how they fit together."

Anders' eyes widened. "Or who is doing the killing."

#

It was after midnight when Anders left and Delilah finally got around to checking her home voicemail messages. She dialed the Verizon access number with dread, believing that her mother's voice would ring out from at least one voicemail message. The only thought worse than having her mother show up was having her mother show up now, in the midst of this mess.

Face it Lila, when it comes to that five-foot-one ball of piss and vinegar, you're nothing but a coward.

But it wasn't her mother's voice that rang forth from her phone. It was Lucinda's.

TWENTY-SEVEN

Delilah called Barb from her cell phone, afraid to tie up the home line. Caller I.D. was no help – whatever line Lucinda had used came up as blocked. In the morning, Delilah would set up a trace on her home line. For tonight, she'd remain by the phone, hoping that Lucinda's kidnappers would call again.

"What did Lucinda say?" Barb said.

Delilah had carefully written down every word, and she read it back to Barb now. "Let this go, Delilah. I was wrong to pursue this. If you don't let it go, it will be Butch all over again." And then more slowly, "This is Butch all over again."

"What the heck does that mean?"

Delilah was standing in her kitchen next to the window that overlooked her backyard. Her eyes scanned for movement. Beside her, the dogs paced back and forth restlessly. Delilah worried about the horses, left out there to their own defenses. She'd turned on all the barn lights, but that was a weak deterrent. Someone looking to drive home a point could do that with a shotgun without ever setting foot on her property.

"Think about it," Delilah said. "Think about Butch."

"Well, the obvious answer is that these people have threatened to beat her if you don't cooperate."

"And if Lucinda had stopped after the second sentence, I would agree. But she didn't. She went on to say, 'this is Butch all over again.'"

Barb was quiet for a moment. "The police."

"I think so. Lucinda never trusted the police. They would back Butch. And now the gag order, the lack of progress . . . the police are not going to solve this murder."

"She's trying to tell us to keep going anyway?"

"Exactly. She found a way to communicate that wouldn't alert her kidnappers. With Butch, we had to continue even though he was beating her. She had been adamant about that."

"We needed the visual proof."

"Yes. Keep going. Don't trust the police."

Delilah ran the water from the faucet until it felt ice cold. She stuck her wrists under the flow in a lame attempt to stifle the persistent sweat running down her body. She didn't want to turn the air conditioners on – too noisy, and right now she needed to hear anything and everything coming from outside. She had a bad feeling that this case wasn't wrapping up. It was just *heating* up.

Barb said her good-byes. They agreed to reconvene in the morning.

"Lock your doors, Lila."

Delilah certainly would. She'd do better than that. Tonight she would sleep with her Glock. It wouldn't be the hottest date of her life, but it just might be the safest.

#

Five a.m. came way too fast. Natasha turned over and reached for Amelia. She was gone. Natasha sat up, her instincts on high alert. She'd dreamed about Miriam all night. Terrible dreams that always led somehow to Sam being hurt or killed or taken. She felt queasy at the thought.

Queasy and pissed.

Natasha threw her legs over the bed. Quietly, she sprinted through the apartment, her heart racing. It was unlike Amelia to get out of bed first. She was a late-sleeper, often not rising until after nine. Sam's door stood wide open. Natasha crept silently through the doorway, the anger turning to panic.

Sam's room was quiet, full of stale air and shadows. Natasha braced herself, preparing for the worst. Her family. Gone. The motherfuckers would pay.

But Sam was in his bed, Amelia's slender body wrapped around his. Amelia snored lightly. Sam slept with his mouth wide open, head against Amelia's shoulder. Natasha felt her heart thawing. Just a little bit.

She was ready to tip-toe her way out of Sam's room when the sound of her cell phone yanked her back to reality. She tried to hit the ignore button. Too late. Amelia rolled over, adorably bleary-eyed and unkempt, her pixy face a mask of serenity. She smiled when she saw Natasha standing there.

"Sam had a nightmare. I didn't want to wake you."

Natasha nodded, at a loss for words.

"Your phone's ringing, Natasha."

Natasha nodded again, feeling silly and sentimental and incredibly protective. She'd let the phone ring itself out. She'd take Amelia to bed and remind her of all the things that made life worth living. Then she'd sleep, curled around her friend, and make pancakes for her two loves in the morning.

The phone starting ringing again. *Fuck.* She dashed into the other room in a race to get her cell before it woke up Sam. She half expected another call from Jake. Instead, Delilah's voice greeted her.

"I'm sorry to call so early, Natasha, but I need you to do surveillance today. Are you available?"

Natasha groaned inwardly. Surveillance was boring. But she'd be paid well. She thought of Amelia and Sam, sleeping peacefully in her apartment. She thought of the house in the burbs, the fenced in yard. And the puppy. A boy should have a dog. She'd follow the fucking president, if that's what it took. Anything that brought in money and was legal suddenly seemed fine to her. "No problem."

"There's a catch."

Okay, so much for legal. Natasha tapped her fingers against the countertop. "Waiting."

"Follow Matthew Anderson."

"Anders?"

"Yes."

"*Our* Anders?"

"Yes, Natasha. *Our* Anders."

Natasha felt stymied by that one. She reminded herself that the gig paid and wasn't illegal. "What exactly am I supposed to be looking for?"

"I just want to know what Anders does. Keep tabs on him at all times, Natasha."

"And if he sees me?"

Delilah's tone was crisp. "You're a professional. Make sure that doesn't happen."

#

Delilah hung up the phone with Natasha, feeling both justified and foolish. But how could she trust

Anders now? And what if he was keeping information from them? This was simply insurance, nothing else. She dialed Barb's cell phone number.

"Can you give me a full day?" she said when Barb answered the phone.

"Yep. Fred's off. He can hold down the fort here."

"Good. Margot will be watching Cashman's house. I want you to tail Jay Patel. I just confirmed that he's home."

"It's not even six in the morning."

"I know. He was less than thrilled to get a wrong number so early."

Barb laughed. Delilah knew that, unlike Natasha, both Margot and Barb were early risers. Barb was probably already showered and dressed, a hot cup of coffee in her hand. She could be at Patel's in an hour, ninety minutes with traffic.

Delilah said, "If you get over there soon, you should catch him. I just want to know where he goes and what he does. If something goes down, Barb, don't react. Got it?"

"Got it. What about you? What will you be doing?"

"I think I found Sister Anna Berger. Or at least I know how to find her."

#

Delilah looked at the address on her phone and compared it to the house in front of her. Right place, but not what she'd been expecting.

Enid Bartholomew's Main Line mansion was actually a one and a half story Cape Cod on the outskirts of Wayne, Pennsylvania. A stone house, with an honest-to-goodness white picket fence and rows of neat annuals lining a path to the front door. An American flag flew at full mast from a pole near the garage. The effect was sweet Americana. It definitely did not jibe with its owner.

A disgruntled Enid answered after a dozen knocks and at least as many pokes to the door bell. She blinked repeatedly at Delilah, as though trying to place her. Recognition finally registered in her eyes, then wariness. Enid took a deep breath and motioned for Delilah to come inside.

The interior was as quaint as the outside. Gingham curtains, floral-patterned furniture, hard wood floors, white trim, lots of candles. And a crucifix over the front door.

"Where is your cousin?" Delilah said, choosing not to beat around the proverbial bush. When Enid didn't respond, Delilah repeated her question. "Where is Anna Berger, Enid?"

"I can't tell you that."

Delilah sighed. "You lied to me."

Enid said nothing. Unlike when they met at the bookstore, this time Enid's perfectly coifed hair was in disarray. Dark make-up smeared under her eyes. She wore a white robe. Her feet were bare. She looked tired and scared and very vulnerable. Delilah almost – *almost* – felt bad for her.

"Why did you lie?"

"I have no idea who you are or what you have to do with Miriam Cross's death. For all I know, you're one of the bad guys."

"I told you. I'm working for Miriam's niece."

"*Please.* No matter how good my plastic surgeon is, it's obvious I wasn't born yesterday." Enid shrugged. "You can tell me whatever you want, that doesn't mean I'll believe it."

"You let me in, Enid. If you thought I was one of the bad guys, there's no way you would have let me into your home."

Enid wrapped long, skinny arms around her chest and rocked back on her heels. She made no reply.

"Look, I know Anna Berger arranged for you to rent that house to Miriam Cross under an assumed name." Okay, Delilah didn't know that exactly, but what the hell.

Enid frowned. "It was a legitimate arrangement. Emily – Miriam - paid rent, like I said. I didn't ask questions, like I said. No lie."

Delilah pulled the biographical information Anders had found on Anna Berger out of her purse. School information, a partial family tree. At first Delilah had dismissed the content as unhelpful. But then she noticed the name Bartholomew. Norman H. Bartholomew was Anna Berger's uncle. Anna Berger's mother, Elizabeth Bartholomew, had married James T. Berger. Anna had no siblings. Norman Bartholomew had an unidentified daughter. He'd lived in Reading, Pennsylvania until his death six years ago. The daughter's whereabouts were unknown.

What were the chances that Enid Bartholomew was the unidentified daughter of the late Norman H. Bartholomew? It fit: Enid's rough-around-the-edges exterior, her raw ambition, not quite fitting in on the Main Line. A kid from Reading may have some problems meshing in the exclusive Philly suburb. Further, what were the chances that the unmarried Enid Bartholomew was Anna's cousin? If it hadn't been for the unusual last name, Delilah would have never put the pieces together.

She held the papers up. "Once I saw the family connection, the rest began to make sense. You own properties. One happened to be available. Anna Berger knew that. Her friend and business associate Miriam Cross needed a place to stay. Fast. Anna thought it was the perfect arrangement. You got a trustworthy tenant and Miriam got a safe house."

No reaction. Enid's gaze never left Delilah's face. Her expression remained unreadable.

Delilah continued. "Neither you nor Anna had figured that Miriam could be traced to Willston. And you certainly didn't expect a murder in your home."

"Are you finished?"

"Anna is missing. I visited her Pocono place. Gone, along with all her stuff." Delilah gave Enid a hard stare. "She could be dead. Just like Miriam."

Enid shook her head slowly. "Anna's fine."

"Then where is she?"

"Why do you care, really?"

"I was honest with you. My client-"

"My cousin is a saint, you know. Not the recognized kind, of course, the kind the priests like to talk about. She's a real saint. Practical. In the trenches, not afraid to get her hands dirty."

Delilah nodded. "Do you know what she and Miriam were doing?"

Enid's face pinched. "Saving lives."

"Whose lives?"

"Women. Children."

"Whom were they saving them from?"

Enid looked away. "I don't really know. Anna kept most of it from me. To protect me, she said. But I told you before. There's always a beater."

Indeed. "Can you tell me where Anna is?"

"No."

"Miriam's niece is missing. The same people who killed Miriam have Lucinda."

"If my cousin dies, their entire project will be in jeopardy."

"Project?"

"I don't know the details, but I do know that this is bigger than Miriam Cross. It's bigger than you, or Miriam's niece. Anna's work is important. Telling you is tantamount to leading the killers to her door."

Delilah shook her head. "What if I told you that Miriam was working on an exposé before she died. Something that would blow some scandal wide open, maybe something related to Anna's work."

Enid cocked her head. "So?"

"So no one will follow me. I can guarantee it. But in order to finish what Miriam started, in order to expose the truth, whatever that truth is, her killer must be brought to justice."

Enid walked over to a window. She peeked outside through white blinds and then turned back to Delilah.

"You can't trust the police in Willston. Someone on the force is dirty."

"I know."

After a long pause, Enid said, "Anna is staying at the Convent of Saint Mary. In Baltimore."

"Thank you."

"It's in a rough section of town."

"I'll be careful."

"My cousin is . . . different. Don't expect her to cooperate."

Delilah nodded. "Will you tell her to expect me?"

Enid smiled. The action softened her features and took ten years off her face - more effective than any plastic surgery. "I can't call her, Delilah. The convent is for contemplative nuns. They don't speak to the outside world." Enid shrugged. "I told you where she is. How to get in is your problem."

#

Back in her car, Delilah had two calls to make. One to Margot. If anyone could get her into Saint Mary's, it was the former nun. The second call was to Big Joe. Delilah knew when she needed help. She'd promised Enid that no one would follow her to Anna Berger's hideout. There was one way to assure that wouldn't happen. Delilah would simply hire her own tail.

TWENTY-EIGHT

Enid had told the truth about one thing: the Convent of Saint Mary was in a poor section of Baltimore. The convent rose from its dilapidated surroundings like a Gothic phoenix. The building itself was a hulking stone structure, more sixteenth-century castle than modern-day urban. Stone spires reached toward a hazy sky. A stone wall surrounded the enclave, its ten-foot tall façade badly in need of repair. Around the religious community, rundown buildings in countless states of rot stood as testament to the poverty in this section of town. Delilah pulled her purse close, glad for the pistol strapped to her ankle.

She rang the buzzer on the front gate and looked up into the security camera, giving the staff on the other side a full view of her face. After what seemed liked hours, Delilah heard a buzz followed by a series of clicks. With a final look around, she pushed against the wrought iron gate that led inside the convent's courtyard.

There, the barren wasteland of the Baltimore slums gave way to a garden oasis. Flower gardens, colorful and fragrant with peonies, irises and narcissus, dotted the courtyard. Raised vegetable beds of intricate shapes and designs bordered a broad stone patio. Three nuns, all in full habits, were kneeling in the gardens - weeding or mulching. It was an idyllic scene that resonated with a note of melancholy for Delilah. Whether because of the absolute poverty outside these walls or because before her was proof that poverty and despair did not always go hand-in-hand, she couldn't say.

Before Delilah had time to consider this further, a young woman in a white habit emerged from the shadows of a long, covered porch. She nodded for Delilah to follow.

Margot had warned Delilah about the expectations placed upon an outsider going to a contemplative convent: no entering a sister's cell, no speaking outside of the visiting room, no immodest clothing. Margot had made a few calls to former acquaintances. It took her much of the morning, but she finally secured a visit to Saint Mary's. No one would confirm that Anna Berger lived there. Delilah was visiting on faith.

The young novice led Delilah through the courtyard and into a dank waiting room-like area. Wooden chairs sat on either side of a half-wall partition. One side was marked for visitors, the other side for nuns. The room had walls of bare stucco and cold cement floors. A single, large wooden cross hung on the rear wall. The only thing that differentiated the two sides was the presence of a water cooler in the visitors' portion. Otherwise, both areas were equally austere.

Wafting from somewhere beyond, the welcome scents of garlic and roasting meat perfumed the air. Delilah's stomach rumbled. She hadn't eaten all day.

Too anxious to sit, Delilah watched as the novice disappeared through an archway. A few minutes later, a slim nun in full habit, including a wimple and veil, walked purposefully into the room. A thick wooden cross hung from around her neck. The woman looked to be in her mid-forties and she spoke with the quiet air of someone used to being obeyed.

"I'm the abbess," she said softly. "What's your business with Sister Anna?"

"I'd like to speak with her."

"It's highly unorthodox."

Delilah remained silent. She knew it was unorthodox. She also knew that if the sisters had let her come this far, they wouldn't turn her away now.

"Remove the weapon from your ankle." The abbess smiled at Delilah's surprise. "Just because I live a cloistered life now, doesn't mean I don't understand the real world. The fabric of your pants folds differently near one ankle."

"Impressive." Delilah reminded herself that Anna Berger came to this convent for a reason. Regardless of their vocation, it took guts to live in this neighborhood. She shouldn't underestimate the sisters.

"Now give me the gun. I'll lock it in my office safe until you're ready to leave."

What choice did she have if she wanted to see Anna Berger? Delilah handed the abbess the weapon.

"This way."

Delilah followed the abbess through the same archway the novice had used earlier. Once through, the two women walked silently down a long, narrow hallway, its plastered walls yellowed with age and bare of any adornment other than another oversized crucifix and a picture of the Blessed Virgin.

At the end of the hallway stood a once-stately staircase leading upstairs. The abbess didn't go up the steps. Instead, she pulled a ring of keys from the pocket of her habit. She singled out a large iron key, the type Delilah had seen in Disney's Cinderella, and unlocked a small wooden door hidden behind the staircase.

"Follow me closely," the abbess said. "The steps are steep and the light is poor."

Delilah again obeyed. She felt along the wall for a railing. There was none. She used the wall to guide her down the steps, listening closely to the sounds of the nun breathing and the *swoosh-swoosh* of the woman's habit against the wooden stairs. The plaster was smooth and cool to the touch.

Two doorways stood at the bottom of the steps. A soft glow of artificial light outlined one door. The other remained black.

"The cellar," the abbess whispered, nodding toward the darkened doorway. "It's quite dark down here right now. Until we get an electrician out to fix the lighting fixture, the sisters are forbidden to come down these steps. For their own safety."

Delilah had to wonder. Their safety . . . or was that a convenient excuse to keep the other nuns away from Anna Berger?

The abbess tapped lightly on the second door. A minute later, someone opened it a crack. Delilah saw a tiny shadow fall across the opening. She heard hushed whispers in a language she didn't understand. The abbess stepped back.

"I'll come back down in forty-five minutes. Be ready."

Delilah thanked her. The abbess gave her a long, penetrating look before nodding and heading back up the stairs. Delilah started to move forward, through the lit doorway, and stopped. It wasn't a nun who was looking at her from across the threshold. Instead, the woman who peered back through the crack was small and dark and Asian.

Delilah recognized her.

Her passport had been in Miriam's box.

#

From what Barb could tell, Jay Patel lived a pretty mundane life. At exactly 7:47, he left his Bucks County home and drove to the Newark train station. There, he boarded the 8:21 train to Penn Station in New York City.

On the train, Patel continued his dull routine. He read the *Wall Street Journal*, was unerringly polite to the conductor, sipped from a metal thermos and blew his nose quietly into a white cloth handkerchief. All in all, Snooze-ville.

Still, what did she expect? That he would pull a .38 out in the middle of the aisle and threaten the other passengers? That he would make a confession to his seat-mate? Barb hadn't won the award for most patient teacher three years in a row for nothing. And those kids had been hoodlums. No, eventually Patel would make a mistake. And Barb would grab him by the hairy Benjamins.

At Penn Station, Patel got in the line to grab a cab. That presented a dilemma for Barb. She couldn't just get in the queue behind him and wait for the next taxi. And she was pretty sure that telling the driver to "follow that car!" wouldn't work in real life.

She decided to circumvent convention. Barb was athletic. She'd worn a pants suit to blend with the morning commuters, but despite the fancy clothes, she could move. And everyone knew New York traffic and gridlock were synonymous. A person could run faster than they could drive.

She scanned the early morning crowd, finally settling on her prey. A scruffy teenager in army fatigues and a ripped t-shirt, maybe a college student, maybe homeless - they looked about the same to Barb - with an old three speed Schwinn with a basket. Barb jogged over to him and offered $25 for the bike. He looked at her like she was mental. She upped it to $50. He started to walk away.

The thing wasn't worth more than $10 in scrap metal, but a look in Patel's direction showed her that he was next in line for a cab. Barb offered $104, all the cash she had on her. The kid looked down at the bike as though deciding whether he could part with an old friend. Finally he shrugged, shoved the bike toward her and pocketed the money.

"Have a good day," Barb called to his back.

She climbed aboard just as Patel's cab took off.

Keeping up with the cab would have been a hell of a lot easier if she didn't have to dodge reckless drivers and weave through foot traffic. By the time Patel got out of his cab, Barb looked and felt like she'd been wrestling alligators. And she had a hole in her good pants the size of Massachusetts.

Patel went inside a building. Barb tucked the bike in an alley, behind a dumpster. The stench would act as a theft deterrent. Then she tried to figure out where she was.

Madison Avenue. Domino's headquarters.

Barb waited ten minutes, watching the building's front entrance to make sure Patel didn't come right back out again. She went inside the ground floor to make sure there were no additional exits. Only then did she head outside to scan the street for a spot to sit. The Starbucks across the street. A few outdoor tables had been crammed along the sidewalk. She rejected the outdoor tables and chose, instead, the counter at the window.

Perfect. The glass was tinted enough to make seeing inside difficult, but she had a clear view of Domino's building and its surroundings.

Barb needed to pee. Number one surveillance rule: no allowance for bodily functions. Men had the definite advantage there. In long car tails, they could pee in a bottle. A little harder for women. Barb carried a camping funnel in her car – for those special moments when she just couldn't wait. It'd be tough to whip that out now.

So she held it.

And she waited.

She watched Domino's building. Nothing. She suspected Patel would be in there at least until lunch. That was three hours from now. She continued to watch and wait.

At 10:14, she couldn't stand the pressure. She needed to pee before she wet herself. She stood, leaving her newspaper at her spot, and ran to the ladies room six feet away. With three daughters and one main bathroom, Barb had mastered the quick pee. She did that now, washed her hands in record speed, and started to jog back to her place.

And that's when she saw him.

He was nearly a block away, standing in the shadows of another office building. Barb would have missed him from her vantage spot at the counter. And even standing at this angle, she wouldn't have noticed him in the hustle and bustle if it hadn't been for the itch on his head, which forced him to remove his baseball cap.

What had Delilah called him? Mr. Clean.

Had he spotted her watching Patel? Unlikely. He wasn't looking toward Starbucks, nor was his gaze on Domino, exactly. He seemed to be looking at something in the distance. She followed the direction of his stare. And that's when Barb got her second surprise.

Anders. Walking toward Domino. She moved forward to get a better look. Anders seemed focused, unaware that he was being followed. He stepped through the revolving door into Domino's building and disappeared.

Barb looked up and down the street. Mr. Clean had stayed in his spot, but his gaze hadn't followed Anders inside. Instead, he seemed focused on a point across the street from Domino. Barb walked the width of the Starbucks, alongside the window, trying to get a look at whatever Mr. Clean seemed to be watching.

At first all she could see were the normal hodgepodge of people that made up New York crowds. And then she saw a familiar body. Clothed in black yoga pants, a black tank top and a logo-less black baseball cap. Barb recognized the sculpted biceps, the straight brown ponytail sticking out of the cap, the nose ring. Natasha.

Mr. Clean was tailing Natasha?

Why the hell was Natasha here? Unless she was watching Anders?

And what was Anders doing at Domino?

Barb's gaze waffled between Mr. Clean, Domino and Natasha.

She had no idea what was going on. But she was pretty sure she was no longer in Snooze-ville.

TWENTY-NINE

Delilah stood in the doorway of the convent's dank basement waiting for the woman in front of her to let her in. The woman looked terrified. Delilah wished she could remember her name. The woman finally stepped aside so that Delilah could enter.

The room felt cramped and barren - exposed stone walls, a low beamed ceiling and an unfinished floor. It smelled faintly of moth balls. A wooden door stood sentinel at the rear of the room.

Behind the woman stood three more women. One, of Asian origin, hands encased in bandages, was small and pretty, with hair so short her head must've been recently shaved. The second woman had deep black skin, prominent features and slender, long limbs. An orange and teal dress hung off her angular frame like a sack, the colors clashing with the fuchsia scarf wrapped around her head.

The third woman had to be, by default, Sister Anna Berger. Her youth surprised Delilah. She could not be much more than thirty-five. Medium height, thin, with long, wavy brown hair pulled into a tidy ponytail. She wore white pants and a white t-shirt, tucked neatly in and cinched with a brown leather belt. A wooden cross hung prominently around her neck. She had a patrician nose and sharp cheekbones, like Enid. But the fierceness in her eyes is what struck Delilah - an intensity at once intimidating and mesmerizing. Delilah had no doubt that those eyes saw the world through a lens that was, to say the least, unusual.

"Sister Anna Berger?"

Anna said, "Shut the door."

Delilah closed the door softly. When she turned back, Anna was gone. The woman who had greeted her stood in front of her, hands on her hips, head tilted to the side.

Finally remembering her name from the passport, Delilah said, "Cinta. Cinta Wahid."

Cinta nodded, sad resignation reflected in her eyes. "Come."

Delilah followed Cinta through the rear doorway and into an underground labyrinth. First they walked through what must have been an old coal cellar. The cement floor was stained black in places, one bare bulb hung from a corner. But the room, though bleak, was immaculate, the floor swept and the walls free of cobwebs. The coal cellar led to another small room, which held a large sink basin, a washer and dryer and a plain card table. Neat piles of white linens sat stacked on the table. Like the other room, it had a cement floor, exposed beams and bare stone walls. The scent of lavender filled the air.

Cinta stopped. "Sister Anna is good," she said. "Please do not hurt her."

"I'm not here to hurt anybody, Cinta."

"Then how you know my name? Are you not United States government?"

Delilah smiled. "No, I'm not with the government. I am a friend to you and Sister Anna."

Cinta met her gaze for a moment and then quickly lowered her head. The gesture reminded Delilah of a dog that had been rescued but the cruelty of its prior owners was always in the background, a constant invisible threat. Delilah tried to give Cinta a reassuring smile, but it felt forced and insincere. Who was she kidding? She didn't have the answers, and she could no more keep these women safe than guarantee her own safety.

But she would try her damnedest.

"Cinta?" Sister Anna opened the door that led from the laundry room into whatever lurked beyond. She beckoned for Cinta and Delilah to follow.

Inside, Delilah looked around. An entire apartment existed underneath the convent. The front room was a living room – dining room combination. Two small, simple green couches and a brown armchair were clustered on one side. A long, narrow table, its wood gouged and scarred in places – probably all they could get through the basement labyrinth – stood on the other. A picture of the Virgin Mary hung on one wall. On another, a large wooden Crucifix, Jesus's face twisted in torment. The walls had been painted arctic white, the floors covered in old pine. Through an archway, Delilah could make out a small galley kitchen.

Anna said, "It's quite something, isn't it? The Diocese built this apartment years ago as a safe house. It hadn't been occupied in years. Abbess graciously agreed to let us stay here." She glanced around the room before looking back at Delilah, her expression cool. She said, "And now we need to leave."

"Not because of me, I hope. I'm no threat to whatever you're doing here."

"Your very presence is a threat. People are looking for me. If they find you, now they can find us. I can't very well put the convent in jeopardy."

"I wasn't followed. I took steps to make sure that wouldn't happen."

"Still. As I'm sure you can understand, we can't afford to trust you. Or anyone, for that matter."

Delilah said nothing, weighing her next words carefully. She understood that these women were in some kind of danger. Certainly, whatever was going on had been enough to get at least three people killed. But why would someone want to hunt down three itinerant foreign workers? Unless they had seen something they weren't supposed to. Or had information. Information that was valuable in the wrong hands.

Delilah said. "I'd like to talk about Miriam Cross."

Anna looked at Cinta who nodded every-so-slightly. Finally, Anna said, "Fine. Please sit."

Anna sat on the armchair, her spine rigid as a barn pole. Cinta disappeared into the kitchen. Delilah sank into the old cushions on the couch, facing Anna.

"Did Abbess explain why I'm here?"

"She said that your contact was persistent and would become a nuisance to the nuns if I didn't see you."

Delilah smiled. "That would be Margot, my employee. We're investigating Miriam's murder."

Anna's face remained impassive.

"Did you know Miriam had been murdered?"

"Of course."

"Can you tell me, Sister, who may have wanted her dead?"

"I have no idea."

"You're certain of that?"

Anna smiled. "Miriam and I rarely spoke. I had no idea with whom she acquainted herself. We were not exactly of the same mindset when it came to most things."

"But you worked together."

"In a manner of speaking."

This was getting nowhere. "Look, Miriam's niece, my employer, is missing. She's been kidnapped, probably by the same people who killed Miriam. I need help if I have any hope of saving her life."

"You're probably too late."

"You said you don't know who the killers are."

"It's pure logic. Miriam met an ugly death. If the same people have kidnapped her niece, then she is probably dead, too – or will be soon."

Delilah sat back, surprised at the coldness in the woman's voice.

"You look shocked, Delilah," Anna said.

"I expected more ... compassion. You are a nun."

Anna smiled. "Technically, I'm not a nun. I'm a sister. There's a difference. Unlike my brethren upstairs" - she motioned toward the ceiling – "I exist in the real world, not closed up and protected behind walls. That has made me a pragmatist. Not without compassion, simply realistic about human frailty."

Anna stood. Delilah watched her walk to a bookshelf lined with magazines, Bibles and religious texts. She pulled a worn copy of *National Geographic* and skimmed its pages until she came to an article. She handed the open magazine to Delilah.

A piece on child soldiers in Sierra Leone. Pictures of hardened-looking kids, some as young as eight or nine, stared back from the pages, their eyes soul-less pits.

Anna spoke with her back to Delilah. "I was there, working with former child soldiers in a camp run by Unicef. Do you know what happens when a fourteen-year-old is forced to rape? He internalizes the hate. It becomes a sort of horrid self-loathing. A difficult thing to dislodge, with God's love or otherwise." She turned to face Delilah. "I've worked at a medical camp for women in Afghanistan. I've seen first hand the torture inflicted on people - women and children, most especially – who have no rights. No voice."

Anna sat back down. "I don't have to tell you the statistics. If I mention things like female circumcision or public stonings, your mind will immediately picture Muslim women. If I mention forced abortions, you will think of China. If I mention domestic violence, you will picture a poor white woman living in a trailer park in Tennessee."

"I don't understand what this has to do with Miriam."

"Exactly. These horrible images, these terrible acts, are real. They are happening now, as we speak. Why? Because we, the so-called normal people, don't stop them. And why don't we stop them? It's not because we don't care. If I ask anyone on the street if they care about a woman in Iran who will be stoned to death for something as ridiculous as sleeping with a man, they will look at me with horror on their faces and say 'Yes, of course I care.'

"But that doesn't solve anything. That woman will still be stoned. A twelve-old-soldier in Sierra Leone will still be made to rape and murder a nine-year-old girl. Those beautiful lives will be lost, including that of the twelve-year-old boy. For when he does that act, his soul will whither."

"Sister Anna-"

"Miriam Cross was not a believer. She and I had only one thing in common: a fierce need to *act*. And that is what we did."

"So you set up the shelter in Hawley?"

Anna smiled. "You did your research."

"I visited the shelter. It looked abandoned."

"It's one of nine shelters we have set up across the United States and Canada."

"But you left that one. You must have gotten word that something went wrong."

"I knew Miriam had been killed."

"Who told you?"

"I can't tell you that."

"Who arranged to send you the women?"

"Miriam. Other shelters have other conduits."

Delilah considered this. "Who are these women? The ones with you now. I assume they're the ones who had been living in Hawley?"

Just then, Cinta came back through the doorway from the kitchen. "It is time for Mary's hands to be re-bandaged."

Anna nodded slowly. She rose. "Come with me."

Delilah glanced at her watch. Less than fifteen minutes left. She was no closer to the truth than she had been an hour ago. But she felt compelled to witness, her hunch that this was bigger than Miriam sadly confirmed.

She followed Anna into a back bedroom. Cinta stood next to a simple bed covered with a white sheet and a brown blanket. On the bed, the other Asian woman sat, her bandaged hands situated on a white towel. A basin of brownish water sat next to her hands. A small yellow sponge floated in the liquid. Delilah assumed it was iodine water, used to disinfect. A pile of clean bandages and a tube of antibiotic ointment sat next to the basin, wrapped neatly in a plastic baggy.

"This is Mary."

Delilah nodded her hello.

"Be brave," Anna said. Mary closed her eyes, her mouth set in a determined line.

Anna knelt on the floor. She unrolled the old bandaging, talking while she worked. "Have you heard of human trafficking, Delilah?"

"Of course." Delilah said. "Many trafficked women end up as prostitutes. Especially abroad."

Anna nodded. "Yes, young girls, too. Sometimes only nine or ten. Many never know anything but sexual slavery, living out short, horrific lives." She shook her head. "But not all are forced into the sex trade. Some, like Mary here, are sold in so-called civilized countries like the United States as house slaves. It's like indentured servitude. They must pay back their asking price, but they are given so little salary – if any - that it may take a lifetime to win their freedom."

Anna continued unrolling bandages, her fingers moving deftly, as though from a memory of their own. "Mary - the name given to her, she doesn't recall her real name - began work in her native India at age seven." She met Delilah's gaze. "While in some countries child labor is closely regulated, in other countries children may work in certain industries not considered hazardous. Domestic work is on the permitted list."

Anna opened the last of the bandaging on Mary's right hand. Beneath, the skin looked raw and blistered. Mary bit her lip while Anna gently moved the wet sponge over the area. Delilah could see echoes of beauty in Mary's eyes, the slender curve of her neck. But time had been cruel. Lines etched themselves around her dark eyes and mouth. Gray hair was woven throughout the short tresses on her scalp. Delilah could not tell if she was twenty or fifty.

"There, there," Anna murmured. "It's okay." She quickly covered the hand with antibiotic ointment, her fingers flying over the tortured skin with butterfly caresses.

Cinta handed her clean bandage and the women worked together to cover the damaged hand. Then they moved to the left one.

"How did Mary end up in the States?"

"We're still not sure. That's what Miriam was working on. We know that people, mostly women, have been trafficked into the States, Great Britain, Canada and other Western countries for years. But recently, the trend has increased. Some of the domestic laborers begin in other countries and then are sold through agencies, ending up here in the end. Others are lured by the false promise of well-paying jobs."

Delilah thought of the picture of a child, stored under a mattress in the shelter in Hawley. She thought of Tula's maid, Maria, and the sacrifices she had made. "And many are desperate, in need of money to send home."

Anna nodded. "Yes. Like Cinta, here. She has two daughters and a husband imprisoned for life. She signed with an agency, was promised enough money to get her children out of squalor. The agency was a set-up. Cinta was systematically raped and beaten to break her spirit, and then she was taken to New York City and sold to a Sri Lankan doctor. He used her as both domestic help and his personal whore." Sister Anna glanced at Cinta apologetically. "Chained to her bed for days on end. She never saw a cent."

Delilah watched Cinta, whose eyes remained on Mary's injured hand. Delilah remembered the blood in the bathroom at the shelter.

"Cinta was pregnant."

This time it was Anna who looked surprised. "She had a miscarriage. The stress of having to run again."

"I saw the blood . . . at the house in Hawley."

"Yes. We had to call in a favor from a local doctor. But, thanks be to God, Cinta was fine."

"I have her passport."

Another surprised look. "It's safe, then. It's proof. Some of these women are smuggled in illegally. They live like shadows, with no real legal existence. Cinta was brought in legally, under false pretenses. Miriam must have obtained her paperwork."

"I have another passport, too."

"Put them in a safe deposit box. Leave word with the abbess somehow. We will be able to use their passports eventually . . . when the time is right."

Both of Mary's hands were re-bandaged now, the whiteness of the gauze like a surrender flag.

"What happened?" Delilah said, nodding toward Mary's hands.

"She disobeyed her employers. They caught her stealing meat meant for their Rottweiler." Anna stood. With a matter-of-fact shrug, she said, "To punish her, they dipped her hands in diluted acid. Then they let the wounds fester, beating her for not doing her chores because of pain and infection."

Delilah felt a stinging, creeping anger. She was not naïve to the cruelty of the world. But how people could treat other humans this way . . . she thought she understood Miriam's need to act. And Anna Berger's stoic realism.

Delilah said, "Have you heard of Domino Venture Partners?"

Anna shook her head.

"Jay Patel? Jack Cashman?"

Another head shake. "Should I?"

"I don't know." Delilah thought for a moment. "Obviously someone wanted Miriam's activities to stop."

"That's clear enough. But I'm afraid Miriam and I shared little information. I didn't tell her where I hid the women after she delivered them to my intermediary; she didn't tell me who was behind the trafficking. This way, if either of us - or any of the others, for that matter – was caught, there would be less of a trail."

"Then there are others?"

"Yes. As I'm sure you figured out by now, Miriam and I were not alone. But no one person knows all of the members."

"Members? You mean of Women NOW."

Anna nodded. "Miriam's exposé was to be the lynchpin to bringing down this particular trafficking ring." Anna sighed. "There are other rings. Too many for one organization to battle. But the only way to combat traffickers is to fight one at a time."

"Miriam could name names?"

"Miriam had a lot of information about who was involved. She didn't tell me, of course, but there were officials and local police, I'm sure. That's how the traffickers get away with it."

Delilah said, "Bribery?"

"Sometimes. It depends on what motivates them. Sometimes the traffickers offer sex with teenagers or maybe a domestic slave of their own." She ran a hand over her hair. "The traffickers are students of human nature. They know how to break people down, they know what tempts them. Satan works through them. That much is clear."

"And all of this information, is it lost now that Miriam is dead?"

Anna seemed to ponder the question. "The work itself will continue. The exposé, however? Only Miriam had the details on this particular ring, I'm afraid."

"If my firm can figure out what happened to Miriam, perhaps we can finish that work, turn it over to the Feds."

Anna flashed her a bitter smile. "If you can do that, Delilah, it would be wonderful. But we won't count on it."

Delilah thought for a moment. She needed to glean any information she could from Anna Berger before her audience was up. "Does the Church know, Sister? Would Church officials have information?"

Anna shook her head. "Doubtful."

"Do they know you're involved in this?"

Anna simply stared back at her, another half-smile gracing her face.

Delilah said, "You look amused."

"There are rules in the Catholic Church. But once you understand the rules, you also understand the holes. This, I'm afraid, is one of those instances."

Delilah pondered this. "If you have to do something you're passionate about, something like this, with a wink and a nod, why be a member of the Church? Why not do it out there" – she motioned toward the outside world – "without the need to be so . . . careful?"

This time Anna laughed. She stood, pushing non-existent creases from her perfectly-ironed pants. "Miriam had fame and fortune. She used the money, the connections she'd made because of her fame, to do this. But let's be clear. Miriam felt passionate about writing, about such intangible concepts as justice and women's rights."

"And you?"

"My passion is for God. The Church, well . . . let's just say that God has given me connections, too."

Delilah nodded, understanding. Anna's focus was clearly on the welfare of these women, which would explain Anna's lack of knowledge about the big picture.

She left that to Miriam. Another thought occurred to her . . . the truth serum in Miriam's system when she died. A desperate attempt to get information from Miriam before they killed her? Delilah thought about the way Miriam had died. She thought of Anders' friend Ahmed and the late Juan DeMarco. She thought of the simplicity of drowning, the messiness of a beheading. Something still didn't add up.

Moments later, Cinta walked Delilah back through the maze of underground rooms to the basement entry. The abbess's soft steps could be heard on the wooden stairs. Taking advantage of the last vestiges of electric light, Delilah reached into her bag. She pulled out an envelope that contained the picture of the little girl she'd found at the Pocono house.

"Yours?" Delilah said to Cinta.

Cinta grabbed the picture and clutched it to her chest.

All the answer Delilah needed.

THIRTY

Natasha watched Anders slip into the Domino building. *Prick*. When she'd agreed to follow Anders, she thought it'd be cake. A few hours in a car outside the Percy Powers office, maybe a stop at his gym or the local book store. But not a trip up the fucking New Jersey turnpike. And what was he doing here anyway? Natasha only had twenty bucks and a nearly-tapped VISA on her. She couldn't follow him all over the damned East Coast.

Natasha leaned against a stop light post and adjusted her baseball cap. She was trying to decide whether to follow Anders up to Domino – she'd found the address on her phone – or wait here. She wanted like hell to confront him, but she didn't feel like hearing Delilah bitch at her again for breaking the rules. She decided to stay put and wait.

And that's when she felt her phone vibrate. Afraid it was Sam's school, she sneaked a peak. A text from Barb: *Mr. Clean at four o'clock.*

What the hell? What was Barb doing here? She texted back: *Where r u?*

Natasha read the reply. Starbucks. Barb was tailing Patel. So it made sense that Patel and Anders were in the same place – if Anders, as she was beginning to suspect, was crooked in all of this. But she was pissed as hell that she hadn't realized that someone was following her.

So what to do? Barb had her back for now. But her instructions were to follow Anders and Barb needed to stay with Patel.

If Anders left Domino and Barb and Natasha separated, there was the chance that Mr. Clean would attack her. After the Philly encounter, Natasha carried three knives. A switchblade taped to her calf for emergencies, a pocket knife in her bag, small but handy, and a five-inch in her back pocket.

She was a big girl. She could handle Mr. Clean. Especially now that she knew he was there.

Natasha texted Delilah. In shorthand, she told Delilah about Anders' trip to the Domino building. When she got no reply, she put the phone away and stared at her target.

Sure enough, six minutes later, Anders emerged from the Domino building. Everything about his body posture – his gait, his stare, the fists he held by his side – screamed anger. But Natasha didn't have time to think about what might have happened in there. She had to head back to the parking garage without Anders noticing.

Natasha followed Anders for a distance. The man was tall and fast and she had to trot to keep pace with him. She was keenly aware of Mr. Clean behind her, though she couldn't see him. But one glance at her phone and a text from Barb and she knew he'd left when she did.

Barb seemed to think Mr. Clean was following her, not Anders. Natasha wasn't so sure.

The parking garage was dank and poorly lit. Natasha took the stairs a few flights behind Anders, keeping her steps light and soft from years of yoga and martial arts training and, before that, the habit of tip-toeing around her explosive father. Once on the third floor, Natasha watched Anders climb into his Toyota. Then she hurried to her car, heart racing. She slipped behind the wheel and started the engine. Following him out of the city would be as much of a challenge as following him into the city had been.

Natasha was shifting into reverse when she felt the hairs on the back of her neck prick up. *Don't be paranoid, stupid.* She hit the gas. Her car wouldn't move. *Fuck.* She tried again. Still wouldn't budge. Something was blocking her.

Natasha hadn't seen anything near the car when she got in, but she hadn't really looked either. She'd been so focused on watching Anders.

Reluctantly, Natasha unbuckled her seat belt. She rolled up her pant leg and un-strapped the switch blade. She held the knife against the palm of her hand and climbed out of the car, her heart pounding. The garage was silent. Every noise echoed. She looked at the back of the car. Nothing on the driver's side, at least from that angle. She made her way quickly to the other side. A big yellow parking boot was attached to her back right tire.

She didn't have any parking tickets. At least not in New York.

Which meant the police didn't do this.
Which meant-

She didn't have time to finish the thought. She felt the metal against her temple just as a knee hit the small of her back, slamming her into the car.

"Don't move," a voice said into her ear.

"And *that's* not cliché," Natasha muttered.

The guy's face loomed over her. She felt his hot breath on her cheek.

"Shut up."

"Another killer line."

The guy grabbed Natasha's ponytail, the gun still at her temple. He yanked, hard, bringing tears to her eyes. He shoved something into her hands.

"Get down on your hands and knees."

Natasha glanced down at the thing in her hand. A key to the boot. This guy was going to kidnap her in her own car. She considered screaming. She thought of Sam. With her gone, Sam's only living relative would be Jake. Or her asshole father, which was even worse. *No fucking way.* Natasha would obey.

For now.

#

Delilah arrived back at the office of Percy Powers LLC three hours later. The door was locked, the place empty. She threw her bag on the front reception desk and jogged to the safe in her office. She unlocked the safe and carefully pulled out the bag that held Miriam's belongings. She sorted through until she came to the CD of Miriam's threesome.

She watched it again.

And again.

She wasn't even sure what she was looking for. Some clue, some tidbit that she'd missed before. But she only witnessed the same raw, brutal sexuality she now associated with Jack Cashman. And the same gentle lovemaking with the man she assumed was with Jay Patel.

If orgy sex could be called making love.
Maybe that was it.
Delilah stuffed the CD back in the safe. She turned the dial to trigger the lock. Then she grabbed her bag again. She headed for her car.

#

Barb's heart pounded into her throat. She'd just watched Anders leave the Domino building and Natasha head out after him. And then, from her spot in Starbucks, she caught Mr. Clean following Natasha. Natasha could handle herself. That wasn't what had Barb worried.

But a second guy following Natasha *did* worry Barb.

He came out of the shadows like a cockroach, slinking along the sidewalk, doing his best to blend into the crowd. There was nothing special about his appearance: stocky, dark-haired, wearing jeans and a gray t-shirt. But with her opera glasses, Barb could make out the bulge in his pants.

And it wasn't the good kind.

Dang. The bastard had a gun. Barb wasn't armed. Natasha surely was. If only Barb could tell her that Mr. Clean wasn't the only one out there. She shot Natasha a text, warning her, and hoped like heck that Natasha checked her phone. Then Barb slung her bag over her shoulder and jogged out to the alley way to retrieve her bike. She said a silent thanks to God when she saw it, still propped behind the dumpster.

She hopped on the bike, ignoring the stink of garbage. Circumstance required speed over caution. A disheveled man holding a sign that said "The end is near! Repent!" blocked her path on the first intersection. She yelled for him to get out of the way. He wouldn't move and for a heart-stopping moment, Barb lost sight of the newest stalker. Then she saw him again, walking quickly down the street, hugging the inner edge of the sidewalk.

He glanced surreptitiously to his left, then his right, before ducking into a parking garage.

Barb pedaled faster. There was nowhere to hide her bike, so she tossed it inside the heavy door that led to the garage's internal stairway and hoped for the best. She took off on foot after the new guy.

The parking garage was dimly lit and smelled faintly of gasoline and car exhaust. She couldn't see the man, but if she employed the same listening technique she employed when eavesdropping on her daughters, she could hear the quiet *flop* when his sneakers hit the concrete. His footsteps stopped on the fourth floor.

Afraid to give herself away, Barb stayed still. She listened for the sound of voices, a gunshot, anything that would tell her what was happening.

For a few minutes, the garage stayed chillingly silent. From somewhere below, Barb heard a car start. The sound gradually faded, until the driver pulled out of the parking garage. Barb let out a breath. Then she heard another engine start, closer by. This one revved, then stopped, revved, then stopped. *Odd.*

Barb moved forward with each revving, using the obnoxious sound to mask her own noise. After the fourth rev, the engine turned off. Silence again. Then some sort of scuffle.

Barb ducked and ran toward the sound. She turned the corner, her solid body curled tightly against the parked vehicles, and caught a glimpse of Mr. Clean standing in the shadows. Surely he saw her, but his blank expression gave nothing away. She froze, surprised. Then she followed his gaze to Natasha's red Toyota.

And the man who stood next to it, holding a gun to Natasha's temple.

Okay, you're out of your element now, Mama. Barb forced her breathing to slow down. *Get yourself together.* She'd been a security guard. Heck, she'd been a gym teacher with inner city kids. This was nothing compared to that. *Think*.

Problem was, she didn't know what Mr. Clean was doing there. Was he a partner to the thug holding Natasha? Were two parties involved in this mess? And where was Anders? Barb would have given her washer and her dryer for a gun right about now.

Darn, she'd settle for a wrench or a screwdriver. Something she could throw at the man.

Throw! Yes, that was it. She needed to distract him.

Barb still had the element of surprise on her side. She snuck a quick glance at Mr. Clean. He still hadn't moved. She dashed across the aisle so that she was diagonal from Natasha and the thug. She crouched down next to a Chevy Tahoe, using the vehicle for cover. Quietly, she opened her suit jacket and tugged off her belt, hoping the metal buckle would do the trick.

Barb watched Natasha take the boot off the car wheel, the gun still pointed at her head. When Natasha stood, the thug grabbed her hair and pulled Natasha's head back. He shoved her toward the driver's seat and whispered something in her ear.

Natasha reached for the car door.

Never get into the car with a stranger. How many times had Barb told her daughters that? It's better to be injured fighting off an attacker than to get into that car with him. And the stats proved that to be the case. Once you were in the car, you were at his mercy.

Natasha opened the door and squatted to get into the sedan. *Now.*

And it all happened at once. Barb flung the belt across the aisle with all the strength she could muster. The metal buckle landed on a windshield, cracking glass. The thug looked back. In a flash, Natasha had a knife out. She buried it in his right arm. The gun fell to the floor. Barb ran from her hiding spot and picked up the gun. She pointed it at the man.

He snarled.

"Finally," Nastasha said to Barb.

"Nice to see you, too."

"What do we do with him?" Natasha gestured toward the thug.

Barb considered this. "Get the knife out of his arm. Evidence."

Natasha nodded. She pulled the weapon out of the man's arm and watched the blood flow against bare skin, staining cotton and denim. The man snarled again. He took a step toward Natasha. Barb took a step toward him, the gun steady and pointed right for his temple.

Barb said, "Don't think about it."

The man growled.

"Police?" Natasha said.

Barb shook her head. "Feds."

Natasha gave her a look that said she understood. She reached into her jeans for her phone, holding the thug's gaze with a look of pure hatred. Eyeing that knife wound, which still gushed blood, Barb knew she'd never want to be on the other end of Natasha's hate.

"Get the number from Lila," Barb said. Barb glanced discreetly in the direction of Mr. Clean, waiting for him to come to this guy's rescue. But the shadows were just that: empty shadows. He'd disappeared.

As Natasha held the phone to her ear, a car horn blared. The guy took advantage of the split second's distraction and pushed Natasha at Barb. He ran. Barb aimed the gun at his back. A silver Prius wound silently around the corner. The man sprinted behind it. Before Barb had a clear shot, he was out of sight.

"Put down the gun," Natasha hissed.

Barb looked up in time to see an elderly woman staring at her from behind the wheel of the hybrid. Barb

smiled and lowered the weapon. The woman gave a worried smile back.
Only in New York.

THIRTY-ONE

Not much had changed about Miriam's Chestnut Hill house. This time, though, Delilah didn't have the luxury of a key. But breaking in through the back door was a simple matter of wedging a pocket knife between the jam and the door. The old lock gave way instantly.

Once inside, Delilah took a quick look around the downstairs. Everything seemed roughly as she had remembered it. Delilah took the steps to the second floor two at a time. After watching the sex tape for the umpteenth time, she felt a niggling sense of *something* gnawing at her gut. Her mind kept coming back to the three deaths: DeMarco, Ahmed and Miriam. Two similar, one different. *There are no coincidences.*

And there's always a beater.

That damn sex tape. Where did the tryst fit in? Or did it? She thought she knew the answer.

Intuition told her that Cashman was hiding something. Logic told her that Cashman and Patel were the two men in the tape. Clearly, Miriam Cross was involved in more than novel-writing. She had not only been instrumental in Women NOW, but had been on the brink of blowing the whole ring wide open. Was that the reason she was murdered? Simplicity said yes. But Delilah could not rid herself of this feeling that there was more to it. She believed a love triangle – a twisted one, at that – to be at the core of Miriam's murder. But how to prove it?

And, more importantly, how to prove it quickly. Lucinda's life hung in the balance.

Delilah walked through the second floor, peeking into bedrooms as she went. Nothing seemed out of place. She scanned the hallway ceiling for the trap door that led to the attic steps. She found it next to the bathroom entrance. After two hard tugs, the steps floated down. Delilah stood still for a moment, listening closely for sounds that said she'd been followed. Satisfied, she pulled a flashlight from her pocket, clicked it on, and crept up the steps.

The stairs creaked. The small tunnel of light thrown by her flashlight cast shadows against the walls. Like many old houses, this attic was a place of quiet rustling and imagined ghosts. Delilah smelled mothballs and dust and, beneath that, the sweet smell of rot. She picked her way through old furniture and neat stacks of newspapers and a few boxes, their contents littered about like the remnants of a yard sale.

But Delilah knew what she was looking for. She had seen it on her first visit, which felt like months ago but had been only days. At that time, she thought nothing of a box of books. Miriam was, after all, an author. And weren't most authors voracious readers?

But as facts emerged, Delilah's curiosity sharpened. Why were these books in the attic, packed away and hidden when Miriam's house brimmed with shelves of books? At first glance, she'd figured they were simply old and irrelevant. But now she had to wonder.

Of course, there could have been a myriad of reasons why they were tucked up in the attic. The books could have been distinctly *not* special. They could have been earmarked for a book sale or a donation. They could have been forgotten in a previous move.

Or they could relate, somehow, to the events that led up to Miriam's death.

Delilah didn't think the presence of Miriam's box in Lucinda's attic had been an accident, as Lucinda believed. Miriam had been purposeful. She knew she was in trouble and had hidden things, some of them in plain sight.

Delilah pushed aside an over-sized wall mirror. Behind it, on the floor, sat an open box of books, the contents arranged just as Delilah had left them. She knelt down and aimed her flashlight on the pile. Delilah's cell phone buzzed. Somewhere below, a pipe gurgled. Fighting an uneasy sense of dread, Delilah glanced at the phone – just Barb with an update, she could get that later - and started sifting through the books, making a mental inventory, looking for patterns. She flipped through each text, looking for stray sheets of paper or notes that could be a clue.

Rosemary's Baby. Robinson Crusoe. Three Elizabeth George novels. *How to Grow an Herb Garden. Romeo and Juliet*, the unabridged version. A textbook on plot from a class Miriam must have taught. *The Complete Short Works of Anaïs Nin* – interesting given Miriam's erotic poetry, but not particularly telling in and of itself. She put that book aside.

Delilah piled the other books neatly between the box and the mirror. She dug further into the cardboard depths, feeling the sides as she went, hoping beyond hope that some piece of evidence lay inside. She was beginning to feel like a fool. Her employer had been kidnapped, the police were somehow involved, and instead of calling in the Feds like she should be doing, she was crouched in an attic pouring over a pile of discarded books.

Brilliant.

And then she pulled out the last three books. Two children's works: *Thumbelina* and *Charlotte's Web*. And a book called simply, *Tantra*.

It was this last book that Delilah paged through. It looked like a text on the secrets of Tantric sex. Her mind immediately flitted to Chinnamasta. The book was filled with sketches of dark men in robes impaling naked women with their large, erect penises. These were interspersed with erudite text about the various schools of Tantric practice. It was a small book, no more than four by six inches, with tiny script and pictures drawn in a mixture of black and white and muted colors. About mid-way through, a page had been folded down. Delilah shined her flashlight onto the earmarked section, not surprised at what she saw. Chinnamasta, the goddess without a head, stared up at her.

The book described her as the sixth Great Cosmic Power, able to transcend the physical – including the mind – to achieve the ecstatic. The book talked about this from a metaphorical standpoint. Someone – Miriam? – had underlined certain phrases, including discussion of the implications for modern people and the marriage of the masculine and the feminine, the physical and the divine.

Like the pages Margot had pulled off the Web, in this book Chinnamasta was pictured standing over a fornicating couple, her decapitated head in one hand, a sword in the other, two goddesses standing watch on either side. Delilah felt a strange mix of fascination and fear growing as she read through the pages. The similarities to Miriam's death – and the events in the months leading up to her murder – could not be ignored. There was the very cause of Miriam's death – decapitation. The uncharacteristic sexual abandon Miriam displayed in the sex tape. And the erotic poetry and short stories Miriam had written in the months before her death.

Evidence of a sexual awakening?

Miriam must have felt a certain kinship with this goddess. But why and how that came to be – and what it had to do with her murder – remained a mystery.

Delilah hastily placed the other books in back in the box. She tucked *Tantra* into her satchel and, on impulse, grabbed the works of Anaïs Nin as well. This she paged through quickly again, looking for a bookmark. She found none. But toward the front, near where the publisher had placed its watermark, was a man's script. Delilah aimed the dying flashlight on the words.

Come undone. For me. Love Always, J

Who was J? Jack? Jay? Someone else?

Delilah removed *Tantra* from her bag. She flipped to the section on Chinnamasta, her gaze falling on words that she'd read twice before but that only now made sense.

She thought she knew who had killed Miriam Cross.

And she was pretty sure she knew why.

#

Delilah's excitement was quashed when she listened to her voicemail messages. Natasha and Barb had a near miss. And Anders visited Domino. It'd been quite a day and it was only 5:15 in the evening. What next?

Delilah called Barb. She told her to go home and stay there, everyone would meet first thing in the morning. Then she called Natasha and Margot and repeated her request. She knew it was time to call in the Feds – she now had the contact from Big Joe – but she was putting that off as long as possible. She couldn't say why, but she had an awful feeling that if the federal government got involved now, all bets were off. Whatever good Miriam was trying to do would be lost and Lucinda would be in deeper trouble. She promised herself she would call tomorrow. By then, she'd have answers. And if she didn't . . . well, she couldn't afford to wait longer than that.

Delilah finished her drive with a call to Anders. Surprisingly, he picked up right away.

"What the hell do you think you're doing?" she said.

"Good afternoon to you, too, Delilah."

"Barb told me you were at Domino today."

"And now you're spying on *me*?"

Delilah hated to lie, but she offered a silent prayer for forgiveness and said, "Barb was following Patel. She saw you go in after him."

"I wanted answers."

"About?"

Silence. Delilah turned onto her street, waiting out Anders's reluctance to share. Finally he said, "Are you home?"

"Almost."

"Good. I'll meet you there."

#

Natasha's head was pounding. She'd been home for almost an hour, but still she couldn't get rid of the icy feeling of gun metal against skin. It had been a very long time since she'd been manhandled by a guy. Years.

Really manhandled – not like the silliness in Center City or Jake's ridiculous attempts to scare her. Today was a reminder of why she'd worked so hard to leave that life.

She sat at a stool next to the small kitchen counter in her apartment, her legs pulled up under her chin, and watched Sam and Amelia play chess. Sam was winning, although whether his victory would be real or a testament to Amelia's reluctance to let him lose, Natasha wasn't sure. But she *was* sure that this was a scene she'd like to see over and over, year after year.

And she'd risked it all today. Because of those motherfuckers. Whoever the hell they were.

Natasha climbed off the stool and walked over to her son and girlfriend. She put a hand on Amelia's shoulder and was rewarded with a sly grin. She knelt down next to Sam and plopped a big, wet kiss on his cheek. He scowled and made a show of wiping it off, but Natasha could see in his eyes that he was pleased.

Then her cell phone rang.

Natasha put her head back and took a deep breath. She figured it was Barb again, with more details on tomorrow's meeting. She wanted to feel annoyed by the intrusion on her private life, but Barb had been pretty fucking awesome today. Natasha had planned to stab the asshole before he could take her anywhere, but it was always risky to get into a car with someone. Looking again at her family, she was relieved she'd never had to chance it.

"Are you going to get that?" Amelia said. "Kid's killing me here, and the phone is breaking my concentration."

Natasha laughed. She reached for the phone, not bothering to check the caller I.D. first. She was surprised to hear Jake's voice on the other end.

"You need to get the hell out of town," he hissed.

Natasha tensed. "Why?"

"They know who you are. You dumb cunt-"
"Don't call me that."
"Fucking aye, Natasha."

Natasha put her hand over the phone. "Be right back," she said to Amelia. Then, in response to her lover's questioning look, she said, "Everything's fine."

But it wasn't fine. It was distinctly *not* fine. Safely in the confines of her bedroom, door shut, Natasha said, "Speak to me, Jake. Now. Tell me what the hell you're talking about."

"I'm risking my life making this call, Natasha. You could at least be nice."

"I am being nice. I haven't hung up on you. So talk."

"You had a run-in with one of Franko's men today. Some slob goes by the name Tank. In New York."

"How'd you know that?"

"You know I hear things. Just listen, okay? For once?" – Jake mumbled a curse under his breath – "Franko's got it out for you. He knows who you are, where you live. Tank was the second of his men you stabbed, Tasha."

"Don't call me Tasha."

"For fuck's sake, will you listen? These men mean business. You've fucked with Franko twice. I don't know what the hell you're up to or why you're suddenly involved in Mob shit, but you need to get out of there. Tonight."

"I can't."

"Then it will be your funeral. You and that bitch you work for."

Delilah. Natasha sat on her bed, her headache worse. Jake could be a drama queen, but he was risking his own life by even making this call. She knew the guy who'd grabbed her today meant business. The car boot was premeditated. He'd meant to abduct her – but for what purpose, she didn't know.

Natasha thought again about the two people in the other room. Aside from Delilah, who'd given her a chance when no one else would, they were all she had. Sam was her life. And she thought maybe, just maybe, she and Amelia could have something long-term. Something real. Something . . . stable.

Was she willing to risk that for whatever shit Miriam had been up to?

No. She wasn't. But she also knew that you couldn't run from your problems. They'd hunt you down and rip you apart in the end. There was only one way to deal with shit. Head on and full throttle.

She said, "Why are you telling me this, Jake?"

Gruffly, he said, "You got my son there, don't you?"

"You mean Jake Morowski has a heart after all?"

"Not a time to be making fun, Natasha."

"I'll move Sam."

"And you?"

"No promises."

Jake grunted. "You always were a hard-headed bitch."

THIRTY-TWO

True to his word, Anders arrived an hour later. Dusk was bending to evening's will and the night air, heavy with the heady scents of lilies and wild roses, promised rain. Delilah had just finished up with the horses. A biting sense of failure coupled with a gnawing concern about Lucinda served to marry physical exhaustion and anxiety. The result was a desire for booze.

She patted Spur one last time. The horses were nervous. They paced in their stalls, pausing every few seconds to paw at the ground. "I know what you mean," Delilah murmured. But their anxiety was ancient – bred in over thousands of years - and stemmed from the coming storms. It would be gone with the last of the rain. She wished things were so simple for her. Delilah switched off the lights in the stable and went out into the dark, accompanied by the dogs. It was then she saw Anders, standing next to his car, a legal-sized accordion folder tucked under his arm, a bottle of wine in his hand.

"I figured you were in there," he said.

Delilah didn't respond right away. She took her time taking his measure. In the dim light of the outside flood lights, he looked thin. His dark hair was pushed back from his face and a day's worth of stubble showed on his chin. Despite herself, she felt the pull she so desperately wanted to deny. And then she felt self-conscious. He always showed up when she looked her worst.

But why should she care? She should have learned that lesson already.

"Are you going to invite me in?" he said.

Delilah gave him a half smile. She tucked a loose strand of hair behind her ear and nodded toward the house. "Come on."

He followed close behind. *Too* close. She hurried up the path, pausing only to thwart the dogs' attempts to maul Anders with kisses.

Inside, Delilah stopped in the kitchen. Anders held out the wine. Delilah took it, glanced at the label – an Australian merlot – and placed the bottle on the counter.

She said, "Thanks, Anders. I could use a drink about now. Wine glasses are in the second cupboard. Corkscrew is in the third drawer on the left. You pour. I'll be back in a few." She looked down at her jeans, brown at the knees from kneeling on the barn floor. "I need to change."

When Delilah returned, damp from the shower and now dressed in clean capri pants and a linen tank, she found Anders in her living room. He stood by the fireplace mantel, his back to her, and was looking at the framed photos that sat on the stone hearth. She knew to an outsider it must seem a shrine to her losses.

Outside, thunder boomed.

"That's my dad," she said. She moved next to Anders and accepted the glass of red wine he proffered.

"You look like him. Same red hair, same blue eyes." He turned to her. "An unusual combination."

"My sisters all look like my mother."

"She's not a red head?"

"Dark hair, dark eyes, curvy figure." Delilah smiled. "My dad was a red-haired maverick, with a salty cowboy personality and a figure like Ichabod Crane. Clearly, I got his genes."

"I think you're beautiful."

Delilah turned away, not because she sensed Anders was lying but because he was being honest. And for some reason, that cut to the quick.

Anders turned back to the photos. He pointed to one. "Michael?"

"Yes."

They both stared at the man Delilah had been set to marry. In the picture, Michael sat on Spur, head cocked, a cowboy hat tilted over one eye. But the other eye stared back at the camera - at Delilah - with mischief and longing. Her Michael. Her one and only love.

"How did he die?"

Delilah shrugged. "We don't know, really. He was kayaking in West Virginia. They found his craft but not him." Delilah took the picture from Anders and placed it gently on the mantle.

"Did they ever—"

"Find his body?" Delilah finished the painful sentence for him. She shook her head. "I searched myself for two months, camping along the river where he'd been. Then I spent almost six years hoping he'd show up, a victim of amnesia. I called nearby hospitals, visited morgues, looked at newspapers. Nothing." She shrugged. "West Virginian rivers are old, the rocks underneath hollowed death traps. It's likely his kayak flipped and he became trapped. But he was an expert kayaker. It makes no sense."

"I'm sorry."

"Me too." Delilah pulled her thoughts away from the past. Booze plus sentimentality would only make her morose. Delilah hated morose. "So what the hell were you doing at Domino?"

"How did you know I was there?"

"I had Natasha following you."

Anders laughed. "At least you're a straight shooter."

"I try to be." Delilah made a shooting motion with her hand. "I needed to know if you were on the up and up, so I asked Natasha to tail you. Never imagined the chaos that would ensue."

"Chaos?"

Delilah recounted the story Barb had told her, including the fact that Mr. Clean had been following Natasha.

"But he didn't attack Natasha? And he didn't get involved when Barb came along?"

"No. Didn't hurt them, didn't help them. Just stood there and watched, then disappeared."

"Interesting. What do you make of that?"

"Mr. Clean and the guy who attacked Natasha are not working for the same people."

"Then what's Mr. Clean's role?"

"That I don't know. When he accosted me outside of the office, he was strong - and not afraid to hit a woman. But-"

"That says it all."

"*But* I went after him first. I sensed him behind me and I kicked him in the chest. He ran off without ever pulling a weapon."

"Doesn't sound like the kind of guy who just shows

up to chat."

"Maybe he was there to deliver a warning." Delilah took a sip of wine before continuing. She preferred white over red, but this one was earthy and rich. "He told me that people far worse than he would be after me if we didn't leave this alone."

"And then Natasha was attacked."

"Exactly. So either Mr. Clean is some sort of ambassador for our Mob friends or he works for someone else."

"And who would that be?"

"Domino. I've believed that all along and I'm sticking with it." Delilah sat down on the couch. She took another long sip of wine and motioned for Anders to sit in the armchair. "Now you, Anders. Why were you at Domino? I was upfront with you. Now I want the truth."

She waited while he picked his file off a side table and then sat down on the couch next to her. He rummaged through the folder until he came to a thick pile of papers secured with a black clip.

"I finally broke down and called Tula. I told her the truth. That Ahmed had called me. That I did nothing to help him. That I don't believe that Ahmed died accidentally." He tossed the binder to Delilah. "It was a tough conversation. But she said she didn't blame me. She said she understood. I think she knew anyway."

Delilah thought back to the night Tula's housekeeper met them with the car. Yes, Tula knew. Softly, Delilah said, "Did you think she would blame you, Matthew? With everything you were dealing with at the time?"

Anders gave Delilah a wistful smile. "Sometimes people are seduced into thinking their reasons for doing something – or not doing something in my case - are justified. We humans have an amazing capacity for rationalization. We can lie to ourselves so convincingly that we come to believe that our lies are truth."

"Is that what you did?"

"I was scared to help Ahmed. That's the naked truth. Did I have valid reasons for rationalizing my inaction? Yes. But underlying everything was cowardice. I knew Ahmed was terrified and I could not invite that terror into my life. Not then."

"And now?"

"And now it seems we have no choice."

Delilah looked at the papers in her hands. They were corporate documents: tax filings and permits and financial statements. For Domino.

"Ahmed was investigating Domino?"

Anders nodded. "Unfortunately, he hadn't written his findings in one place."

"Or if he did, someone took them."

"Maybe. That's why I was in New York. Visiting Tula and trying again to get an audience with Domino." Anders reached over and reorganized the papers in Delilah's hands. "All Tula could locate were these notes and papers, some of which are publically available, some of which are not."

"So if someone found out that Ahmed was gathering information, information not generally accessible, they may have caught wind that he was up to something."

"Exactly."

Delilah skimmed the top document, a corporate tax filing. She wasn't sure what she was looking at, but one thing caught her eye. The existence of foreign subsidiaries.

"I thought Domino was a U. S. company?"

"It is." Anders pulled another document from the file. He paged through until he came to a set of spreadsheets. Delilah squinted at the rows of numbers. "But two years ago, they invested in several foreign joint ventures. Explains the two foreign-based partners you saw on the business cards." He turned a page. "The financials are hard to follow. I imagine there were bribes involved."

"That's illegal."

Anders laughed. "You of all people should know that illegality isn't always a deterrent. Especially where money is concerned."

"True. So where are these joint ventures?"

"Indonesia. India. Thailand. The Balkans."

"Developing countries."

Anders nodded. "And human trafficking hot spots."

"It all seems to come back to that, doesn't it?"

"Yep. But there's more." Anders stood. He walked across the room, paused at the darkened windows – rain was pouring down in sheets now - then return to his spot on the couch. He handed Delilah a brochure. "Look at this."

She read through the document and then looked up, surprised. "Juan DeMarco's fundraising dinner? Was this with Ahmed's things?"

Anders nodded. "Look at the next page."

Miriam Cross's name was printed across the top as the featured speaker. Ahmed had highlighted her name in pink.

"Ahmed was at the dinner?"

"No. I would have remembered seeing his name, but I double checked to be sure."

"Could he have attended under an alias?"

Anders was thoughtful. "Possible, I suppose."

"But whether or not he was there, this proves some connection to Miriam. Ahmed may have been looking for an opportunity to meet her."

"And then Ahmed was killed, weeks later."

Delilah stared at the brochure, willing it to impart its secrets. "Wait, this doesn't make sense."

"How so?"

"The dates don't add up."

Anders leaned in closer so that he could look at the brochure. Delilah felt the warmth of his shoulder against hers, the pressure of his thigh on her leg. She flashed to the night they spent together, the press of his lips. The hardness of his body.

Get it together, Lila.

She moved over slightly, away from him. "I've been working off the assumption that DeMarco's dinner was the beginning of everything. That Miriam met Cashman and Patel there, found out about the domestic slave trade sometime after this dinner. But Ahmed was clearly seeking her out for a reason. And that was *before* the dinner."

"So that means one of two things" - Anders held up a finger - "either Miriam was already involved with Sister Anna and Ahmed knew it."

Delilah nodded. "Or Ahmed told her about Domino and wanted her to help him. He introduced her to what was going on."

Just then, Sampson startled from his spot near the fireplace. He sprinted to the window and started to bark. His gentle giant of a brother, Goliath, the Great Dane, perked his ears and ran to the window beside him.

"Something has them worked up," Anders said.

Delilah rose. She looked out the window. Only blackness stared back. Blackness and rain. "It could be the storm."

Anders shook his head. "You should stay at a hotel."

"Hogwash."

"No one says hogwash anymore, Delilah."

"Yeah, well, it's out of fashion to coddle women, too."

"I'm not coddling. Someone tried to hurt Natasha today. You don't even have an alarm system."

"Yes I do" - she pointed to the dogs - "and they have

the added benefits of no timer delay and total loyalty."

"And having to feed and care for them." But Anders smiled and reached down to pet Sampson, who was by now curled on the couch next to him, current crisis averted. The little Jack Russell mix turned over to give Anders better access to his tummy.

Delilah watched Anders scratching her dog. Something about his gentle caresses nudged at her brain. She remembered the books she'd found at Miriam's Chestnut Hill house. "Wait here," she said.

She pulled the two books from her backpack, hung on a peg in the kitchen, and walked back into the living room. She sat back down on the couch, careful to keep her distance from Anders. It was late and the wine was messing with her head. She needed to keep her wits about her.

"Check these out." Delilah opened the book called *Tantra*. She pointed to the sections about Chinnamasta. Anders skimmed the prose. His eyes widened.

"Where did you find this?"

"In Miriam's attic. Last time Lucinda and I were at Miriam's Chestnut Hill house, I saw a box of books. I had gone through them quickly, but I hadn't really focused on the titles. I went back tonight." She picked up the second book and turned to the marked page. "Take a look at this."

Delilah handed Anders the Anaïs Nin work. Anders read the inscription aloud. "Come undone. For me." He flipped the page. "Hmmm. Signed simply 'J.'" He met Delilah's gaze. "J for John or for Jay?" He shrugged. "Could be anyone, I suppose."

"I don't think so." Delilah took the book from Anders. She held the book up to the weak light flowing from a table lamp until she found what she wanted. "There. It's hard to read."

It was a date. Six years ago.

Anders looked at her questioningly. "Doesn't that just support the 'could be anyone' theory?"

"I don't think so. I think it was Jay Patel."

"Because?"

"Because she loved Jay Patel. You could tell in that video. The person who gave her these books . . . well, there was a degree of trust."

Anders looked skeptical. "How do you explain the dates? We assumed that Miriam met Jack Cashman and Jay Patel at Juan DeMarco's dinner. Or at least because of DeMarco's dinner. But this predates the dinner by *five* years."

"I know it doesn't quite fit at first, but just try to follow my logic. What if Miriam knew Jay Patel first? What if she found out about Domino's connection to the slave trade through Jay?"

"But Domino just set up those corporations in the last two years."

Delilah shook her head. "Maybe those are just the legitimate businesses. Domino could have already been involved in human trafficking before they started the so-called employment agencies. For all we know, Domino itself – the whole venture - is a front for the Mob."

Anders looked thoughtful. "How do you explain Ahmed? He highlighted Miriam's name for a reason. This still doesn't add up."

Delilah stood. She walked to the fireplace mantel and picked up Michael's photograph. So young, so handsome, so full of life. Not fair. Then whoever said the world was just.

And that's when it hit her. Who ever said the world was just? People could be seduced into thinking they could trust someone only to find out they'd been betrayed. Death was one form of betrayal. But there were others.

"Patel could have gotten the idea from Miriam!"

Delilah spun around and tried to control the excitement in her voice. "What if she and Jay had been lovers for awhile? What if Miriam had already been involved in fighting the slave traders? Women NOW has been around for years. Sister Anna has been at this for a long time. Maybe Patel got the idea from Miriam."

Anders nodded. "That would explain why Ahmed was reaching out to Miriam. He wanted to warn her. To let her know Domino was involved."

"And let's not forget the Mob. We know Franco's in this somehow. Miriam could have been helping Anna Berger, working on a book, oblivious to the fact that her own lover had gotten a business idea from her."

Anders repeated the inscription from the book. *"Come undone. For me."*

"Miriam came undone alright. In the end, this was her complete undoing."

Silence enveloped the room. The implications of Miriam's choices loomed large. Lucinda had described her aunt as a celibate. In reality, she was hungry . . . for love, for sex, for something novel. And that hunger led to her demise.

Anders rose. He walked to where Delilah was standing and looked hard into her eyes. His hands found her own. He leaned in and kissed her. She kissed back.

What are you doing, Delilah? She shook her head. "Matthew, don't."

"I'm not a married man, Delilah. Not really. I haven't been for a long time."

"It doesn't matter."

"Because you're still promised to a dead man?"

Delilah slapped him, hard. Anders stepped back.

"Oh my God, I'm sorry," Delilah said.

"Don't be. I was out of line." Anders backed toward the kitchen and the door, rubbing the side of his face. "I get it, Delilah. My feelings for you are real. But that doesn't matter. Because you can't let go." He shook his head. "We all have our demons."

"Matthew-"

"We'll stick to business. That's your comfort zone, after all, right?" He put his hand on the door knob. Delilah reached an arm out, as though to stop him. She felt dizzy, misunderstood. She wanted him to stay and she wanted him to go. She wanted him to hold her and she wanted him out of her life forever.

All business now, Anders said, "The whole scenario we've cooked up sounds pretty far-fetched. We need something concrete to back it up."

"Matthew-"

"I had no luck at Domino today. I suggest we ambush Patel at home tomorrow. Before he even gets out of his house." He opened the back door. "I'll be here at five to pick you up."

"Matthew!"

But Delilah's voice was drowned out by the sound of the old wooden screen door slamming shut and the distant boom of thunder.

#

Delilah didn't sleep that night, the scene with Anders an emotional punch to the gut. Instead, she sat in her office and stared at the chart she'd made listing out everything they knew about Miriam Cross's life - and death. As the night wore on, Miriam's life began to blend with her own. The senselessness of it all overwhelmed her.

She thought about Matthew's words: was she promised to a dead man?

No. That was ridiculous.

But was it? Why had she slapped Anders? Where had that kind of anger come from if not the sting of truth?

Delilah put the chart away. She was letting Miriam's

death and the pressure of locating Lucinda get to her. Miriam's betrayal was not her betrayal.

Or was it? True, neither her father nor Michael had sold her out. But wasn't death the greatest betrayal of all?

Exhausted, Delilah tried to sleep. The heat felt oppressive. After an hour of tossing and turning, she got up again. Too tired to focus, she turned on her computer and clicked her way onto the Web. She spent the rest of the night researching human trafficking. The things she read turned her sadness into fury.

Because of the very nature of the trade, exact numbers weren't available. Millions of women, men and children each year were duped or forced into becoming prostitutes, domestic slaves and day laborers. Delilah thought about those women living in the basement of a convent in Baltimore. Each of them had left a life in their home country, hopeful that they were turning a corner, making a better world for themselves and their families. Instead, they were raped, abused, broken. They became lost women, without homes, fearful for children living thousands of miles away.

That wasn't a life. That was hell.

As she read, a few of the loose ends that had been bothering Delilah made sense. The men at Miriam's house in Philadelphia must have been mobsters waiting for a delivery of escapees to Miriam in this underground railroad of sorts. Even though Miriam's was dead, they knew others were involved. They'd thought the decoy house may have been a meeting spot and they wanted the chattel that, in their twisted minds, they'd already paid for.

And the foreigners Miriam's neighbor saw at Emily Cray's Willston home? Surely escaped slaves, too. And their couriers.

Delilah's stomach clenched with disgust.

She thought of Cashman's maid, with her haunted eyes and broken body. Another victim? Could a man of Cashman's background do something so awful? Anna Berger said the Mob handlers were schooled in human nature. Had they sweetened a deal with Domino by giving Cashman a slave of his own, someone he could torture without fear of consequence?

Her mind flicked to all-too-common headlines: School principal arrested for child pornography. Priest accused of molestation. Police officer indicted for rape. Of course Cashman could have bought his housekeeper. People in positions of power did horrible things. And because of their power, they often got away with them.

The thought made Delilah shudder. For unlike the women with Sister Anna, now at least safe, Cashman's housekeeper remained in bondage.

And how many others were out there? Forced into servitude because of a market system that would support it and enough corruption to let it continue. Perhaps Anna Berger's theory was right: for most people, ignorance *was* bliss. Knowledge without the ability to help was painful and people are programmed to avoid pain. What had it been like for Miriam to live with that knowledge, to exist in a world where you knew the horrors your fellow people were capable of inflicting? And if Delilah's theory was right and Domino took advantage of that knowledge to make money, consequences to human lives be damned, what was it like for Miriam to live with herself, betrayed by the very man she loved?

It was with these thoughts that Delilah finally dozed off at 3:48 in the morning, Goliath and Sampson at her feet. She awoke what felt like seconds later to the pounding at her door. Anders, she thought groggily. Back for Round Two.

THIRTY-THREE

Barb's phone rang at 5:12 a.m. Her husband had been on call the night before and he sounded exhausted. He also sounded worried, which was very unlike Fred Moore.

"I can't say much right now Barb, so listen closely. Okay? You know I never interfere with your work. But this thing you're working on? The thing with the author? You gotta pull the plug."

"Why? What do you mean?"

"I mean my job is on the line. All the questions I've been asking about the murder scene and the autopsy got the attention of the wrong people. The boss called me up today. Said that my wife's interfering with police business and if she doesn't stop . . . he left it at that, but I got the point."

Barb cradled the phone closer to her ear. She whispered, though she wanted to shout. "They have no right, Fred, and you know it."

"Yeah well, I'm not afraid to fight a good battle for justice and all, you know that, Barb, but I got a sense of something bigger behind this, if you know what I mean."

The Mafia? Barb thought about Lucinda's call, her hint that the police were involved. She considered again the lack of media attention on Miriam's death, the shoddy investigation. She didn't want to put Fred's job in danger, but she refused to be bullied, either. If the bad guys won this battle, they'd have control. And the police force her husband worked for, the one he risked his life for day after day, could *not* be compromised by the Mob. It was better to do something else than be owned by the very people you were paid to fight.

"I won't stop, Fred. Anyway, it's too late for that."

"Just say you'll stop, Barb."

"I won't stop, I told you that."

"I'll speak slowly, Barbie Doll. Say you'll stop."

And then she got it. Fred only called her Barbie Doll when they were sharing a joke. He knew his wife and no more expected her to stop than he expected her to suddenly vote Democrat. But he needed to be able to report back that he'd done his domestic duty.

"I'll stop, Fred."

"Thank you, Barbie Doll. Now go back to sleep."

#

Delilah and Anders drove to Richboro in silence. Delilah sat in Anders old Land Rover, her head turned toward the window, and watched the rural scenery unfold in the awakening light. Sidewalk neighborhoods gave way to long stretches of road flanked by farms. And on the back roads, farms gave way to new million dollar developments. Many of these were the commuters' homes, houses paid for by New Yorkers thrilled at the value they could get for their money here in Pennsylvania, even though the time spent commuting limited the time they could spend in their gargantuan homes. To Delilah it seemed an odd choice. But then, she chose to live in a ramshackle old house miles from her neighbors. To each her own.

Tired of the tension, Delilah made use of the time to call Margot, Barb and Natasha. She cancelled the morning meeting and asked Barb and Margot to hold tight until after she and Anders met with Patel. Barb filled her in on Fred's call. Delilah didn't like it. The bad guys were closing in, getting a little too comfortable pushing Percy Powers LLC around. And Delilah couldn't reach Natasha. She didn't like that, either. Especially because Natasha was her own ticking time bomb. God only knew what that woman was doing. Delilah left Natasha a message. She'd try her again later.

She asked Anders if he had a plan.

"Your call, boss."

"Don't do that. I'm not your boss. It's condescending."

Anders sighed. "How do you want to handle Patel?"

Delilah told him. Anders said nothing for a minute. "It's risky."

Delilah told him about Barb's husband's call. "It's only a matter of time before they come after us. Right now, no one wants to expose their hand. They're still hoping we'll shut up and go away. But that won't last. They'll get impatient and try to shut us up for good. We need to act quickly."

Anders smiled. "You're showing your cowgirl."

Delilah didn't return the smile. "Just good business."

"You packing?"

"My new motto: Never leave home without a gun."

Anders laughed. The mood in the car seemed to lift

a notch.

Anders turned down Mill Road and made a left at a For Sale sign that marked the expanse of yet another doomed farm. He drove about a mile before pulling over. They were at the mouth of Willow Hill Estates, a compilation of million-dollar-plus houses on two acre lots. Barb had told her that Patel's house was the fourth one on the right.

Anders took an audible breath. "Ready?"

"Let's go."

#

Natasha kissed Amelia good-bye and gave Sam an extra long hug. They were at the Rolling Hills Inn in Lancaster, Pennsylvania, in a room with no view and even less atmosphere. Two double beds, covered in green and taupe comforters, clashed with a gold armchair, a wooden armoire, and plum-striped drapes. The place smelled like stale cigarette smoke and antiseptic cleaner. But she figured the patchwork hills of this part of Pennsylvania would put distance between Sam and Amelia and the dangers lurking in Philadelphia. She hoped to hell she was right.

Natasha pulled her girlfriend to the side before leaving. Amelia had been less than willing to trek an hour and a half outside of town without a reason, so Natasha had been forced to tell her at least part of the truth. She left out the small fact that it was the Mafia after her. Some things, she'd learned, were better left unsaid.

Now she took Amelia's hand. "You won't leave the hotel, right?"

"Tasha-"

"Promise me. I packed plenty of food. You can order all the movies you want. Just make it an adventure for Sam, okay? I don't want him to be scared."

Amelia pouted. But one look at Natasha, and

Natasha was sure she could see just how serious the situation was. Amelia nodded slowly. "I'll make sure he has no idea what's going on."

Natasha smiled. "Thank you."

"Be careful, okay?"

Natasha waved away her concern with bravery she didn't feel. "I've been in worse situations." And she had. But that was for another day.

"Just promise."

"I promise."

Amelia leaned in to kiss her and Natasha gave her a gentle kiss back. "One more thing. If something should happen to me - and it won't, so don't worry - but if I get hit by a bus or something, will you be Sam's guardian?"

Amelia looked surprise. She nodded. "I wouldn't have it any other way."

"Because I don't want his father to get him, you know. And my parents are dead to me."

Amelia put her fingers to Natasha's mouth. "Shh. I love Sam. Now be careful, okay? And be back tonight."

"I'll do my best." But that was one thing Natasha couldn't promise.

#

Patel was still home. At least his car was still there. At her request, Anders parked a few doors down from the Patel's four thousand square foot abode.

"Do we go in?"

"No. We wait." Delilah looked at Anders. The hurt in his eyes belied his easy manner. She felt another pang of regret over last night. And the silly thing, she told herself, was that Michael would want her to be happy. She said, "Trust me. Just keep the ignition on and be ready to pull out when I say go."

It didn't take long. Six minutes later, Jay Patel closed the door to his home and strode toward his car. Delilah watched the man closely. Patel wore a crisp business suit and carried a leather briefcase. His gait was purposeful.

They needed to time this well. Too soon and he would retreat to his house. Too late, and he'd speed off in his car.

Patel put his hand on the door to the Mercedes. He opened it and slid behind the wheel.

Delilah said, "Now. Pull out quickly and block his driveway."

Anders hit the gas pedal.

Clearly surprised, Patel climbed back out of the car. He stood in his driveway, staring at Anders' car. Patel's expression changed from confusion to anger and then to fear. Delilah wanted fear.

Delilah got out of the Land Rover. She heard Anders do the same.

"Mr. Jay Patel?"

He nodded.

"Delilah Percy Powers. I'd like to ask a few questions."

Patel looked from Delilah to Anders and back again. "You're the private investigator. Your ladies were here several days ago. I told them all I know."

"We have a few more questions. It won't take long."

"Please leave. Before I call the police."

Delilah smiled. "I don't think you'll do that, Mr. Patel. While you or your friends may have some officer on the payroll, if you call 9-1-1 at this hour, you'll get a cruiser. Some low level cop right out of the academy who's too young and too green to owe you any favors. And when he arrives, we'll simply tell him we were lost and asking directions." She looked at Anders. "Right dear?"

"Right."

Patel seemed to consider this. Delilah was bluffing, of course. For all she knew, Patel had a special police connection whom he could call 24-7. Or no connection at all.

"What is it you want to know?"

Delilah walked until she was just feet from Patel. The man had a pleasant, baritone voice with a smooth British accent. Very highbrow. Very educated. It was also the voice from the sex tape. While he was not a man Delilah would be attracted to - too thin for her tastes, and a little too put together - she could see why Miriam had fallen for him. He had soulful brown eyes and impossibly long lashes and he emanated a quiet self-assurance that was almost magnetic.

Finally, Patel said, "Do you want to come inside?"

Delilah eyed the Meridian Security sign in his yard. She wanted Patel nowhere near his family, where he could pass signals to call the police or he himself could push a panic button, if he had one. She also didn't want his wife to look out and call the police. Which meant they needed to get Patel out of here quickly.

Delilah said, "No, but we'd like you to come for a ride with us."

"Out of the question."

"We'll go somewhere public and nearby. Where we can talk."

Patel eyed her warily. "Where would that be?"

"Dunkin' Donuts."

Patel's eyebrows shot up. "You are not serious."

Anders spoke. "We're very serious. We can talk there undisturbed. That's all we want. To talk."

"If my car is here-"

Delilah said, "Get in the car with Anders. Front seat. Give me your keys. I'll move your car, and when we're finished, we'll return you to your car. Promise."

Patel again seemed to weigh the decision. "And if I refuse?"

Delilah didn't want to, but he was forcing her hand. The longer they stood here, the more suspicious it would look to his family and neighbors if they happened to glance outside. And before long, the whole neighborhood would be waking up. She could not afford a scene.

So Delilah unbuttoned her cardigan and let Patel get a peek at the holster strapped to her chest. "We're getting desperate, Mr. Patel. If you refuse, things could get ugly."

Anders nodded. "At the very least, we share some information, perhaps a certain tape, and your wife learns of your infidelity. At worst" - he nodded toward the house, letting the threat hang between them.

Patel glanced at his watch. Finally, he handed Delilah the fob for his car. Then, after glancing once more toward his home, he slid into the front seat of the Land Rover.

"One more thing," Delilah said while Patel's door was still open. "Your phone."

"No."

Delilah looked at Anders. He shrugged.

"Then give it to Anders while he drives. You can have it back at Dunkin' Donuts."

Reluctantly, Patel handed Anders his phone. Delilah started the Mercedes and followed Anders' SUV through the neighborhood. About a quarter mile from Patel's street, Delilah pulled over and parked the car in a strip mall parking lot. Then she climbed into the back of the Land Rover and handed Patel his keys. They drove the mile to Dunkin Donuts in silence.

Once inside, she led Patel to a corner booth. Anders ordered coffee, which Patel accepted with a surprised flourish.

"You're very considerate kidnappers."

Delilah smirked. "Too bad we can't say the same about the thugs your company hires."

"I don't know what you're talking about."

"Stop lying, Patel." Delilah looked at Anders. "Show him."

Anders took Domino's financial papers from the briefcase he had brought into Dunkin Donuts. He spread them out on the table so that Patel could get a clear view.

Patel said, "I'm not sure what you think this proves, Mr. Anderson."

Anders looked at him. "I never told you my name."

Patel smiled. "No need. You were the gentleman who showed up at Domino yesterday. We do have a surveillance camera. To keep out the undesirables."

Anders smiled at the dig. "You refused to speak with me."

"It does no good to speak with the liberal media. And that's what you represent, no?"

"No." Anders voice was threatening. "I represent my friend Ahmed Rajav. Recognize *that* name?"

"I'm afraid I don't."

Anders slammed his fist down. "You fucking got him killed, jackass." Heads turned toward their table. Delilah shot Anders a look that said, *keep it calm.* They needed information from Patel. They'd start with honey, saving the threats for later.

"Look, Mr. Patel, let's review what we know, save us all a little time," Delilah said. "We know you and Miriam were lovers. We have that on tape." She waited for a reaction from Patel. Getting none, she continued. "We know that Miriam was writing a book on human trafficking. We know that Domino has set up subsidiaries in developing countries that have high rates of human trafficking. We know that one of its so-called businesses is recruiting foreigners and selling them here in the United States."

"You know no such thing."

Delilah smiled. "We also know that you hired a

gentleman to tail us. A tall, gaunt looking bald man who has most recently kidnapped Lucinda Mills."

This time, Anders shot her a look. Delilah was guessing, but Patel didn't need to know that. Patel fidgeted in his seat. He opened and closed his eyes. The first real reaction they'd gotten from him.

"We also know," Anders said, "That Domino is somehow connected to the Mob. And that the Mob has something to do with Juan DeMarco." He leaned over the table so that his face was just inches from Patel's. "One *dead* Juan DeMarco."

"You don't seriously think I killed Juan DeMarco."

Delilah cocked her head. "You admit knowing him."

Patel gave her a long look. "You are very persistent, Ms. Powers. I must admit, when I first heard that Lucinda Mills had hired a private investigator, I assumed it would be some buffoon who drank too much and was unable to procure a real job." He shook his head. "I have not before seen such an odd group of employees, but you don't give up. I admire that."

"Stop with the bullshit, Patel. This isn't about my team. It's about you. It's about the fact that you murdered Miriam Cross."

Patel's shock was palpable. "You think I killed Miriam?"

"A neighbor saw you at her Chestnut Hill house before her disappearance. You were arguing. The police were called. Then there's the sex tape. You had everything to lose if she went public with the human trafficking story *or* your affair."

"I didn't kill Miriam."

"What about this?" Delilah pulled the Anaïs Nin book from her bag. She showed him the inscription.

He took the book from Delilah, leafed through the pages, and put it on the table. His eyes look woeful. He remained quiet.

326

"And this book." She handed him *Tantra* and watched the expression on his face when she opened to the section on Chinnamasta.

He looked at Delilah questioningly. "What does this have to do with anything?"

"Did you give Miriam these books, Patel?"

"I did not kill Miriam."

Anders spoke up. "Let's let the Feds decide that. I think the evidence against you is pretty incriminating. And they'll have access to information we don't."

Patel sat back in his chair. He fingered the Anaïs Nin book, picked it up, and turned back to the inscription. When he spoke, his voice was soft, barely a whisper. Delilah leaned in to hear.

"I didn't write this inscription. Nor did I give Miriam the book on Tantric sex. Our relationship wasn't like that."

Delilah said, "Then what was your relationship like?"

Patel looked up and smiled, but his gaze was distant, his mind clearly elsewhere. "Miriam was a breath of fresh air. She loved to talk about books and politics, economics and philosophy. She was an intellectual, yes, but unlike other intellectuals of her kind, she had passion and fire. She was not afraid to act." He looked down at his hands, studied his wedding ring. "I was madly in love with Miriam Cross, I'm afraid."

"So you killed her out of jealousy?" Anders said.

"I did not kill Miriam, Mr. Anderson. I've already told you that."

"Then who did?"

"If I had to guess? The Mafia."

Ander said, "So there is a connection between Domino and the Mob? You little shit-"

Patel looked at Delilah with pleading in his eyes. She, in turn, said, "*Matthew.*"

Patel said, "Jack introduced Miriam to me. At the

time, I believed it to be an act of kindness on his part. My marriage was arranged, you see. And while I love my wife, we are not particularly compatible. She and I . . . well, let us say that we are more like siblings than husband and wife."

Delilah nodded for him to continue.

"But Jack wanted sexual excitement. I believe he has an addiction, if you can call it that. Always something new, something bold. He wanted to have a threesome. At first I was horrified by the idea. But he offered up Miriam, said she was willing. I had met her twice by then and was quite enamored. So I agreed."

"And that was the tape?"

"That was one of the tapes. We met three times. That was the last. Jack became violent and I refused to join again. I didn't know he was such a . . . sadist."

"Why would Miriam, a woman who seemed so strong, so independent, be attracted to a man like Cashman? Why would she put up with the violence?"

Patel considered Delilah's question. "I suppose that is the million dollar question, as you Americans say. I wish I knew the answer. Miriam was a very controlled woman. Jack offered her a release, I suppose. She was able to be someone else for a while." He gave a rueful smile. "We all want that on occasion, yes? To be someone else for a while."

Anders said, "Why did Miriam have the tape?"

Patel shrugged. "I could not say. I thought Jack had all three."

Delilah said, "You allowed yourself to be recorded? You seem smarter than that."

Patel nodded. "You are quite right. The first time, I didn't know I was being recorded. But lust does crazy things to a person's mind. I was wooed into thinking we had a circle of trust. I was a willing accomplice that third time. And I am afraid it was quite foolish."

"Miriam blackmailed you?"

"Of course not. Jack blackmailed me."

Now Delilah was confused. "For what?"

Patel paused. When he spoke, it was with an air of resignation. "Jack knew Miriam was involved with helping trafficked women. He also knew trafficking could be a lucrative business."

"Was Domino in trouble financially?"

"We had made a few bad deals. Nothing that would ruin us, but Jack was never one to turn away easy money. He wanted in. He used Miriam and her knowledge to get in touch with the right people. At first, she had no idea. She thought Jack was merely interested in her work. Jack set Domino up as a middleman in the slave trade. 'No risk, lots of profit,' is how he spun it to me."

"But you didn't want to get involved?" Delilah said.

"I would never betray Miriam that way. I refused. But Jack needed me onboard. This all happened after our three-way affair was over, but I am certain now that he set it all up."

"He threatened to use the tapes against you if you didn't go along with his plan?" Anders said.

"Exactly. He thought we could strike a quiet deal. That no one would ever know - especially Miriam."

"But along came Ahmed."

Patel nodded. "Your friend Ahmed stumbled across one of our employment agencies while in Thailand. He put two and two together. Profitable American venture company – and we were quite profitable by then – exploits local population and all that. Ahmed contacted Miriam. And I am afraid you know what happened next."

Anders said, "Who killed Ahmed?"

"I think that's obvious."

"The Mob," Delilah said, "So Domino was one of the Mob's suppliers?"

"I'm afraid the correct verb is 'is.' The traffic continues."

"Pigs," Anders muttered.

Patel shook his head. "If not Domino, another supplier. The Mob has discovered that trafficked foreign women and girls make easily-subdued prostitutes. These girls are desperate, poor, often uneducated and can be . . . convinced, with the right tools. But prostitutes have a short shelf life. The Mob wanted to diversify."

"Domino offered an alternative."

Patel nodded. "These women also make willing domestics. And a wealthy couple will pay a great deal for a long-term worker. Someone reliable, someone they can trust."

"You mean slave, not worker." Delilah could feel the blood heating her face. "Someone they can beat and humiliate and subjugate."

"It's not always that way. Sometimes the arrangement is mutually beneficial."

She shook her head. "Never when the power is distributed that unequally. Domino preys on women and girls who are either too poor to know better or who are so desperate to feed their families that they will agree to move across the world and work for better wages."

"Only there are no wages," Anders said. "Are there?"

"What happens once the domestics get to their Mafia handlers, I cannot say. We are merely the matchmakers, if you will."

"You disgust me." Delilah shook her head. "How could you go along with that?"

"I am a pragmatic man. These people are poor. Their governments cannot support them and often these jobs give them a roof over their heads and a meal in their bellies." He shrugged. "It's often better than what they had in their homeland."

"You keep telling yourself that, Patel." Delilah thought of the women in Anna Berger's hideout, of burned hands and rape babies. *"No one* wants to be a slave. You lie to yourself so you can sleep at night."

Patel gave Delilah a long, cold look. "If I had not gone along with this, Jack would have told my family. He would have shared the images of . . . of the three of us. Then I would have truly lost my honor, lost everything. And Jack would have found a way to do it anyway."

"So instead you lost your morals. And Miriam."

Patel lowered his gaze. "Yes, sadly. That was the argument that Miriam and I had, over which the police were called. Miriam was devastated by what Jack . . . at what *we* had done. She wanted me to leave the business. I tried to explain. I thought perhaps I could stop it from the inside. She refused to understand. Blamed herself. Then she disappeared."

Anders said, "So you killed her."

"For the last time, Mr. Anderson, I did not kill Miriam. I tried to protect her, just as I tried to protect your friend here" - he nodded at Delilah - "and Miriam's niece."

At this, Delilah perked up. "So you do know where Lucinda is."

Patel looked defeated. Eventually, he said, "Roger has her. She is safe. I tried to warn you. I am afraid it's too late. We will all end up like Miriam."

"Give us Lucinda."

"You must stop looking into Miriam's murder. The people behind her death are making a lot of money. Miriam got in the way. Ahmed got in the way. Juan DeMarco refused to cooperate. Look where they are now."

Anders shook his head. "We're too far in to back out now. We could never feel safe unless these bastards are in custody."

"Is it possible, Patel," Delilah said, "that Jack killed Miriam? It sounds like he had motive as well. She was, after all, interfering with business. The beheading-"

He looked troubled. "No. Impossible. Jack was abroad when she died. He was negotiating another employment agency in India."

"You know that for certain?"

"I have no reason to question. We picked up our first employee from this agency yesterday."

Delilah tried not to think about the implications of that sentence. Another employee for Sister Anna to rescue. Another woman living a nightmare. "Give us Lucinda. Today. We will have someone meet your man Roger."

Patel looked back and forth between Delilah and Anders. "Only if you promise to drop the murder. As I said, that is my condition."

Delilah agreed. Anders looked at her sharply. She ignored the look. She would explain later.

"Five o'clock tonight." She named the meeting place and described Barb. Patel agreed.

At least she'd have her employer back, safe and sound.

#

"What the hell did you do that for?" Anders said when they were back on the road and alone. "You weren't serious about simply dropping Miriam's murder?"

"What would you have me do? I want Lucinda back. Miriam is dead. Nothing we do will change that."

"But-"

"But nothing. I have three employees whose lives are in danger. Natasha left me a message. The Mob has made threats on her life, on her family's life. We're playing a dangerous game. A good detective knows when they're ahead. We have the information we need. If we stop now, we can save Lucinda and keep my people safe."

"But Ahmed."

Anders slowed to a stop at a red light. Delilah put her arm on his. "We know who killed Ahmed. The Mob. Probably Franco's guys, the same guys who killed DeMarco. Probably the same guys who killed Miriam."

"I want to see them behind bars."

Delilah nodded. "I do, too."

"Not based on what you just did."

Delilah felt her temper flare. "Look, you don't work for me anymore, remember? You can do whatever you want now. Write Miriam's book if you want. As for Percy Powers, I have a connection with the FBI. Tomorrow I'll turn over everything. About Domino, about the Mob. We let the Feds finish the job. They'll have evidence they can use to lock up Ahmed's murderers."

Anders looked skeptical. Delilah couldn't blame him. Their only real witness – Patel – was scared. Maybe he would testify if the Feds offered him protection, but he had more than his business to lose. So many of Patel's choices were about protecting his honor. And with the Feds involved, the whole sordid mess would come out. But then again, Patel had spilled to Delilah and Anders. Perhaps he also knew when to fold.

Anders gunned the engine. "And now?"

Delilah didn't even hesitate. "Right now I have an opportunity to save another life. I'm going to take it."

Anders glanced at her. "Who?"

But Delilah was already calling Barb. Time to move ahead with her last move.

THIRTY-FOUR

Barb had heard from Delilah an hour ago. It was now 1:48 in the afternoon. She and Natasha needed to meet Mr. Clean - real name Roger - at five o'clock at a bar in Philly. But Barb couldn't reach Natasha. She tried her cell again and left a message. This was one task she didn't relish doing alone.

Barb put down the laundry she'd been folding and walked to the front door. She thought she saw movement outside in the yard, between the garage and the tool shed. But a long look outside reassured her that she was simply going nuts.

Delilah had told her about the threat to Natasha and her family. She also told her about the meeting with Patel. Still, Barb wasn't completely convinced that they had all the loose ends tied up. She understood the connection between Miriam and Patel. It sounded like the guy really cared for Miriam, in his own warped way. She even understood the role Domino played in this whole mess. People were motivated by greed. It was an all too common theme.

But what Barb didn't get, what she would never understand, was how a sensible, intelligent, independent woman like Miriam Cross could involve herself with Jack Cashman. How could she *allow* herself to be duped?

The phone rang and Barb jumped. *Don't be such a baby.* She was letting her imagination get the best of her. She checked the caller I.D. Fred. It was better he not know where she'd be tonight - he would give her a hard time. And justifiably so. But this was the end. Once Lucinda was safe, they would turn in their evidence and get out of the game of *Who killed Miriam Cross?*

She wasn't sorry to see this case end. She was just sorry they couldn't hand over the killer on a silver platter. Or a morgue slab.

Barb let the call go to voicemail. Then she went to the kitchen sink and ran the water until it was cold. While she waited, she watched a red-breasted robin eating from the feeder she kept outside. Her yard was big and wooded and private, usually a plus in her eyes, but today she'd give anything for a bustling neighborhood. Again she thought she caught movement outside her window, but when she looked twice she noticed a squirrel, digging beneath a tree.

That's it. She admitted to herself that she was spooked. She had almost two hours before she'd pick up Lucinda. It would take an hour to get downtown. That gave her an hour to kill. She couldn't stay here. The silence was feeding her case of the crazies. She'd go shopping. Target was an excellent place for company. And then she'd head into Philly. With or without

Natasha.

#

Delilah and Anders arrived at Cashman's house at 3:04. Later than Delilah wanted, but it'd taken that long for Margot to make the necessary arrangements. Delilah scanned the street, looking for Margot's Miata. She saw it immediately. Margot was circling the block.

Anders pulled into Cashman's driveway. "Turn off the engine," Delilah said. "This may take a few minutes."

Anders glanced at his watch. "I'm afraid you don't have long. Who knows when Cashman will be back? Especially if Patel warned him."

Delilah nodded. "I doubt Patel talked, though."

Delilah was banking on Cashman's addictive personality. Sex addition, work addiction. Cashman was a guy who thrived on the kill. He probably wouldn't roll in from New York City until well after eight. But from everything she knew about Jack Cashman, she also knew he was a player. And players like to play - which could mean an early arrival home for a shower and a change of clothes before an evening out with some unlucky woman. So they needed to act fast.

Margot parked behind them and climbed out of her car. She carried a black overnight bag, which she held up. "Your car or mine?"

Delilah had thought this through. "Yours. You'll take her. You have been less involved with the case. There's less possibility that someone will tail you."

Margot nodded. She looked somber, her usually serious demeanor a few notches closer to stern. "Anna Berger filled me in. Horrific."

"Is she meeting you or is she sending someone else?"

Margot shook her head. "Someone else, I think. Close by. I am sworn to absolute secrecy on the meeting place. Anna's paranoid."

Anders said, "I guess she needs to be."

Delilah looked from Anders to Margot. To Anders, she said, "Stay in the car, okay? Unless we need you. I'm afraid your presence will only scare her."

Anders nodded. "Understood. If Jack shows up?"

"We'll have a confrontation on our hands." Delilah glanced at Margot. "Ready?"

Margot smoothed her habit. "Ready."

At Delilah's request, Margot had worn the habit, kept from her days in the convent. Margot had declined at first, saying it would feel deceitful. But Delilah convinced her that it was for the greater good. Cashman's maid was expecting to be taken to a nun. She would be more likely to trust women, and especially a woman of God.

At least that was the hope.

Delilah went first. She knocked on the front door. No answer. She rang the doorbell. No answer. The door was locked, so she rang again and waited. A minute later she rang several more times in quick succession, trying to convey a sense of urgency. She was rewarded with movement. The door opened a crack.

"Mr. Cashman no home."

"I don't want Jack, Rosa. We're here to help you."

Two brown eyes widened on the other side. "Mr. Cashman is no here."

"Rosa, I know this is scary and overwhelming, but we are here for you." Delilah repeated the sentence in Spanish she'd gleaned off of Google Translator, hoping it would help quell the woman's anxiety. But instead, Rosa slammed the door.

"What now?" Margot said.

Delilah forced herself to take three long, deep breaths. *Think, Lila.* Delilah could almost smell the woman's terror. The devil she knew and all.

Taking the chance that Rosa was still on the other side of the door, Delilah said, loudly, "Rosa, I know

Miriam told you she would rescue you. I know Miriam was going to take you to Sister Anna and make sure no one could hurt you again. I am here with Sister Margot and she knows Sister Anna, too. We are going to take you to meet Sister Anna."

When there was no response, Delilah said, "I've been there, Rosa. I've seen where Sister Anna and the others women live. Women like you, who have families they haven't seen in years. Women who have been deceived and hurt. But the place they are now is clean and safe. They learn skills, they get a new identity if they want. They return home." She paused. "We can help you. But you need to hurry. Before Mr. Cashman gets home."

Still no response. Perhaps Rosa had gone upstairs, or really was too scared to act. Or maybe Delilah had the whole situation wrong to begin with. But she didn't think so. Delilah shook her head slowly, unwilling to give up, the clock against her. And then the door opened. Rosa stood before them, her short-sleeved maid's uniform perfectly clean and pressed. A sharp contrast to her skin, which was mottled with burns and bruises, some old. Some fresh.

"Oh my God," Margot muttered.

"Rosa, do you have anything you absolutely want to bring with you?"

Rosa said, "Clothes. Toothbrush."

Margot shook her head. "No need, my love. We have clothes and personal items for you. You can leave that."

"No pictures?" Delilah said.

Without emotion, Rosa said, "He burn them."

Delilah took another deep breath. She held her hand out for the other woman. "Come. We need to leave quickly."

"He will be gone for two days. He tell me that."

"Did he tell you not to answer the door?"

Rosa nodded.

"Did he threaten you with . . . with more of this?"

"He say I will have an accident."

Margot started to say something and Delilah shook her head. "Let's get her out of here. I don't want to risk it."

Margot said, "What will you do about Cashman?"

Delilah sighed. "I'd like to say he'll spend the rest of his life in prison when the FBI gets through with him. But the truth? He'll hire a good lawyer, say Rosa was clumsy and deny knowing anything about human trafficking. He'll say the employment agencies are just that. He and Patel may get off scot free."

"But the sex tape and Rosa -"

"Neither man is clearly identifiable. I don't think that tape accomplishes anything other than hurt Miriam's memory. As for Rosa" - she stole a glance at the broken woman between them, who seemed to be lost in thoughts of her own - "That's the good news. Sister Anna is protective of her women. No one, including our own government, will have the opportunity to detain Rosa again."

Margot shook her head. "So justice won't be done?"

"I didn't say that. Domino will come under scrutiny. Anders may decide to write that book. Perhaps the FBI can piece together their business dealings with the Mafia. We'll give them everything we have. It may not be enough." Delilah shrugged. "But I prefer to think like an optimist.

THIRTY-FIVE

Delilah could feel the noose twisted around her neck loosening, at least a little bit. While Anders was driving her back home, Margot called and confirmed that Rosa was safely in Sister Anna's hands. And Lucinda was safe, too. *Hallelujiah.* For tonight, Lucinda would stay with Barb and her family as a precaution, but tomorrow she'd return home . . . under Big Joe's continued watch. At least for a few days. Until this whole mess was turned over to the FBI.

Tonight, Delilah would pour herself a large glass of Pinot Grigio, slip into cotton pajamas and, after a hot bath and a juicy steak, she'd sort through all the evidence they'd collected. She had the number Joe had given her for the Fed connection. She remembered the guy from the police academy: straight, serious, and no bullshit. Exactly what she was looking for. She'd give him what they had plus a timeline that she'd create and *voila*. No more Percy Powers involvement.

So why did she still feel so unsettled?

For one, they hadn't pinpointed Miriam's killer. The Mafia felt like a generic answer, which didn't sit quite right with Delilah. Two, the way Miriam died still bothered her. A beheading. Not that the Mob wouldn't engage in that sort of horror, but it seemed too symbolic for Delilah's taste. And, of course, number three was Natasha. Where the hell was that woman? She was supposed to have accompanied Barb today, but never returned Barb's calls. Since then, no calls, no voicemails, just one text confirming that she was okay.

And there were other things, things Delilah couldn't quite put her finger on. But she brushed her misgivings away. Sometimes gaps existed, even after a job was completed. You had to learn to live with the gray.

Anders pulled onto Delilah's street and stopped before turning into her driveway. "So I guess we part ways?" he said. He'd been quiet for most of the drive. Delilah knew he had his own issues with the way this had wrapped up, not the least of which was guilt over Ahmed's murder. But that could not be helped.

"Can you do me one last thing?" Delilah said. "Just confirm that Cashman was out of the country when Miriam was killed."

Anders nodded. "Already on my to-do list anyway." He killed the engine. "Delilah . . . I'd like to see you again. Maybe under different circumstances?"

Delilah turned to him. In the dying daylight he looked at her the same way Michael used to, with a gentle, sweet hunger in his eyes. But he wasn't Michael, she reminded herself. Michael was dead and Anders was here. Real, warm and alive. And despite the trials they'd been through on this case, he was solid, steady. And so damn attractive.

Still, she wanted to start fresh. And right now, until this case was put to bed, she couldn't do that. When she didn't reply, Anders looked hurt. He turned his gaze back toward the road and twisted the key in the ignition. Delilah reached out, caressed his arm. Slowly, softly, she turned his head toward her and kissed him. She felt his body respond. Her own heart raced.

She pulled back and smiled. Her voice shaky, she said, "This weekend? Dinner? We can take it slowly. I think we both need the time and space to see where this might lead."

Anders nodded. "I'd like that."

He pulled back onto the road and down Delilah's driveway. The second they neared the house, any warmth from her exchange with Anders dissipated. The noose tightened anew.

There, next to her Jeep, sat her mother's silver Lexus. And Joan Powers stood on the porch, a scowl on her face the size of Montana.

"Mother," Delilah said, her quiet evening alone disappearing along with her sanity.

"Delilah. And who is this young gentleman?"

Delilah introduced Anders as her friend and colleague. She watched her mother take in his well-worn jeans, his lanky build, the several days' worth of stubble, his soft brown eyes.

Before her mother could skewer Anders with questions, Delilah gave him a dismissive handshake. "Call me tomorrow?"

He nodded, took one last glance at her mother, and got back in the Land Rover. Delilah watched him leave, mentally conjuring up ways she could send her mother back on the four-plus hour journey home.

She came up empty.

"Delilah, I'm famished. I brought an evening dress. If you'd like to change out of those beat-around clothes and get a proper meal, I'll treat you. I don't imagine you get that often." She made a show of looking at the house. "It will be nice to catch up."

"Can't, Mother. I have to take care of the horses."

Joan scowled again.

"Let's go inside," Delilah said. "I'll show you to your room. And I can make us a nice steak and salad for dinner. Would that be okay?"

"Is your kitchen clean, Delilah? I remember that last placed you stayed. I found mouse droppings under the cabinets."

Delilah unlocked the front door and let her mother inside, silently bracing herself for the evening ahead. "No mice, here, Mother." *Yeah, right.* One look at the two hundred year old foundation should tell her mother otherwise.

But her mother was already onto other topics. "This house is a rambling mishmosh of architectural styles. You need a good interior designer - and a contractor to open up these rooms. But what you really need is a husband, Delilah. A nice, *successful* husband. One who will take care of you? Get you a proper house in a proper neighborhood."

Delilah rolled her eyes. She was in for a very long night.

#

Natasha could feel the resentment building. With Amelia and Sam safely tucked in for the night, she was free. The more she thought about the threats, the more pissed off she became. Fuck Franco and his beasts.

Natasha left Tony K's shop at 6:48 p.m. Her backpack loaded, she took a second to check her reflection in one of the unplugged televisions at the front of his store. Tony ran a legit television repair shop in

North Philly, just off of Broad Street. But he also ran a not-so-legit gun and knife shop out of the back of the shop. Natasha and Tony went way back. She knew he'd hook her up.

Still looking at the television screen, Natasha pulled a stray hair away from her face and tucked it behind her ear. She didn't like the crazy she saw looking back from her reflection. She'd given up crazy a long time ago.

Outside, she jogged past a hair shop specializing in weaves, a restaurant with a sign for all-you-can-eat fried shrimp, its serving window blocked by steel bars, and two check cashing stores. Her car was parked outside one of the check cashing stores. She got in quickly and locked the doors behind her.

She wanted to use her phone to pull up Google Maps. She knew her next stop, but not how to get there from here. But she didn't dare use her phone again. Could be tapped, could have a tracer. Better to be paranoid than dead. The truth was, Jake had scared her. If he was right, she'd pissed off the wrong person. And now her recklessness - because knifing two of Franco's men *was* reckless - could mean the end for the only people in this world she gave a shit about.

Jake had made it sound like a personal vendetta. Natasha didn't believe that. She did believe, though, that Miriam Cross's killer was still out there. And he would kill again if it meant keeping her and the rest of Percy Powers quiet.

And so Natasha pulled away from the curb, seatbelt carefully buckled - she was a family woman now, after all - and headed north on Broad. She'd take Broad to Route 611. That should get her in the general vicinity of where she needed to be. She'd figure out the rest.

She just wanted to be there by dark.

THIRTY-SIX

Dinner was tense. Instead of a steak, a glass of wine and a hot bath, Delilah had a heavy dish of take-out pasta and two hours of her mother's lectures. Under the guise of maternal benevolence, her mother insisted on paying for a restaurant meal. But Delilah suspected that that had more to do with the age of Delilah's appliances and the rundown state of her kitchen than any particular kindness on her mother's part.

Delilah finished the last few bites of fettuccine *fra diavolo* and pushed her plate back. Joan had moved onto the topic of Delilah's sisters and Delilah was not-so-patiently listening to the benefits of Sarah's restful life in Georgia with her gentleman farmer husband and litter of kids. To Delilah, a houseful of kids and a yard full of chickens and pigs did not sound particularly restful. But she'd learned long ago to keep her mouth shut. She couldn't win a verbal duel with Joan Powers.

"So, Delilah, you are probably wondering what brought me all this way."

Yes, Delilah thought. Please tell me the real reason for your trip or go to bed and let me finish my case notes on the Cross murder. Please. But instead she said, "I am curious, Mother."

"While you have a lovely home here" - the pained look in her eyes said otherwise - "and a job, Paul and I have decided that you should move home."

"This is my home."

"Home as in Virginia, Delilah. With us, your family."

"I'm happy here."

"You're not happy, you're surviving. There's a big difference. I should know."

Delilah took a deep breath. "Is this about Daddy again? About all the ways you were deprived in Wyoming?"

"I loved your father."

Delilah turned away. Any discussion with her mother usually ended here and Delilah never let it get any further. What good would it do?

"Don't make that face, Delilah."

"What do you want me to say?"

"This is why I can't talk to you. You don't listen."

"I'm listening, Mother. Tell me just how unhappy I am. Better yet, remind me again of how much I'm like my father. A constant disappointment."

Her mother moved closer to the table and leaned in. "Look around you, Delilah. You live on a farm, alone. Alone! What woman lives on a farm alone? Do you want to grow old this way, the eccentric lady on the hill with her horses and her police job?"

Delilah looked at her empty plate, at the window across the room, at anything but her mother. She felt that old anger ready to burst through her pores. She took deep breaths, willing it away.

"Is that what life is all about, Mother? Marriage? What about independence? What about the fact that I put *myself* through law school? That I own a successful business? That I bought this house with my own money, money I worked hard to earn? Don't those things count for anything?"

But her mother would be undeterred. "You will be lonely and alone. You're almost thirty-six. What about kids? The window is closing." She smiled. "Look at my marriage to Paul. Don't you want that for yourself?"

That was too much for Delilah to bear. Between gritted teeth, she said, "So maybe I should find myself a nice married man and break up a marriage? Isn't that what you mean?"

"What are you saying, Delilah?"

Delilah couldn't stop herself. "Isn't it obvious? I may have been young, but I wasn't stupid."

Now Joan looked angry. She closed her eyes while she spoke. "What are you saying?"

"Dad. Paul. You and Paul were . . . together . . . *before* Dad died."

Joan stood. "Is that what you think?"

"The timing. Only six months and you're remarried? And I saw you! I saw you and Paul hugging. At the hospital while my father lay dying! How do you explain that, *Mother*?"

But Joan remained eerily quiet. She walked to the window, looked outside, before turning slowly back to Delilah. "Is this what your anger is all about, Delilah? I thought it was about Michael. I'm not stupid, either. I know you blame me for Michael's death. Because I convinced you not to go on that trip. But it could have been both of you, Delilah. Don't you see that?"

"Don't change the subject. You and Paul. You weren't faithful to dad."

Her mother looked suddenly defeated. She sank back into the chair. "It's true."

Delilah felt ill. "Oh my God."

Joan held up a hand. "Partly true. Paul and I already knew each other. We were close. Your father knew."

"What?"

"He knew, Delilah. Paul and I were friends. Your dad knew there were . . . feelings. He accepted that. Your father, well . . . we were different, he and I. We wanted different things. Would our marriage have lasted if he had lived? I don't know. But Paul and I were never . . . intimate. And there was you to consider. You and your father, well, you were everything to him."

Delilah shook her head, tears burning at her eyes. She *was* her father's child. And for an instant, she felt a universe of incomprehension for how he'd fallen in love with this woman. James Percy, Delilah's quiet, loving father. Never measuring up. Never doing enough, never enough of a success. Why did he stay?

But she knew the answer. When she thought of the way he'd looked at her mother. The adoration in his eyes. He loved his wife. Even if she wasn't good for him.

Like Delilah's continued her love for a ghost. And like Miriam's love for Jay Patel.

And then it hit Delilah like a load of hay. The domino effect of unhealthy love. It could cause a sane man like her father to stay with a woman who despised his way of life. And it could cause a sadistic man like Jack Cashman to kill.

Which meant one thing.

She had a sudden and overwhelming urge to find out if her hunch was right. Her gut said she needed to do it now.

"Mom, can we . . .can we continue this conversation later? I know I'm being abrupt, and I'm sorry-"

"I'm leaving tomorrow."

"You just got here."

Joan sighed. "Delilah, I'm obviously not going to convince you to change. You've made choices - and it's your life. But you will have to live with the consequences."

"I'm happy, Mom."

"Happy?" Joan shook her head. "Perhaps I will never understand you."

Suddenly, Sampson and Goliath started to bark from the other room. Not their deer-in-the-woods bark. Something far more menacing.

Delilah put her hand up for her mother to be quiet. Delilah heard other noises besides the dogs' barking. A bang came from outside. She thought of Natasha's message. If the Mob was after Natasha, it was likely they were after her, too. Delilah ran to the cellar door, off the back of the kitchen, and opened it.

"Get down there now. Hurry!"

"I will do no such thing."

The sound of glass shattering blasted from another room. Then two gun shots following by a yelp. Joan's eyes widened to saucer-sized pools.

"Delilah, what's happening?"

"The cellar Mom, now! There's a door at the back that leads to a coal bin. Go in there. Don't turn on the light!"

"I can't-"

"You can and you will," Delilah whispered. "I will come and get you. I promise. Go!"

Two sets of footsteps were making their way toward the kitchen. Delilah's mother gave her one terrified look before backing toward the cellar door and disappearing inside its black depths. Delilah closed the door softly behind her and glanced around the kitchen wildly. She didn't have a gun - both were now locked in her bedside table. She opened a kitchen drawer and tucked a paring knife into her jeans pocket and grabbed her meat cleaver. On impulse, she also pulled the small meat thermometer out of its drawer and jammed this into her other pocket.

Not much, but they'd have to do.

#

Natasha watched the two men break the window into Delilah's study. She tensed, gripping the gun tighter. She'd wanted to jump out and confront them when the men first arrived, but she'd just gotten here, having parked along the main road a mile back and hiked through the woods. So she waited.

She was on her stomach, about thirty feet from the house. She hadn't been surprised to see the Franco thugs. She *had* been surprised to see Jack Cashman. She itched to get in there. But they'd left a thug behind and she needed to take care of him first.

Natasha edged closer to the house. She heard a dog yelp and the sound sent shivers through her spine. *Fuckers.* Quietly, she rose to a standing position. She'd wait until the look-out was settled in. Then she'd make her move. The element of surprise was on her side. She needed to keep it that way.

#

The kitchen door slammed open. Cashman was the first to enter. Behind him was a short, stocky man with black hair and a noticeable limp. A moment's deduction told Delilah that he was the thug whom Natasha stabbed. The thug leered at her. Both men held guns. Delilah eyed the silencer on the end of Cashman's piece. He meant to kill. She just hoped they didn't find her mother - and that her mother had the good sense to stay in the cellar.

But this wasn't to be.

"Where's the other one?" Jack said.

"What other one?"

"There are three cars outside, Reds. I saw two shadows sitting in this room. Where's the other one?" When Delilah didn't answer, he said, "You can tell me or I can give Donald here the order to shoot on sight. Your choice."

Delilah gripped the cleaver behind her back.

"She's got a knife," Donald said.

"Drop the knife, Reds," Cashman said. "And tell me where your compatriot is."

"She has nothing to do with this. Do what you need to do to me, but leave her out of this."

The cellar door opened. Delilah's mother stood in the doorway, eyes wide, head back.

"Leave my daughter alone," she said.

Jack nodded in her direction and the other man grabbed Joan's arms. "What do you want me to do with her?" he asked.

"Just hold onto her for now. Give me some time with this one" - he motioned the gun toward Delilah - "but we may need the old lady later."

Donald nodded. He pushed Delilah's mother toward the kitchen door. Delilah, sensing that it was better to speak to Jack alone, let them go. She thought of the truth serum used on Miriam. They wouldn't kill Joan until they had what they wanted from Delilah. Information. Her mother was safe, for now. Delilah tried to give her mother a reassuring look. It fell flat.

With Donald out of sight, Cashman pulled a kitchen chair out and sat down. He pointed for Delilah to do likewise, keeping the gun aimed squarely at her heart.

"What the hell were you thinking?" he said. "You could have just dropped this whole thing and walked away. We would have let you go. But instead, you fucked with my property. Why'd you have to go and do that?"

"I don't know what you're talking about."

"Don't be a dumb bitch, Delilah. I know exactly what you and that old broad did. I have a security camera."

"Of course you do. It makes it fun to torture your maid and watch it later. Does that get you off, Jack? Do you jerk off to those videos?"

"Shut up."

"Why should I? You're going to shoot me anyway."

"Rosa was never tortured."

"Save your bullshit, Cashman. We know what you did to her. We know about Domino's involvement with trafficking. And we know that you killed Miriam."

"You can't prove a damn thing."

"That's the thing. We can. And it's all being neatly bundled up and handed to the authorities as we speak."
Okay, a small lie, but hey-

"The authorities?" Cashman laughed.

"The Federal authorities."

Delilah could see the wheels turning in Cashman's head. He raised the gun for emphasis. "Who exactly has all this information?"

Delilah stayed silent.

Cashman smiled. "It doesn't matter now. You're dead. Your mother's dead. And if I have anything to do with it, one by one your girls will be dead."

"Women. They're women."

"I don't think you're in a position to correct me."

"You killed Miriam. You were never in India. That was a ruse."

Another smile. "Miriam was an unfortunate side effect. Whatever happened to her was of her own doing."

"You loved her."

Cashman squirmed. "She was a means to an end."

Delilah shook her head. She was buying time, but for what, she wasn't sure. Even if she managed to get Jack, her mother was vulnerable in the other room. She listened for sounds of struggle coming from the living room. Silence. Not even the dogs. Her poor dogs, who were just trying to protect her. She felt the anger building.

She said, "You loved Miriam. You didn't kill her because she was a threat to the business. After you got whatever information you could by drugging and beating her, you murdered her - because she fell in love with Jay Patel."

Cashman remained silent.

"Miriam chose someone else, Jack. Even after you poured your heart out to her."

Cashman stood. "Bitch." He aimed the gun at Delilah's temple. "You have no idea what you're talking about."

"Chinnamasta. The Tantric goddess Miriam was so obsessed with. Because with Jay Patel, she understood what it meant to be sexually alive-"

"Stop."

"She understood what it meant to lose herself to love and sexual abandon."

"I said stop!"

"And you'd been trying to make her feel that way for years. The books. I saw the inscription, 'Come undone. For me.' That was you! You'd been chasing her for years. But face it, Jack. You weren't good enough."

Jack was looking at her with pure malice. In her mind, Delilah saw Rosa's swollen, bruised arms. She thought of the women in Sister Anna's shelter, women with children and mothers and lives who were forced into refugee status by men like Cashman. For what? Money? The rush of power and success? Hate and pity mixed like cement in her veins. She couldn't stop herself. If she was going to die, at least she'd have her say.

"You're a pig, Jack. Nothing but a spoiled, sadistic pig who killed a woman because you couldn't have her." She spat on the table. "I always wondered why Miriam was killed in a different manner than the others. And then it dawned on me. The beheading? Your little inside joke. A way to get back at Miriam – and Patel. You even called off the Mob hit. You wanted to kill Miriam yourself, you sick bastard."

Cashman sneered. He flipped the safety.

"Even Patel couldn't bring himself to believe you were capable of something so heinous." She knew she was pushing, but she couldn't stop herself.

"*Shut up!*" His finger hovered over the trigger.

Delilah heard glass shatter, then a scream from the other room. Jack turned toward the sound. Delilah took the moment to spring from the chair, pulling the paring knife from her pocket at the same time. She lunged toward Jack. He aimed the gun at her, but didn't have time to steady his hand before she was on top of him. She jammed the knife into his arm. He howled.

Delilah kneed Cashman in the groin. He used his good arm to backhand her across the face. She lost her balance and tripped backwards, against the table. He fell on top of her, his body dead weight against her own. She felt his hands around her neck. She tried to reach into her pocket for the meat thermometer. All she had left. His grip tightened. She felt herself losing consciousness. *Fight it, Delilah.* She thought of her dad, telling her to get back up, keep going. To focus.

She concentrated. Through the haze, she pictured the thermometer. She directed all of her energy toward getting her hand into her pocket, touching the sharp point of metal, grasping it. Her lungs burned, she felt dizzy.

Focus, Delilah!

Jack was over her, a madman's grin on his face. Her senses felt heightened. She smelled the whiskey on his breath, saw the deep blue of his eyes. She blinked. *Focus.* Her hand was around the thermometer. She pulled it out slowly. She felt her eyes closing. Sounds were coming from the other room. Yelling. A door slamming. She pictured her father. *Focus.*

Finally the thermometer was out of her pocket.

Cashman pressed his thumbs down into Delilah's neck. She used her last bit of energy to swing her arm up. She jammed the point of the meat thermometer into Cashman's eye.

He screamed.

Delilah pushed him off of her. She gasped for breath. Someone ran into the kitchen. She felt hands under her arms, fingers grabbing her ankle.

Then she heard the quiet pop of a silenced gunshot from another room. Panicked now, she thought of her mother. She forced her eyes open. And that's when she saw her mother standing over her, concern blending with the mascara that stained her face.

"Delilah? *Delilah*? I think you killed him."

Delilah forced herself into a sitting position. Breathing came hard, talking even harder. "Are you okay?"

Her mother nodded slowly, tears leaking from her eyes. Delilah saw Natasha standing behind her, Cashman's gun down by her side. Natasha had the disheveled look of a madwoman. But Delilah had never been so happy to see anyone in all her life.

Natasha said, "It's not over."

Delilah rubbed her throat. Her mother was looking at her with horror, so Delilah could only imagine the bruises already mottling her skin. She tried to shake off the lingering haze. "Why are you here?" She said to Natasha. "Never mind. Later. What do you mean it's not over?"

"There were three of them. Cashman and the asshole who came inside. And one standing guard. I chased him into the woods, but he's still out there."

"How long ago did he run?"

"Ten minutes maybe."

That was a hell of a lead. Delilah looked from her mother to Natasha. She knew these woods better than anyone. Quickly, she jotted down Joe's number and handed it to Natasha.

"Call this man. Tell him who you work for. Tell him Delilah said it's time to call the Feds. Ask him to have someone come here. Now. Tonight." She looked into Natasha's face and saw the haunted look of an angry, abused teenager. She bit back unproductive guilt. "It *will* be over."

#

The woods on Delilah's property were dense in the summertime. Pine trees elbowed maple, oak and birch trees for sun, but the old-growth trees limited the light available to the forest floor, reducing the undergrowth. That made riding easier. Delilah had spent many days in the woods on horseback, meandering through the trails and over the small creek that ran through her property. Tonight she would take advantage of the new moon and her instinctive knowledge of the forest.

Ignoring her mother's protests, she set out after the third goon. He hadn't taken the car, parked at the edge of the driveway. That meant he was the getaway driver. He didn't dare leave without his fellow perps. That told her that Jack expected this to be a quick and easy job. She smiled with satisfaction. It was easy for people to underestimate a group of female detectives.

Delilah had taken Millie out of her stall. Somehow it

seemed right to use the formerly abused filly to hunt down an abuser. She patted the horse on the side and gave her a gentle nudge. "Let's go, little lady."

She had her gun. And some rope. Time to play cowgirl.

Millie cantered easily through the woods, years of practice lending her a sure-footedness, even in the dark. Delilah pictured the layout of her property. The guy could have taken off for the road, but without a car, he would have had to walk miles before coming to a gas station or convenience store. Delilah figured it was more likely that he was simply hiding out somewhere close enough to the house so that he could join his fellow thugs when the job was over.

Unless he knew they were already dead. In which case, he'd try to get as far away as possible, as quickly as possible. But the first scenario seemed more likely. The car was still there. If he knew his friends were dead, he would have taken off already.

Delilah would take care of that. She opened the car door - unlocked - and felt around for the keys. They were still in the ignition, ready for a quick escape. Delilah pulled the keys out and tucked them into Millie's saddle bag. She headed into the woods.

Delilah decided to make a large circle around the house and work her way inward as quietly as possible. She encouraged the horse into a fast-paced walk, listening closely for noises that would give away her prey.

Night sounds permeated the evening air. Delilah could identify all of them. The hoot of her resident owl, the steady hum of crickets and the occasional yowl of a feral cat prowling what was, for it, a wooded grocery store. These woods had been Delilah's home for years. And riding was second nature. She ignored the throbbing in her neck and skull, the sharp, stabbing pain in her ribs when she breathed, and focused all of her effort on listening, on guiding Millie through the darkness. On finding the bastard.

She found him on her third pass. Delilah's eyes had adjusted to the new moon-darkness. She saw a shadow leaning up against a tree trunk. Millie's sudden hesitation told Delilah it was more than a wayward branch. She urged the horse forward.

When she was within twenty feet of him, he realized someone or something was there. He spun around, gun at the ready. But he had been staring at the well-lit house and his eyes weren't accustomed to the darkness. Delilah took advantage of the opportunity. She charged, urging Millie on to full speed. He shot blindly, expecting a person, not a horse. He missed. When Delilah was close enough, she kicked out, knocking him down, using Millie's bulk to trap him near the tree. He tripped on a root, dropping his gun.

Delilah hopped off the horse. She picked up his gun and stuffed it in the saddle bag. The man was momentarily stunned, clearly not expecting a woman to come charging out of the woods on horseback. But it didn't take him long to regain his composure. He began to stand, fists clenched at his side. Delilah pointed the gun in his face.

"Don't try anything, asshole. I'd prefer you alive, but I'm happy to hand over a corpse."

"Who the fuck are you?"

She unclipped the safety, ignoring him.

"Fuck you." The man ran at Delilah, head first. She didn't hesitate. First rule of the ranch: be ready to act at all times. Hesitate, and an animal dies. Delilah aimed and shot just before the bastard made impact.

His knee exploded. He screamed and fell to the ground. Twenty seconds later, Delilah had him tied to the tree. Delilah took off her blood-soaked t-shirt, ripped it, and used the strips for a tourniquet, which she twisted around his leg, above the wound. He swore at her the whole time, a barrage of insults that deserved a clock to the jaw. But Delilah let him go. She wanted him alive - the best way to prove his connection to the Mob and to Domino.

And anyway, she'd been called worse.

Delilah climbed back on the horse. Despite the evening heat, she was shivering. The adrenaline that had been coursing through her veins was abating, and she felt tired and sore and very lightheaded. Hard to believe that less than an hour ago she was having a tumultuous dinner with her mother. And now it was all over.

The whole damn case was over.

Well, almost.

THIRTY-SEVEN

Delilah scheduled a meeting with her team six days later, before the end of her prescribed recuperation period. She was feeling better. The contusions on her neck had calmed from angry purple to a pale red and her cracked rib didn't sear with every breath. Besides, her house felt lonely without Sampson and Goliath. She'd buried her canine heroes under a maple tree in her yard, within viewing distance of the barn. But the silence was palpable.

So Delilah welcomed today's tasks.

Relieved to be back at Percy Powers, Delilah sank into a chair at the conference table. Barb, a worried expression on her face, was already seated beside Margot, who seemed calm and composed as usual. Natasha was there, although she'd been unusually quiet. Delilah had invited Anders, too. Today was about closure and she figured he deserved closure as much as anyone.

"Lucinda is home," Delilah said. "Her kids are still upstate, where they will stay until the FBI is finished with its initial investigation."

"How is she?" Barb asked.

"She's happy to have this mess solved. Seems Patel had been telling the truth. Mr. Clean was his misguided attempt at protecting what was left of Miriam's legacy."

"A little late," Margot said.

Delilah nodded. "Perhaps. At least Mr. Clean – A/K/A Roger Crutchfield – treated her civilly. Lucinda knew he was trying to protect her. She just didn't know who was behind it."

"How is she dealing with the truth about her aunt," Barb said.

"As well as can be expected." Delilah shrugged, and the action triggered a fresh ripple of aches down her spine. "She feels like she never really knew Miriam. And that's been hard."

"And what about Patel," Barb said. "Was he arrested?"

"He's currently on house arrest. I haven't spoken with him, but Carl, my Fed connection, says Patel feels responsible for this whole mess."

Margot frowned. "He should."

Delilah sighed. "We can certainly see a dozen places where, had he acted differently, Miriam might still be alive. I guess the irony is that he fought so hard to keep everything under control, going so far as to hire a kidnapper, yet in the end, it all blew up."

"You can't run from your demons," Natasha said.

Margot gave her a long look before nodding her agreement.

"And Domino?" Barb said.

"Domino's assets have been frozen. I've been warned that the investigation could take years. It's part of a larger trafficking net. An international cooperative effort."

"And Franco's role?" Anders said. He'd been quiet until then. Delilah could see he was upset. He stared at her neck with an almost paternalistic anger.

"He's a slippery bastard. But the goon we caught at my house is one of Franco's henchmen. He provides a connection between the Mob and Cashman and perhaps Franco and the police." To Anders, Delilah said, "No promises that we'll get Ahmed's killer unless Patel cooperates, which he might." She looked into Anders' eyes. "Though I imagine you have some plans of your own? Maybe to continue Ahmed's work? And maybe Miriam's exposé, too?"

Anders didn't say anything, but Delilah had learned to read that look. Something good would come out of this, one way or another. She hoped he would be able to humanize the plight of the slavery ring's victims, give them voices and lives so that others would understand their pain. That's what Miriam would have done. She took a long look at Anders. Yes, she thought, Matthew would do that, too.

She'd ask him when they were alone. She realized she was very much looking forward to being alone with Matthew Anderson.

"I still can't figure out why Miriam kept that sex tape," Barb said. "Much less why she got involved with two men."

"She'd spent a long life controlling her impulses," Margot said. "She found freedom with Cashman and Patel."

Natasha gave Margot a funny look. Delilah, too, had to wonder if Margot, the former nun, could somehow relate to Miriam's plight. Did Margot have a past of her own?

"As to why she kept the tape, I guess it was for safe keeping," Delilah said. "In case she needed it later."

"Insurance?" Natasha said.

Delilah nodded. "So that's it." Delilah stood, signaling an end to the meeting. "And the good news? Miriam's will should go through and we should get paid."

"Was she worth a lot?"

"Enough. Lucinda won't be wanting for much anymore. And Women NOW will continue. Miriam saw to that." Delilah walked toward the door. Her steps were labored, her breathing still a bit ragged. She missed the adrenaline that got her through that night a few days ago. It had tempered the wounds that smarted now.

On her way out, Barb touched her arm. "Are you sure you're okay?" she said. "I'm sorry . . . that I wasn't there to help."

"I'm fine. And don't be sorry. You were wonderful. I was proud of all of you."

Barb smiled. "*I'm* the one who was proud. You ladies know how to kick some butt, as my daughter would say." She paused, her expression turning serious again. "Is your mother still at your place?"

Delilah shook her head. "She left two days ago. Paul flew in and drove her home."

"How did she handle this?"

Delilah considered her mother's long silences, her uncharacteristic censoring of the constant critique of Delilah's life. She'd seemed almost . . . human. And Delilah had felt her own anger and hurt melting. Simply a shared post-traumatic response or the beginning of healing? Delilah wasn't sure.

"She needs time. My mother's used to a different sort of life."

"She needs to figure out what a great daughter you are."

Delilah gave Barb a wary smile. "How's Natasha? She seems to be brooding."

Barb looked back into the room they'd just left. "Not brooding, exactly. Shell-shocked. For all her tough girl act, she's never killed anyone before. She's taking it hard."

Delilah understood. Although Delilah could honestly say that she'd killed Cashman in self-defense, the action changed her. She'd taken a life. It left a void in her soul that was beyond explanation, even though Cashman had been a very bad man.

And underneath that beautiful body and emotional shell, Natasha was still a kid. A kid on her way to becoming a woman. What happened four nights ago would weigh heavily on Natasha, make her question her life and her actions. As it should.

Delilah would talk to her. Invite her and her family out to the farm. She could use the company, too. It would do them all good.

But right now, she had another mission. She explained to Barb that she had to leave.

"Where are you going?"

"Back to where I started," Delilah said. "There's still one question I couldn't answer. But I think I've figured it out."

#

The house on Lacy Lane was looking more alive. It was a sunny summer day and a dry breeze ruffled through the trees. Someone had painted the house's trim, and the bright white enlivened the fading façade. No one would know a woman had been murdered here. Delilah figured that was the point.

Delilah pulled up to find Enid on her hands and knees, planting impatiens in the flower beds that lined the front of the small ranch home. Enid stood and watched Delilah get out of the car, her expression indelible. Delilah nodded a hello. She had come for answers - that was all. A quest to satisfy her own need for understanding. She tried to convey that to Enid with her body language. But Enid, sensing danger, looked ready to flee.

"I just came to chat," Delilah said.

"I have nothing more to say to you."

"Is Anna safe?"

Wariness crept into Enid's eyes. "As far as I know."

Delilah gazed off in the distance, first at the neighbor Janie's house, then back at the home that once sheltered Miriam, then living as Emily Cray. She said, "Jack Cashman is dead."

"I know."

"Why didn't you tell me that you and Miriam had been college roommates?"

"Because it wasn't relevant."

"But it was." Delilah bent down to pick up a container of impatiens. Carefully, she touched the tip of silky white petals. "The timeline always bothered me. At first I thought that Miriam had learned about the local slave trade from Cashman and Patel. That seemed to make sense. Miriam let herself be seduced by some pretty bad men. She tried to make up for it with Women NOW."

Delilah shook her head. "But then I realized that Domino got the idea from Miriam. In fact, Cashman probably formed the business to spite her. Which meant" - Delilah put the flower down and looked at Enid – "that Miriam had already been involved with Women NOW, with Sister Anna, when she met Cashman and Patel. I couldn't find a nexus between Anna and Miriam, though. But a funny thing happened. When I asked someone to pull Miriam's niece's phone records, you know what he found? Your number. And the history showed you had called Lucinda right after Miriam died.

Why would that be, Enid?"

When Enid didn't respond, Delilah continued. "I've had quite a bit of time on my hands lately, recuperating and all, so I did a little searching into your history." Delilah smiled. "I realized that you were the connection between Miriam and Anna."

"Miriam and I were best friends."

"*Were.*"

Enid stared at her hands. Long, slender hands that appeared young even without the surgeries the rest of her body had obviously endured. Surgeries aimed at winning the love of a man who was incapable of love.

"See, what I realized," Delilah said, "Is that Miriam *didn't* die for a great cause. She died because of plain old jealousy. Jack's . . . and yours."

"I never wished her ill. I tried to help her."

"You told Jack where Miriam was living. You set her up in this house under the alias of Emily Cray and then, knowing full well that Jack was angry and jealous over Miriam's rejections and her feelings for Jay Patel, you told Cashman where she lived." Delilah looked at Enid, incredulous at the other woman's calm. At her ability to lie, even to herself.

"Jack said he wanted to talk to Miriam. Reason with her."

"You *knew* about Miriam's involvement with Anna. You *knew* that Jack had used that connection, had exploited it for his own benefit. You *knew* that Miriam was in danger. Miriam trusted you. She thought you were helping her." Delilah shook her head. "At the very least, you compromised all that Anna and Miriam had worked for. Why, Enid? Was it worth it?"

Enid turned away. She knelt down on the ground and began digging a small hole with a sharp metal shovel. Her actions were frantic, her face a mask of indifference.

"Why?" Delilah repeated. "I know you had been

married once. I know you divorced. Was it for Jack Cashman? Did you introduce Jack to Miriam and unwittingly start his obsession with another woman?"

Finally, Enid looked up. "Do you know what it's like to give up everything for a man? And then to get nothing in return?"

Perhaps Delilah did. She held Enid's gaze for as long as she could bear. But the raw pain was too much and she had to turn away.

After a long silence, Enid asked, "Are you turning me in?"

"I don't think I can without compromising Women NOW."

"I didn't know what Jack intended to do. I really didn't know." Enid shook her head. "I still don't know that for sure that it was . . . him."

"*Bullshit.*"

Enid dug with more gusto, slender wrists punching into the ground in jerky motions. "What could I do? Miriam was already dead by the time I had an inkling of what had transpired."

"Why didn't you make an anonymous call? Instead, you called her niece, never having the courage to speak with her. You could have done something to lead the authorities to Domino. They would have figured out the rest from there."

Enid didn't respond, but Delilah already knew the answer. Enid had been protecting Jack. But most of all, Enid wanted Jack's love – something she thought she could have with Miriam gone. But things don't work that way. Enid lost a friend and her self-respect along the way, all for nothing. Certainly not for love.

Enid looked back at her flowers. "For whatever it's worth, Miriam had been like a sister to me."

Delilah watched Enid choose a yellow flower. She stood there for a long moment, amazed at how life could simply go on. Enid would plant this garden, she would re-rent this house, she would live on the Main Line where she didn't quite fit in and she would continue to tell herself that none of it was her fault. That she loved a woman she had led to the grave.

Without another word, Delilah turned and headed back to the car.

The horses would have an afternoon walk today. The first in days. She and they would lose themselves in the refuge of a long, lazy summer evening. Delilah slid into the Jeep, contemplating the nature of love. Her love for the horses was pure. Her love for Michael had been once, too, but she'd let it twist and morph into something obsessive and unhealthy. And Anders . . . maybe there was room in her heart now for another. Maybe.

But Enid's love for Jack had been obsession, as was Jack's love for Miriam. Obsession that ended in death.

And with that thought, it dawned on Delilah why Miriam had kept the sex tape. It wasn't for insurance, as she'd told Barb. That tape served as a reminder to Miriam of her own weaknesses. Miriam Cross, renowned author and philanthropist, had been as capable of losing her way as the next person.

Delilah stepped on the gas, shifting the Jeep into second gear. In the end, Delilah supposed they all needed a reminder now and again.

ACKNOWLEDGMENTS

Where to start? I'm grateful to so many people for the role they've played in supporting or inspiring my writing life.

First, I'd like to thank my husband, Ben, for insisting that we stay in Driggs, Idaho on that fateful vacation several years ago. Not only has he been patient and supportive when it comes to my crazy idea to be a writer, but his love of the outdoors helped to inspire Delilah and her gang of private investigators.

I'd like to thank my agent, Frances Black of Literary Counsel. I knew the first time I spoke with Fran that I wanted her to represent me. She's been a constant source of support, wisdom, encouragement and fantastic New York City restaurant suggestions. I consider her a friend as well as an agent and feel very blessed that, from the beginning, she understood my vision for this series. I'd also like to thank her colleague Jennifer Mishler, who, with the help of a little caffeine, has the energy and enthusiasm of three people.

I am forever grateful to my early readers, especially Mike Wiecek, Mark Anderson, Marnie Mai, Jennifer Brown, Kathleen Balbier, Suzanne Norbury, Jared Butler, Greg Smith, Sue Argenziano, Ben Pickarski, Angela Tyson, Kevin Savage and Rowena Copeland. Their thoughtful feedback has made this a better book.

A huge "thank you" to my parents, Gary and Angela Tyson, who never tried to stop my reading addiction. I know my father would be so proud (but practical) if he were still with us today, and my mother has always encouraged my brother and me to pursue our dreams.

And a big "thanks" to my extended family, too. What a blessing to have so many cheerleaders on my side!

Gratitude goes to Donna Sabella, PhD, RN, my cousin and an expert on human trafficking. She patiently answered my seemingly endless questions about the topic and helped to put a face on a heinous problem. Human trafficking is a very real issue. If you want to help, check out my website (www.watyson.com) for a list of resources.

And, of course, I'm grateful to mystery readers, who share my love of the genre. Without you, a writing life would not be possible. Read on!

Made in the USA
Lexington, KY
05 November 2013